THE DEVIL IS STILL LAUGHING

The dog had squeezed under the bed and was yelping. Squashed between the headboard and the wall, the old woman lay unconscious. Léa had great difficulty heaving her up and laying her on the mattress. She was ashen and a little blood trickled from her right nostril. The left side of her face was bruised and discoloured. Léa leaned over her: her breath came unsteadily through her half-open mouth. The opening of her white cotton nightdress revealed red marks where hands had grabbed the flabby flesh of her neck.

Aghast, Léa stared at the outstretched body of the woman who once comforted her and gave her little secret treats when Ruth or her mother had punished her. The memory of cuddles in the huge old fireside armchair in the kitchen at Montillac made her burst out sobbing and shout in a childlike voice:

'Donie, Donie, answer me . . .'

Dragging herself out of the numbness into which she had sunk, the old woman opened her eyes. Léa flung herself at her.

'Sidonie, please, talk to me . . .'

Slowly she raised her hand and placed it on Léa's bowed head. Her lips opened and closed, but no sound issued from them.

THE DEVIL IS STILL LAUGHING

The Blue Bicycle Book Three

Régine Deforges

Translated from the French by Ros Schwartz

A STAR BOOK
published by
the Paperback Division of
W H Allen & Co Plc

A Star Book
Published in 1988
by the Paperback Division of
W H Allen & Co Plc
44 Hill Street
London W1X 8LB

First published in Great Britain by
W H Allen & Co Plc, 1987

Printed and bound in Great Britain by
Anchor Brendon Ltd, Tiptree, Essex

ISBN 0 352 31997 6

To my father,
to Franck, my son.

Acknowledgements

The author would like to thank the following for their collaboration, often unknowingly given: Jean-Pierre Abel, Paul Allard, Henri Amouroux, Robert Antelme, Louis Aragon, Robert Aron, Alix Auboineau, Lucie Aubrac, Michel Audiard, Colette Audry, Marc Augier, Claude Aveline, Marcel Aymé, François Barazet de Lanurien, Maurice Bardèche, Georges Beau and Léopold Gaubusseau, Pierre Bécamps, Suzanne Bellenger, Jacques Benoist-Méchin, Christian Bernadac, Georges Bernanos, Pierre Bertaux, Nicholas Bethell, Maxime Blocq-Mascart, Georges Blond, M. R. Bordes, Jean-Louis Bory, Alphonse Boudard, Pierre Bourdan, P.-A. Bourget, Robert Brasillach, Georges Buis, Calvo, Raymond Cartier, Louis-Ferdinand Céline, Jacques Chaban-Delmas, Marguerite Chabay, René Chambe, Richard Chapon, Jean-François Chegneau, Bertrande Chezal, Winston Churchill, Maurice Clavel, René Clément, Guy Cohen, Colette, Larry Collins, Arthur Conte, E. H. Cookridge, Lucien Corosi, Gaston Courty, Jean-Louis Crémieux-Brilhac, Croix-Rouge française, Jean-Louis Curtis, Adrien Dansette, Jacques Debû-Bridel, Marcel Degliame-Fouché, Jacques Delarue, Jacques Delperrié de Bayac, Abbé Desgranges, Maja Destrem, David Diamant, *la Documentation française*, Friedrich-Wilhelm Dohse, Jacques Doriot, Paul Dreyfus, Raymond Dronne, Claude Ducloux, Ferdinand Dupuy, Jean Dutourd, Georgette Elgey, Dr Epagneul, Jean Eparvier, Robert Escarpit, Raymond Escholier, Hélène Escoffier, Marc-André Fabre, Mistou Fabre, Yves Farge, J.-N. Faure-Biguet, Henri Fenet, Richard de Filippi, Marie-Madeleine Fourcade, Ania Francos, Jacky Fray, Henri

Frenay, André-Frossard, Liliane and Fred Funcken, Jean-Louis Funk-Brentano, Jean Galtier-Boissière, Paul Garcin, Romain Gary, Charles de Gaulle, André Girard, Jean Giraudoux, Alice Giroud, Léon Groc, Richard Grossmann, Georges A. Groussard, Gilbert Guilleminault, Georges Guingouin, André Halimi, Hervé Hamon, Robert Hanocq. René Hardy, Max Hastings, Philippe Henriot, Jean Hérold-Paquis, Rudolph Hoess, Sabine Hoisne, Hoover Institute, Raymond Huguetot, Bernard Irelin, Jacques Isorni, Jeanine Ivoy, Capitaine Jacques, Claude Jamet, Maréchal Juin, Bernard Karsenty, Joseph Kessel, Jacques Kim, Serge Klarsfeld, Karl Koller, Maurice Kriegel-Valrimont, Jean Lacouture, Jean Lafourcade, Christian Laigret, Christian de La Mazière, Henri Landemer, Roger Landes, Dominique Lapierre, Jean de Lattre de Tassigny, Jacques Laurent, Eric Lefebvre, Roger Lemesle, Alain Le Ray, Jean Mabire, Grégoire Madjarian, René Maisonnas, Franz Masereel, Pierre Masfrand, Micheline Maurel, Claude Mauriac, François Mauriac, William Peter McGivern, Léon Mercadet, Edouard and François Michaut, Henri Michel, Edmond Michelet, François Mitterrand, Jean Moulin, André Mutter, Jean Nocher, Henri Noguères, Pierre Nord, Jacques Oberlé, Albert Ouzoulias, Guy Pauchou, Jean-Jacques Pauvert, Robert O. Paxton, Gilles Perrault, Philippe Pétain, Jacques Peuchmaurd, Eric Picquet-Wicks, L. G. Planes and R. Dufourg, Theodor Pliever, Edouard de Pomiane, Roland de Pury, *Sélection du Reader's Digest*, Lucien Rebatet, P. R. Reid, Colonel Rémy, Jean Renald, Françoise Renaudot, Ludwig Renn, André Reybaz, Patrick Rotman, David Rousset, Claude Roy, Raymond Ruffin, Cornelius Ryan, Maurice Sachs, Georges Sadoul, Saint-Bonnet, Antoine de Saint-Exupéry, Saint-Loup, Saint-Paulien, Henri Sanciaume, Jean-Paul Sartre, Régine Saux, Simone Savariaud, Lily Sergueiew, Service d'Information des crimes de guerre, William L. Shirer, Jacques Sigot, Knut Singer, Sisley-Huddleston, Michel Slitinsky, A. Soulier, Philip John Stead, Lucien Steinberg, Pierre Taittinger, Guy Tassigny, Elisabeth Terrenoire, Geneviève Thieuleu, Edith Thomas, Charles Tillon, H. R. Trevor-Roper, Pierre Uteau, Jan Valtin, Pierre

Veilletet, Dominique Venner, Jean Vidalenc, Camille Villain, Gérard Walter, Pierre Wiazemsky, Princess Wiazemsky, Prince Yvan Wiazemsky, Karl Wilhelm, Olga Wormser.

Wo wir sind, da ist immer vorn
Und der Teufel der lacht nur dazu.
Ha, Ha, Ha, Ha, Ha, Ha, Ha!

Wherever we go, we're always in front
And the Devil is still laughing.
Ha, Ha, Ha, Ha, Ha, Ha, Ha!

Summary of the story so far

Early in the autumn of 1939 Pierre and Isabelle Delmas were living happily on their wine-growing estate in Montillac near Bordeaux with their three daughters, Françoise, Léa and Laure, and Ruth, their faithful governess. Léa was seventeen and very beautiful. She had inherited her father's love of the land and the vineyards where she had grown up in the company of Mathias Fayard, the son of the estate manager. He was her playmate and was secretly in love with her.

On 1st September 1939, at Roches Blanches, the estate of the d'Argilat family, friends of the Delmas, there was a party to celebrate the betrothal of Laurent d'Argilat and his gentle cousin, Camille. Léa's aunts and uncles were there with their children: Luc Delmas the lawyer and his children, Philippe, Corinne and Pierre; and Adrien Delmas, the Dominican monk who had a reputation for being something of a revolutionary. Léa's admirers Jean and Raoul Lefèvre were at the party too. Léa was the only person who was not in a festive mood on this occasion: she was in love with Laurent and could not bear the idea of his engagement. She met François Tavernier, an elegant, cynical, rather ambiguous character who seemed very sure of himself. Out of spite, Léa became engaged to Camille's brother, Claude d'Argilat. The same day, war broke out and there was a general mobilization.

In despair, Léa attended Camille and Laurent's wedding where she was taken ill. She was treated by the family doctor, Doctor Blanchard. She postponed the date of her wedding but her fiancé was killed at the beginning at the war. Léa went to Paris to stay with her great-aunts, Lisa and Albertine de Montpleynet. There she met Camille again, also François Tavernier, for whom she felt a mixture of loathing and attraction. She made the acquaintance of Raphaël Mahl, a homosexual Jewish writer, an opportunist and a rather disturbing character, and of Sarah Mulstein, a young German-Jewish woman who was fleeing from the Nazis.

Laurent left for the Front and Léa promised she would look after Camille who was pregnant and in poor health. In spite of Camille's delicate condition, she and Léa fled the Occupation and joined the general exodus on the roads. Conditions were hazardous and there were frequent air-raids. Chance had it that the distraught Léa bumped into Mathias Fayard who, for a brief moment, gave her warmth and affection. She also met François Tavernier who initiated her in the pleasures of physical love. The signing of the Armistice made it possible for the two women to reach the Bordeaux region where Camille's son Charles was born, with the help of a German officer, Frederic Hanke.

But on the day of their homecoming, they found the household in mourning. Léa's beloved mother Isabelle had been killed in an air-raid. Her father gradually lapsed into insanity while on the estate, which had been requisitioned by the Germans, a precarious existence beset with hardship and difficulties went on. Léa, Camille and little Charles met Laurent at the home of the Debrays who had been hiding him since his escape from Germany. He was about to go underground. Rifts set in, dividing families and villages: there were the staunch Pétain supporters on the one hand, and, on the other, those who believed in the fight for freedom. Léa instinctively belonged to the latter. Unaware of the danger, she acted as a messenger for the underground fighters. But her sister Françoise was in love with one of the occupying Germans, Lieutenant Kramer. Mathias Fayard maintained a stormy relationship with Léa which was complicated by the fact that his father had his eye on the estate. Spurned by Léa, he volunteered to go and work in Germany.

Exhausted from the responsibilities weighing on her shoulders, Léa returned to Paris to stay again with her great-aunts, Lisa and Albertine. Her time was divided between carrying messages for the Resistance and being wined and dined in occupied Paris. In the company of François Tavernier, she tried to forget the war for brief moments at Maxim's, L'Ami Louis, or at the little clandestine restaurant belonging to the Andrieus. She also saw Sarah Mulstein who opened her eyes to what was going on in the concentration camps, and Raphaël Mahl who had become a collaborator of the most despicable type. She satisfied her lust for life in the arms of François Tavernier. But Montillac needed her: she had to cope single-handed with the shortage of money, Fayard's greed, her father's insanity and the threats hanging over the d'Argilat family. In the underground cellars of Toulouse, thanks to Father Adrien Delmas, she met up with Laurent and abandoned herself to him. On her return, she was interrogated by Lieutenant Dohse and Commissioner Poinsot. She was only saved through the intervention of her Uncle Luc. Françoise ran away when her father refused to give his permission for her to marry Lieutenant Kramer. Grief-stricken at losing his daughter, Pierre Delmas died. Father Adrien, Uncle Luc, Laurent and François Tavernier met briefly for his funeral. After a last embrace, fragrant with the smell of Montillac soil, Léa found herself facing her precarious future alone with Camille, little Charles and the aged Ruth.

During the night of 20th September 1942, at the height of the German Occupation, seventy members of the Resistance were awaiting execution in the cells of Fort Hâ, near Bordeaux. A little later, on a rainy morning, they faced the firing squad, singing the Marseillaise for the last time.

At Montillac, life was hard, despite the efforts of Camille to get the estate back on its feet and thwart Fayard, the manager, who dreamed of taking over the place.

In Paris, Léa stayed with the Montpleynet sisters. She met up with her old acquaintance Raphaël Mahl, still a Gestapo informer. She was also reunited with the enigmatic François Tavernier for whom she always felt an inexplicable passion. She tried to forget her troubles in black market restaurants and it was on one of these occasions that she witnessed the arrest of her Jewish friend, Sarah Mulstein, by the Gestapo. Sarah was tortured but with the help of Raphaël Mahl she was able to escape. Before smuggling her out of Paris, Léa and François hid her in the Montpleynet sisters' apartment.

While the Gestapo were looking for Laurent, Camille was

arrested. She was imprisoned in Fort Hâ and then in the camp at Mérignac where she fell ill. Léa returned to Montillac and devoted herself to securing Camille's release. The Gestapo finally let Camille go, having extracted no information from her.

Léa discovered the sad reality of horror and torture through Mathias Fayard, her childhood friend, who volunteered to go to Germany, and through the Lefèvre brothers who, like her, had joined the Resistance. The Mathias of her youth died in a sordid hotel run by a sleazy prostitute . . .

A large number of young men and women in the Bordeaux region were now working for the Gestapo. The local people were divided by an atmosphere of hatred. In this depressing situation, Léa waited for François Tavernier who finally arrived at Montillac where he attended a luncheon in honour of a young French Gestapo worker, who had become an acquaintance of Léa's naïve younger sister, Laure. They contrived to throw him off the scent, but that afternoon Doctor Blanchard was shot by the same young man. For the first time in three years, Laurent d'Argilat and François Tavernier found themselves face to face. They both agreed to send the inhabitants of Montillac to Paris.

The French had begun reading again but the bookshops were empty. It was the jazz age, a kilo of butter cost three hundred and fifty francs* and coffee was anything between one and two thousand francs.† On the Eastern front, the Germans were retreating. Caught up in a social whirl, Léa was enjoying herself so as not to have to think about her dead and missing friends. After a short stay in Paris, she took the train back to Bordeaux.

Raphaël Mahl, abandoned by his friends in the Gestapo, became number 9793 in a prison cell in Fort Hâ. There he gleaned scraps of information, in particular about the presence of members of the Resistance and British airmen who had not been identified by the Germans. He cold-bloodedly denounced them.

One night, his body, which had been horribly mutilated by his cell-mates, was thrown on to a rubbish tip and buried under a pile of refuse.

François Tavernier joined Léa at Montillac but had to leave again almost at once. Léa was left alone . . .

* about £3
† about £10 to £20

14

Time heals all things. One day, the tears will have stopped flowing, the furies abated, and the graves will have disappeared. But France will remain.

Charles de Gaulle
Mémoires de Guerre. Le Salut.

Chapter 1

For Léa, it was the beginning of a long wait.

It was early 1944. The weather, which had been mild and wet at the beginning of the year, suddenly turned cold on 14th February and the thermometer dropped to −5°C in the mornings. For two weeks, the north wind vied with the snow. Towards mid-March, the air finally became warmer and spring was definitely around the corner. At Montillac, Fayard anxiously studied the sky. There was not a cloud in sight, and it had not rained for a long time. This drought was the despair of the farmers who had no fodder for the animals, and now it looked as though this year's harvest would be ruined.

Relations between the inhabitants of the 'castle' and Fayard, the estate manager, had been on the brink of breaking down since an accountant had examined the estate's books. Fayard had been forced to admit that he had been selling wine to the German authorities even though he had been expressly forbidden to do so by Léa and her father before her. In his defence, the fellow had emphasized that they would be the only wine-growers in the region not to sell to the Germans; that they had sold them wine well before the war began and that most of the high-up Jerries in the area were large wine merchants in their own country and many of them had connections in Bordeaux that went back twenty years. Some of them were old customers: did Mademoiselle not remember that old acquaintance of Monsieur d'Argilat who had dropped in during the grape harvest of 1940?

Léa remembered him quite clearly. She also remembered

that her father and Monsieur d'Argilat had requested the honest Munich wine merchant, who had become an officer in the Wehrmacht, not to visit them for the duration of the war. Fayard admitted that he had put the revenue from these sales 'to one side' as, knowing Mademoiselle's feelings on the subject . . . but he insisted he had always intended to return the money to her. In any case, part of the money had been used for the maintenance and purchasing of equipment. Mademoiselle had no idea how much even the smallest barrel cost!

Oh yes she had! She was perfectly aware how much things cost. The old bank manager in Bordeaux had been relieved to receive the generous cheque François Tavernier had given her. He could not see himself suing the daughter of his old schoolchum from the Lycée Michel Montaigne for writing cheques without sufficient funds or non-payment of bills. Unfortunately, the roof tiles of the right wing of the house had been blown off in a storm and the estate's account was again overdrawn. The expert sent by Tavernier had given her an advance, thinking he would soon be reimbursed, but neither he nor Léa had heard from Tavernier since mid-January. Now it was nearly the end of March.

The accountant advised that, given the circumstances, Léa should either negotiate with Fayard or sue him for embezzlement. Léa refused to do either. If it had not been for little Charles, who brought some joy to Montillac with his games and his laughter, the atmosphere would have been sinister. Yet everybody made an effort to conceal their worries from the others. Only Bernadette Bouchardeau, her aunt, sometimes allowed a tear to roll down her emaciated cheek. Camille d'Argilat was glued to the wireless, day and night, listening to the messages on Radio-London, waiting for a sign from Laurent. Since Dr Blanchard's death, Sidonie, the cook, had become much frailer, moving only from her bed to the armchair by the door. From there, she would look out over the estate, gazing at the vast plain where the smoke could be seen rising from Saint-Macaire and Langon. The long hours of solitary silence ticked by to the rhythm of the trains crossing the Garonne. The old cook decided eventually

to return to Bellevue. Every day, Ruth took her food and Léa, Camille and Bernadette took it in turns to keep her company. The sick woman would grumble and tell them they were wasting their time sitting with her, that they had more important things to do than look after a helpless old woman. But they all knew that these visits were all she had to live for. Even calm Ruth was affected by this atmosphere of sadness and anxiety. For the first time since the beginning of the war, she was beginning to have doubts. The fear of seeing the Gestapo or the militia appear kept the tough northern woman awake at nights.

As for Léa, she threw herself into digging up the kitchen garden and pulling up the weeds from the vineyards in the hope of killing time. When that was not enough to exhaust her and soothe her spirit, she cycled for miles through the undulating countryside. She only returned home to collapse on the divan in her father's study where she tossed and turned in restless sleep. When she awoke, Camille was nearly always by her side with a glass of milk or a bowl of soup in her hand. The two friends would exchange smiles, silently watching the fire burning in the hearth for hours. When the silence became too heavy, one of them would switch on the huge wireless set perched on a chest of drawers near the bed and try and tune into London. Increasing interference was making it harder to hear those cherished voices speaking of freedom.

'*Honour and the Fatherland. Monsieur François Morland, a prisoner escaped from the stalags, and member of the management committee of the Union of French Prisoners of War speaks to you . . .*

'*Repatriated and escaped prisoners of war, my comrades in the Resistance groups, first of all, I want to tell you the good news . . .*'

The speaker's voice was drowned by the crackling.

'It's always the same: we'll never hear the good news,' said Léa as she banged and thumped the wireless set.

'Wait, you know that won't do any good,' remonstrated Camille, gently pushing her friend away.

She switched the wireless on and off several times. She was just about to give up when the same voice came back on the air:

'I told General de Gaulle on your behalf of the faith which inspires us. On your behalf, I told Chief Administrator Frenay, who escaped like us, of all the things that give us a reason to live. It is to these men's credit that they believe in the future. They have long understood the hope in our hearts . . .'

The interference began again and only a few scraps of phrases were audible. Then the broadcast came to a sudden halt.

'But their demands are even greater, and more generous. Because, in the camps, and in the commandos, they have learned to recognize each other, they want to see their country rid of signs of weariness and old age. Because they have come together, they want a country where classes, categories and hierarchies are dissolved in a just system which is stronger than any charity. Because, in the towns and countryside of their exile, they have shared the same poverty as people of all races and nations, they want to share with them the benefits of future existence. Ah yes! Comrades, we are fighting for everybody. It is for all this that we have chosen to struggle. Let us remember the vow we took on our departure, when we left our loved ones behind. They said to us: "Whatever you do, do not betray us, make sure you tell France to put on her most determined face and come and meet us."

'Those of you who have escaped, or been repatriated, those from the mutual aid centres, those from isolated underground groups, the time has come to keep that promise.'

'Another idealist!' exclaimed Léa. 'Ah! The face of France is determined all right! Let Morland come and see what a lovely face it is . . . puffy with fear, hatred and envy, deceitful eyes, her mouth dripping with slander and denunciations . . .'

'Calm down! You know very well that France isn't just that, but it is also men and women like Laurent, François, Lucien, Madame Lafourcade . . .'

'I don't give a damn!' shrieked Léa, 'they're the ones who'll die if they're not already dead, and it's the others who'll be left.'

Camille turned very pale.

'Oh! Be quiet . . . don't say that . . .'

'Shh! It's the personal messages.'

They huddled so close to the wireless set that their heads were touching the varnished wood.

'Everything is rising up against me, everything assails me, everything tempts me . . . Ginette's ducks arrived safely . . . I repeat: Ginette's ducks arrived safely . . . Barbara's dog will have three puppies, I repeat: Barbara's dog will have three puppies . . . Laurent drank his glass of milk . . . I repeat: . . .'

'Did you hear that?'

'Laurent drank his glass of milk.'

'He's alive! He's alive!'

Laughing and crying, they flung themselves into each other's arms. Laurent d'Argilat was alive and well. It was one of the agreed messages to let them know there was no need to worry.

That night, Léa and Camille slept peacefully.

A week after Easter, their friend, the butcher in Saint-Macaire who had helped Father Adrien Delmas to escape, came to visit them in his gas-fuelled van. It made such a din that they heard him coming well before he drove into sight. When the vehicle turned into the drive, Camille and Léa were waiting for him on the kitchen doorstep.

Albert walked towards them beaming. He was carrying a large parcel wrapped in a spotless white cloth.

'Good morning, Madame Camille, good morning Léa.'

21

'Hello Albert. How lovely to see you! It's at least a month since you last paid us a visit.'

'Well, Madame Camille, you can't just do as you please these days. Can I come in? I've brought you a nice joint and some calf's liver for the little one. Mireille has made you some hare pâté. I think you'll find it tasty.'

'Thank you, Albert. If it weren't for you, we wouldn't eat meat very often. How is your son?'

'He's fine, Madame Camille, just fine. He said it's quite tough going and that he's been suffering badly from chilblains, but they're better now.'

'Hello Albert. You'll have a cup of coffee, won't you?'

'Hello Mademoiselle Ruth. I'd love a cup. Is it real coffee?'

'Almost,' said the governess, picking up the coffee pot which was keeping warm on a corner of the stove.

The butcher put his bowl down and wiped his lips on the back of his hand.

'You're right, it's almost real. Come closer, I've got some important news. Well . . . yesterday, I received a message from Father Adrien. We may be seeing him round here again soon . . .'

'When?'

'I have no idea. They've managed to help the Lefèvre brothers escape from hospital.'

'How are they?'

'They're being treated by a doctor near Dax. As soon as they're better, they'll join Dédé le Basque's Resistance group. Do you remember Stanislas?'

'Stanislas?' asked Léa.

'Aristide, if you prefer.'

'Yes, of course.'

'He's back in the area to form another network and punish the traitors who denounced our friends.'

'Are you working with him?'

'No, I'm working with the La Réole group but as we're on the boundary between the two sectors, I act as go-between for Hilaire and him. One of you should tell Madame Lefèvre that her sons are well.'

'I'll go,' volunteered Léa. 'I'm so happy for them. Was it very difficult to get them out?'

'No, we had accomplices inside the hospital and the police officers on duty were Lancelot's men. Did you hear Monsieur Laurent's message on the BBC last night?'

'Yes. After such a long period of worry, it looks as though all the good news is coming at once.'

'Only good for some. I can't help thinking about the seventeen young lads from Maurice Bourgeois's group who were shot by those swine on 27th January.'

They all remembered the 20th February edition of *La Petite Gironde* with the headline: TERRORISTS EXECUTED IN BORDEAUX.

'Did you know them?' stammered Camille.

'Some of them. From time to time we helped each other out, even though they were communists and we're Gaullists. There was one lad I was very fond of, Serge Arnaud. He was the same age as my son. It's hard to die at the age of nineteen.'

'When is all this going to come to an end?' sighed Ruth, wiping her eyes.

'Soon, I hope! The trouble is, there aren't many of us. The Gestapo are a cunning lot. Since the wave of arrests, deportations and executions in the Gironde region, Aristide and the others are having a hard job finding volunteers.'

He was interrupted by the sound of a bicycle bell. The door swung open. It was Armand, the postman.

'Good morning, ladies. I have a letter for you, Mademoiselle Léa. I hope it'll make you happier than the one I delivered to old Fayard.'

'Another letter from the bank,' sighed Léa.

'Do you know what was in it?' asked Armand. 'You'll never guess . . . a coffin.'

All except Albert exclaimed:

'A coffin!'

'That's what I said. A little black cardboard coffin. I think Fayard's name was written on it.'

'But why?' asked Camille in astonishment.

'Why? Because they're sent to those who collaborate with

the Jerries to let them know that when the war's over, they've got it coming to them.'

'For the sake of a few bottles of wine,' murmured Camille scornfully.

'It's not just a few bottles of wine, Madame Camille,' snapped the butcher.

'What do you mean, Albert?' asked Léa.

'We're not certain, but on two occasions, Fayard was seen coming out of the Langon Kommandantur.'

'We've all been there for some reason or another.'

'I know, Madame Camille, but there are rumours, especially about his son. When I think I used to know him when he was a kid. I can still picture the pair of you chasing through the vineyards, pelting each other with grapes. Do you remember, Léa?'

'Yes . . . It already seems such a long time ago . . .'

'That won't improve Fayard's ill temper,' said Ruth, pouring the postman a glass of wine.

'It certainly won't. He turned red as a beetroot and then white as a ghost when he saw what was in the envelope. I didn't wait to hear any more. I got out.'

He drained his glass in one gulp.

'This won't do. I'm sitting here chatting and I haven't finished my round. Well, goodbye folks. See you soon.'

'Goodbye Armand. See you soon.'

'I should be on my way as well,' said Albert.

Léa saw him to his van.

'They're parachuting some arms in soon. Can you go and check that the hiding place in the grotto hasn't been discovered? There should be a case of ammunition and another of grenades.'

'I'll go tomorrow.'

'If all's well, draw a white chalk cross on the fence round the angel at the crossroads.'

'All right.'

'Be careful, your uncle would never forgive me if anything happened to you. Beware of old Fayard.'

*

24

In the chapel, everything seemed normal and the cases were intact. Despite the fine weather, the grotto was deserted.

During the night of 15th April, heavy rain had furrowed the steep paths leaving little heaps of loose gravel in the hollows. Léa made her way back through the cemetery. She stopped before her parents' grave and pulled up a few weeds that had escaped Ruth's attention. The square was empty. She could hear children's shouts. 'It's recreation time,' she thought as she pushed open the church door. The freezing damp made her shudder. Three old women looked up from their prayers as she went in. What was she doing there? Sainte-Exupérance in her niche looked even more like a big wax doll with dusty clothes than ever before, and that was precisely what she was. Where was the emotion she had felt as a child? Where was the wonderful image of the little saint whose name she had adopted as her *nom de guerre*? All that had became ridiculous and dangerous. She began to feel increasingly ill-tempered. She had an urge to drop everything and join Laure and her carefree young friends on the Boulevard Saint-Michel or the Champs-Elysées, drink cocktails with strange names and colours, dance in clandestine clubs and listen to banned American records instead of cyling across the fields and vineyards carrying messages or grenades, going over the accounts and listening to the wireless set for news of François, Laurent or the unlikely landing! She was tired of living in dread of the arrival of the Gestapo or the militia, fearing Mathias's return and worrying about the shortage of money. François Tavernier was probably dead since he had not kept his promise . . . the very thought was almost enough to make her fall to her knees.

'Oh God, not that, please!'

Léa left the church overwhelmed with anxiety.

She felt immensely weary. Her badly made wooden-soled shoes felt like lead weights dragging at her feet. When she walked past the last farm on the outskirts of the village, the mangy dogs followed her, barking, and then, reassured, returned to their kennels. At the 'Angel crossroad' she looked round to make sure nobody was there and made a white cross

on the rusty railings. The Verdelais clock tower struck six.
Huge dark clouds were rolling across the sky.

Was it the call of the vast tormented sky? Léa found herself
on the path that led to Sidonie's cottage. She felt dwarfed by
the immenseness of the landscape. How right the old lady
had been to want to return to Bellevue! Here, the soul flew
off towards the distant moors, the great ocean and the infinite
heavens. In these familiar surroundings she always experienced a feeling of peace, a desire to rest, to dream, to medi-
tate, as Adrien Delmas would have said.

She was startled out of her daydreams by a groan. Sidonie's
dog, Belle, was cowering against the door whining.

Léa held out her hand to the animal who stood up and
growled.

'Don't you recognize me?'

On hearing her familiar voice, the animal went to Léa and
lay down at her feet. She let out a sinister howl. Suddenly
worried, Léa pushed open the door and went inside. The
room was in a turmoil: it looked as if a hurricane had hit it.
The furniture was overturned, the crockery smashed, and
papers and linen were strewn everywhere. The sheets had
been torn off the bed and the mattress overturned, indicating
that the cottage had been given a through going-over. Who
on earth could have attacked the humble possessions of a
sick old woman like that? Léa knew the answer but could
not bring herself to say it.

'Sidonie, Sidonie . . .'

The dog had squeezed under the bed and was yelping.
Squashed between the headboard and the wall, the old
woman lay unconscious. Léa had great difficulty heaving her
up and laying her on the mattress. She was ashen and a little
blood trickled from her right nostril. The left side of her face
was bruised and discoloured. Léa leaned over her: her breath
came unsteadily through her half-open mouth. The opening
of her white cotton nightdress revealed red marks where
hands had grabbed the flabby flesh of her neck.

Aghast, Léa stared at the outstretched body of the woman
who once comforted her and gave her little secret treats
when Ruth or her mother had punished her. The memory of

cuddles in the huge old fireside armchair in the kitchen at Montillac made her burst out sobbing and shout in a childlike voice:

'Donie, Donie, answer me . . .'

Dragging herself out of the numbness into which she had sunk, the old woman opened her eyes. Léa flung herself at her.

'Sidonie, please, talk to me . . .'

Slowly she raised her hand and placed it on Léa's bowed head. Her lips opened and closed, but no sound issued from them.

'Please try . . . tell me who did this . . .'

The hand grew heavier. Léa glued her ear to Sidonie's mouth.

'A . . . a . . . away . . . g . . . get away . . .'

Her hand became even heavier. Léa tried gently to disengage herself, murmuring:

'What do you mean?'

The hand slid as if with regret from Léa's thick hair and fell heavily against the wooden bedstead with a dull thud.

Belle howled like a creature possessed.

Léa's tears stopped as she stared incredulously at the beloved wrinkled old face which had suddenly become strange and hostile.

It was not true . . . barely a second ago she had felt the warm breath against her cheek . . . and now . . . that indecent mass of flesh with her nightdress hitched up . . .

Angrily, she smoothed down the nightgown.

Why didn't that dog shut up! Why was she howling like that? Stupid animal. She wasn't crying, was she?

She heard a noise behind her and spun round. A man was standing in the doorway. She stood rooted to the spot in terror. What was he doing in this devastated cottage with Sidonie's corpse not yet cold? Suddenly she understood. Sheer fear swept aside her pride.

'Please, I beg you, don't hurt me!'

Mathias Fayard was no longer looking at her. He pushed her out of the way with one hand and walked over to the bed, his face pale and his fists clenched.

'So they dared!'

How tenderly he joined the gnarled hands and closed the eyes of the woman he used to call as a child 'Mama Sidonie', who was so adept at saving him from having his ears boxed by his father. He knelt down, not to say a long-forgotten prayer, but because he was overwhelmed with sorrow.

Léa watched him fearfully, but when he turned towards her with tears running down his grief-stricken face, she fell sobbing into his arms.

How long did they remain kneeling and clinging to each other beside that corpse? It would take with it to the grave what remained of their childhood.

Belle climbed on to the bed and, whining, licked her mistress's feet.

Mathias was the first to regain control of himself.

'You must get away.'

Léa did not respond. The young man took a grubby handkerchief out of his pocket and wiped his friend's eyes and then his own. She let him get on with it, apparently unaware of what he was doing. He shook her, at first gently and then almost violently.

'Listen to me. You must get away from Montillac. Someone has denounced you and Camille.'

When she still did not respond, he felt like slapping her.

'Good God! Can't you hear me? Dohse's men and the militia are coming to arrest you.'

At last! She seemed to be taking in what he was saying and to see him. Grief and exhaustion gradually gave way to an expression of incredulity and horror.

'And you're the one who's come to warn me!'

He hung his head at her outburst.

'I overheard Denan giving orders to Fiaux, Guilbeau and Lacouture.'

'I thought you were working for them?'

She had suddenly regained her strength and her scorn.

'Sometimes. But whatever you may think, I don't want them to get their hands on you.'

'Is it true that you're familiar with their methods?'

Mathias stood up and looked at Sidonie's corpse.

'I thought I was.'

Léa followed his gaze and she too got to her feet. Her eyes filled with tears again.

'Why her?'

'I heard Fiaux say they received a letter, accusing her of hiding your cousin Lucien and of knowing where the Lefèvre brothers are. But I didn't think for a second that they'd come and interrogate her. I only thought of you, of warning you. What I don't understand is why they didn't go up to the house afterwards.'

'How do you know they didn't?'

'I took a shortcut through the vineyards to come here. I'd have seen or heard their cars. Unless they're hidden in the little pine wood.'

'I didn't notice anything. I went past there on the way back from Verdelais.'

'Come on, let's get out of here.'

'But we can't leave Sidonie like that.'

'There's nothing more we can do for her. When it's dark, I'll go and tell the priest. Hurry up.'

Léa kissed the cold cheek for the last time and left the dog to guard the body. She was still whining.

Outside, the sky too looked threatening.

At the end of the terrace, Mathias stopped her.

'Wait here for me. I'm going to make sure it's safe.'

'No, I'm coming with you.'

He shrugged and helped her up the steep slope. Everything seemed quiet. It was now so dark that they could hardly make out the façade of the house.

Léa noticed that he stayed close to the sparse foliage of the tree arbours to keep out of sight of the farmhouse and the sheds. He certainly did not want his parents to see him.

A thin light shone under the french window which opened on to the terrace. Camille must have been watching out for her because the door was suddenly flung open to reveal her, dressed in her navy blue coat as if she were about to go out.

'Here you are at last!'

Léa pushed her out of the way as she went inside.

'Sidonie's dead.'

'What?'

'This fellow's friends came and "interrogated" her.'

Clasping her hands to her breast, Camille stared at Mathias in disbelief.

'Don't look at me like that, Madame Camille. We don't know exactly what happened.'

'Listen to him! We don't know exactly what happened! Do you think we're stupid? We know very well what happened, do you want me to spell it out for you?'

'There's no need and it won't bring Sidonie back. There are more urgent things to attend to. You must leave.'

'How do we know it's not a trap and that you're not going to take us straight to your Gestapo friends?'

Mathias's jaw was set and he started towards her with his fist raised.

'That's right, hit me, do their job for them . . . you enjoy hitting, don't you?'

'Madame Camille, shut her up. Every second we waste here . . .'

'How do we know we can trust you?'

'You don't. But you, who love your husband, will you believe me if I tell you I love Léa and that in spite of everything that divides us, all the things I've done, I'm prepared to die to keep her from harm.'

Camille laid her hand on the young man's arm.

'I believe you. What about me? Why are you trying to save me?'

'If you were arrested, Léa would never forgive me.'

Ruth came into the room carrying a crammed knapsack which she handed to Léa. 'Here, I've put in some warm clothes, a torch, and two jars of preserves. Now leave.'

'Leave, leave,' crooned little Charles with his woolly hat pulled down over his ears.

'Go on, hurry up,' urged Ruth, shooing them out.

'But you're coming with us!'

'No, somebody has to be here to open the door if they come.'

'I don't want you to stay. Not after what they did to Sidonie.'

'Sidonie?'

'They tortured her to death.'

'My God!' exclaimed the governess, crossing herself.

'Make up your mind quickly, Mademoiselle Ruth. Are you coming or aren't you?'

'No, I'm staying. I can't abandon Monsieur Pierre's house. Don't worry, I can deal with them. Only one thing matters to me . . .'

'Between us, it'll be easier to make them believe you've left for Paris,' said Bernadette Bouchardeau, who had just come into the room.

'Your aunt is right. If they're here, your absence will seem more natural.'

'But they might be killed!'

'That's no more likely than if you stay.'

'That's true,' said Ruth. 'Go on, it's dark now. Mathias, I hold you responsible for them.'

'Have I ever lied to you?'

'What are you planning to do?'

'Take them to Albert's so he can hide them.'

'Why to Albert?' Léa almost shrieked.

'Because he's a member of the Resistance and he'll know what to do with you.'

'What makes you say that?'

'Stop taking me for a fool. I've known for a long time that he hides British airmen, that he knows where the parachute drops are and that he helped the Lefèvre brothers to escape.'

'And you haven't denounced him!'

'I don't believe in denouncing people.'

'Your bosses can't be very pleased with you.'

'That's enough!' shouted Camille severely. 'You can argue later. For the time being, we've got to get away before they come. Ruth and Madame Bouchardeau, are you sure you won't come with us?'

'Quite sure, Camille dear. I want to stay here in case Lucien or my brother needs me. And anyway, I'm too old to wander around the countryside sleeping under the stars.

You ought to leave Charles with us, we'd look after him well.'

'Thank you very much, but I'll feel more secure if he's with me.'

'I'm going to my parents' house to make sure they don't see us leave. I'll meet you in fifteen minutes in Montonoire where I've left the car.'

Mathias went out through the kitchen.

The two young women and the child gulped down some soup, buttoned up their coats and kissed Ruth and Bernadette Bouchardeau for the last time before setting off into the night.

They were hiding near the black car where they had been waiting for Mathias for nearly twenty minutes.

'He won't come. I tell you, he won't come.'

'Yes he will. Shh! Listen! Someone's walking along the road.'

Camille, who was crouching by the car, hugged her little boy closer.

It was so dark that the masculine figure merged with the sky.

'Léa, it's me.'

'About time too!'

'I couldn't get a word in edgeways with my father shouting and my mother groaning. I almost had to run away. Quick, get in.'

Charles was clutching Léa's old teddy bear which Ruth had come across in the attic and patched up. He clambered into the car, laughing. He was the only one who found the situation amusing.

Never had the streets of the little mediaeval town of Saint-Macaire seemed so dark and narrow. The blue glow of the concealed headlamps was not bright enough to light up the road ahead. At last, they pulled up outside the butcher's house. Mathias switched off the engine. There was not a glimmer of light, not a sound . . . only the oppressive silence of the impenetrable night that seemed as if it would go on for ever. Inside the car, they all held their breath, their ears pricked up, even Charles whose face was buried in his mother's neck. There was a click, Léa jumped. It was Mathias, cocking his pistol.

'It's best if you go and see,' he whispered.

She slid nimbly out of the car and knocked on the door. At the fifth knock, a hushed voice asked:

'What is it?'

'It's me, Léa.'

'Who?'

'Léa Delmas.'

The door was opened by the butcher's wife in her night-gown, a shawl over her shoulders; she was holding a torch.

'Come in at once, child. You gave me the fright of my life. I thought something had happened to Albert.'

'Isn't he here?'

'No, he's gone to Saint-Jean de Blaignac for a parachu . . . But what on earth brings you here at this time of night?'

'The Gestapo . . . I'm with Camille d'Argilat and her son. Mathias Fayard drove us here . . .'

'Mathias Fayard? Here? We're done for!'

Pushing Camille and Charles ahead of him, Mathias walked in and closed the door behind him.

'There's nothing to be afraid of, Mireille. If I'd wanted to denounce you, I'd have done so a long time ago. All I ask of Albert and his comrades is to hide these people, I don't want to know where, until I find another solution.'

'I don't trust you. Everyone knows you work with them.'

'I don't give a damn what everyone knows. It's not a question of my safety but of theirs. If it makes Albert and the others feel happier, they can take my parents as hostages.'

'Good grief!' Mireille spat out scornfully.

Mathias shrugged.

'I don't care what you think of me. What matters is preventing the Gestapo from arresting them. If Albert wants to speak to me, he should leave a message at the Lion d'Or in Langon. I'll meet him wherever he tells me. Now I must be on my way.'

33

When he went over to Léa, she looked away. Only Camille felt sorry for him, he was obviously suffering a great deal.

'Thank you, Mathias.'

The three women stood motionless in the kitchen doorway until the noise of the engine died away. Still clutching his teddy bear, little Charles had fallen asleep on a chair by the fire which had long since gone out.

It was three o'clock in the morning by the time Albert came back from the parachute landing with Riri the gendarme, Dupeyron the garage-owner and Cazenave the road-digger. Each man was wearing a sub-machine gun slung over his shoulder.

'Léa . . . Madame Camille . . . what's happened?'

'The Gestapo are looking for them.'

The four men froze.

'And that's not all,' said Mireille, her voice growing shriller, 'they've murdered Sidonie and it was young Fayard who brought them here for you to hide.'

'The bastard,' groaned Dupeyron.

'He'll denounce us,' stammered the gendarme.

'I don't think he will,' said the butcher pensively.

'He said that if we didn't trust him, we could take his parents hostage,' mumbled Mireille.

Camille felt obliged to intervene.

'I'm sure he won't betray anybody.'

'You could be right, Madame Camille, but we can't take any risks. I think, my dear Mireille, that we are going to have to take to the woods.'

'You don't mean it! What about the shop? And our boy, supposing he wants to join us, supposing he needs us! You go if you want, but I'm staying.'

'But Mi . . .'

'Don't keep on, my mind's made up.'

'Then I'll stay too.'

The buxom woman flung her arms round her husband's neck. He hugged her close as he tried to hide his emotion.

'Heh! I say, can you imagine me slaughtering old mother Lecuyer's ox?'

This made them all smile.

'That's all very well, but what are we going to do with them?' asked the gendarme, indicating Léa and Camille.

Albert drew his comrades over to the other side of the kitchen. They whispered together in a huddle for a few minutes. Riri and Dupeyron went out.

'When they come back, we'll leave, if all is well. We're going to take you to some friends of ours for a few days. We know we can count on them. After that, we'll see. A lot depends on what Mathias tells me when I see him.'

He turned to his wife.

'Mireille, prepare a nice big basket of food.'

'There's no need, we have plenty,' said Camille.

'Never mind, you don't know how long you'll have to stay in hiding.'

The garage-owner returned:

'It's safe to go, everything's quiet. Riri's keeping watch.'

'Right, let's go. Mireille, don't worry if I'm not back before daybreak. I'll take the nipper, Cazenave'll take the basket. Come on, say goodbye.'

The van was extremely uncomfortable as it bumped about over the ruts.

'Is it much further?' groaned Léa.

'Not far now, it's just before Villandraut. The whole region is safe. The local Resistance are friends of ours. Your uncle knows them well.'

'Do you think we'll be staying here long?'

'I've no idea. We'll see when I've spoken to Mathias. Here we are.'

After a short drive between low buildings, they pulled up outside a house that was set a little apart from the others. A dog barked. A door opened. A man carrying a gun came up to them.

'Is that you, Albert?' he asked in a low voice.

'Yes, I've brought you some friends who are in a spot of trouble.'

'You could have warned me.'

'It wasn't possible. Have you got any room at the moment?'

35

'You're lucky, the English left last night. Is it for long?'

'I don't know.'

'Women and a kid,' he mumbled, 'I don't like this. We're always having trouble because of those bloody females.'

'Charming!' said Léa between gritted teeth.

'Don't take any notice,' said Albert, 'old Léon's always grumbling, but there isn't a better shot in the area nor a kinder heart.'

'Don't stay outside like that, the neighbours are all on our side, but these days, a rotten apple can easily get into the barrel.'

The room into which they were shown was very long and low with a floor of dried mud. There were three large, high beds surrounded by faded red curtains hanging from the wooden beams on the ceiling. Between the beds were carved wooden chests and a huge table cluttered with traps, red and blue cartridges, a sub-machine gun in bits lying on a newspaper, dirty dishes and old rags. The chairs were all different and the stove was black from years of use. The fireplace was huge and on the mantelpiece were the inevitable engraved cartridges from the Great War. There was a worn stone draining slab by the sink over which hung yellowing calendars covered with fly droppings. The 1944 calendar seemed quite out of place with its gaudy colours. That was the only furniture in the room which glowed yellow in the light from the oil lamp. There was no electricity on the farm.

The simplicity, coupled with the strong smell of the tobacco leaves hanging from the ceiling, took the two women aback and they stood gaping in the doorway.

'I wasn't expecting more guests so soon, I haven't had time to change the beds,' said Léon, taking clean sheets out of one of the chests.

'Is there another room?' Léa whispered in Albert's ear.

'Oh no!' retorted their host, who had sharp ears, 'there's no other room. This is the best I can offer you, young lady. Here, come and help me make the beds. You'll see, they're comfortable. Real goose down. Once you're inside, you won't want to get up again.'

The sheets were rough but smelled of sweet grass.

'If nature calls, it's behind the house, there's as much room as you like,' he said mischievously.

'What about the washing?'

'There's a bowl outside and the well isn't far.'

The expression on Léa's face must have been funny, as Camille burst out laughing, despite her tiredness.

'You'll see, we'll be fine. Let me help you.'

Charles did not wake up, even when his mother undressed him and tucked him into bed.

Chapter 2

Camille and Léa had not slept so well for a long time. Even Charles, who was usually the first to awaken, was still asleep although it was late morning. The light shone through the thick red curtains, making a warm rosy glow. They could tell it was a fine day. The door must have been open – they could hear reassuring farmyard noises, hens clucking, the squeaking of chains and the clanging of the bucket being lowered into the well, the cooing of turtledoves, a distant whinnying, a child calling its mother. It seemed as though nothing could disturb such perfect tranquillity. Somebody came into the room and poured coal into the stove. Shortly afterwards the aroma of real coffee filled the air. The smell was enough to entice Camille and Léa out of bed and they simultaneously drew back the curtains surrounding them. At the sight of the two dishevelled young women, Léon let out a groan that sounded like a laugh.

'Well, well, I've had to resort to drastic measures to get you out of bed: nothing but pure Colombian coffee.'

Léa almost fell off the bed in her haste. She had forgotten how high it was. She grabbed the bowl Léon offered her. She raised it to her nostrils and breathed in the wonderful smell with pleasure.

'I put two lumps of sugar in, I hope that's not too much.'

'Two lumps of sugar! Did you hear that, Camille?'

'I heard,' she said, coming over to them. She seemed so thin in her long white nightgown – it made her look like a hospital patient.

Léon handed her a bowl of coffee too. He was delighted that they were so thrilled.

38

'How did you get hold of all that coffee?'

'The English airmen gave me a packet of it when they left. And that's not all.'

From the chest which appeared to serve as a larder, he took out a large loaf of bread.

'I think you'll enjoy this, it's white bread, real brioche!'

He took his knife from his pocket, opened it slowly and cut three generous slices. Léa buried her nose in the thick light bread and greedily breathed in its sweet smell as if she were afraid it might disappear for ever. Camille stared at her share with the same earnestness that she put into everything she did.

'Bread . . . bread . . .'

Charles was standing up in bed holding out his hands. Léon picked him up and, sitting him on his knee, cut him a slice.

'That's far too much for him, Mosieur Léon, he'll never eat all that,' exclaimed his mother.

'I wouldn't be surprised if he did, a sturdy little fellow like that. Here, drink your coffee before it gets cold.'

The old farmer was right, Charles ate all his bread.

They spent three days in the country. The weather was fine though a little chilly.

Albert returned on the evening of the 21st. He had met Mathias in Langon. The young man had agreed to follow him blindfold, with his hands tied behind his back, and to be bundled into the boot of a car and taken to a Resistance hideout near Mauriac. There, he had answered the butcher and his comrades' questions without hesitation. Satisfied with his replies, Albert had dropped him that night near the station at La Réole.

'Have the Gestapo been to the house?' asked Léa.

'They haven't, but Superintendent Poinsot's men have.'

'Was Maurice Fiaux with them?'

'No.'

'What happened? How are my aunt and Ruth?'

'They're fine. They interrogated them politely without really taking any notice of their answers, according to Ruth.'

'What did they want?'

'They wanted to know if they'd heard from Father Adrien. Not a word about you or Madame d'Argilat.'

'That's odd! Why did Sidonie tell me in her last breath to get away, and why did Mathias think we were going to be arrested?'

'Because, he told us, he had overheard a conversation between one of the militia chiefs and Fiaux saying that you probably had a lot to do with the Lefèvre brothers' escape and that you must know the whereabouts of Father Adrien and your cousin Lucien.'

'So why did they go to Sidonie's place first?'

'The police received a letter denouncing her – I've got an idea who sent it – saying that she hid members of the Resistance.'

'Why didn't Mathias warn us sooner?'

'Apparently Denan kept him in his office for several hours.'

'But who is this Denan?' interrupted Léa.

'A nasty piece of work is Lucien Denan! He arrived in Bordeaux with the exodus. Until 1942, he was a sales assistant at the department store Dames de France, in the haber-dashery department. As soon as work was over, he would go to the central intelligence office and record all the information he had gleaned about the shop's employees. He soon became their top intelligence gatherer. He left the store and was nominated Assistant Inspector for Jewish Affairs, and subsequently regional delegate. When the Bordeaux militia was set up, he became chief of the 2nd Section. They say he also works for the German Intelligence service under the name of "Monsieur Henri". That's who he is. To go back to young Fayard, as soon as he was able to get away, he took a car. Unfortunately for Sidonie, he arrived too late. They buried her this morning, poor thing. There weren't many of us at the funeral.'

Léa could not hold back her tears.

'Ruth did everthing very nicely,' continued Albert. 'I've taken in her dog but I'm afraid it won't be long before Belle goes to join her mistress.'

'Are they looking for us or aren't they?' asked Camille.

'According to Mathias, officially they aren't. But that doesn't mean a thing. I think it's best for you to stay in hiding for a while.'

'Does he know where we are?'

'Of course not. We don't trust him to that extent. I'm meeting him in Bordeaux, at Saint-Jean station, on the 24th. I'll try to come and see you the following day. Until then, lie low.'

The weather was magnificent and warm although the mornings were very cold. Intoxicated by the seaside smell of the pine trees, Léa and Camille felt as if they were on holiday. They let themselves sink into a state of mental and physical lethargy. They spent their days in the forest, picnicking under the trees, snoozing in a hollow in the sandy ground, playing hide-and-seek with Charles, oblivious to reality. They came down to earth with a bump when a comrade arrived to tell old Léon that the butcher and his wife had been arrested. Mireille had been taken to Fort Hâ, while Albert was at 197 Route du Médoc (renamed Avenue du Maréchal Pétain) for interrogation.

Camille turned pale. She remembered the dreadful time she had spent in the dungeons in that sinister fortress, with the cries of the tortured ringing in her ears.

'When was he arrested?'

'On his way to meet young Fayard in Bordeaux.'

'Mathias denounced him!' cried Léa.

'We don't think so. As a security measure, we told Aristide. Two of his men were watching the station and another was waiting for Mathias Fayard near the meeting place. Everything seemed normal. I arrived with Albert and Riri five minutes before the appointed time. We got caught up in the crowds getting off the Paris train and were separated. Riri and I saw Mathias arrive. He seemed to be alone. We turned round. Ten or so yards away, Albert was surrounded by an officer, two German soldiers and three Frenchmen in civilian clothes. We heard him saying: "You are making a mistake."

'The crowd parted in front of the group and that was

41

when, I think, Mathias realized what was happening. He turned pale, took a few steps towards them and then stopped. I was close to him.

‘ "Bastard," I said to him, "we'll get you for this."

'He looked at me as if he didn't understand.

‘ "I had nothing to do with this, I don't understand. It's a coincidence."

‘ "You're going to pay for this coincidence."

‘ "Don't be so stupid. I'm the only person who knew about our meeting."

‘ "What proof is that?"

‘ "Think what you like, let's follow them, I want to know where they're taking him. Come with me."

‘ "So you can have me arrested too!"

‘ "Here, take my pistol. All you have to do is shoot me if you think I'm going to betray you."

'And he handed me his gun, just like that, without even trying to hide it. I grabbed it, saying:

‘ "You must be out of your mind!"

'I checked that it was loaded and put it in my pocket. We headed for the exit. Riri joined us. From the look on his face, I thought he was going to finish Fayard off there and then.

‘ "Explain to him," said Mathias calmly as he walked towards a front-wheel drive vehicle parked at the foot of the steps.

'Meanwhile, only a few yards away, Albert was being pushed into a Citroën 15 with a German number plate. I got in with Mathias while Riri walked away.

‘ "Isn't he coming?" asked Mathias.

‘ "He doesn't trust you. He'll follow with some friends of ours who aren't far away."

‘ "Well, they'd better hurry up," he said, pulling away behind the German car.

'I got out the gun and pointed it at Mathias, ready to shoot at the slightest doubt. I turned round several times, wondering how Riri and our pals could possibly follow us. Ahead of us, the Jerries were driving at high speed.

' "Shit," said Mathias, "they're not going to the Cours du Chapeau Rouge."

' "What's in the Cours du Chapeau Rouge?"

' "One of Poinsot's offices."

' "So?"

' "That means they're going to hand him over to the Germans and it's harder to escape from their clutches than from the French police."

'We turned off the Cours Aristide-Briand and went down the Cours d'Albret. I thought: "They're taking him to Fort Hâ," but no, they continued. We drove past the prison. When we reached the Rue Abbé-de-l'Epée, Mathias asked me if I could see my friends behind us. There were just a few bicycles and a German van but no other cars. As we drove up the Rue de la Croix-de-Seguey, I realized where they were heading. At the Médoc barrier, we were stopped by German police. I put the gun back in my pocket; my stomach sank. Mathias showed them a card and they motioned him through. The streets of Le Bouscat were almost deserted and there were no cars. Mathias slowed down to put a greater distance between us and them. Still no sign of my pals. When the Jerries stopped, we stopped too, about a hundred yards from them. We saw them push Albert into what we knew was the Gestapo interrogation centre. There was nothing we could do. I looked at Mathias, he was still very pale and his hands, clenching the wheel, were mottled. I felt like killing him on the spot. He guessed what I was thinking for he said:

' "There'd be no point. You'd only get yourself arrested too. We've got to tell his wife and the others. I swear I haven't betrayed anyone. The traitors are in your midst."

'I let him drive on. We went slowly past number 224, the mansion where Commander Luther lives, almost opposite number 197. All was quiet.'

The man drained the glass Léon had poured for him.

'What happened next?' asked Léa.

'We went back to the station, to see if the others were there. After having a look round, Mathias said:

' "Let's not hang around here, we'll draw attention to ourselves. Let's go to Saint-Macaire and tell Mireille."

'We drove along the right bank of the Garonne. Just outside Rions, we were stopped by militiamen looking for saboteurs who had blown up something in the town. As we left Saint-Maixent, we were stopped again, this time by Germans. When we finally reached Saint-Macaire, it was more than three hours after Albert's arrest.

' "We'd better go through the port," said Mathias.

'At the foot of the old ruined castle, he stopped the car and hid it in a cave that served as a shed for people who made their own wine. We scrambled up the slope, and found ourselves behind the church.

' "Don't make a sound," he said, without appearing to notice the gun that was still pointing at him.

'There wasn't a soul to be seen in the narrow streets, most of the shutters were closed even though it was broad daylight. Two shots rang out and echoed through the streets.

' "That came from the direction of Albert's house," cried Mathias.

'Hiding in a doorway, we witnessed Mireille's arrest as she was pushed into a car by a German NCO. Outside the butcher's shop, a dog lay bleeding to death on the pavement. A soldier laughed as he kicked the carcass which rolled to a halt not far from where we stood. I heard Mathias murmur:

' "Belle . . . they've killed Belle . . . " '

'Sidonie's dog!' cried Léa. 'Poor creature.'

'Then what did you do?' asked Léon.

'I made him go back down and drive me to Bazas where I handed him over to George's men until we reach a decision.'

'How did you find out where they took Mireille?'

'When we arrived at George's place, a comrade who's a police officer in Bordeaux had just told them about the double arrest and where each of them had been taken.'

Overwhelmed by the news, they sat in silence. Léon was the first to speak. He turned to the two young women who were hugging little Charles. The child's anxious eyes darted from one to the other.

'You're no longer safe here.'

44

'Why do you say that?' asked Léa irritably. 'Albert would never betray us.'

'He'll hold out as long as he can, I'm sure, but it's a risk we can't afford to take. Don't forget they've arrested his wife as well. If they torture her in front of him, he'll talk.'

'He's right.'

Suddenly, Léon reached for the rack and grabbed the gun that was usually hidden under his bed, aiming it at the door. They all fell silent. They heard a scratching sound and the door opened to reveal a man in a lumber jacket.

'My goodness,' said the man in English, 'Léon, don't you recognize me?'

The old man put down his gun grumbling:

'Aristide, you shouldn't just turn up like that, it's dangerous.'

'You're right. Hello, Léa, do you remember me?'

'Very well. It's nice to see you again.'

'You must be Madame d'Argilat?' he said, turning to Camille.

'Yes, how do you do?'

'I've got good news for you. Your husband left Morocco with the division formed by General Leclerc for a landing. He arrived in Britain on 21st April at the port of Swansea in South Wales. The General himself went to greet them.'

Happiness transformed Camille. How beautiful she was, thought Léa. She felt a surge of affection and kissed her. How long ago it seemed since she hated the wife of the man she thought she loved, who had been her lover for one night in the pink brick cellars of Toulouse. With no ulterior motive, she shared the happiness of the woman who had become her friend.

'Thank you for bringing me such good news, monsieur.'

'I think I'm in a position to say that you'll have more good news soon. Meanwhile, you must get away from here. I'd gladly take you to stay with a friend of mine in Souprosses, but I think she's being watched by Grand-Clément's men who are looking for me.'

'Supposing we went back to Montillac, since they're no longer looking for us?'

'We can't be sure. It's better not to take any risks.'

'For a few days, we can go to the dovecote,' said Léon. 'It's well hidden in the forest, they'll never find it. It's not very comfortable, but . . .'

'Life is more important than comfort,' said Aristide. 'Pack clothes and food for a few days, we're leaving right away. Have you got blankets there?'

'I think so. I'll take a clean one for the child.'

'What are you going to do with Mathias?' Léa asked the English agent.

'If it were up to me, I'd put him on woodcutting duty,' grumbled Léon.

'We can't just get rid of him. We'll have to interrogate him. Even I, who normally trust nobody, am inclined to believe he had nothing to do with these arrests.'

'All the same, he works for them.'

'He's not the only one, I'm afraid! But, until it's proved to the contrary, he hasn't killed anyone.'

'We're ready, monsieur,' said Camille, gripping a small holdall.

Colonel Claude Bonnier, the regional military representative, known as Hypotenuse, had been sent to France by the Central Intelligence and Action Bureau in November 1943 with the task of reorganizing the Resistance movement in the Aquitaine region after Grand-Clément's betrayal.

He was captured in Bordeaux by the Gestapo in February 1944 while he was at his radio headquarters in the Rue Galard, about to send a message to London. The operator, who had been arrested as the result of being denounced, had, in turn, denounced Hypotenuse who walked into a trap laid by Lieutenant Kunesch.

He was taken to Le Bouscat, to the headquarters on the Route du Médoc where he was interrogated at about 6 p.m. by Dohse in person. He had obstinately refused to admit that he had been sent by London and insisted that his name was Claude Bonnier alias Bordin, even though he had been identified by Toussaint, the Lespine brothers, Durand and

Grolleau, and he denied having ordered the execution of Colonel Camplan, suspected of treason.'*

After about twenty minutes, Dohse, annoyed, had ordered him to be taken to solitary confinement. He would continue the interrogation after dinner. He was locked up, still handcuffed. In the middle of the night, a message was sent to Dohse in the officers' mess: something strange was going on in Hypotenuse's cell. When he reached the cellar at 197 Route du Médoc which served as a prison, Bonnier was lying on the ground, his body jerking about, foaming at the mouth, face and lips streaked with mud, groaning weakly. The chief warder was leaning over him. He straightened up.

'*Er hat sich mit Zyankali vergiftet.*'

'*Das seh' ich auch, Dummkopf! Haben Sie ihn nicht durchsucht?*'

'*Selbstverständlich, Herr Leutnant, aber die Kapsel muss in seinem Jackenfutter versteckt gewesen sein.*'

'*Wie hat er das fertiggebracht, mit gefesselten Händen?*'

'*Er muss die Kapsel mit den Zähnen erwischt haben, aber dann ist sie ihm entfallen. Die Flüssigkeit hat sich auf dem Fussboden ausgebreitet und er hat sie augfeleckt. Daher stammt auch der Staub in seinem Gesicht, und deshalb war er auch nicht sofort tot.*'

'*Rufen Sie schnell einen Arzt!*'

'*Zu Befehl, Herr Leutnant!*'†

---

* Hero of the 1914–18 war, Eugène Camplan joined the Resistance in its early days. In 1943, Colonel Touny assigned him the task of coordinating the Free French forces in the Bordeaux region. He was named head of the southern subdivision of the B2 region. Suspected of treason (meetings with Dohse and Grand-Clément), by Bonnier, he was executed by Bonnier's men in January 1944, near Ruffec in the Linaux woods. After the war, as the result of a prolonged inquiry, Colonel Camplan, 'the victim of a tragic misunderstanding', was officially exonerated and declared to have 'died for France'.

† He's poisoned himself with cyanide.

I can see that, you idiot. Wasn't he searched?

Of course he was, sir. No doubt he'd hidden the capsule in a fold in his jacket.

How did he manage that if he was handcuffed?

continued overleaf

The warder left the room, shouting:

'Einen Arzt, schnell, einen Arzt!'*

In the neighbouring cells, the prisoners put their hands over their ears in vain to try and keep out the cries and moans. Were the twenty-year-old Resistance fighters feeling remorse at the suffering of the man they had denounced while being manipulated by Dohse? Probably not. It seemed right to them that the man who had killed their leader, Colonel Camplan, should pay for it with his own life.

Claude Bonnier died at dawn without having talked.

Deeply impressed, Friedrich Dohse had murmured:

'The London ones are no ordinary men.'

Paradoxically, Bonnier's terrible death, which should have paralysed the movement, galvanized the fighters in the shadows and revived their strength.

The same thing happened when Albert was captured.

The butcher was no ordinary man either.

He had joined the Resistance out of a firm conviction that the Germans had no business in France and that men like himself ought to do everything they could to chase them out, if in the future they wanted to hold their heads up high in front of their children. Son of a soldier who had fought at Verdun and died as a result of his wounds, he had adopted one of his father's favourite sayings. Each time he went for a walk on the Pian slopes which looked out over the region, the old man would stop to contemplate the beautiful fertile land and say quietly:

'It is worth laying down our lives for France.'

But Albert did not have a cyanide capsule, and Dohse did not step in between Poinsot's torturers and him. They tortured him with the most sophisticated methods, with the help of butchers' knives.

He must have picked the capsule up with his teeth and dropped it. He dragged himself across the floor and licked the liquid, which would explain the dust all over his face and the fact that he did not die immediately.

Quick, call a doctor.

Yes, sir.

* A doctor, quick, call a doctor!

48

At first, he had tried to joke:

'This is God punishing me for having killed so many animals.'

They hacked at him with the knives and laughing, they pushed pieces of garlic into the cuts.

'A nice leg of lamb!'

They sprinkled salt and pepper on his bleeding chest and tied him up 'like a roasting joint'. When they were tired of 'working on this lump of meat', which had become inert and from which they had not been able to extract a single word, they kicked the body down the cellar steps and shut him up in the cell in which Bonnier had died. He came round to hear his torturers say with a coarse laugh:

'If he doesn't talk tomorrow, we'll cut his wife up in front of him.'

'I'll talk,' was his only thought.

During the interminable night, the slightest movement caused him so much pain that he was unable to suppress his cries. For hours and hours, he gnawed the rope that bound the upper part of his arm. Despite the damp cold of the cellar, he was soon sweating from the effort. Just before dawn, the rope gave way. His tortured body was exhausted, he lost consciousness . . .

When he came to, the sun was rising. He started to undo the ropes which were embedded in his wounds and caked with blood. This new pain was so unbearable that it got the better of his determination, and he cried as he had not cried since the death of his father when he was nine years old. His strong frame shook with loud, ridiculous sobs. He fell back on to the filthy floor, and sank into the depths of despair . . . If his torturers had come back to interrogate him just then, he would probably have talked.

Under his cheek, his tears made a puddle which seeped into the dust . . . His fingers worked the muddy mixture. 'The earth . . .' It was from the earth that he drew the strength and the anger he needed to finish freeing himself from the ropes. A ray of light crept in through a badly-covered air vent. Near the opening was a large metal ring that Albert managed to grasp by raising his arm. A pipe ran

49

the length of the wall; he climbed up it and tied one end of the rope to the ring. With the other, he made a slipknot which he put over his head. He let himself go . . . His feet waved in the air. A last-minute effort at survival made him try to climb down the pipe. The thin rope tightened round his neck and crushed his larynx. Albert took a long time to die.

In the neighbouring cell, two members of the Sainte-Foy-la-Grande Resistance group sang, in a husky voice that became louder and louder:

> *Ami, si tu tombes,*
> *Un ami sort de l'ombre*
> *A ta place*
>
> *Demain du sang noir*
> *Séchera au grand soleil*
> *Sur les routes*
>
> *Sifflez compagnons*
> *Dans la nuit la liberté*
> *Nous écoute.**

> * Friend, if you fall,
> A friend will step out of the shadows
> To take your place
>
> Tomorrow, black blood
> Will dry in the hot sun
> On the roads
>
> Whistle comrades
> For in the dark night, freedom
> Is listening to us.

The *Song of the Partisans* (Chant des Partisans), with words by Maurice Druon and Joseph Kessel, music by Anna Marly, was broadcast for the first time by the BBC on 9th February 1944, and read by Jacques Duchesne with the title 'Freedom Song' (Chant de la Libération). It was broadcast twice after that with Anna Marly's music, in April and in August 1944. Written in London, this poem was first published in the *Cahiers de la Libération* (Freedom Notebooks), a clandestine review founded in occupied France by Emmanuel d'Astier de la Vigerie in September 1943.

Albert's wife and comrades did not learn of his dreadful death until the day after Bordeaux was liberated.

Chapter 3

Dear Léa,

I don't know how things are at Montillac, but here in Paris, everyone is going mad. We are all living in the hope that the Allies will land and never has the population hated the Anglo-American forces and their wretched air-raids more. The raid on the night of 20th April was particularly terrifying. I was at the home of some friends who live on the top floor of an apartment block in the Place du Panthéon. For more than an hour we sat there watching the show drinking champagne and whisky. It was more spectacular than the firework displays on the 14th July. Not a single stained-glass window was left intact in the Sacré-Coeur. More than six hundred people were killed. Our aunts were very upset. So was I, it made me feel bad but I prefer not to think about it, otherwise I'd be like them: I'd spend my time praying in the cellar, in the metro or in the cinemas that stay open till six o'clock in the morning to serve as air-raid shelters. There are air-raid warnings nearly every night and even during the day. It's no way to live.

As for food, luckily I manage, otherwise all of us in the Rue de l'Université would starve. It must be easier at Montillac. My friends and I talk of nothing but Doctor Petiot and the murders in the Rue Lesueur. I have night-mares about it. So does Aunt Lisa who keeps all the news-paper clippings about the whole nasty business. They say that the English dropped explosive cake tins on Charente. Did you hear about it? Even though most people think it's anti-British propaganda, some say the English are quite capable of such a thing. Paris received a visit from my ex-hero. Field-Marshal Pétain came in person to be acclaimed outside the Town Hall. Aunt Albertine and I had the most awful trouble stopping Lisa from going to see him.

I see Françoise and her baby from time to time. Otto had forty-eight hours leave last week. He still hasn't been granted permission to get married. I think Françoise is very upset but she hasn't said anything to me about it. She pretends to be enjoying herself with women who she thinks are in the same position as herself, but in fact they're just soldiers' whores. I advised her to return to Montillac until the end of the war, and she replied that it was out of the question. You ought to write to her. Otto has gone back to the Eastern Front. I'm going to try and send you some cigarettes and a length of lovely blue material.

This'll make you laugh: I've begun reading. A friend lent me a book that was published before the war, I think. It's the story of a family and an estate just like ours except that the story's set in America, in the deep south during the Civil War. It's called *Gone with the Wind*, it's great. You ought to get it from Mollat's in Bordeaux.

How are Camille, Charles, Ruth and Aunt Bernadette? Give them my love. Don't forget a big kiss for Sidonie too. Have you heard from Laurent? Have you seen that funny François Tavernier again? Are Uncle Luc and his charming son still pro-German? What has become of Mathias? I can't believe he's working for the Gestapo. And are his dear parents still stealing from us? I haven't managed to get the money you asked me for. I talked to Françoise and our aunts, but you know how badly off they are: they've only just got enough to live on. When we told Otto, he was genuinely distressed not to be able to help out, but his father has cut him off without a penny, he's only got his pay. Perhaps you should think over Fayard's suggestions. What does Camille say? I know you'll fly off the handle at me for suggesting we sell Montillac or at least part of it. I'm going to sign off now because some friends have arrived to take me to the cinema. We're going to the Helder to see *Le Voyageur sans Bagages*.*

Write soon, lots of love,

Laure.

PS In spite of the air-raids, you should come back to Paris, it would give you a break. I'd like to take you to listen to some jazz in a cellar in the Latin Quarter.

Léa smiled as she finished reading the letter. 'My little sister really has no idea,' she thought. She unfolded a third sheet of notepaper covered with elegant handwriting.

My little girl,

I'm sending this with Laure's letter to tell you how much I'm thinking of you and that beloved house where you and your sisters were born and that your poor father and dear mother were so attached to. Lisa and I are very worried about the difficult situation you are in. We've been through our accounts again and again but we are virtually penniless. We own nothing other than our apartment in the Rue de l'Université. In order to eat, we had to sell our mother's finest jewellery at ridiculously low prices, and the pieces that are left have only a sentimental value. The investments we made before the war have proved disastrous and our banker has run off with the gold we entrusted to him. In other words, short of selling the apartment, we can't help you. Lisa and I are desperately sorry not to be able to do anything. Have you thought of asking your uncle Luc's advice? I know you don't see eye to eye, but out of respect for his brother's memory, I'm sure he'll help you as best he can. Too many dishonest folk are trying to take advantage of women who, because of the war, find themselves having to cope alone with situations they have not been prepared for. The war will soon be over. If only you can hold out until then!

Laure causes us quite a lot of anxiety, she's always out, she comes home late at night, dealing in goodness-knows-

* Traveller without a suitcase

54

what, we worry about her almost as much as Françoise, whose prospects of marriage seem to be fading. What will become of her afterwards?

Write to us more often and tell us how you and dear Camille are. We are delighted that she is with you. Give my regards to your aunt, Madame Bouchardeau, and to Ruth. My beloved child, forgive us for not being able to help you. Lisa and I pray for you every day. God bless. Lots of love,

Your Aunt Albertine.

Léa screwed up the letter which fell to the floor. She felt desperate, abandoned. There had to be something she could do.

The young women and the child spent only two nights at the dovecote. On the morning of the third day, Léa was awoken by a familiar voice which, in her sleepy state, she was not able to identify.

'This girl sleeps like a dormouse!'

'Father, what a pleasure to see you.'

'Uncle Adrien!'

'My sleeping beauty!'

Crouching on her blanket, Léa would not let go of her uncle's hand as she stared at him with a mixture of joy and disbelief.

'I thought I wouldn't see you again until the end of the war.'

'The end isn't far away.'

'When did you get here?'

'I was parachuted in last night. I landed not far from here. Aristide was waiting for me and he told me about Albert and Mireille . . .'

'We've got to do something.'

'Aristide and his men have joined forces with the men from La Réole. They're taking care of it. For the time being, there's nothing we can do.'

'I can't stop thinking that it was our fault they were arrested,' said Camille.

'I don't think so. When the Gestapo arrested certain members of the Resistance, they found documents in their homes. Others talked under torture or threat. When I learned in London the name of the young fellow who's Poinsot's right-hand man, I was immediately afraid for Albert and Mireille. He had known they were members of the Resistance for a long time.'

'Why didn't he speak out sooner?'

'That's where this character reveals a particularly perverse streak: he wants to capture all the leading figures of the local Resistance single-handed and take them to his masters.'

'If you know who he is, why doesn't someone do away with him?'

The priest's emaciated face which now sported a splendid moustache dyed black, making him unrecognizable, clouded over. Léa noticed how he suddenly tensed. Poor Uncle Adrien, despite the war, he remained a priest for whom killing an enemy, even if he was a traitor, was to break God's sixth commandment: Thou shalt not kill. Ah! If only she were a man . . .

It was Camille who put her thoughts into words.

'I think I know who you are talking about. I'm only a woman, but I'm ready to kill him if you give me the order.'

Léa stared at her friend in astonishment. Camille, whom she had thought of as a wet blanket for a long time, would never cease to amaze her. As long ago as Orléans, had she not shot the man who attacked them?

Father Delmas gazed at the young woman with affection and emotion.

'It's not a task for someone like you. He's surrounded by bodyguards who are as cruel as he is.'

'But they wouldn't be suspicious of me!'

'Let's drop the subject, please.'

'No, let's talk about it. Camille's right. He wouldn't be suspicious of us.'

'You don't know what you're talking about. Those people are dangerous, very dangerous, and we have enough experienced men to do the job if the need arises.'

'But . . .'

'Camille, don't go on about it.'

There was no arguing with Adrien. He smiled and went on:

'I've got a surprise for you. Can't you guess?'

'You . . . you've seen Laurent?'

'Yes, when I visited General Leclerc.'

'How is he?'

'As well as can be expected. I agreed, although it's strictly forbidden, to carry a letter for you. Here you are.'

With an unsteady hand, the young woman took the crumpled envelope Adrien Delmas held out to her.

'Whatever you do, don't keep it. As soon as you've read it, destroy it. Are you coming, Léa? Let's go for a walk.'

Left alone, Camille turned the blank envelope over and over. Finally, she tore it open with uncharacteristic violence. She took out two sheets of cheap squared paper:

My darling wife,

What I am doing is madly careless for both of us and for our friend but I can't stand the long silence any more. Every single night I dream of us and our child, I imagine both of you in my father's house, when at last we can be together again. It is for that long-awaited moment that I am fighting. These last few months in Africa with men of determination and a leader whom many find tough but all worship, have made me believe in the future.

We are living in remarkable comfort in the middle of a beautiful estate. The officers live in the castle and the men in comfortable barracks placed at our disposal by the British government. We have a training ground of four thousand hectares. I always think of you when I enter the General's office in the library. Half of the books are exquisitely bound eighteenth-century French works. You would like this room. Its high windows look out over lawns surrounded by huge trees and greener than any grass you ever see in France.

Since our recent move here, the General has decided to dine in the company of his senior officers, which entitles me to attend these gloomy silent meals, our leader not being a talkative man. On top of that, there's another honour we all dread, that of being chosen for the "great cretin's walk" if the weather permits, or for the "little cretin's walk" if the weather is bad. One has to walk three kilometres which can be doubled or tripled according to the General's mood. His silences are interspersed with reminiscences of Chad, of Ksar-Rhilaine, of his two escapes, or of his bicycle ride across France. The other evening, he asked me to talk about my son. It was so unusual for him to ask about his men's families that I sat there speechless for a moment. That made him angry: "Why don't you answer me? You're as bad as the rest of your comrades, you can't stand my walks and my monologues on my campaigns. But I am capable of showing interest in other subjects apart from the war." That is no doubt so, but not one of us can believe it. So I told him about you, about Charles and about our region and the people who live there. I couldn't stop talking. He didn't interrupt once. At the castle door, he clapped me on the shoulder and said with that smile that makes his eyes crinkle and takes years off him: "You see, I do know how to listen. Good night."

Our days begin at dawn and end late. We are all overtrained and a little on edge. Tomorrow evening, we're going to the concert in the cathedral to hear Brahms's *Requiem* and Beethoven's *Fifth Symphony*. I'll think of you more than ever and allow the music to bring me closer to you.

Darling, take care of yourself and our child. Tell our lovely friend that it is a great comfort to me to know that she is with you. Give her my love. I pray to God that we may soon be reunited. Talk to my son about me from time to time so that he will recognize me when I hug him. These lines are the last you will hear from me; don't keep them. I kiss your gentle face and your beautiful hands. I love you.

Laurent.

Tears of joy ran down Camille's face. Ever since she had

known him, even when he was away, he had always been present and loving. When it was all over . . .

A shot rang out. The young woman was dragged out of her lovesick daydreams with a jolt. She went into the clearing. Old Léon and three young men wearing berets were pushing a panic-stricken lad ahead of them with their rifle butts. He was clutching a bloody hand to his chest. They thrust him in front of Adrien and Léa.

'He's a spy,' said one of the comrades.

'It's not true!'

'Bastard! Why were you hiding?'

'And this pistol? Is it for shooting rabbits?'

'The area isn't safe . . .'

'You said it, stupid fool!'

The butt of a gun struck his injured hand. His yell brought Camille rushing to the prisoner's side.

'Don't hit him! He's wounded!'

'Speak, lad, what are you doing in these parts?'

'I wanted to join the Resistance.'

'Don't listen to him, he's a spy, believe you me.'

'Leave him to us, we'll get him to talk.'

'Please, Father, stop them . . .'

So far, Léon had not said a word. Sitting on a tree trunk, with his beret pushed up, he was contemplating the scene and drawing on his extinguished cigarette-end. He stood up reluctantly.

'He's bleeding all over the place . . . Madame Camille, find a rag to make him a bandage. Don't cry lad, the two of us are going to have a little chat.'

Charles, whom they had all forgotten, tugged at Léa's skirt.

'Why did they hurt the man?'

Camille returned with a clean tea towel. She bandaged the injured hand.

'That'll do,' said Léon. 'You others go back on guard duty. Father, I think you'd better pack your bags.'

'I agree with you.'

'Don't move, lad.'

59

The prisoner, who had stood up, let himself fall to the ground again groaning.

The old farmer, without taking his eyes off the boy, went over to the priest and whispered:

'Do you know the Ciron gorge?'

'Yes.'

'We've got men out that way. Do you need a guide?'

'Only to get out of your hideout. After that, I know the area.'

'When you get to Bourideys, go to the house with blue shutters, it belongs to a friend of mine. Tell him Léon has gone mushroom picking, he'll harness the cart, get in touch with Aristide and take you to the caves.'

'It's not far, we can go there on foot.'

'Not with the women and the kid.'

'You're right. What are you going to do with him?'

'Interrogate him, of course!'

'You know very well what I mean.'

'Father, that's our problem. This is my sector. I ought to know, too many of our men have been captured lately.'

'I know. Aristide's received orders from London to execute Grand-Clément . . .'

'He's not the only one to have collaborated with the Jerries.'

'Too true, unfortunately! That's why I'm here. Grand-Clément and those he dragged along with him have done all the damage they can but I'm trying to convince myself that behind his relations with Dohse there was . . .'

'Father, behind his relations, as you say, there was the betrayal of good patriots, the denunciation of communist comrades and the handing over of tons of arms sent by the British. That's more than enough for me: a bastard like that deserves to die like a dog.'

The priest shrugged wearily and went over to the prisoner.

'Talk, lad, it'll be best for everyone if you do.'

'Especially for you,' sneered Léon, poking the injured boy with his gun.

Camille and Léa appeared, carrying their bags. Léa had piled up her belongings in a large blue cotton square which she tied by the four corners. She slung the bundle from the barrel of Léon's hunting rifle. With her flowery dress, her straw hat and her espadrilles, she looked like a comely peasant woman carrying the farmhands' lunch to the fields.

'Jeannot,' called Léon.

A bearded young man appeared from behind a pine tree.

'Show them the way to the road. Keep your eyes and ears open. This lad may not have come alone.'

'All right, boss.'

'Goodbye, monsieur. Thank you for your hospitality.'

'You're welcome. Now, leave.'

Camille looked at the old farmer, the hut and the forest with an emotion that took her by surprise. The young woman, who was usually so reserved, kissed Léon impetuously, her eyes full of tears.

'I'll never forget the few days I've spent here. I hope to return one day. Farewell.'

Why did the clearing, bathed in sunlight, suddenly seem so cold to Léa?

'Come on, let's go,' she said, taking Charles's hand.

They walked through the woods for nearly an hour. Adrien Delmas carried the child on his shoulders. The road to Bourideys was clear. They soon arrived at the house Léon had told them of and found the man who was to take them to the caves. The horse, harnessed to the carriage, seemed put out at having to pull so many people. It whinnied and shook its bridle fiercely and progress was very slow. Despite the animal's ill humour, they soon reached Préchac. As they turned into the village, two gendarmes stopped them.

'Oh, it's you, Dumas!'

'Hello Renault, hello Laffont. What's the matter?'

'Who are these people?' asked Laffont suspiciously.

'Leave them alone, they're friends. I'm taking them to the caves. They've been sent by Léon des Landes. But you haven't answered my question, what's going on?'

'What's going on is that you can't go to the caves.'

'Why?'

'The Germans and the militia are combing the area.'

'Apparently someone important from London's been parachuted in recently.'

Camille clasped her son to her. Léa absently played with a curly lock of hair. Adrien Delmas stroked his black moustache . . .

'Have they arrested any of our people?'

'Not yet, but they're well-informed, the bastards. If it hadn't been for a kid from Marimbault who went fishing at dawn and came to Les Gillets to warn our comrades, they'd have all been done for. They nearly caught Lancelot and Dédé le Basque.'

'Shit! What am I going to do with this lot?'

Laffont motioned to Dumas that he wished to speak to him alone.

'Are you sure of the chap with the moustache?'

'Of course I am! Otherwise old Léon wouldn't have sent him to me. I even believe he may be the fellow who was parachuted in.'

'All right. We'll take care of them. We'll give them a lift in a police car. You'd better make yourself scarce, it's not a good idea to hang around here. Everybody out, ladies and gentlemen. Have you got somewhere to go?'

'Yes, Brouqueyran, near Auros. You must know it?'

'Yes, we know it, all right! If you're going to La Sifflette's place, let me shake your hand, she's my cousin, a fine woman . . .'

'You and your family get on my nerves . . . It's dangerous to stay here.'

'You're right, you're right . . . go and get the car. Come on, the rest of you.'

'Bye bye!' cried Charles, waving at the cart driver who was making his horse turn round.

They did not exchange a single word during the five-mile ride from Préchac to Captieux. Little Charles fell asleep on his mother's knee. As they entered the little market town, Laffont, the Brigadier from the gendarmerie, turned to Father Delmas.

'Have you got identity papers?'

'Yes.'

'And you, ladies?'

'Yes. Why?' asked Léa.

'If we are stopped by a German patrol, say that you're going to spend a few days with relatives, the Puch family in Grignols.'

'Who are these people?' asked Adrien.

'Good folk who've saved many a life.'

But all went well and they arrived in Brouqueyran without hindrance. They were welcomed at the tobacconist's-cum-café-cum-grocer's-cum-general store-cum-baker's belonging to the woman called La Sifflette, the Brigadier's cousin.

The owner had been nicknamed La Sifflette, the whistler, because of her habit of whistling while serving drinks and because of her fondness for surreptitiously 'wetting her whistle' as she stood behind the counter. 'Hello cousin, have you brought some more people for me?' she said.

'Yes I have, as usual, cousin.'

Léa glanced around the room. Behind the old wooden counter, the shelves where the groceries used to be stacked were empty. There were just a few scattered dusty cans. On the floor, leaning up against the wall, was one sack of grain and a reel of wire. In the centre of the room stood a large buffet table with wooden benches, and on the worn floor tiles there was a thin layer of sawdust.

'Can I speak to you in private?' Adrien Delmas asked the owner.

'Let's go into the courtyard then, we won't be disturbed. Make yourselves at home. Laffont, pour them a drink and give the little cherub some lemonade.'

They were not out of the room for long. When they returned, Charles was drinking his lemonade with Laffont's cap pulled down over his ears. La Sifflette burst out laughing at the sight of him.

'With a recruit like that, the war will soon be over!'

'We'd better be on our way . . . Our comrades will be wondering what's happened to us. Goodbye kid. Can I have my hat back?'

'No, I want to keep it.'

'Come on darling, give it back. It's too big for you,' said Camille, trying to take it away from him.

'No! No!' shrieked the child.

'Will you let go,' grumbled Léa, snatching the cap and returning it to its owner.

The child screamed even louder.

'Shut him up or I'll bash him,' cried Léa, twisting his arm.

Charles was so surprised by her angry tones that he forgot his woes and fell silent.

'You mustn't talk to children like that, mademoiselle. He's not to know, poor little thing,' said La Sifflette, picking him up.

Laffont put his cap on and left with Renault.

As soon as they had left the café, Father Delmas, who, since his arrival in the forest had not let out of his sight a heavy-looking battered old suitcase, asked La Sifflette if there was somewhere quiet.

'Above the barn there's a loft we never use. We keep old clothes and broken furniture there. You can have that room because it has two doors.'

Charles and Léa were glaring at each other. They were sulking. Camille could not help smiling at them.

'Honestly Léa, I'm beginning to wonder who's the biggest baby. Don't forget, he's only four.'

'So what! That's no excuse for screaming like that.'

'You're horrid, you're horrid. I don't love you any more. You aren't my best friend. I won't marry you when I'm grown up.'

'I don't care. I'll find someone who's much handsomer than you.'

'It's not true. I'm the handsomest! Aren't I mummy?'

'Yes, my love, you're the handsomest and I'm sure Léa thinks so too.'

'She's not answering. You see! She doesn't love me any more!'

It was all too much for the lovesick child, he burst into tears.

'No, Charles, don't cry! I was only joking. I love you, I love you more than anything else in the whole world,' cried

Léa, snatching him away from his mother and smothering him with kisses.

'Do you mean it?'

'Of course I do, my darling.'

'Then why did you hit me?'

'I'm sorry, I was tired and irritable. I promise I'll never do it again. Kiss me.'

And for a few minutes they kissed, cuddled and laughed while Camille looked on affectionately.

'So, have the lovebirds made it up?'

La Sifflette went over to the bar and whistled as she poured herself a little drink which she gulped down.

'You must be hungry. I'll make you a nice wild mushroom omelette with a salad from the garden. I've got a little cake left too. How does that sound?'

'It sounds lovely, madame, thank you very much. Can I help you?' asked Camille.

'There's no need. You look after the child. Go and make yourselves at home in your room. It's at the top of the stairs, second on the right.'

'Thank you for everything.'

'Basta! You can thank me later. Shh! Someone's coming.'

Three elderly men, dressed in old black cotton jackets typical of the Bazas region, came into the room.

'Hello everyone.'

'You've got visitors, La Sifflette. More of your relatives?' said the man wearing a battered hat, with mock seriousness.

'Leave her alone, Loubrie. It's none of our business.'

'You're right, Ducloux, especially with things as they are.'

They continued their lighthearted banter in local dialect.

'So, you old boozer, what can I get you?'

'Have you got any more of that white wine you had yesterday?'

'It's too expensive for a bunch of old misers like you. Yesterday, it was on the house. It mustn't become a habit!'

'What a tight-fisted woman! Stop moaning and give us a little drink.'

La Sifflette took them three glasses and a bottle of rosé.

'I say, have you heard? The Jerries are roaming all over the place!'

'So I hear. My cousin, the gendarme, was here earlier and he was telling me.'

'What are they looking for?'

'How should I know? Go and ask the bastards!'

'Do you think I'm crazy? I don't want them to take me for one of those bloody terrorists!'

'There's no danger of that! They'd soon find out you're a braggart.'

Loubrie's companions guffawed.

'You can't fool La Sifflette!'

'She knows you too well, you old petticoat-chaser!'

'You old fools! You've been listening to gossip. All the same, La Sifflette would do better not to take in so many strangers! The villagers are beginning to talk.'

'If you think you can frighten me with your tittle-tattle, you old rascal, you're mistaken.'

'I'm not trying to frighten you but to warn you. The Jerries are getting jumpy. They're not daft. They hear the English planes like the rest of us.'

'And even if they didn't hear them, there are swine who keep their eyes and ears open and keep them informed.'

Loubrie drained his glass in one gulp. A little wine dribbled down his stubbly chin and he choked. Ducloux thumped him on the back.

'My my! What a mucky pup! You mustn't get so worked up. If your conscience is clear the lads in the Resistance won't harm you, they're good fellows so they say . . . Here, let me wipe your collar otherwise Raymonde's likely to give you a thrashing, she's such a stickler for cleanliness,' said La Sifflette, laughing.

Loubrie pushed away the hand that was trying to wipe his collar and got to his feet grumbling:

'Stop fussing over me as if I were a baby.'

The three old men left to the raucous laughter of the owner who locked up the café behind them. Léa, Camille and Charles came downstairs.

'Now we'll be left in peace. I don't trust those nosey-parkers. This evening I'll go off and find out what's going on. What a lovely child he is . . . Where's your daddy? Gone to the war, of course . . .'

Chatting all the while, La Sifflette made their omelette. The goose fat began to sizzle in the frying pan on a corner of the grimy old stove.

'Mademoiselle, would you lay the table?' she asked Léa. 'The plates are on the shelf in the sideboard. It'll be ready soon.'

'Mmm! It smells delicious. It reminds me of my childhood when Sidonie used to make us omelettes with chanterelles or ham,' said Adrien Delmas who had just come into the kitchen. 'Madame, tonight, you'll have to tell the people from Auros and Bazas to be on the lookout. I'll tell the folk in Villandraut and Saint-Symphorien. Léa, you go to Langon and Saint-Macaire and tell them. Poinsot and his men know about all the arms caches and hiding places. The Germans are searching the Ciron gorges to create a diversion. Maurice Fiaux and Lieutenant Kunesch are in charge of the operation. Dohse and the militia are absolutely determined to stop Aristide setting up another network. They're trying to use Grand-Clément but even the most gullible members of the Resistance are wary of him. London has reissued the order to execute him, as well as Fiaux. Come on, let's eat, it's going to be a long night.'

'Father, I want to help too.'

'No, Camille, not you.'

'Why not?'

'You have a duty to Charles. Besides, he can't stay here on his own.'

Camille sighed and bowed her head.

'Of course not. You're right.'

'Hurry up and finish eating, the omelette's getting cold. Do you like that, poppet? I'm going to cut you a soldier to dip in your egg. Father, how do you find my omelette?'

'Terrible!' he replied, laughing.

Chapter 4

The star-spangled sky was magnificent. Before crossing the Garonne in Langon, Léa stopped outside the church and dismounted from the bicycle borrowed from La Sifflette, an old boneshaker that looked like a relic from the Great War. She had delivered her uncle's message to the cook at the Nouvel-Hôtel without mishap: '*The waters of the Ciron no longer flow into the Pouy-Blanc lagoon.*'

'Tell him I understand. You're doing a fine job, Mademoiselle Léa, your papa would have been proud of you.'

Pierre Delmas's daughter was overcome with a sad happiness. How quiet everything was! It was hard to imagine that close by, perhaps only a few yards away, men were lying in wait, ready to kill as soon as they received the command. When she reached the crossroads, Léa did not turn right to go to Saint-Macaire, instead she turned left and went under the viaduct. She could not help it, she had to see Montillac again.

The ancient bicycle creaked and groaned as she rode up the hill. Léa had to get off and push. The La Borde crucifix with its dark arms still dominated the Prioulette estate. It was at the foot of this cross that she had been assigned her first mission by her uncle. How long ago that seemed! The dark shapes of the trees made her heart beat twice as fast. Her home was there, so close. She stopped at the entrance to the drive that led to Montillac, fighting against the urge to run and take refuge in the old house, and hug Ruth before going back. A dog barked, then another. A light appeared in the Fayards' doorway. She could clearly hear the voice of the estate manager ordering the dogs to be quiet. It was not wise to stay there. She climbed on to her contraption again and turned back.

It was one o'clock in the morning when Léa opened the gate of the level crossing in Saint-Macaire. She stifled a scream when the crossing-keeper's dog went for her, barking amid the rattle of its chains. She ran across the rails, leapt on to her bicycle, took off down the main road and turned into the road that led to Benauge. When she reached the Cours-de-la-République, she stopped outside the garage owned by Dupeyron. It was the gendarme, Riri, who opened the door. As soon as he recognized her, he pulled her inside.

'Mademoiselle Léa, what brings you here?'

'I have a very important message for you: *The waters of the Ciron no longer flow into the Pouy-Blanc lagoon.*'

'Shit! We've got to warn all the others in the area.'

'I've told them in Langon. By now, the people in Villandraut, Saint-Symphorien, Bazas and Auros will also have heard.'

'Just as well. Dupeyron, you take charge of contacting Cazenave, I've got to get back to the gendarmerie.'

'What! Aren't you coming with us?'

'I can't desert my post, it's not fair on my comrades. Things are hard enough as they are.'

'Have you any news of Albert and Mireille?'

'Not really, mademoiselle. We know that Mireille is interned in the Boudet barracks, and that she's not too badly treated, but we haven't any news of Albert. Mathias Fayard and René were the last to see him. Since then, we haven't heard a thing. Nobody has seen him come out of the house in Le Bouscat. No doubt you know that Mathias managed to escape last night, which forced the lads from Mauriac who were guarding him to disperse all over the area.'

'Do you think he'll denounce them?'

'I've no idea. I don't understand youngsters any more. They all seem to be going crazy. I know Mathias well, we used to play football together, we used to go partridge shooting, we were almost comrades although I'm older than him. He's not a bad lad. His stay in Germany changed him completely. He came back with political ideas. Politics are a bad thing, especially at the moment. But I don't think he's particularly dangerous. It's Maurice Fiaux who frightens me. He's a nasty piece of work, he likes evil. And he knows the area well. Goodbye, mademoiselle. Tell the person who sent you that we're doing the necessary and that if he needs to contact me, he knows where to get hold of me . . . Wait, before you go out, I'm going to make sure the coast is clear . . . All right, you can go. A safe ride back, mademoiselle. Goodbye . . .'

A cold biting wind had risen which hampered Léa's progress. Yet, as she pedalled through the Constantin woods, she was perspiring all over. Her icy hands gripped the rusty handlebars. At the hamlet of Le Chapitre, one of the worn tyres burst. The bicycle skidded.

Her hands and knees grazed, Léa lay in the road for a long time without the strength to move. Only the noise of a wheel squeaking as it went on spinning broke the stillness of the night.

It was the cold that finally forced her to get up. She could feel blood trickling down her legs. Her knees hurt, but not as much as her hands. She retrieved her bicycle but it was useless as both wheels were buckled. In a rage, she threw the old contraption to the side of the road and continued her way on foot, hobbling painfully.

Just outside Brouqueyran, the rumbling of an engine made her hurl herself into the ditch. Three cars sped past, a few yards from her. Friends or foes? How could she tell?

The dust had barely settled when she heard the slamming of doors and the sound of voices. They had stopped in Brouqueyran. I hope Uncle Adrien isn't back yet! she thought as she ran towards the village.

'Go on! Break down the door.'

Léa stopped in her tracks at the sound of that voice. She was suddenly very frightened. Run . . . she had to run away . . . She fell to her knees and did not even feel the pain. Before her eyes, the men had smashed in the door while others were searching the tumbledown buildings surrounding the old café. She prayed they would not find the radio transmitter. The transmitter! But what did that matter! Camille and Charles were alone in the house! She stood up and ran openly towards the café . . . Camille's cries stopped her.

'No! No! Don't hurt him.'

A man stepped out carrying the struggling child. His mother followed, clutching at the man. He kept kicking her away but he was unable to make her let go.

'Mummy . . . mummy . . .'

Hidden behind a wall, Léa was trying to grope around in the dark and find a gun.

Flames leapt from the house, illuminating the scene. No uniformed men . . . Two armbands bearing the emblem of the militia . . . two young faces glowing in the light from the fire which was spreading rapidly. Sub-machine guns waving around like toys . . . Bottles being loaded into car boots . . . laughter . . . French voices belching, swearing and shouting abuse . . .

'You're going to tell us where the others are, bitch!'

'And La Sifflette, you've never set eyes on her, eh?'

'Albert . . . Mireille . . . Lucien . . . Aristide . . . Your damned priest, those names mean nothing to you?'

'I don't know what you're talking about. Give me back my child!'

'You can have him back when you've talked.'

'Leave her alone, Jérôme, give back the kid. We'll make her talk in a safe place. That was bloody stupid of you setting the place on fire, now the whole local Resistance network will know what's going on.'

'Shit! Don't worry, Maurice, we're ready for them.'

'Mummy!'

'Give him back to her for Christ's sake! Get in.'

Hugging her son, Camille climbed into one of the front-wheel drive vehicles. Maurice Fiaux took the wheel.

'We're going to La Réole,' he shouted to the others.

Crumpled against the wall, Léa watched the cars drive off into the night in the direction of Auros.

It was thanks to the flames that Adrien Delmas found his niece, shivering with cold and fever.

'Where are Camille and Charles?'

'Fiaux, Maurice Fiaux.'

She shook her head, her teeth chattering, unable to utter another word.

The priest helped her up and walked dumbfounded towards the flames. La Sifflette appeared from nowhere like a witch.

'My God! Where's the little one and his mother?'

'I don't know. Apparently Maurice Fiaux and his gang have been here.'

'What have those devils been up to? Father! She's wounded!'

'I know. So there's nobody here?'

'If I know them, I bet they've run away like scared rabbits. Poor us! To think it's for the sake of those good-for-nothings that people like you risk your lives.'

'Be quiet! You're risking your life too, and you've lost everything you have. Is the church open?'

'No, but I know where the priest hides the key. I say, Father, look! The barn hasn't caught fire yet! Perhaps your transmitter . . .'

He gently laid the unconscious Léa down by the cemetery wall and ran towards the barn shouting:

'Camille . . . Charles . . .'

La Sifflette took the key from a hole in the wall and opened the church door. She managed without too much difficulty to drag the young girl inside and up to the altar. There lay a threadbare carpet which had once been thick and luxurious, a present from the Squire of Mirail. It was still more comfortable than the cold uneven flagstones. She stretched Léa out on the carpet. She groped around and found some matches behind the heavy volume of the Gospel. After several attempts, she managed to light one. La Sifflette lit the two large candles on either side of the tabernacle, picked up one of them and went to rummage around in the tiny sacristy. The only thing she could find to protect the injured Léa from the damp and cold was the pall marked with a white cross, used to cover coffins at funerals.

As she went out, she automatically crossed herself.

*

The fire seemed to be dying down. The wailing of the fire-engine could be heard coming from Bazas. The reassuring sound only made the owner of the Brouqueyran café-cum-tobacconist's-cum-grocer's-cum-general store shrug her shoulders.

'You were right, the transmitter was still there,' said Adrien Delmas, showing her his heavy suitcase. 'Here's the fire brigade. I'll have to hide it.'

'You'd better keep yourself out of sight too. Here, take the church key and lock yourself in. If they ask me for it, I'll say it's lost.'

'No news?'

'No . . . I was going to ask you the same thing. They must have been taken to Bordeaux.'

'I don't know if that's the best thing that could have happened to them or not.'

'You mustn't say things like that, Father . . . even they wouldn't hurt a little child!'

'May the Lord hear you.'

La Sifflette did not hear the priest's disillusioned comment, she was already running out shouting to meet the fire brigade.

Léa regained consciousness in the flickering candlelight. Numb with cold, she was no longer even shivering. She raised herself up on her elbows. The surroundings, the pall, the candles . . . For a moment, she thought she was dead. A furious anguish made her leap to her feet and fling her macabre covering to the floor. The local priest would doubt-less have thought she was an apparition of the Virgin. Just then, her uncle entered the church. 'How beautiful and fear-some the child is . . . straight out of a horror story,' he thought before turning the key in the lock.

'Who are you?'

'Don't be afraid, it's me.'

'Oh, uncle . . .'

Adrien walked towards her, put down his suitcase and made Léa sit on the altar step. He drew her towards him and covered her with the pall.

'Tell me what happened.'

In a low but unfaltering voice, she told him everything.

He bowed his head in grief, reproaching himself for not intervening in time. From outside, they could hear the muffled voices of the firemen trying to put out the blaze.

'You're sure he said La Réole?'

'Yes.'

'Why La Réole? . . . There's something I can't quite put my finger on . . . He should have taken them to Bordeaux.'

'How did they find out?'

'As usual, someone informed them. They thought they'd arrest the lot of us. Are you sure there weren't any Germans with them?'

'I don't think so. They were all speaking French and none of them was in uniform.'

'That seems to corroborate the information we received in London: the Gestapo has no idea what Fiaux and his gang are up to. They act on their own account, which makes them all the more dangerous and unpredictable.'

'But why would he do that? Without orders.'

'As usual, there are several answers.'

'But you know him well!'

'Yes . . . that's precisely why he frightens me. He wants to take revenge on society; he wants to become a feared and respected leader. What's more – and he has already proved it – he enjoys killing, torturing and humiliating.'

'We can't leave Camille and Charles in his clutches . . .'

They were interrupted by a knock at the door.

'Open up, it's me, La Sifflette.'

Gun in hand, Adrien Delmas unlocked the door.

La Sifflette came in, pushing before her a young man wearing a fireman's helmet that was too big for him.

'We're lucky that old Déon broke his arm. This is his son, Claude, who came in his place. I know him, he works for Léon des Landes's Resistance group, he's going to try and get in touch with him. I told him about the child and his mother.'

'Good. Apparently, they've been taken to La Réole.'

'To La Réole! I hope you're mistaken! There are rumours that the local Gestapo have lent a cellar in the high school to

74

some Frenchmen for the interrogation of communist Resistance fighters.'

'Is there any proof?'

'No, it's gossip, that's all.'

'Uncle, I forgot: Mathias has escaped.'

'So perhaps there's a hope . . .'

'I must go, monsieur, my colleagues will start wondering where I am.'

'You're right. Leave messages for me with the priest at Auros. Ask for Alphonse Duparc. Is that clear?'

'Yes, monsieur. You'll hear from us tomorrow.'

The door closed behind La Sifflette and the fireman.

'Uncle Adrien, what did you mean about Mathias?'

'You get some rest, and let me think in peace.'

'Come on, come on, our gendarme friends are here.'

Léa struggled to open her eyes.

'Here, child, drink this, it's hot.'

La Sifflette was holding a tumbler containing a brew resembling coffee.

She sipped a mouthful and almost spat it out again.

'What is it? There's alcohol in it.'

'It's laced coffee. It disguises the taste of the oats. Go on, drink it, otherwise you'll catch your death of cold in this damp church.'

Léa drank it although she was on the verge of nausea. It was true that it made her feel better. Without too much difficulty, she stretched out her legs. The scabs on her knees made her skin taut.

Outside, it looked as if it was going to be a fine day. The café had been reduced to ashes and was still smouldering. The gendarmes Laffont and Renault were leaning against their car, looking grimly at the charred remains.

Adrien Delmas was studying a map.

'Where are we going, uncle?'

'To La Réole.'

Léa looked at him blankly.

'We're going to cross the Garonne in Castets, it'll be wiser.

75

Then we'll go to the farm above La Réole via the country lanes.'

'But why go to La Réole?'

'Because this part of the country is surrounded. We no longer have a safe hideout. From the farm, it'll be easy for me to get in touch with Hilaire.'

'I haven't been back to La Réole since the death of the Debrays.'

La Sifflette scratched around in the rubble with the help of a pitchfork, looking for anything that might have survived the blaze. Not a single complaint or sound escaped her lips. But her distress was evident from the way she was scrabbling in the ashes which were still warm. Her whole life had gone up in smoke; there was not a scrap of her existence left.

'Come on old girl, it's time to leave,' said Laffont, placing his hand gently on the handle of the pitchfork.

'You're right, it's no use raking over old memories.'

With a weary gesture, she threw down the tool and got into the car with not so much as a glance over her shoulder. None of the neighbours had come to ask after her.

From the farm, you could see what was coming, as Jean Callède would say. They received a warm welcome from Madame Callède. La Sifflette helped her with the cooking. Madame Callède's famous grilled sausages washed down by the local wine had fed many a Resistance fighter.

Léa and La Sifflette were not able to benefit from their hosts' quiet hospitality: on the eve of their arrival, a message had come through from London: *'Honour will get the better of audacity'*, indicating that there would be a parachute drop the following night. The two women insisted on taking part. At the request of Father Delmas, the men reluctantly agreed. They generally considered women to be useful for hiding weapons and parachutes in the kitchen and nothing more. As for Adrien, he had to go and join old Dieuzayde of the Jade-Amicol group and Aristide, Dédé le Basque, Lancelot and Georges, to examine a plan to rescue Camille d'Argilat and her child and eliminate Maurice Fiaux.

There were about ten of them surrounding the field, including Léa and La Sifflette. Posted at regular intervals, they crouched in the undergrowth, invisible in the dark. Each held a torch. Others had spread out to guard the paths leading to the field, their ears pricked up for the slightest sound. The wait seemed interminable. Suddenly . . . there was a far-off purring sound.

'Here he is,' whispered Callède. 'Careful.'

The purring grew louder. A whistle. Almost simultaneously, the torches were switched on . . . one . . . two . . . three . . . four . . . five . . . were switched off, one . . . two . . . three . . . and were switched on again. The purring swelled to a rumble . . . a dark shape hovered over the field marked out by the beacons, descended, seemed to hang in the air. Its engines became muffled . . . A shadow detached itself from the plane . . . a bang . . . the parachute opened . . . Others followed . . . The containers hit the ground with a metallic clang. The supply plane disappeared but the last two parachutes remained attached to the cockpit, white flags unfurling over La Réole. If that did not alert the Gestapo and the gendarmes . . . The men busied themselves with the containers. Not a trace of the drop was to remain. La Sifflette and Léa removed the parachutes, folded them and put them in a cart pulled by two oxen. The men loaded the containers into three vans to drive them to the Bienvenue sawmill. Some guns were hidden in the piles of sawdust, others in the barns and the tobacco sheds. Nothing moved in La Réole. La Sifflette was driving the cart. Léa hid the parachutes in a barn, under the straw. Everything was quiet on the farm but nobody could sleep. They could all see the white sails floating over the river and the old town.

The following day, at dawn, Dupeyre arrived on his bicycle and came breathlessly into the kitchen.

'The Germans are beginning a campaign, Rigoulet told us. Make sure the guns are well hidden and get the two women away from here.'

'But where on earth can we take them? To the Rosiers'?'

'No, they're too close. Take them to Tore's place, in Morizès.'

Shortly after their departure, the Germans arrived. They searched the place high and low and pushed Callède and his wife around in vain. Jean Callède was trembling with fear. In the panic, he had forgotten two parachutes from an earlier drop that were rolled up inside old tarpaulins and Sten bullets in sugar packets. Even though they had found nothing, the Germans took Callède, Loue, Dupeyre, Bienvenue, Charlot and Chianson away for interrogation at the Gestapo headquarters in La Réole.

When the convoy pulled up outside the college, chance had it that the mayor of Gironde-sur-Dropt was there. He knew all the prisoners and was unaware of their clandestine activities. He asked to see the commander and offered to be guarantor to the prisoners. They were all released except Pierre Chianson. No doubt he had been denounced for the parachute drop in Saint-Félix-de-Foucade.

Like La Sifflette, Léa had only the clothes she had been wearing on the night of the fire. Her belongings had all been burned. She decided, without telling anybody, to go to Montillac and when everybody was asleep, she borrowed a bicycle.

It was a beautiful, mild night. Just outside Sainte-Foy-la-Longue, she stopped to contemplate the shimmering waters of the Garonne snaking across the vast plain, the stars reflected in the water. As always when confronted with this familiar landscape, she was choked with emotion. She always felt the same wonder and awe. The same feeling of being at total peace with the world. The same feeling that nothing terrible could happen to her in such a place. A certainty which emanated from the earth as it slumbered . . . Everything would be all right. Uncle Adrien would find a way of rescuing Camille and Charles. The thought of the little boy who wanted to marry her was like a dagger in her heart. The countryside became blurred. She rode off again, her heart heavy. In Saint-André-des-Bois, she almost knocked down a young man who was urinating in the middle of the road. He ran away as she swore at him.

Léa hid the bicycle in the grass behind the plinth of the crucifix, opposite the house. She crossed the road and went through the meadow to avoid going down the gravel drive which would have been too noisy. A thin shaft of light was visible behind the shutters of her father's study. 'Ruth must be doing the accounts,' she thought as she approached the window. She could hear muffled voices. Try as she might, she was unable to identify the speakers or understand what was being said. That laugh! That laugh again . . . Without worrying about being heard, she walked around the house. The heavy shutters over the front door were half open. In the dark, she skirted round the obstacle course of furniture in the drawing-room and pushed open the study door.

'Léa!'

Little Charles hurled himself at her.

'Darling . . . my little poppet . . . How wonderful! When did you come back?'

'This evening. Mathias brought him here.'

'Mathias?'

'We played hide-and-seek. Mummy didn't want to play with us, but now you're here, we can go and look for her. You will play, won't you?'

'Yes, yes.'

Mathias was there all right. He looked even thinner, he was impeccably dressed and clean-shaven, but his hair was dishevelled.

'Ruth . . .'

Without letting go of the child, Léa embraced the old governess whose face was wet with tears.

'My darling, I'm so happy. I thought I'd never see you again. So many misfortunes have befallen this house. But isn't it dangerous for you to be here?'

'Probably, but I didn't have a thing to wear . . . Mathias, how did you find Charles? Why didn't you save Camille too?'

'I couldn't save both of them. Camille's exhausted. It was she who asked me to take care of her son.'

'That's unbelievable!'

'But it's true. She also told me to tell you that if she dies, she wants you to be a mother to him.'

'I don't want her to die!'

'I'm going to do my best to rescue her. I had to negotiate with Fiaux for ages to get him to let go of the kid. He wanted to keep him to force the mother to talk. He interrogated her without managing to get anything out of her other than: "I don't know anything about it." But if he had beaten the child as he intended to, he'd have made her talk.'

'He was horrid, that man,' stuttered Charles who had begun to cry. 'He pulled my hair and kicked mummy hard in the tummy . . . and after that she didn't move any more. I kissed her lots and lots and then she woke up . . . then I wasn't frightened any more. Then it was dark . . . She sang: "Rock-a-bye baby on the tree top, when the wind blows the cradle will rock . . ." '

Léa felt a surge of violent hatred. She could feel, trembling and sobbing against her breast, the little boy she had helped into the world. Abuse directed at her childhood friend welled up inside her and she felt capable of murdering him. Killing him, along with the others . . . She felt an unsuspected strength flow through her body, a desire to fight, to kill . . .

'I know what you're thinking, but the main thing is to save Camille.'

'How, do you have any ideas?'

'Yes . . . I'm going to try and get her transferred, but we haven't got long, she's at the end of her strength. If I succeed, I'll let you know. Where are you hiding?'

'I can't tell you.'

'You must.'

'Nobody knows where I am.'

He looked at her scornfully.

'It's hardly surprising that with discipline like that your friends so often get caught.'

'They don't get caught unless they're denounced.'

'You poor thing. If you think the Germans need that! All they have to do is listen to talk in the cafés.'

'It's French people who eavesdrop for them!'

'Not always. You are so careless that they'd have to be blind not to notice anything.'

Ruth intervened.

'Please, don't argue. Listen to me, Léa: I think we can trust Mathias.'

'Maybe, but I can't tell him where I am and he knows that perfectly well.'

'Well, tell your uncle and Aristide or Hilaire's men the following plan: as soon as I've obtained Camille d'Argilat's transfer to Bordeaux, I'll let you know. I'll tell you the composition of the convoy, the number of men – in my opinion, I don't think they'll be very many – the time of departure and the itinerary. You and your comrades will have to ambush the convoy and save Camille.'

Léa, who was still hugging little Charles, now asleep, asked in a low voice:

'Do you really think it's possible?'

'Yes.'

'Can I ask you something? Why do you stay with Fiaux and his gang? For money?'

Mathias shrugged.

'You won't believe me if I tell you.'

'Go on, tell me.'

'From my present position I can better look after you.'

'You're right, I don't believe you.'

'You see!' he said with a wry smile, and shrugged again.

'What are we going to do with Charles? Isn't it dangerous to have brought him back here?'

'No, since Fiaux knows he's here. Besides, I've asked my father to keep an eye on him.'

'And he agreed?'

'He didn't have much choice.'

Léa gently laid Charles on the old sofa and sank into one of the fireside armchairs.

'Ruth, I'm hungry and I'm thirsty. There isn't any food in the house by any chance, is there?'

'Of course, love, I'll light the fire.'

'Leave it, Mademoiselle Ruth, I'll do it.'

'Thank you, Mathias.'

A bright flame soon leapt up and, for a few moments, the only sound was the crackling of the dead vines. That cheerful noise, the warmth, and the familiar surroundings dispelled the animosity between Léa and Mathias for a while. As they sat gazing into the embers, their eyes met. The expression in Mathias's look was one of adoration, of passionate love; in Léa's confusion and utter weariness.

The young man was fighting the desire to take her in his arms, knowing that she would reject him. As for Léa, she wished she could wipe out the vile memory of that night in a sordid hotel in Bordeaux, and snuggle up to him and tell him her troubles as she used to do when she was a little girl and they would take refuge in the children's room or the hayloft.

Without even being aware of it, they sighed in unison, expressing all their inconsolable grief.

Ruth returned with a tray containing two bowls of soup, some home-made pâté, bread and a bottle of Montillac red wine. They devoured this frugal meal with an appetite that was a credit to their youth. As always when she was enjoying a meal, Léa forgot the danger of her situation.

'Your pâté's really good,' she said with her mouth full.

'It's true, it's excellent,' agreed Mathias.

They finished eating in silence, savouring this peaceful moment. When the bottle was empty, Léa asked:

'Ruth, I've lost all my clothes. Can you pack a bag for me? Would you have a couple of dresses for someone who's about the same size as Aunt Bernadette? How is she, by the way?'

'Not too well. She complains that she doesn't hear from Lucien very often and her rheumatism's very bad.'

'Poor thing . . . Will you look and see if you can find some dresses and woollens for me?'

'I'll have a look.'

Charles turned over in his sleep. Léa covered him with the tartan blanket which her father used to wrap round himself when he worked in his study in the winter.

'We have to find a place where we can meet.'

'What about the church in La Réole?'

'No, it's too risky for you. Fiaux and the others know you, they might arrest you.'

'Where then?'

'Do you know the cemetery in Saint-André-des-Bois?'

'Of course,' she said impatiently.

'Do you know where the vault of the Le Roy de Saint-Arnaud family is, just to the right of the entrance?'

'Yes.'

'The trunk of the cypress tree to the left of it is hollow. I'll leave messages in it. Go there every day. If you want to contact me, use the same tree. Is that clear?'

'I'm not stupid, but supposing they won't let me go?'

'It's up to you to find a way of persuading them. Camille's life is at stake.'

Ruth came back carrying a large bag.

'But that's much too bulky!'

'I'll tie it to the carrier. Where's your bicycle?'

'Behind the crucifix.'

'I know. Ruth, have you got any string?'

'Yes, I thought of that.'

While Mathias went off to attach the bag to the bicycle, Léa leaned over the sleeping Charles and stroked his blond hair.

'You will take good care of him . . .'

'I'll try . . . we've hardly got any money left. Your Aunt Bernadette has put her pine woods up for sale, but in the meantime . . .'

'I know, Ruth, what can I say? Sell the furniture if you can find a buyer, I haven't got anything.'

A tear rolled down the child's cheek as he moaned in his sleep.

'I'm sorry, darling, I'm a crazy old woman to bring the subject up at a time like this. I'll manage.'

'I'll never be able to thank you for all you've done for us . . .'

'Will you be quiet! A fine thing that'd be if I expected thanks! Some letters arrived during your absence, I've put them in the bag.'

'You can leave as soon as you're ready. The bag's firmly

fixed on, you could cycle across the whole of France and it wouldn't budge,' said Mathias, coming into the room.

'Goodbye Ruth, give my love to Aunt Bernadette.'

'Goodbye darling, God bless. Mathias, I'm leaving her in your hands.'

'You needn't fear, Mademoiselle Ruth, she'll be all right.'

As they reached her bicycle, Mathias picked it up and asked:

'Would you like me to come with you?'

'You know you can't. I have to leave now.'

Reluctantly, he let go of the handlebars. They remained motionless and silent for a second; they were both miserable. Léa shivered.

'Leave quickly, you've probably got quite a way to go and I don't like to think of you alone on the roads at night.'

'Mathias, I don't understand, what's happening to us?'

'What do you mean?'

'You and me, having to hide . . . becoming enemies . . . And at the same time . . .'

'At the same time, what . . . ?'

How hopeful he sounded . . . He'd better not think that she had forgiven him.

'Nothing. These are strange times we're living in when we don't know who our friends are, because even our dearest friends can betray us.' Mathias refused to hear the bitterness in her voice. He only noticed the words 'dearest friends'. He was her dearest friend, he was in no doubt about that. What did it matter if she thought he was a traitor, betraying what, anyway, because he would never, ever betray *her*. The rest was only politics and that had nothing to do with his emotions.

He waved goodbye and went back to the house without looking round. Disconcerted, Léa watched him disappear.

Chapter 5

In Morizès, everybody had gone to bed. Léa stayed up alone in the kitchen where a bed had been made up for her. She watched the dying embers in the fireplace as she smoked a cigarette made from tobacco that Callède had secretly harvested. The strong, bitter smoke irritated her throat and made her eyes water but soothed her anxiety about Camille being so ill. The Gestapo had been forced to allow her to be transferred to the hospital of Saint-Jean in La Réole. Nobody had been allowed to see her.

Father Delmas had met Mathias and accepted his help. Aristide and his men had given their consent. Since then, they had just been waiting. Maurice Fiaux and his gang had returned to Bordeaux.

Léa got up from the low chair and switched on the wireless. They had not been able to tune in to the BBC for several days because of the interference. After twiddling the knobs for a few minutes, the familiar but barely audible voice of Jean Oberlé came out of the speaker:

'*The poet Max Jacob has died in the camp at Drancy. He was imprisoned there because he was a Jew. And yet, he converted to Catholicism thirty years ago. Ever since, his works have been full of the most intense and sincere Catholic sentiments. But do the Germans take any notice of that?*

'*The Germans stick yellow stars on the chests of those they torture. For them, it is a dishonourable label, the only worthy one being their swastika. Catholics or Jews, they are all the same to them, and Hitler is their God. What do the guards at Drancy care that Max Jacob is dead, for them it just means one less Jew . . .'*

Even poets, thought Léa as she switched off the wireless.

As she undressed in the half-darkness, she remembered that her uncle had told her about his encounter with Max Jacob in Saint-Benoît during a brief visit there. Apparently he had the naïve faith of the newly converted. He was dead, like Raphaël Mahl and perhaps Sarah, all three Jews. She felt momentarily ashamed at having associated, even in death, the despicable informer and collaborator Mahl with the brave fighter Sarah and the vulnerable poet. But there was in Raphaël a despair that had always moved her. Despite his pains to make himself an object of hatred, he had not succeeded and his appalling end had absolved him for ever. She missed him, in the same way as she missed a friendly presence that evening.

She slid between the rough sheets that were still a little damp. The feeble glow of the embers made the room look slightly unreal and comforting. Through her half-closed eyes she saw a different fire in a very different room . . . the weight of the red eiderdown reminded her of a vicuña wool blanket . . . The coarse cloth of the sheet teased her nipples through her nightdress. She turned to the wall to shut out the flickering light. Whatever she did, she must not think about him, or remember the way he caressed her, kissed her body, that body whose desires she had such trouble controlling. It was such a long time since a man . . . She sat up in a rage as she felt the irrepressible urge to make love well up inside her. She tore off her nightdress and furiously satisfied her body's demands.

The following day, Adrien Delmas arrived in Morizès accompanied by Lieutenant Pierre Vincent, known as Grand-Pierre, the leader of the Resistance group in Puy, near Monségur, and three of his men who had come for supplies. They were all very excited as they talked about the blowing up of the petrol station in Saint-Martin-de-Sescas by fourteen of their men on 5th May. The lieutenant and the priest found it hard to restrain them. Léa watched them enviously; at least they were able to act . . .

After their departure, Adrien Delmas went over to his niece.

'Thanks to Abbot Chaillou, the hospital chaplain, I was able to see Camille. She's much better. She is extremely courageous, not a single complaint. She's worried about you and her son.'

'Could I see her?'

'I think that'll be rather difficult and unnecessarily dangerous for both of you. Day and night there is a Gestapo guard outside her door. But one of them likes a bottle of good Sauternes.'

'Well, let's get him drunk.'

This brought a smile to Adrien's face.

'We'll see. There are more important things to think about. We've got to get her out of there.'

'What does Aristide say?'

'For the time being, he's very busy on his farm trying to recruit more men, avoid Grand-Clément and his men who are trying to eliminate him, and keep the various groups in order. But, as soon as we need him, he'll send the necessary men.'

'Have you heard from Mathias?'

'No, not since he told us about Camille's transfer.'

'It's my turn to go to Saint-André-des-Bois.'

'Don't forget, if you find yourself in difficulties there, you can call on Jules Coiffard who lives in the big house by the roadside. He and some neighbours smuggle people out and act as a letterbox. This afternoon, I'll be in Chapelle-de-Lorette. The militia and the Germans are stepping up their efforts in the area since the fall of the American Flying Fortress in Cours-Monségur. The destruction of the depot in Saint-Martin-de-Sescas didn't exactly please them either. The Gestapo has released a dozen or so agents in the area. It's thanks to one of them, a certain Coubeau, who used to run the grocer's in the Rue de la Croix-Blanche, and who passed himself off as a Canadian officer, that the gendarmes arrested Captain Lévy whom they handed over to the Gestapo in Toulouse.'

'Was he tortured before being executed?'

'I don't know, but it's highly likely.'

'When will it all be over?'

'God . . .'

'Don't you talk to me about God,' she cried, 'you don't believe in him any more than I do!'

'Be quiet,' he groaned, thumping her shoulder.

What had become of the quiet, gentle, affable man she had known all her life? His gaunt face, burning eyes, his features twisted with suffering, his lips firmly shut to keep in a burning secret, his once beautiful hands now gnarled, clenched as if to repress their urge to strike, that could not be the preacher whose voice had thrilled thousands of Christians all over the world, whose passionate voice had long dominated the half-hearted bishopric of Bordeaux, and whose fatherly affection had so often helped Léa and her family.

'You're hurting me.'

He let go and rested his forehead on the mantelpiece. His shoulders were stooped; he suddenly looked old. How helpless and alone he seemed. That was it, he was alone, desperately alone faced with himself, and alone among the uncultivated men whose ideas were usually so different from his. He was the person to whom Léa was the most deeply attached since the death of her parents. Consciously or not, she listened to what he had to say. He was a sort of spiritual guide, someone whom she could not let down, a human ideal that was difficult to attain. If doubt, fear and hatred took over in this man, it represented a whole world of balance, intelligence and kindness that had collapsed. And that, she could not bear. A blind anger brought beads of sweat to her brow and made her heart beat faster.

When he turned round, after what seemed to Léa like an eternity, their wrath was slightly appeased.

'I'm sorry, my darling. Tiredness . . . no doubt. At the moment I lose my temper over the silliest trifles. Will you forgive me?'

'Yes, uncle,' she replied, still trembling, as she snuggled up to him.

But she was aware that an invisible barrier had come between them.

At last, some good news: the arrival of Raoul and Jean Lefèvre, the two suitors of her youth whom she had not seen since their dramatic arrest together with Dr Blanchard, on the day that Marie was assassinated in the village square in Verdelais.

The three young people were unable to tear themselves away from each other, they were so thrilled to find each other alive.

The evening meal was a festive occasion for all. Léa squeezed in on the bench between her long-lost friends, her eyes sparkling with pleasure and the Callèdes' white wine. She laid her head on Jean's shoulder and then Raoul's, stroked their hands under the table and rubbed herself against them seductively. She laughed, talked nineteen to the dozen and blossomed with happiness as she had not done for a long time, bursting with youth and beauty.

'Well, it's a treat to see you like this. My wife and I were beginning to wonder if you knew how to laugh,' said their host. 'You're just the same as you used to be,' said Jean, kissing her neck.

'You're even more beautiful,' retorted Raoul, kissing her in turn.

The two brothers had been sent by Léon des Landes to join Dédé the Basque and his men who were preparing to sabotage La Réole railway station. It was in Chapelle-de-Lorette that they had learned their friend was in Morizès. They told of their escape, saying that Albert and the others had been brave and cunning. The mention of Albert's name dampened the spirit of the joyous reunion for a moment, but the memory of the jovial butcher from Saint-Macaire, of whom there was no news, dispelled the sadness. To cheer everyone up even more, Callède opened another bottle of wine.

It was late when the guests parted company. Raoul and

Jean had arranged to stay overnight. They were to spend the night rolled up in a blanket in front of the fire.

Long after the others had left, they were still talking, drinking and smoking as they chatted. Settled on Léa's bed, they were unable to part company and go to bed.

Hemmed in by the two young men on the narrow bed, Léa was overwhelmed by a feeling of well-being, delighting in their company and the warmth which she could feel from their bodies. She ruffled their curly hair while they inhaled the warm smell of her neck, covering it with little kisses. For all three of them, it was simply a desire to be together as their bodies became entwined like those of young puppies at play. They were so thrilled to be reunited that they had forgotten that they were men and she a woman, that they were young, and the underground existence of the war had hardly favoured their love lives. Without any premeditation, the boys' kisses became more loving, their hands became bolder as they discovered their friend's body. Instead of fighting them off, she abandoned herself to their caresses with that husky laugh that used to have such an effect on them when they were younger. Those four hands caressing her skin opened up sunny places, making the sadness and anguish of the last few days fade away. No more fear . . . no more war . . . no more death . . . When Jean penetrated her, she stifled her cry by embracing Raoul.

At daybreak, they were awoken by the cold as they lay there naked. Leaning over their friend, the two brothers looked at each other in horror, their eyes full of tears.

'I'm cold,' Léa murmured.

Raoul got up and threw a bundle of dead vines on to the embers which were still hot. Soon a bright fire was roaring.

'Forgive us,' stammered Jean, his face buried in Léa's hair.

As for Léa, she was silent as she pensively ran her finger along the scar that ran from the young man's chest to his stomach.

'Come here,' she said to Raoul who was pulling on his clothes.

Looking sheepish, he sat down on the bed.

'You shouldn't regret what happened. On the contrary, the three of us have always loved each other, we grew up together and you two have always shared everything.'

'But not you!'

This cry from the heart made her laugh. The war had not changed Jean. He was still that possessive little boy, torn between his love for her and love for his brother.

'Don't laugh,' said Raoul, 'we behaved dreadfully.'

Léa's expression became grim and her voice hard.

'Don't say that. It's not us who are dreadful but circumstances. Tomorrow you might be killed, or I might. It's natural that we live life to the full on the rare occasions when that's possible. I'm not ashamed of making love with both of you, I'm not sorry, I have no regrets. The only thing I regret is not being able to do it more often.'

'Shut up, you're immoral.'

'And you're stupid. There's no such thing as morality any more.'

'If there's no more morality, can you tell me why you chose the Resistance rather than collaboration? You could be living peacefully in Paris, trailing around the tea salons with Françoise . . .'

'Raoul!' exclaimed Jean.

' . . . or selling your wine to the Germans instead of roaming the countryside carrying messages, hiding guns and risking arrest, torture . . . Can you tell me why you're on our side if morality's dead?'

'Leave her alone!'

'Be quiet, Jean, I'm going to try and answer him. It's not a question of morality, or at any rate, it isn't for me. Do you remember, before the war, all this business with the Germans, the Allies, the Maginot line and Poland bored me, I didn't want to know about it. And then you, Jean, Laurent and others went away . . . There was the defeat. Camille and I being bombarded as we fled across France, all those people dying around us, Josette's body, riddled with bullets, blood gushing from her throat, that man who attacked us . . . the death of Madame Le Ménestrel and her two children, mummy dying in the air-raid . . . papa . . . But even all those horrors might not have been enough to make me share your and Uncle Adrien's ideas if it had not been for the presence of the Germans in Montillac, in that house which belongs to me. Each time I saw them on the terrace, in the vineyards or in the sheds, I felt dispossessed, humiliated. I felt they had no right to be there. I then began to understand the meaning of losing the war, of the Occupation, and I couldn't accept it. You see, there's nothing noble about it.'

'Perhaps not, but not all French people have reacted the way you have.'

'Perhaps because they're not attached to a piece of land that they feel is in their blood, that is part of them.'

'You're like your father, you're in love with Montillac,' said Jean, kissing her. 'You're the one who's right. Let's think of last night as a wonderful moment when we forgot about morality and the war.'

'Come on Raoul, don't look so miserable. We didn't do anything wrong.'

The young man gazed at the two people he loved more than anything else in the world with genuine sadness. But his love for Léa was now making him jealous of his brother, which he would never have believed possible. It cost him a great effort to smile.

After drinking a bowl of hot milk and eating a piece of bread, they left for Chapelle-de-Lorette.

On 11th May, the brothers joined Grand-Pierre's Resistance fighters. There was a clash between the Germans and the Resistance in Sauveterre-de-Guyenne. Jean was wounded and his brother took him to the Château de Madaillan and then, as it was not safe to stay there, to the priest in Blasimon, Maurice Gréciet, who agreed to hide him. Raoul and his companions hid for a while in the La Colonne woods near the Château de Villepreux, before going back to their camp in Le Puy.

It was not Léa who found the message from Mathias announcing Camille's transfer to the Boudet barracks in

Bordeaux on Monday 15th, but a lad sent by Callède. Her departure had been arranged for one o'clock in the afternoon. The day before the planned escape, Léa, dressed in nurse's uniform, visited Camille with the priest Chaillou, taking advantage of the fact that it was Saint Joan's Day, and the hospital was under-staffed. The German on duty, the one who had a weakness for Sauternes, was having a drink with a nurse who was graced with abundant charms, just his type. This woman had promised to keep him away from his post for twenty minutes or so, while a nun from Saint-Vincent-de-Paul kept watch outside the hospital gates and another by the chapel.

Léa was expecting to find Camille tired and thin, but even so, she was appalled at the state of her friend. She was nothing but skin and bones, and her sunken eyes had dark purple shadows under them. Léa forced herself to smile, kissed her and . . . burst into tears.

'Come on, I'm not as hideous as that, am I? You look marvellous in that outfit. Don't cry, I'm much better, aren't I, monsieur?' she asked, turning to the priest.

'Yes, madame,' said the priest, looking away.

Léa would not have been able to answer. With an effort, she managed to smile again.

'Hurry up, you haven't got long. I'm going to see if our drunkard is behaving himself.' The priest went out.

The two friends were left alone, clasping each other's hands, too moved to talk much. Camille was the first to break the silence.

'The priest's right, we haven't got long. How's Charles? I hope he isn't too unhappy. Have you heard from Laurent?'

'Charles is fine, he isn't unhappy. We haven't heard from Laurent recently but as long as he's in England, there's nothing to worry about.'

'What about François Tavernier?'

'No news,' replied Léa, as her stomach contracted.

'I'm sure you'll hear from him soon. He's not the sort of man who'd let himself get caught. Trust him. How are things with you?'

'You only think of others,' Léa said with a mirthless laugh. 'What about you?'

'I'm fine.'

'Tomorrow, we're going to try and rescue you. Will you be strong enough?'

'Yes, I want to see my son again.'

'Well, listen to me.'

Léa briefly told Camille of the plan worked out by the Resistance . . . but that plan was not to be carried out.

When she returned to Morizès, Léa told her uncle and the five Resistance fighters that they'd have to give up the idea of attacking the ambulance, as Camille was too weak to be able to run away when the vehicle stopped. She and the priest, Chaillou, had thought of a better plan.

Chapter 6

The long-awaited rain finally began to fall.

The vehicle was parked with all its lights off in the Rue Perdue opposite the hospital. Rigoulet and La Sifflette were waiting in a van in the Place Saint-Michel. In the back sat a young Resistance fighter holding his breath and gripping a Sten gun. Two men were hidden in the Rue des Ecoles and another opposite the house of the Black Prince.

'Watch out, here they come.'

A man and a woman were running down the Rue Saint-Nicolas. The man, who was fairly tall, was carrying someone, which hampered his progress.

The rear doors of the car opened as the driver briefly flashed the headlights twice. The van driver returned the signal. They started up the engines.

'She's fainted.'

'Mathias, lay Camille on the back seat.'

'Hurry up, it won't be long before they find out she's gone.'

'Thank you, lad. What you've just done makes up for your mistakes. Come and join us, you'll be welcome.'

'I'm not sure, Father. Anyway, it's too late for me.'

'What are you going to do?'

'Keep watch. Now, go. Goodbye Léa.'

'Goodbye Mathias . . . Thank you.'

The car pulled away. The van followed close behind. They got away just in time, for lights were beginning to come on in the hospital windows. Whistles could be heard mingled with shouts while the vehicles turned off in the direction of Bazas. Less than a mile from the old town, they turned left and stopped in Saint-Aignan at a farm belonging to sympathizers. They carried Camille, who was still unconscious, inside the house. Rigoulet, having ensured that all was well, set off again alone for La Réole while the car continued in the direction of Bazas.

It was Father Delmas who had organized the operation and convinced his comrades that the Germans would not imagine that their prisoner was so close at hand. Besides, they needed time to arrange a safe hiding place and an escape route to Switzerland. He decided that Léa, La Sifflette and two men would stay with the sick woman.

This escape, combined with the blowing-up of the petrol reserves, the clash in Sauveterre and the numerous acts of sabotage and attacks put the Germans and the militia on the alert. Little towns and villages witnessed the arrival of men in grey-green and navy blue uniforms who came and searched their houses, barns and churches. They paid visits to Saint-Pierre-d'Aurillac, Frontenac, Sauveterre, Rauzan, Blasimon, Mauriac, Pellegrue, Monségur and La Réole. Many members of the Resistance were arrested between 17th May and 20th May. Seventeen members of the Buckmaster group were tortured, killed or deported. Fourteen of them were never to return.

On 19th May, La Sifflette, and Léa, with a headscarf over her hair, drove Camille to Morizès in a haycart. Her condition was stable. They were just in time. The following day, the Rosiers, in whose house they had been staying, went to the market in La Réole. When they returned to Saint-Aignan, the mother and daughter went home to cook lunch while the father had a drink with the postman and his assistant, Manuel. Suddenly they heard the sound of a motor vehicle coming along the road. They had fled in the middle of the night only ten days ago, when tipped off by comrades. But this time, it was more dangerous. They could make out the black roof of a front-wheel drive vehicle approaching the farm. Without stopping to pack anything, the Rosiers and their daughter fled across the fields to Morizès where they were taken in by Tore. The postman ran off in another direction. Nobody was arrested, but the Germans discovered seven tonnes of arms in the tobacco-drying shed.

Léa realized that Camille's health would not improve while she was separated from her son. With Madame Rosier and La Sifflette's help, she decided to go and fetch Charles. The three women went off on bicycles. Léa parted company from the others in Saint-André-des-Bois. La Sifflette was to meet her in two hours.

The wine store was a hive of activity. Fayard and three strange men were loading crates of wine on to a van. On catching sight of her, the estate manager almost dropped the case of wine he was holding in astonishment.

'Hello Fayard. Business is good.'

He put the case down and removed his beret, revealing his balding white head.

'Good day, mademoiselle,' he stuttered, 'so you're back?'

'Don't worry, not for long. But friends of mine will be in touch with you soon.'

Why had she said that? It just came into her head when she saw the look of fear on his face. She was also thinking of a punitive operation carried out by a Resistance group in the Lot-et-Garonne region against a black market dealer who was suspected of denouncing members of the Resistance. She felt a wicked delight in watching his calloused hands shake. This man's love of the land and greed had led him to deal with the enemy to the point of becoming an informer. To think that he might take Montillac from her!

She angrily turned on her heel and started walking towards the house.

The weather was muggy and stormy, but the old house had retained a little of its wintry coolness. Everything was peaceful, unchanging: there was a smell of polish in the air mingled with the smell of white roses, the first of the season, growing up the side of the wine shed that was exposed to the sunlight. It was Isabelle Delmas who had planted the early-blooming, fragrant climbing roses. That bunch on the hall table . . . 'If I close my eyes, I'll see mummy come walking in.'

'Léa!'

Charles came running towards her with outstretched arms, followed by Ruth.

'You're back. Where's mummy? I want to see mummy.'

'You're going to see her, darling. I've come to fetch you.'

'Fetch the child! You're not serious?'

'Ruth, I have to. Otherwise Camille will never get better.'

'But it's much too dangerous.'

'Please Ruth, I haven't got long. Pack some clothes for him.'

'Come with me, I've several things to tell you. Charles, go and find Aunt Bernadette.'

'No, I want to stay with Léa.'

'Do as Ruth tells you. If you're good, I'll take you to see mummy.'

'Really?'

'I promise.'

The little boy went out of the room calling Bernadette Bouchardeau.

As she packed, the governess told Léa what had happened during her absence.

'Your uncle Luc and your cousins came here last week. They wanted to inform you that they had had a visit from Fayard's lawyer regarding the sale of Montillac.'

'And what business is it of Uncle Luc's?'

'Apparently Fayard has received Françoise's consent . . .'

'What!'

'I said "apparently". That's what the solicitor said. Since Laure is a minor and Luc Delmas her guardian, and since you had gone off to join the terrorists thus outlawing yourself, it is up to your uncle to take the responsibility of deciding whether to sell or not.'

'But that's absurd!'

'Perhaps, but your uncle and your cousin, who are lawyers, say that it makes sense, all the more because of your absence.'

'I see. It'd suit everybody if I were arrested and disappeared for good.'

'I'm sure it'd suit Fayard, but not your uncle. You're his

brother's daughter and he would like you to keep the estate. He's changed a lot, you know, since Pierrot left . . .'

'Changed! You could fool me! The last I heard, he was still a collaborator!'

'I don't think he is. He supports Pétain, that's all.'

'All the same, he still let his daughter marry a German!'

'True. And yet he's a good man.'

'There are a lot of good people like him about. Let me tell you something. I find it easier to understand Fayard. Fayard is after the land, he merely sees the war as a means of getting what he wants, getting rich. He doesn't give a damn whether they're French, Germans or whatever, he collaborates with whoever seems in the best position to help him succeed in getting his hands on the estate. He doesn't even realize that he, a veteran of the Great War, is betraying his country. In Uncle Luc's case, it's more serious. He's an intellectual, he knows the meanings of words and the seriousness of the consequences they can lead to. His love of order, bourgeois values and his profession make him respect the authorities. As far as he is concerned, only Pétain is legitimate and Pétain has asked the French to collaborate. I also think Luc is totally lacking in imagination, otherwise he would see that sooner or later Germany will lose the war and that today's terrorists will be in power tomorrow.'

'But that's precisely what he doesn't want. He says that if the Americans land and de Gaulle is victorious, France will fall into the hands of the communists, and it's the Russians who'll be laying down the law in our country. The way he sees it, only Germany can protect Europe from the communist scourge. He is deeply convinced of it.'

'And of course my dear cousin thinks exactly like his father.'

'Worse, he wants to join the German army.'

'I'd be very surprised. Philippe has never been known for his bravery.'

'To get back to the subject, your uncle thinks that to avoid selling, you should write a letter saying you refuse to sell. It's not certain that it would be enough, but it would delay things.'

'I'll discuss it with Uncle Adrien and Camille.'

'Well, don't take too long over it. Look at me . . . you don't look too well. You seem tired.'

'I often cycle twenty or thirty miles a day. It's all uphill around here. If the war goes on much longer, I'll have calves like a racing cyclist and I'll be able to compete in the Bordeaux Grand Prix. And I'm very worried about Camille.'

'Poor thing! She's an unlucky one. Did they . . . ? You know what I mean?'

'Torture her? Not really, not in the way swine like Denan do. Do you know, those militia bastards have invented a new word which sounds more elegant and charming than torturing? It's "touyaguer" – it's become their favourite pastime.'

'Touyaguer?'

'Yes, it comes from Touyaga.'

'Touyaga?'

'It's the name of a chartered accountant who was denounced and consequently arrested by the militia. Pierre Touyaga was burned, beaten with a club, they peeled off his skin and pulled out his nails, then burned his feet and genitals. Marcel Fourquey of the 2nd Division of the Bordeaux militia was so pleased with his work, and that of his assistants, Guilbeau and Beyrand, that he invented a new verb. Now, in Bordeaux, the militia no longer torture, they "touyague".'

'But that's appalling!'

'Camille was only given a light "touyaguing": slaps, kicks and punches. She was saved by her frailty. They couldn't continue "touyaguing" her without killing her. But since then, she hasn't got any better. I thought that Charles's presence might help her.'

'But won't he be in danger, given the precarious existence you're leading?'

'I don't think so. The Resistance are watching the area closely and with the recent arrests, the Germans have withdrawn into their quarters. The greatest danger comes from men like Fiaux and Denan. I know that Aristide has had orders to kill them and that Uncle Adrien is here to see that he succeeds. But by that time, Camille and Charles will have fled to Switzerland. Is there any hot water? I'd love to wash my hair. I can't get used to washing in cold water.'

After bathing and washing her hair, Léa felt like a different woman. Despite the advice on hygiene given by the Resistance leaders and over the air on the BBC, the camps and farms which acted as refuges were not very clean. Some leaders tried to instil a military discipline: saluting the colours, physical exercise, handling of arms, clothes as neat as possible, respect for superiors, and personal hygiene and cleanliness in the camp, but that was only possible in the large groups such as those in the Limousin, Vercors and Brittany, where training was intense.

In the Aquitaine region, at the beginning of 1944, there were not many fighters in the groups. After May, things changed, and Aristide was able to transmit details of the total strength of his numbers to Baker Street. In all, 1,595 men were perfectly acquainted with their mission and determined to fight. Although small, this number was to increase to 15,000 men. Meanwhile, Colonel Buckmaster seemed satisfied.

Léa was overjoyed to abandon the old bicycle borrowed from Tore and recover her blue bicycle. On the carrier she fixed a wicker chair for Charles. Now she had to act quickly. Fayard could well have alerted the Langon Gestapo.

Ruth and Bernadette Bouchardeau were shattered to say goodbye to the little boy, their one source of happiness, who was wriggling and laughing in his chair.

'Keep still, you'll make us both fall off.'

Léa joined La Sifflette at the bottom of the Bernille hill.

The joy of the mother and child at being reunited compensated a little for Adrien Delmas's anger at the three women's recklessness. La Sifflette took all the blame, saying that as the eldest, she alone was responsible. The priest pretended to accept her reasons.

Chapter 7

Maurice Fiaux and his gang had not got over Camille's escape from the Saint-Jean hospital. Father Delmas knew that the militia and the Gestapo had managed to infiltrate certain Resistance groups in the south as well as the north, which had not been too difficult a task, the young Resistance fighters often being as thoughtless as they were confident. One glass of wine too many, a pretty girl they wanted to impress, a good word for the Resistance or for General de Gaulle, an open, comradely manner: any of these things might result in information to be gathered during the course of a normal conversation, enabling Dohse and Robert Franc to make arrests. There was even a rumour that one of Grand-Clément's men had penetrated the commandos recruited by Aristide. The leaders saw traitors everywhere. London issued execution orders.

So far, the former Resistance leader had managed to avoid all the traps set for him, but the British agent was determined to get rid of him and all those who worked with him. Already, one of his deputies, André Basilio, had been killed on 22nd May. They had to act quickly, for Grand-Clément knew that Aristide was back: on the eve of Basilio's execution, the English agent had found himself face to face with André Noël, a former member of his network who had gone over to the enemy, captivated by the theories of Dohse – and the man whom he still considered as his leader – on the Bolshevik threat that menaced France. The order was given to eliminate Grand-Clément and Noël, but they disappeared: the two men had left for Paris. As for Dohse, he had the town searched in the hunt for the Resistance leader, without success.

Father Delmas and Aristide knew that the landing was not far off. The English officer had received orders in April to listen to the French language programme on the BBC on the 1st, 2nd, 15th and 16th of each month when messages regarding the landing might be broadcast. Everything had to be ready for this possibility and preparations had to be made calmly and with the utmost secrecy. This was impossible. Since the beginning of the year, small, fairly well-armed groups had been taking every opportunity to plague the occupying forces: sabotage, attacks on sentries, escaped prisoners, and so on, putting the Germans and the militia in a permanent state of alert and jeopardizing the safety of the Aquitaine Resistance groups.

It was in this climate of waiting and tension that a message from Mathias Fayard, addressed to the priest, reached Aristide's headquarters in Blaye-Saint-Luce. There was a moment of panic at the farm in the Garonne estuary: how had he found out about this place where they had all thought they were safe? They could get nothing out of the messenger who was the idiot son of one of the local fishermen imprisoned in Fort Hâ for having distributed clandestine newspapers, well before Aristide's return. To be on the safe side, they kept the retarded boy with them.

The contents of the letter were most alarming. According to Mathias, Maurice Fiaux knew the exact whereabouts of most of the Resistance camps to the east of Bordeaux, the number of men and the quantity of arms at their disposal, and also the names of their leaders. For reasons that he alone could explain, he had not passed this information on to either the Gestapo or the militia.

'How does Fayard know all that?' cried Aristide.

'This is what he says:

You know, Father, that I keep an eye on Fiaux so that I can better protect Léa. I hid in the attic of the house where he lives in Le Bouscat. His room was just below me. The ceiling was nothing but a thin board, all you have to do is listen and you can hear everything that's being said. That's where I overheard his conversation with his two bodyguards yesterday. Some of the things he said make me think that he is going to try and sell this information to the head of the Gestapo as he doesn't trust his militia comrades "who would take the dough for themselves" as he says. I thought of killing him, from where I was hidden, that was not impossible, but then I thought that if I missed, he and the others would certainly not miss me and then there'd be nobody to warn you and protect Léa. Act fast, he must be prevented from talking. I would gladly carry out the task, but he is suspicious of me, he won't allow me near him. This letter, signed by me, is proof that I am not lying and that I am not trying to lure you into a trap. If you want to see me, leave a message at my parents' in Montillac or at the Chapon-Fin. Ask for René, he's the kitchen assistant. He knows how to get in touch with me and he'll get a message to me the same day. I would like to make it clear that I am not doing this for the Resistance, but for Léa. Yours, with respect.'

'This is absurd,' said Lancelot, 'I don't trust the little fool an inch.'

'What do you think, Father?' asked Aristide.

'He's telling the truth.'

'How can we be sure?'

'Yesterday, in Castillon-la-Bataille, we arrested a young lad we suspected of double-crossing us. When I interrogated him, he sneered that we were done for, that the militia knew the exact whereabouts of the Resistance camps and would soon be moving into the attack. Just then, the radio operator came to fetch me to decipher an urgent message from London. When I came back, he was dead.'

'Dead?'

'Yes, our lads began to beat him. Did one of them try to stop them by threatening them with his gun? I couldn't find out the truth. The fact is, a shot was fired, killing him outright.'

'You aren't going to start feeling sorry for him?'

'The death of a person is always a sad thing.'

'No doubt it is, but there is a war on. In war, people kill

and people die. Sometimes you have to kill one man to save tens or hundreds of others.'

'That's what they always say in war, to justify deaths. I saw so many lives sacrificed in Spain on the same pretext . . .'

'Perhaps you're right, Father, but we have no choice. The Allies will soon be landing, we can't risk having the Resistance attacked and dismantled. We must get rid of Maurice Fiaux, his bodyguards and Mathias Fayard.'

'Why him?'

'I don't share your trust in him.'

'I've known him since he was a child, his love for my niece made him commit some serious blunders . . .'

'Do you call working for the Gestapo and the militia a serious blunder?' broke in Lancelot.

'I propose we put it to the vote,' said Dédé le Basque, who had not spoken so far.

'All right,' said Aristide, 'who agrees that the four of them should be executed?'

All except Adrien Delmas raised their hands.

'Then it's agreed. Lancelot, put some men out on their trail, tell them to track them down and then report back. In forty-eight hours at the latest, we must know about their habits, where they live and the weak spot in their defence. Is that clear?'

'Perfectly clear. You ought to go to Jard-de-Bourdillas in the Landes de Bussac until the bastards are out of the way.'

'Perhaps. I'll decide later. I don't think I'm in too much danger here. We have men in Saint-Ciers, Montendre, Saint-Savin, Saint-André-de-Cubzac and Bourg. The HQ is well protected. Father, I'd like to speak to you in private.'

Aristide seemed even younger and smaller in build compared to the lined face and tall emaciated figure of Adrien Delmas.

'How is Madame d'Argilat?'

'Much better.'

'I'm glad to hear it. Have you managed to arrange her departure for Switzerland?'

'Not yet. A lot of *passeurs** have been arrested, and getting a sick woman right across the south of France is no easy job.'

'I've contacted London to try and get hold of a plane, but they told me it was too risky for the moment. However, if what Fayard says is true, she and your niece can't stay in Morizès any longer. We could try and send them to Luze, near Arcachon.'

'I'd rather they stayed in Daniel Faux and Lieutenant Vincent's sectors. Léa knows the area well. If there's trouble, she'll know where to hide. Besides, I'm expecting my contact for Switzerland in La Réole.'

'As you wish. But I'd still rather they were closer to Lorette.'

'Very well, I'll move them out tomorrow morning. It's Whitsun, let's hope the Lord's light will shine down on us.'

'Rendezvous here on Monday, at six p.m., to finalize how we are going to execute Fiaux and his associates. Father, can I say something?'

'Go ahead.'

'You ought to see a doctor, you look very tired.'

'We'll see about that later,' the priest said with a faint smile.

The following day, Father Delmas celebrated Mass in the church of Chapelle-la-Lorette in front of most of the Resistance fighters, of all denominations, including the group made up of Cauthure, Camille and Léa. Charles had been left in the care of Mother Faux, who, aided by La Sifflette, was cooking her 'mutton and beans' which the hungry young folk so adored. Madame Carnélos, whose farm, perched above Lorette, served as lookout post and arms cache, was cleaning small fish from the Garonne. Around the buildings with their thick walls, trenches had been dug and converted into shooting positions. Loudspeakers were rigged up outside the attic windows and others were hidden behind the wall around the well belonging to the Faux family's house.

Since the assassination of Captain Lévy by the Toulouse

---

* People who were paid to smuggle fugitives out of France

Gestapo, many young people had joined the Resistance. Colonel Becq-Guérin, who had succeeded him, continued his work and initiated new recruits in the handling of arms. Most of these were farmers, workers and students dodging compulsory labour in Germany.

As they left the church, Léa inhaled the smell of 'mutton and beans' with delight. It was one of her favourite dishes.

'I'm so hungry,' she cried, rubbing her stomach uninhibitedly.

'So am I,' rejoined Camille who now had a little more colour in her cheeks.

Léa looked at her with a mixture of surprise and pleasure.

'It's ages since I've heard you say you're hungry.'

'I feel as though I've come alive again. Praying did me good and gave me strength. I feel we're safe here.'

As in the clearing in the forest, Léa shivered, despite the hot Whitsun sunshine.

'Look who's coming to join us.'

'Raoul! Jean!'

The two brothers kissed Léa with a slight awkwardness which she swept aside as she embraced them with a happy laugh. Jean was unable to suppress a cry.

'Oh! I'm sorry, I forgot . . . Did I hurt you? Are you in a lot of pain? Is it serious . . . ?'

'No, but it's still painful.'

'Jean was very lucky. The bullet very nearly went straight through his heart. Camille, we're very glad to see you looking better. How is Charles?'

'He's here with me.'

Deep in conversation, they reached the Faux's courtyard where tables and benches had been set up. The Resistance fighters were already seated and impatiently waiting for their food. They rose to give the young women their seats, but Léa preferred to sit in the shade of the linden tree with the Lefèvre brothers. Camille sat next to Charles whose plate was already full.

The meal was very gay and the guests thoroughly enjoyed themselves. The sentries were relieved so that they could eat what had been left for them by their comrades. To make up for the small portions of 'mutton and beans', Madame Faux gave them double helpings of cake, which was as popular as her famous dish. When it was time for the chore of washing up, Léa slipped away and hid in a barn, dragging Raoul with her.

'Kiss me.'

'But what about Jean?'

'Be quiet, he's injured. Kiss me.'

They rolled in the hay and, for a while, they were only concerned with the physical pleasure they derived from each other's bodies.

In the evening, the Resistance fighters made their way back to their respective camps and Father Delmas left for Bordeaux on a motorcycle requisitioned from a garage owner in Langon.

That Whitsun 1944 the exceptionally warm night seemed to belong to the priest as he straddled his motorcycle and rode through the vine-covered slopes. The heat was suffocating. It was marvellous weather for the grapes, but disastrous for the other crops which were suffering terribly from the lack of water. A few flashes of lightning promised rain, but the storm blew over.

As he rode through a little wood, at the bottom of a valley, Adrien Delmas was assailed by a strong smell of moss and mint and by the cold damp of the undergrowth. Even after all these years, he never ceased to be amazed by this abrupt transition from land constantly shaped by human hands to these wooded hollows which shut out sun and sky, with tangles of hostile undergrowth and treacherous roots and stagnant pools of water inhabited by crawling creatures. These places, which seemed all the wilder because of the contrast, made him feel momentarily uneasy. Even when summer was at its hottest, one did not feel like resting in the shade of those malevolent trees. He did not remember ever stopping in such a place. But that evening, his spirit and his heart were in harmony with the dark and damp surroundings.

He switched off the engine and braked. The warmth of the machine felt friendly and restrained him for a second from leaning it against a tree and abandoning it. He parted the branches and the creepers and entered the shadows. His feet squelched as he made his way over the peaty ground. A shrivelled, uprooted oak tree barred his path. He sank on to the rotten trunk; he no longer had the strength to fight against the overwhelming despair he felt. Since his belief in God had suddenly left him, one morning at dawn, in Spain, as he faced those young people, little more than children, who were being shot, his burning eyes had not shed a single tear. How many sleepless nights had he spent calling for help to the God he no longer believed in? Yet he continued praying to him daily, seeking to be reunited with that glorious faith through the familiar words. He had confided in one of his Spanish friends, a priest like himself, who had gazed at him with compassion and embraced him.

'I pity you from the depths of my soul, but I cannot do anything for you. I am experiencing the same turmoil and it is so painful that I've thought of killing myself . . . It's only the thought of the suffering it would cause my mother that has stopped me.'

They parted company even more distressed. Since then, Adrien Delmas had never brought up the subject again, trying to forget his suffering in action. He was unable to do so. His grief was so great that he prayed for death with all his might. The time had perhaps come to go out and meet it.

He had always found the deaths of others unbearable, even those of traitors and murderers. And yet, in that dank dark place, he had just reached a tremendous decision: he would kill Maurice Fiaux, thus preventing him from denouncing the Resistance groups organized by his friends. Once he had made up his mind, this man, this priest, who before the war had campaigned against the death sentence, experienced peace, something he had not felt for a very long time.

He outlined a plan: he could find out the boy's address from his mother. Fiaux would not be wary of him and anyway, he would be only too delighted to arrest this Resistance leader who had so far managed to escape both the German and the French police. After the murder, he would not have time to flee and one of the young militiaman's henchmen would shoot him.

At peace, he left the little wood.

The following day, he volunteered to kill Maurice Fiaux. Those who knew he was a priest stared at him in astonishment, then horror, and tried in vain to dissuade him. He insisted that he was the best person to do it, saying that he was the only one who could approach the victim and execute him with the least risk. As that was not enough to convince them, he reminded them of his rank in the secret army and the orders from London. They gave in, reluctantly and with great sadness. He secured the postponement of Mathias Fayard's execution, although he was to remain under close surveillance.

A hitch delayed the final encounter: on 30th May, Fiaux left Bordeaux for Paris. According to his mother, he was to be back in Bordeaux by 6th June at the latest. What was he up to in the capital? He had been invited to a meeting by Darnand as a reward for his zeal . . .

Chapter 8

'Philémon requests his six bottles of Sauternes.'

Aristide leapt out of his chair and almost pulled the knob off the wireless set that he had been twiddling for a while, trying to tune in to the BBC for the sixth broadcast he had been ordered to listen to. It was seven p.m. on the evening of 2nd June 1944.

'I repeat, Philémon requests his six bottles of Sauternes.'

There was no doubt about it, that was message 'A' intended for his area informing them of the imminence of the landing, and the order for the Resistance groups to be in a state of alert. That evening he assembled his staff: Lancelot, François and Jacqueline, Dany and Marcel. He convened the group leaders at three o'clock at 29 Rue Guynemer in Caudéran, a suburb of Bordeaux.

The following day, they were all at the meeting. Aristide received them individually and gave them precise instructions. First, Cadepoint, the leader of the railway workers, was given orders to sabotage engines, points, signals and tracks over a radius of a hundred and twenty-five miles. Pierre Roland, representing the Bordeaux dockers, was instructed to destroy the electrical fittings controlling the mines placed along the quaysides by the Germans. Henri Mesmet announced that Léon des Landes had five hundred men willing to fight but that only half were armed. The officer reassured him: they were expecting three parachute drops in the next two days. No problems of that kind for

111

Captain Duchez of the Arcachon group, his men were well-armed and well-trained in the use of heavy artillery: machine guns, mortars and bazookas. The four representatives from the Lège, Andernos, Facture and Arès groups each had between seventy and a hundred suitably armed men. In the Mérignac group, there were only about twenty people left after the wave of arrests, but Pierre Chatanet came to offer their services. Their mission was to cut the telephone lines. The leaders of the groups from La Réole, Bègles, Pessac, Lermont, Bordeaux Saint-Augustin and Blaye were there too. Dédé le Basque's irregular forces had been feverishly waiting for the moment when they could go into action. The operation consisted of hampering the German troops stationed in the south-west as much as possible in their march towards the landing place, when it was publicized.

As they left Caudéran, their hearts were full of hope. They were optimistic but impatient too. After four years of occupation, a few days' wait seemed too long to that handful of men who had refused to accept defeat.

Léa finished having a hasty wash and flung the contents of the bowl into the courtyard.

'Hey! Watch out!'

She froze on the spot.

'What's the matter, have you turned into a pillar of salt?'

A burst of laughter brought her down to earth. The bowl clattered to the ground, shedding splinters of blue enamel.

'François!'

That subdued but wild cry went through François like a dagger. With a roar that was most uncivilized, he caught her in mid air.

She was there . . . in the flesh and blood . . . warm . . . smelling of cheap soap and that unique cherry tree fragrance that was hers. He sniffed her, emitting little animal sounds, nibbling her, burying his face in her hair, devouring her tongue and her lips . . . Shamelessly she rubbed up against him, letting out a moan that aroused him even more . . . He pushed her away and held her at arm's length, on the point of climaxing, and devoured her with hungry eyes. Ah! The bitch! How he had missed her. The memory of her body had kept him awake for whole nights, while he lay uncomfortably with a painful hard-on which neither his hands nor the hospitable female military auxiliaries in the British Army had been able to relieve. At first, he was amused at being in such a state of arousal for a spoilt kid who was not even there, but as the months went by, it sent him into a rage which he vented on the young British girls or on London whores.

When he touched her, all his breeding deserted him . . . he felt a burning desire to rape . . . no caresses, or preliminaries . . . to take her . . . there, in that farmyard, under the mocking gaze of the Resistance fighters who were pretending to be engrossed in the handling of their Stens. They repeated the instructions to themselves over and over again so as not to seem embarrassed:

'To load the magazine, place the gun so that the catch (f) enters the slit (g). Place the four fingers of the left hand on the lever (a) so that the third finger is in the hole (b) in the catch and the index is on the tip (c). Lower the catch (d) on which the little finger is placed and insert a cartridge in front of the opening (e) with the right hand. Raise the catch with the third finger and push to insert another cartridge. Repeat until twenty-eight cartridges have been loaded . . .'

One man dropped his cartridges. Blushing, he picked them up and moved away. Most of his comrades followed him.

Standing on the doorstep, La Sifflette stood there with her hands on her hips, watching the couple with an approving smile. There was no doubt about it, they were made for each other, those two! It took a strapping fellow like that, who resembled a poacher, to tame this beautiful, insolent girl who looked at men with an expression that seemed both innocent and hungry. The sooner she left for Switzerland with Madame d'Argilat, the better, or else the lads would end up killing each other over her.

'Hey! You lovebirds, this is no place for kissing and

cuddling, there are plenty of places you can go round here. Hey! Do you hear me?'

'Forgive me, madame,' said François Tavernier, tearing his gaze away from Léa.

'There's no need to apologize. If I were a handsome male confronted with a female like that, I'd do the same . . . but I wouldn't stand there in the farmyard, I'd carry her off to the tobacco-drying shed up there, where there's freshly cut hay.'

'Thank you for your kind information, madame. Léa, do you know the tobacco shed in question?'

'Come with me.'

La Sifflette watched them run off down the gravel path.

The five hundred yards between the farm and the shed seemed endless. In their haste, they stumbled in the ruts, twisted their ankles, cursing and laughing as they ran. He had one arm round her waist; his free hand held a kitbag and a gun. The door was locked with a rusty padlock. Using the barrel of his gun as a lever, he broke it open.

The heady smell of the dried tobacco and the freshly cut hay assailed them and aroused their senses all the more. François flung down his bag and gun, tore off his jacket and pushed Léa into the hay. They fell together, fighting as they sought each other's bodies, impatient. They came together brutally, with such violence that they both cried out. They were submerged by sheer physical pleasure: it felt as if they were being washed out to sea by a powerful wave and then dropped back, dislocated and unsated, on their rustic bed.

'Get undressed.'

Without taking his eyes off her, he removed his clothes. Naked, his penis erect, he went over and wedged the door shut with his gun. Now, he wanted to make sure he would not be disturbed. He wanted to take his time and savour Léa's body to the full.

When his huge appetite for her was finally appeased, it was late afternoon. They had not spoken other than to exchange words of love that have become clichés from being repeated

114

so often. There was a loud knocking at the door. He grabbed his gun.

'Who is it?'

'Major, it's me, Finot. I was told you were here.'

Tavernier put down his gun and started to get dressed.

'What do you want?'

'We have to leave, Major, otherwise you'll miss your plane.'

'Good God! Couldn't you have come to fetch me earlier?'

'But, Major, nobody knew where you were!'

Léa, who was lying there naked, raised herself up on her elbows.

'Are you leaving?'

'I took advantage of a mission in the area to look for you. At Montillac, nobody could or would tell me where you were. Luckily, I remembered Madame Lafourcade and her sons. Maxime agreed to telephone, and . . . I found you.'

'But now you're going away again.'

'Yes, but I'll be back.'

'Major!'

'Coming!'

'François . . . !'

'Ssh, little girl . . . no tears. Everything's going to be all right, the war will be over soon.'

'But . . . we haven't had time to talk to each other!'

'I know, my love, we'll talk to each other later.'

He picked her up and held her close, she was so vulnerable in her nakedness.

'Kiss me . . .'

'Major!'

When he drew away from her, he could taste salt. He was not sure whether it was from her tears or from his own.

He and his driver raced down the slope to the farmyard where an old black Mercedes was waiting. He jumped into the car. It pulled away. He turned round. On the doorstep, a young woman who looked like Camille d'Argilat stood holding a little boy by the hand, waving to him.

François had been parachuted in the previous day for a

mission connected with the landing. He took off that night for London aboard a British Army Blenheim.

When Léa came back from the tobacco shed that evening, with dark shadows under her red eyes, Camille, who had come to meet her, kissed her and said simply:

'You're lucky.'

They went inside the farmhouse holding hands.

In fact, Léa had become accustomed to this frugal clandestine existence, even though she occasionally complained about the primitiveness of her surroundings and the overcrowding. Camille, on the other hand, who never complained, was beginning to suffer from this tough life. More than anything else, she dreaded the camp being attacked. Her health had improved, but she was still so weak that she found it difficult to walk. Her faith in God and the thought of her husband and her son kept her going.

It was on the evening of 5th June that message 'B', so eagerly awaited by Aristide and his friends, was broadcast. It was one of three hundred messages given out that night by the French Resistance to its men. '*A rose behind the ear*' announced the Allied Landing in Normandy and the mobilization of the entire French Resistance.

Operations were set in motion at once: at dawn, the guns patiently stored in barns, tobacco sheds, wine cellars and caves were rapidly distributed. The underground cables linking the headquarters of General von der Chevallerie, the Commander of the 1st Army stationed in Bordeaux, to the Mérignac base and to the troops' barracks, and, later, the cables linking the Luftwaffe to the Chut battery, were destroyed. At Pessac station depot, Pierre Chatanet and his men blew up nine engines, delaying the departure of three thousand German soldiers for the Normandy front for several days. They also disrupted the Lacanau to Saint-Louis line. As for Georges's group, they blew up the railway line between Le Puy and Lonzac, the railway bridge between Montendre and Chartressac, cut the German Army's telephone cables in

Le Souge, destroyed eight 150,000–volt electricity pylons near Ychoux and three 120,000–volt pylons in Boir.

The Arcachon group, led by Major de Luze and Captain Duchez, blew up two high-voltage pylons, depriving the southern part of the railway network of electricity, and the telephone and telegraph cables of the seaside resort were also destroyed, cutting it off from the rest of the world. Dédé le Basque and Léon des Landes constantly harassed the German convoys which were trying to travel north along the secondary roads towards the beaches of Normandy.

During the evening of 6th June, at the Carnélos farmhouse, they were listening to the voice which had been upholding the honour of France for four years, although interference sometimes made it impossible to hear what he was saying:

'*The final battle has begun!*

'*After so many battles, so much violence and pain, this is the decisive onslaught, the one we have all been waiting for. Of course it is the battle for France and it is the battle of France!*

'*For the sons of France, wherever they may be, whoever they are, their plain and sacred duty is to fight with all the means they have at their disposal. It is a matter of destroying the enemy who is crushing and sullying our country, the hated enemy, the dishonoured enemy.*

'*The enemy is going to do everything within its power to escape its destiny. It is going to fight to hold on to our land for as long as possible. But for a long time now, the enemy has been a retreating beast . . .*

'*For our nation which has been fighting with her hands and feet tied, against an oppressor who is armed to the teeth, good order in battle demands several conditions . . .*'

The three conditions were not heard by those listening. They only heard the end of General de Gaulle's speech:

'*The battle of France has begun. The nation, the empire and the army have one common will, one common hope. Behind the cloud which is so heavy with our blood and our tears, the sun of our glory is reappearing.'*

When the words of the *Marseillaise* blared out, naturally, they all rose to their feet. Some people cried unashamedly. Later, after a member of the staff of the Supreme Command of the Inter-Allied Expeditionary Forces had given instructions to the people living in the landing zone, Jacques Duchesne spoke on the programme 'Frenchmen speak to the French'.

'It is no accident, my friends, that this evening, you have not heard: "Today, the 277th day of the invasion", and so on. It is not an omission that you have not heard "1,444th day of the French people's liberation struggle". It took 1,444 days for this liberation to begin. But you will never hear those two phrases again.'

They all applauded the words 'never again'. A little more patience, and they would never be afraid again, they would never have to go into hiding again. A few more days, a few more weeks and they could go back home, go back to the vineyards, the factories, the office or simply to their own homes. In a month or two, the prisoners would come back, in time, perhaps, for the grape harvest. That night, the inhabitants of Antoine Carnélos's farm all had sweet dreams.

Nothing made them suspect a German attack.

The weather was overcast and heavy that afternoon of 9th June. Léa and Charles were laughing as they returned from the Candale woods, famished after a long walk picking wild strawberries. They had found a dozen or so that were barely ripe which they had shared equally. The little boy adored Léa. She acted as if he were a teenage brother and joined in his games with the solemnity of a child. They had decided to have a picnic, but they had eaten Mother Faux's snack hours ago. That was why they came back sooner than expected, in the hope that there'd be some leftovers from lunch back at the farm.

They could already smell the daily 'mutton and beans' which Léa, glutton that she was, was beginning to detest. Suddenly, a burst of machine-gun fire made them freeze in their tracks.

'They're playing around,' said the child with the important air of someone who is in the know.

'I don't think so. Wait, stay here . . . don't move, I'm going to have a look.'

'No, I want to come with you.'

Another burst, then another.

'It's coming from the farm! Promise me you won't move, I'm going to get your mother.'

She raced down the slope and stopped behind the big cherry tree that overlooked the Carnélos's farm. A hundred yards away, in the cornfield, the grey-green helmets of the German soldiers emerged. They were accompanied by militiamen in their distinctive navy blue uniforms and black helmets. One of them stood up with a shout and then fell back, crushing the tender young corn with his weight . . . A burst of gunfire came from the farm. From upstairs, the guns of Daniel Faux and his comrades were sweeping the field . . . Men fell, others took their places. From one of the ground-floor windows, Camille, armed with a gun, fired . . . 'Charles! Charles . . . where are you?' 'He's safe, he's with Léa.' Resistance fighters ran past the cherry tree. Léa followed them. Camouflaged at the entrance to the woods, they flung a few grenades in the direction of the enemy.

'Léa! Léa!'

'Shit, the kid!'

Charles, terrified by the noise and the shouts, was rushing through the trees. Léa chased after him. Fear lent wings to his little legs. The fierce gunfire continued . . .

'Charles . . . Charles . . .'

He could not hear . . . he bounded like an elf . . . 'Stop, please, stop . . .' He had gone past the corner of the wall . . . He disappeared from view . . . 'Oh God, protect him!'

'Mummy! Mummy!'

'Charles!'

Camille let out an animal yelp and rushed out, dropping her gun. La Sifflette tried to hold her back. She struggled, screamed . . . Suddenly, there was silence. The child was standing in the farmyard. Léa ran past the corner . . . Someone flung her flat on the ground . . . Camille appeared in the doorway . . . she ran, arms outstretched towards the child, who was running to her . . . how beautiful they were . . . it took an eternity for them to reach each other, like a ballet in slow motion. Charles spun round. A red flower spread on his white shirt, his arms slowly rent the air, he tottered . . . One of his grass-stained white sandals fell off, no sound issued from his open mouth . . . But Camille could see that he was calling her . . . 'Don't be afraid, Mummy's here . . . darling, careful, you'll fall . . . Oh! darling, have you hurt yourself? You're bleeding! It's nothing . . . Ah . . . I can't see you any more . . . something warm's running down my forehead . . . on my lips . . . it tastes salty . . . Where are you? Ah! There you are! What are you doing lying on the ground? It's true, you fell over. Have you hurt yourself? Mummy'll look after you . . . You're so brave! You're not crying. Wait, I'll carry you. How heavy you are . . . I'm not very strong yet, you see. I'll call Léa . . . she'll come and help me . . .'

Léa saw her name on Camille's bloodstained lips. She struggled to answer the mute cry . . . Jean Lefèvre was holding her down with all his strength.

'Let me go! Camille needs me!'

'There's nothing we can do.'

Bullets hailed down round the mother and child. The young woman's body fell on top of her son. Léa broke free from Jean. She reached them at the same time as La Sifflette who began to drag Camille into the house. La Sifflette fell . . . Léa picked up Charles and sped into the woods. She ran . . . she dared not look at him. Blood made her fingers sticky. She ran.

She ran until she reached Deymier. There she was taken in by a woman whose son had been killed in 1940. Her arms and legs were scratched to pieces by the brambles and her clothes were torn. Gently, the woman took the child from her.

'He's alive.'

In Lorette, the order to withdraw came at about six o'clock that evening. The Germans had forced them to use the heavy artillery. After mining the camp, the group dispersed in the woods, taking the injured with them. They removed their hats and bowed their heads before Camille and La Sifflette's bodies, but had to leave them behind. A few moments later, the enemy stormed the house. The roof, blown off by explosives, fell in on the attackers.

The enemy suffered heavy losses: forty-eight Germans and twenty-eight militiamen had been killed. The Resistance fighters met up in Lamothe-Landerron. The fifteen injured were evacuated. They had not all been so lucky.

Despite the bravery of René Faux, who had been wounded in the knee hiding Robert Liarcou, the latter was discovered with a shattered knee. He was dragged over the gravel. An enemy nurse wrapped the injured knee in straw and made a splint from two planks. He was thrown unconscious into a truck where chairs, provisions and bicycles were piled. He was driven to the school in La Réole, the Gestapo headquarters. There he found his companion, Paul Gérard, lying in a pool of his own blood, his limbs all crushed. He had been discovered at the Faux's house. The Germans beat him to death. He died that night, stabbed several times by a militiaman. His body, carried in a sack, was thrown into a mass grave dug along the bank of the Garonne.

At dawn, when they came to fetch him, Robert Liarcou thought he was going to be shot. After stopping off at the Gestapo headquarters in Langon, he was taken to Fort Hâ where he was left without treatment, supported by two members of the Resistance who were also wounded: Laforestière from Puissegrain and Marcel Guinot from Bergerac. A few days later, his guards dragged him to the infirmary where Dr Poinot was permitted to examine him. When he saw the extent of the wound, he tried to persuade the commander to allow the young man to be taken to hospital. The commander only agreed after five or six haemorrhages. His leg was amputated in Béquet hospital on 14th July, after thirty-six days without treatment. In August, he was taken back to Fort Hâ.

He, at least, survived. Three of his comrades, likewise taken prisoner in La Réole, were deported. They were not to come back. They were called Bolzan, Labory and Zuanet.

Charles had lost a lot of blood, but in spite of his slight build, he had a strong constitution. He was wounded in the shoulder, but he recovered very quickly.

Chapter 9

Maurice Fiaux was more surprised than wary when he saw Father Delmas standing on his doorstep. After a brief glance outside, he ordered his bodyguards to leave him alone.

'I'm not in any danger in a priest's company, am I Father?' he said with a mocking smile. 'What do you want of me?'

'Germany's lost the war. People like you will be shot. In the meantime, we need you. I've been ordered by London to make you an offer. If you agree, you can save your skin.'

Fiaux looked at the priest doubtfully.

'What proof have I got that this isn't a trap?'

Adrien Delmas looked at him with scorn.

'You have my word. I am concerned with saving human lives. Let's go out for a walk. I don't want to risk being overheard by your henchmen.'

Maurice Fiaux hesitated for a moment, then suddenly made up his mind.

'As you wish, Father . . . but I will have to get someone to follow us . . .'

'If I were you, I'd do nothing.'

'Is there money to be made?'

'Perhaps,' said Adrien Delmas, barely able to conceal his disgust.

'Very well, let's go. Anyway, I'm big enough to look after myself,' said Maurice Fiaux, brandishing an impressive automatic pistol.

As they went down the stairs, they passed two young men smoking on the landing.

'If I'm not back in an hour, tell Superintendent Poinsot. Tell him I had an appointment with an important member of the Resistance who gave us the slip in the Mérignac camp. He'll know who I mean.'

'Don't you want us to come with you?'

'There's no need.'

The weather was very close on this late afternoon of 9th June. The Rue de la Porte-Dijeaux was bustling with office workers on their way home. Pale children were splashing about in the filthy water in the gutters.

'Where are we going?'

'To the embankment, it's quieter.'

Maurice Fiaux faltered.

'I've given my word,' said the priest bitterly.

'What you have to say to me must be pretty important for you to take the risk of being recognized and arrested. Have you seen your charming niece recently? I heard she was playing at soldiers somewhere near La Réole. I forget where. Ah yes! I remember: Lorette. That's the place isn't it? I would never have believed a young lady from a good Bordeaux family would mix with communists. Apparently, Madame d'Argilat has become a communist too . . . I heard her little boy sings the *Internationale*. But I couldn't believe that. The son of a London hero! It's true, you haven't set them a very good example. Already in the days when you used to visit my mother's employer, you had Bolshevik ideas. It's strange for a Catholic priest. Lucky they're not all like you.'

'There are a lot more of us than you realize.'

'We know who they are. Do you remember Father de Jabrun? He was a Jesuit. Was he one of your friends?'

'Yes.'

'Apparently he died last year at Buchenwald.'

And so he was dead, Louis de Jabrun with whom he used to spend hours before the war discussing Eckhart's *Traités* or Jakob Boehme's *Les Confessions*, or those of Saint Augustin. Another of the finest men he had ever met had disappeared.

'As for Father Dieuzaide and Father Lasserre, if I were in their shoes, I'd be saying my prayers.'

'Perhaps you ought to be saying yours,' thought Adrien Delmas with macabre humour.

They walked along the Quai Richelieu and the Cours d'Alsace et Lorraine in silence. Father Delmas turned into the Rue de la Porte-des-Portanets.

After a few paces, Fiaux stopped, suddenly anxious. His grip on his pistol tightened.

'Drop that! It's only a humble French pistol, but it shoots accurately.'

'You're mad! What do you want of me?'

'Go in there.'

Delmas pushed him roughly into the sordid hall of an eighteenth-century building that had once been magnificent. A disgustingly dirty stone staircase led to the upper floors.

'Where are we going?'

'To the second floor, last door. Don't put your hand back in your pocket.'

No staircase had ever seemed so steep. Fiaux walked up. He was tense, imagining, without really believing it, that he was going to get a bullet in the back. Adrien Delmas dragged his feet with such effort that he broke out in a sweat.

'It's not locked, go in.'

After the dirtiness outside, the huge room seemed excessively clean. The furniture consisted of a camp bed, a table, a military tin trunk and two chairs.

'Sit down,' said the priest, relieving him of his gun.

'No.'

'Sit down,' said Delmas, seating himself on one of the chairs. Pale but with a steady gaze, Fiaux obeyed.

'What do you want of me?'

'To kill you.'

He sat and gaped in astonishment. A trickle of saliva ran down his chin. He gripped the sides of the chair, his legs went weak. He began to shiver.

'You don't have the right.'

'Did you have the right to kill, to torture, to denounce people the way you have?'

'I was obeying orders!'

'So am I.'

'No, it's not true! You want to protect your family . . .'

'Shut up. If you're a believer, commend your soul to God.'

Maurice Fiaux slipped off his chair and fell to his knees.

'But you can't kill me! Not you!'

'Yes I can. If it's a sin, I'll take responsibility for it.'

'I beg you, you knew me as a child . . . Think of my mother . . . What will you tell my mother?'

It was true, he had a mother . . . Get it over with quickly.

Before his eyes, Fiaux was reduced to a quivering heap from which emanated a foul smell. Poor kid, he thought as he pulled the trigger. The bullet pierced his left temple and he died instantaneously.

Adrien Delmas contemplated his deed with visible emotion. He turned the body over and went through his pockets. In the crocodile-skin and gold wallet he found the list of members of the Gironde Resistance groups, and in nearly every case there was the name of the head and the number of men. The Lorette group was circled in red with the figure 9, and the Libourne, Targon, Villandraut and Podensac groups were marked with a red dot. If that list got into the hands of the Germans, that would be the end of the Resistance in the whole of the south-west. Aristide had to be informed at once.

Before leaving the room, he automatically traced the sign of the cross over the body.

Late that night, Father Delmas found the Englishman's head-quarters which had been changed every day since the landing. There he learned of the deaths of Camille and La Sifflette. Nobody had any news of Léa or little Charles, except that he had been hit at the same time as his mother. They had disappeared during the German attack.

Although Léon des Landes broke the news gently, it was a great shock for the priest. He almost fainted. They ran over to support him and he stood up again. Why hadn't he killed that devil earlier? Why had he hesitated for two days before finishing him off? Because of him, because of his idiotic scruples, women, and possibly a child, were dead and others injured. Who knew if the next day, or even that night, others would share the same fate because he had dithered over taking the life of a brute?

Overwhelmed, he gave a report of the circumstances of Maurice Fiaux's death. A painful silence followed his curt and precise account.

'I'm going to La Réole to find out what has happened to Léa and Charles. Have you any messages you want me to carry?'

They all knew it was useless to try and stop him. Dédé le Basque and a young Resistance fighter accompanied him to the edge of the village where a sentry procured him a bicycle.

'Have a rest and go later, Father.'

'No, I must go now. Farewell, my friends.'

Dédéle Basque was worried as he watched him ride off into the night.

It was several hours after daybreak before Adrien Delmas cycled into view of the rooftops of La Réole. He walked down the sloping streets of the little town, pushing his bicycle. He went into the Hotel Terminus in the Place Jean-Jaurès. A little higher, overlooking the Garonne, was the college, the Gestapo headquarters. It was in that hotel that the *passeur* for Switzerland was supposed to leave him a message.

He sat down heavily at one of the tables in the restaurant. Without his having to ask for anything, a waitress set a slice of bread and some pâté before him.

'Would you like some wine?'

'If you like.'

The girl returned with an open bottle and a glass. While she poured the wine, he asked:

'Have you see Hélène?'

She darted him a quick glance of relief before replying.

'Yes, she'll be coming soon.'

That meant that everything had been arranged for the departure of Camille and her son.

'Don't you feel well? You've gone all white!'

'No, I'm all right . . . just a little tired. When is she coming?'

127

'I don't know. Very soon, I think.'

At that time of day, the restaurant was empty. The sound of clattering plates reached them through the half-open kitchen doors.

'I must finish laying the tables for lunch,' she said aloud. 'You shouldn't be seen in town. Have you heard what happened yesterday?' she whispered.

'Yes, how many were killed?'

'They say two or three women and a little boy.'

'Any wounded?'

'About fifteen.'

'Where are the others?'

A voice shouted from the kitchen.

'Germaine, you're idling. Lay the tables.'

'Yes, madame, coming . . . They're somewhere between Mongauzy and Lamothe-Landerron.'

'Germaine . . .'

'Coming, coming, I'm taking the customer's money.'

'Here you are. Thank you. Keep the change.'

'Thank you, monsieur.'

Adrien Delmas left the restaurant and collected his bicycle. At the suspension bridge, he met a German patrol. He got back on to the bicycle and rode off in the direction of Marmande. His legs ached from his thirty-mile ride the previous night. He would not be able to carry on pedalling much longer. Zigzagging along the road, he reached Mongauzy. He stopped outside the church, a red blur in front of his eyes and his face crimson. Everything was going round and round. Something was ripping through his chest. As he fell, he saw the face of the man he had assassinated, contorted with fear.

He regained consciousness in the local priest's bed.

'What a fright you gave me, monsieur.'

'How long have I been here?'

'Three days.'

'I must leave.'

'Don't you move! The doctor said it was very serious. He's

128

coming back today. Monsieur! Get back into bed! There, you can see for yourself, you can't get up.'

'But I have to.'

'I don't know why you're in such a hurry to leave, and I don't want to. But you're safe here, and the doctor, and the schoolteacher who helped me carry you here, are people you can trust.'

Adrien Delmas looked at the man in the worn green cassock which had a few buttons missing. He was a good man, a country priest. What would he have done if he had known?

'Ah! I see you're feeling better. Don't talk! I have to examine you first. When did he regain consciousness, Father?'

'About a quarter of an hour ago.'

The doctor examined the patient attentively. He was very elderly and should have retired long ago. His long, bony fingers felt Adrien's thin body with expert precision. When he had finished, he carefully put away his stethoscope and wiped his glasses, which seemed to the priest to take forever.

'Well doctor, don't keep us waiting.'

'It's not too good. How old are you?'

'Fifty-five.'

'My poor fellow, you have the heart of an exhausted man of my age. You must have absolute rest. I'm going to prescribe some medicines and I hope the chemist has them. I'd gladly give them to you, but I gave all mine away a long time ago and, after what happened the other day, my medicine cupboard is bare.'

'You mean the assault on the Resistance . . .'

'Yes, there are a lot of casualties.'

'Are there any women among them?'

'Wounded? No. Two unfortunate women were killed.'

'And the child?'

'I haven't seen a child, either dead or alive.'

Adrien Delmas closed his eyes and brought his hands to his chest.

'Don't talk any more, it's too tiring for you.'

'Doctor, one more thing. Haven't you heard anything

about a young girl and a little boy who are in hiding somewhere in the area?'

'No, other than a young Resistance fighter with a head
wound who kept saying over and over again: "Léa, don't go,
Léa, don't go." '

'She's the one I'm looking for. She's a very pretty girl of
twenty . . .'

'No, I haven't seen any pretty girls. Why are you looking
for her? Is she a relative of yours?'

'Yes, she's my niece.'

'As a favour, I'll find out for you. People round here
know me. If they know anything, they'll tell me. But on one
condition: that you rest quietly.'

'I promise.'

'Good. If I find out anything, I'll let the priest know.'

'Thank you, doctor,' stammered Adrien before losing
consciousness.

'Poor man. I don't think he'll last long. Pray for him,
Father. He must have suffered a lot to be so worn out.'

'Do you have any idea where to find this girl and child?'

'No, but I'm going to go to Jaguenaux where they're
looking after the wounded. I'll drop in again this evening.
Goodbye, Father.'

'Goodbye, doctor.'

'Keep an eye on your guest.'

The doctor was unable to return until the following day. He
looked devastated.

'Nobody knows a thing. The last time they were seen alive
was when the farm was attacked. The child was dead or
injured. Some say that the Germans could have flung them
into the burning building. At the moment, the place is under
guard, nobody can go near it.'

Adrien Delmas was listening, unable to utter a word.

'Why would they have done that? They're soldiers, not
animals.'

'My dear Father, they're worse than animals! They are the
unclean beast your scriptures speak of.'

'What's going on, doctor? You look very upset.'

'What's going on, Father, is that they have massacred all the inhabitants of a village in the Limoges area.'

'It isn't possible!'

But the tears streaming down the elderly face told him that it was.

The priest crossed himself and laid his hand on the old man's shoulder.

'May God forgive them.'

The doctor drew himself up with anger.

'May he forgive them, you say! But if your bloody God exists, he can't forgive that. I've seen plenty of disasters, plenty of horrors in my long lifetime. I've seen lads dying, their limbs ripped off, in the mud of the trenches, I've seen people mutilated, the casualties of the Great War . . . I've seen my best pals reduced to a pulp on the fields of Verdun! I know about war, and death, it disgusts me, but I accept it as an inevitable part of man's nature. But the massacre of women . . . children . . . , especially of children, that I do not accept.'

'Calm yourself, doctor.'

'You want me to calm down! But do you know what they did in Oradour-sur-Glane? Tell me, do you know? Last Saturday, the 10th June . . . people were hurrying to get their tobacco rations. They had assembled all the schoolchildren for their medical. Some refugees had arrived the previous evening, about two hundred of them. It was after lunch that they arrived in trucks, in combat dress, pointing their guns at the houses. The Major, a certain Otto Dickmann, had the mayor brought before him, and then the village policeman . . . Accompanied by two SS, he walked round the village beating a drum . . . "Calling all inhabitants . . ." then he gave his message: "Calling all inhabitants, the men, the women and the children must assemble immediately in the fairground, with their identity cards, for an identity check." The SS dragged the old and the sick from their beds and pushed them to the fairground with the barrels of their guns, as they pushed the peasants brought from the neighbouring fields, the families from the nearby hamlets, the fishermen and the little children who were not walking fast enough . . . Soon, all the inhabitants were gathered together. A few shots from the other end of the village made the stupefied crowd jump. Gunmen took up their positions all around. Women and children sobbed. They separated the men and the women. The mothers hugged their children to their breasts, clinging to the handles of the prams. Surrounded by ten SS, the women and children were escorted to the church. The priest had never seen so many people. The men were made to line up in three rows. In the silence, they could hear the Limoges tram ringing its bell as it approached the bridge. A shot . . . A soldier shouts in excellent French that terrorists have a large arms cache in the village and that, under threat of reprisals, they were to inform them where the arms were hidden. An old farmer said he had a hunting gun . . . "We're not interested in that," said the soldier. The men were divided into four groups of forty to fifty. Two were sent to one end of the village and two to the other. They were herded into seven barns. The Germans laughed and chatted as they pointed their machine guns and sub-machine guns at them. Suddenly, with a great shout, they opened fire. The bodies piled up on top of each other, the bullets glanced off the walls and the wounded shrieked. The shooting stopped. They finished off anything that was still moving with pistols. Soldiers brought straw, bundles of wood, a wheelbarrow and a ladder. They set fire to the bales of straw which they threw on to the heaps of bodies, some of which were still twitching, and closed the doors. The same scene was repeated in the seven barns. In the church, four hundred women and children, perhaps five hundred, watched in horror as a group of soldiers dragged in a large crate with strings hanging from it . . . They set fire to the strings and went out. An explosion . . . Thick black smoke filled the church. Screaming in terror, half choked, women and children ran everywhere. The guns rattled through the open door . . . grenades went off . . . hair caught fire. Gone was the smell of dust and incense, it was replaced by the smell of blood, shit and burnt flesh. Lads of twenty were throwing bundles of sticks and straw into that writhing human mass . . . A flame-thrower spat out its fire . . . A woman, whose daughter had died by her side, dragged herself along . . . Two children, who had taken refuge in the confessional, were shot. Mothers and children, intertwined, were burned alive . . . Can you hear those screams? Tell me, can you hear them? Can you see the walls of that holy place stained with the victims' blood? The traces of those poor fingers sliding along the stones? Those shattered faces? Those broken limbs? That baby screaming in its pushchair before becoming a human torch? Tell me, CAN YOU SEE THEM?'

They could see them so clearly that the priest had fallen to his knees in prayer and the old doctor closed his eyes in horror. Without a word, he turned his back on them and disappeared into the darkness, bowed under the burden of all the world's sorrows.

Adrien Delmas had got out of bed, the taste of nausea in his mouth. With a great effort, he gently raised the old priest and laid him on the bed he had just vacated. He got dressed and checked that his pistol was working. Before going out, he looked at the prostrate priest and left without a word.

He walked for a long time across vineyards and fields without attempting to seek cover. People he met greeted him as usual in the country. He did not answer. They turned round, astonished, a little worried. One didn't know who one might meet on the road these days. He asked for a glass of water at a farmhouse and politely thanked the farmer and his wife. They felt uneasy as they watched him leave. The woman rapidly crossed herself, saying:

'He looks as though he's seen the devil.'

The thin figure had disappeared in the distance long before the woman went back into the house.

At dusk, he stopped in a little damp mossy wood and rested against a tree trunk. He absently caressed the bark as he loved to do as a child in the Landes. But those pine trees left their bitter resin and their lingering smell on his hands. He shivered at the recollection. He dispelled those sweet memories and cleared his mind completely, definitively. No

133

more thoughts. Then, his face upturned towards the empty
sky, he took out his gun.

Chapter 10

The disappearance of Adrien Delmas was an added source of worry for Aristide. Nobody had seen him since the meeting when he had informed them of Maurice Fiaux's execution. They feared he had walked into a trap set by the militia or the Gestapo. But their spies were unable to gather any information. Despite their comrades' advice, neither Aristide nor Dédé le Basque agreed to alter the dates of meetings or actions planned. They were both convinced that, even under torture, Adrien Delmas would not talk. Lancelot rebuked them for having such faith.

Since the 'agreement' between Dohse and Grand-Clément which had already taken a severe toll on the Resistance groups in the south-west, most of the leaders lived in fear of betrayal. Some of them saw traitors everywhere. Renaudin, the man who was the representative of the National Liberation Movement whose task it was to coordinate the Resistance forces, was surely a traitor. He was seen too often in the company of Grand-Clément or his men. Apparently he was in charge of a network of three thousand men.

One day, Dédé le Basque who was travelling by tram to a meeting in a park in Bordeaux accompanied by Lancelot, found himself face to face with André Noël and Renaudin as he was alighting. Noël, who had been sentenced to death by the Resistance, went up to him with a big smile:

'Hello Inspector! They say that since you left the police force you've become involved in important activities.'

'Do you want a sample right now?' retorted Dédé le Basque as his hand reached for his pocket.

'Watch it! Don't be stupid. Everything's changed since the

landing. I have some important news for you. Come to the Place de la Victoire tomorrow at 11 o'clock, and we'll discuss a joint action.'

The following day, Dédé le Basque went to the meeting accompanied by Marc, a Resistance fighter from Toulouse, and four armed men. Nobody turned up. At one point, they thought they glimpsed Renaudin on the corner of the Rue Elie-Gintrac. They waited in vain for a while and finally decided to leave. At that moment six SS burst out from behind a half-lowered iron blind in front of a draper's shop. They seized the four Resistance fighters before they had a chance to reach for their guns. Dédé le Basque and Marc managed to run away while the Germans dragged their companions into the shop. Three Germans set off in pursuit of the fugitives. Dédé le Basque was hiding in a doorway; they ran past without seeing him. As soon as they had rounded the corner, he rushed into the shop firing his gun. The Resistance fighters threw themselves upon their guards and disarmed them. Unable to take them prisoner, Dédé le Basque ordered them to clear off. The few passers-by who had not taken refuge in the nearby buildings or run away at the first shot, had watched the scene impassively.

As soon as they reached Aristide's headquarters, Dédé le Basque and Marc made their report. On reading it, Aristide was totally convinced of Renaudin's treason. Yet another arrest reinforced his conviction, if there had ever been any doubt, that of Pierre Roland. He was in charge of sabotaging the electricity network enabling the detonation of explosives which were to destroy the port and part of the town of Bordeaux. So far, he had only been able to carry out minor sabotage operations. He had suggested that Aristide ask Colonel Buckmaster by radio to bomb the sector where the cables had been located. The day after the message had been sent, fifteen or so bombers from the 15th USA Air Force had destroyed the entire circuit.

Two days after the bombing, Pierre Roland had been arrested and taken to Le Bouscat, to 197 Route du Médoc. He had been tortured to death, but he had not talked. In the face of the threat that hung over all of them, Aristide, overwhelmed by grief and anger, assembled a team of four determined men. For three days, they followed Renaudin. On 29th June, everything was ready: they killed him on the corner of the Rue du Héron and the Rue Mouneyra. A police officer, who thought they were a group of muggers, ran after them shouting. He injured two men, Mouchet and Langlade. Mouchet shot the policeman from where he was lying on the ground and killed him, while Jules and Fabas managed to get away before the German soldiers and French police arrived on the scene. The two prisoners were tortured by the Gestapo. Mouchet was executed and Langlade died from the tortures he suffered.

Later, on 11th August, it was André Noël's turn. He was lured into a trap set by Triangle. In his case, the Resistance fighters chosen to execute him were not content just to kill him, they beat him up, no doubt trying to avenge their dead or deported comrades. When they finally decided to kill him, the traitor was unrecognizable. They disposed of the body by throwing it into the Garonne.

As for Grand-Clément, his whereabouts remained a mystery.

In the village of Deymier, Léa was unable to get over the shock of Camille's death. Each night she woke up in tears calling to her friend. Madame Larivierre, the woman who had taken Léa and Charles in, tucked her up again and tried to soothe her with kind words. She would sleep for a short while before finding herself in the grip of the nightmare which had often recurred after the killing of the looter in Orleans, only now there was the added horror of the bloody image of Camille, Charles and La Sifflette being shot.

Madame Larivierre had told her that the Resistance fighters had dispersed and that some of them had met up around Blasimon and Mauriac. The good woman could not, or would not, tell her any more, other than to say that Camille and La Sifflette had been buried in provisional graves in La Réole. She agreed to get a letter to Ruth in which Léa asked her to give the bearer some money and clothes.

The young boy who delivered the message returned

looking sheepish, followed by Ruth who had locked him up until he told her where the letter had come from. Madame Larivierre grew very angry and thundered that the Germans would come and arrest them and they'd have to get out within the hour. Ruth paid the earth for a bicycle for Léa and settled Charles on to her own carrier, saying:

'I would have come to fetch you by train but the railway line has been blown up again.'

Léa warmly thanked her hostess who watched her leave with a sigh of relief.

They reached Montillac late the following evening, partly because Léa was very weak and partly because of the difficulty of cycling on the narrow winding roads over the hills. Ruth managed to get her inside without being seen by the Fayards. Léa was confined to bed with a high temperature for two days. As for Charles, Ruth forbade him to go out and he wandered around the house, a sad sulky figure, asking for his mother.

When Léa was able to speak, she told Ruth in a flat voice, without shedding a single tear, about Camille's death and the combat she had witnessed.

'What's happened to your uncle and the Lefèvre boys?'

'I don't know. Uncle Adrien has not been back since François Tavernier's visit. I thought you'd have heard from them.'

'No. Your aunt Bernadette received a postcard from Lucien, that's all. We know that your uncle Luc is very worried about Pierrot who's in Paris, apparently. After you left, a letter from Laure arrived. I took the liberty of opening it.'

'What does she say?'

'Nothing much: that food supplies in Paris are down to almost nothing, that the metro isn't running because there isn't enough electricity, that the suburbs are bombed almost every day and that the Germans are getting more and more jumpy. Your aunts are well.'

'Is that all?'

'Yes, except that she's waiting for you in Paris.'

'Doesn't she mention Françoise?'

'No, but I had a letter from your sister. Otto's fighting in Russia and she hasn't heard from him for three months.'

'He won't come back.'

'Why do you say that?'

'We're all going to be killed like Camille,' Léa replied, pulling the sheets over her head and turning to the wall.

Grief-stricken, Ruth looked at the girl she loved huddled under the covers. What could she do? She felt old and helpless. Overwhelmed by Camille's death, she did not know what to do for the best for Léa's safety. She could not stay there. Fayard might find out at any time and denounce her. She could not think of a sufficiently safe hiding place. Most houses belonging to sympathizers were under surveillance.

Seeing that Léa was still motionless under the covers, she decided to leave the children's room, where Léa had specifically asked to be taken.

During the evening of 15th July, Léa and Ruth were ensconced in Pierre Delmas's study, all the shutters and windows bolted despite the stifling heat, listening to the BBC. Jean Oberlé was talking about the assassination of Georges Mandel by the militia.

'After the murder of Philippe Henriot, he's the second member of parliament from the Gironde region to be killed in a few days,' said Ruth who was putting the finishing touches to a shirt she was making for Charles from an old dress.

'Aunt Lisa's the one who'll be upset about Henriot's death, she so loved the sound of his voice.'

There was a scratching at the shutters that made them freeze on the spot.

'Did you hear?'

'Yes, switch off the wireless.'

Léa obeyed, on the alert, her heart thumping. The scratching started up again.

'Go and hide, I'll open the window.'

'Who is it?' she whispered.

'Jean Lefèvre,' came a muffled reply, 'we're wounded.'

'Quick, open up.'

139

The reddish sun had barely set behind the Verdelais hill, tinging the countryside for a few moments longer with that pinky gold that made the summer evenings so beautiful. The soft light bathed the two young men spattered with dust and blood, disguising the state they were in. Léa, forgetting her exhaustion, leapt out of the window, for they were too weak to climb in unaided. With Ruth's help, she pushed them inside. Raoul slipped to the floor, unconscious.

'He's lost a lot of blood. We must call a doctor,' said Jean before he too collapsed.

It was too much for the strong Ruth, who burst into tears.

'This is no time to cry. Go and get a doctor.'

Ruth wiped her eyes vigorously.

'Will he come? They're too afraid of the Gestapo.'

'You don't need to tell him they're injured, say . . . I don't know . . . somebody's slashed their leg with a scythe, or an axe!'

'What about when he sees them?'

'He's a doctor. They'll certainly die if we don't do anything.'

'You're right, I'll go and telephone . . .'

'Is the telephone working?'

'Yes.'

'Well, what are you waiting for? I'll go and get some towels.'

In the dimness of the drawing-room, Léa bumped into her aunt Bernadette Bouchardeau.

'What's going on? I heard a noise.'

'Since you're here, you'd better help us. It's Jean and Raoul, they're wounded.'

'Oh my God! Poor souls.'

'Go and get some towels and the first-aid kit. Be careful not to wake Charles.'

In the study, Jean was coming round.

'. . . that's right, doctor, the Montillac estate, at the top of the hill to the left . . . Hurry . . . He's coming. He's the new doctor in Langon.'

'Thank you, Ruth, how's my brother?'

140

The two women did not answer. Ruth slipped a cushion under his head.

Bernadette came into the room carrying some sheets and the first-aid box. She almost fainted at the sight of the two young men covered in blood, and burst into tears as Ruth had done.

'Oh no!' shouted Léa, snatching the sheets from her aunt. 'Go and get me some boiled water.'

When Dr Jouvenel arrived, he found the patients with clean hands and faces. He was very young and looked as though he were still a student. He turned pale as he looked at them.

'Why did you tell me there had been an accident?'

'We weren't sure you'd come if we told you the truth,' said Léa.

'Mademoiselle, I am a doctor, I have to treat everybody, whether they're Resistance fighters or Germans.'

'These are Resistance fighters,' said Léa softly.

With no further ado, he examined Raoul who was still unconscious.

'Give me some scissors.'

He cut off Raoul's trousers which were stiff with blood. The three women were unable to restrain a cry. His whole belly was one gaping wound.

'The poor thing . . . I can't do anything here. He must be taken to hospital. He's lost too much blood.'

'Doctor, that's not possible,' said Jean who had dragged himself over to his brother's side. 'If the Gestapo get him, they'll torture him.'

'I'll prevent them.'

'Then they'll arrest you.'

Dr Jouvenel shrugged.

'Jean . . .'

'I'm here, Raoul, don't worry, we're safe, we're going to take you to hospital.'

'I heard . . . don't bother . . . I'll die before I get there . . .'

'Be quiet, you're talking nonsense, you're going to get better.'

'Léa, is that you?'

'Yes, Raoul.'

'I'm glad . . .'

'Don't talk,' said the doctor, applying a makeshift dressing.

'Doctor, it makes no difference, you know it doesn't. Léa, are you there? Give me your hand . . . I'm all right, doctor, you look after my brother . . .'

'I've finished. I'm going to send for an ambulance.'

'Wait a bit, doctor. See to my brother.'

'Do as he asks,' said Ruth.

Jean had a bullet in the shoulder, another in his thigh and a badly crushed hand.

'You're going to have to go to hospital too, I haven't got any instruments for extracting those bullets.'

'Too bad, just dress the wounds.'

'You might get gangrene.'

Léa called softly:

'Raoul! Raoul!'

'Don't cry, Léa . . . I'm happy . . . I'm dying beside you . . .'

'Be quiet!'

'Jean, are you there?'

'Yes.'

'That's good. Léa, I love you . . . So does Jean . . . It's better like this . . . After the war you can get married . . .'

'After the war, you're the one she'll be marrying, old chap. She's always preferred you, haven't you, Léa?'

'Is that true?'

'Yes,' she murmured, fascinated by his emaciated face, his shining eyes, his pinched nostrils and the grey pallor spreading over the face of this young man who had been her lover for one crazy night.

'Léa . . .'

Oh! the sudden weight of his head! In a flash, she relived Sidonie's death. How handsome he was, despite the stubble of a few days that marred his features. He was smiling. Gently she placed her lips over his mouth that was still warm.

When she looked up, her head was spinning. She leaned on the doctor's arm.

'Go and lie down.'

Lying on her back, she looked at Jean who was crying and hugging his dead brother to him. Her aunt and Ruth were crying too. As for Léa, she was choked with grief but was unable to cry.

The doctor, assisted by Ruth and Léa, dug a grave in the crumbly earth by the wine sheds, behind the privet and lilac hedge. The corpse, wrapped in a sheet, was laid in the hole and covered with earth. The Verdelais church clock struck three in the morning.

Jean did not react when the doctor gave him a tetanus injection. He also gave him a tranquillizer which made him fall rapidly into a comatose sleep.

Léa accompanied Doctor Jouvenel to the spot where he had left his bicycle. There was no point in his hiding; the Fayards were bound to have noticed his arrival.

'You should get away as soon as you can,' he said.

'And go where?'

'Have you got family anywhere else?'

'Yes, in Paris.'

'It's difficult to get there at the moment, trains are few and far between, but if I were in your shoes, I'd try all the same.'

'But I can't leave them on their own!'

'I'll see what I can do. I'll help you if I can. I can drive you as far as Bordeaux.'

'Thank you, doctor, I'll think about it. Is Jean seriously wounded?'

'No, it's not too serious. But he must have those bullets extracted soon. Goodbye, mademoiselle.'

'Goodbye, doctor.'

Jean Lefèvre slept until lunchtime in Pierre Delmas's study. He eagerly drank the bowl of coffee substitute brought by Ruth and ate a huge piece of clafoutis.

'Ah, you're awake,' said Léa, coming into the room. 'Are you in a lot of pain?'

'No, I'm going to be on my way.'

'Where are you going?'

'I don't know. I'm going to try and find the others, if they haven't been captured or killed.'

'What happened?'

'You haven't got a cigarette, have you?'

From the pocket of her flowered rayon dress, Léa took an old tobacco pouch and a packet of Job cigarette papers and held them out to him.

'That's all I've got.'

His fingers were shaking so badly that he was unable to roll the tobacco in the thin paper.

'Give it to me.'

Léa expertly rolled the cigarette, moistened the edge and lit it for him. He smoked in silence for a few seconds.

'It all began last Monday, July 10th. Raoul and I were with Grand-Pierre's group. We had picked up a message on the BBC. I can still hear the announcer's voice: "*Le Tapefort is frightening . . . we repeat, Le Tapefort is frightening . . .*" Maurice Blanchet turned to Maxime Lafourcade and said:

' "You can round up the group, it's tonight all right."

'I asked Maxime what that meant and he replied:

' "There's going to be a parachute drop near the Bry farm in Saint-Léger-de-Vignague." '

'It was good news because after the clash in Saint-Martin-du-Puy, we were short of ammunition. At about ten o'clock that night, there were twenty or so of us around the field. Five men were watching the adjacent road and two more were in a van concealed in the woods. The others were waiting impatiently for the arrival of the plane. At last, after half an hour, we heard the sound of the engines of a Flying Fortress and switched on our torches. When the signal was given, three comrades and I rushed over to the first container which was full of Stens and dressings. In the second, there were grenades, tobacco and sabotage equipment. We were about to open the third when we heard the warning whistle.

' "It's them!" cried a sentry.

' "Hurry up," said Maxime.

'We managed to load the contents of a fourth container on to the van. Maxime gave the order to retreat just when the Germans opened fire on us. We joined Duras's group and it was only the following morning that we learned what had happened to four of our comrades.'

Jean puffed nervously at his cigarette which had gone out. Léa lit another one for him. He continued in a dull voice:

'Maxime had stayed behind with Roger Manieu, Jean Clavé and Elie Juzanz to cover our retreat. They had mounted a machine gun between two containers and, thanks to the ammunition that had been dropped, they swept the field. The Germans retaliated, but did not show themselves. Four militiamen led them to within less than forty yards from our comrades, in spite of the ravages caused by the machine gun. All four were wounded but they tried to escape. It was too late and they had used up all their ammunition. The Germans knocked them out with the barrels of their guns and watched laughing as those bastards from the militia tortured them. They pulled out their fingernails, flayed them, scalped them and to finish with, they had to muster up their remaining strength to dig their own graves . . .'

Léa, dry-eyed, watched Jean who was sobbing.

'Then what happened?'

'They set fire to the Bry farm and left singing for Mauriac. We and the Duras group were stationed fifty yards away, on the Blasimon road. We machine-gunned and threw grenades on to the camp. The Germans and the militia threw themselves down on their stomachs to retaliate. That's when Raoul was wounded in the shoulder and I was hit in the leg. Two of our comrades died close to us: Jean Koliosky and Guy Lozanos. We retreated, gunning a few down as we went. When we reached the cemetery in Mauriac, we were injured a second time. The priest, Gréciet, took us in and gave us first aid. When he saw how serious Raoul's injuries were, he called Doctor Lecarer in La Réole, a member of our network. But because of German road blocks, he wasn't able to take us to his house and he left us in Pian, and from there, we made our way here on foot. You know the rest.'

The two friends sat in silence for a long time, holding hands. Ruth marched into the room, interrupting their mournful reverie.

'I'm worried, there's nobody at the Fayards' place. It's all locked up. You've got to leave, children.'

'Where do you expect us to go?'

'To your aunts in Paris.'

'I can't leave now, I've got to go to Verdelais and tell my mother.'

'I'll do that, Jean.'

'Thank you, Ruth, but I must be the one to tell mummy about Raoul's death.'

'I understand, love. What are you going to do afterwards?'

'Carry on fighting. Forgive me for leaving you, Léa, I've got no choice.'

'Take my bicycle, Jean, it'll be quicker.'

'Thank you. I'll bring it back if I can. Farewell, Léa. You should leave too.'

Without replying, she embraced him. Bernadette Bouchardeau and Ruth kissed him too and advised him to get medical treatment for his wounds.

Chapter 11

Léa had just finished packing a few clothes for Charles and herself, and a little case containing what was left of her mother's jewellery, in a sailor bag which was easy to carry over the shoulder. Ruth brought her some sandwiches wrapped in a white napkin and a Thermos flask filled with water.

'I've given Charles a bag of cherries and the rest of the clafoutis.'

'Please come with us, Ruth.'

'No, darling. Someone has got to stay and look after the house and your aunt.'

'I'm frightened of leaving you two alone here.'

'What can happen to two old ladies like us? There's no need for you to worry, everything will be all right.'

'Still no news of the Fayards?'

'No.'

'What time is Dr Jouvenel coming?'

'At three o'clock. The train should be leaving at four if the tracks have been cleared.'

'Do you think we'll be able to get a seat on the Paris train from Bordeaux?'

'Dr Jouvenel said he would ask his friend who works at Saint-Jean station.'

'Léa, when are we going?' asked Charles as he came tearing into the room.

'Soon, we're waiting for the doctor.'

'Is he taking us to see mummy?'

'I don't know. Maybe. Go outside, I'll be with you in a minute.'

Léa closed her bag and looked around her. 'I'll never see this room again,' she thought.

With heavy heart, she shut the door of the children's room which had been her refuge from so many childhood sorrows and soothed her anger on so many occasions.

There was not a cloud in the sky. The midday sun beat down, as hot as the previous day. Some of the vines had been scorched. Why had Fayard abandoned Montillac just now, when there was so much work to be done?

'Ruth, I'm going to take our luggage down to the workmen's hut by the roadside. Then the doctor won't have to drive into the estate.'

'As you like. Here's a little money for the journey. It's all I have.'

'Thank you, Ruth, but how are you going to manage?'

'We don't need money. There's enough in the kitchen garden for us to be able to eat and the hens are laying at the moment. And your aunt should be getting her pension next month. Hurry up, lunch is nearly ready. Wear a hat, the sun is very strong.'

Léa did not want to upset the elderly woman so she went to fetch her straw hat from the hall. The cool dark hall was a pleasant change from the dazzling heat of the courtyard. She loved this place stretching from north to south, where all the household used to meet each other. It was always a little untidy for everyone would leave an article of clothing, a toy, a book, a newspaper or their sewing lying on the table and chairs. 'When the war's over, I'll have to have it redecorated,' she mused, contemplating the white walls on which hung a series of old engravings representing various monuments in Bordeaux, and yellow and white Louis XVI china plates decorated with mythological figures.

She stared at her reflection in the tall, tarnished mirror. How thin she had become! François wouldn't like that, he liked curvaceous women. But what surprised her most was the expression in her eyes, which was both hard and lack-lustre. She recalled Raoul's dead eyes . . . Camille . . . Sidonie . . . Doctor Blanchard . . . his maid, Marie . . . her father . . . her mother . . . the Debrays . . . Raphaël Mahl . . . all those people she loved were dead. Who else had died? Albert and Mireille? Uncle Adrien? Laurent? Lucien? Her kind cousin, Pierrot . . . ?

'Léa, where are you going in your hat?'

Charles's shrill voice tore her away from her ghosts.

'I'm going to take the luggage out and go for a stroll. Do you want to come with me?'

'Oh yes! Léa,' said the little boy, snuggling up to her.

They had left the bag and the little holdall in the hut and, hand in hand, they walked down towards the vineyards below the terrace.

'Look, my sandal's come undone.'

Léa knelt down and fastened the buckle.

'Don't move!' she whispered suddenly, flinging the child to the ground.

Along the cypress-lined drive, seven or eight men in navy blue uniforms were walking doubled up, holding sub-machine guns in front of them. When they reached the end of the terrace, they stopped. Above them a man leaned out . . . Léa stifled a scream. Behind him, German soldiers ran silently. From where she was hiding, Léa could only make out their grey-green helmets. The Wehrmacht officer signalled to the militiamen who were climbing up to the terrace.

Charles tried to break free from Léa's grip.

'Let me go, you're hurting me.'

'Please, be quiet. The Germans are inside Montillac.'

His little body began to quake.

'I'm frightened. I want my mummy.'

'Be quiet, otherwise they'll capture us both.'

He was quiet, crying silently and unaware that he had wet himself.

Everything was quiet under the relentless sun on the plain. Léa was not sure whether she had dreamed up the German soldiers and militiamen, it was so peaceful. No matter how hard she tried, the only sound she could hear was the song of the cicadas. Perhaps Ruth and Aunt Bernadette had seen

149

them coming and been able to run away in time. An inhuman cry dispelled that hope. Without thinking, Léa leapt up and started running towards the terrace holding Charles by the hand, cursing her floral dress which was visible from miles away. They hid behind a cypress tree. Germans and militiamen were coming and going in the courtyard, kicking in and breaking down the doors of the wine sheds with the barrels of their guns. Bursts of gunfire shattered all the windows and furniture was flung out of the first-floor windows. 'Why are they doing that?' she wondered.

Léa was too far away to hear or see clearly what was going on. The courtyard was partly concealed by the square pillars. A van drove up, scraping the stone of one of the pillars. The looting began. Shouts, laughter and shots reached their ears, sounding unreal in those familiar, sun-drenched surroundings. In the vegetable garden, by the Fayards' cottage, two militiamen were chasing the hens. Suddenly, horror: a flaming figure appeared, screaming, at the top of the tree-covered walk, spun round and crumpled on the gravel path . . .

Léa clutched the motionless child to her . . . Her eyes bulging with terror, she watched the writhing body of one of the two women she had left a few moments earlier . . . Was it Ruth or Bernadette? The flames were so high that it was impossible to distinguish the face . . . anyway, there was no face left . . . it was melting. The screams had stopped issuing from the hole that had been a mouth. All that remained was a burning black skeleton. A German soldier pushed it ahead of him with a piece of steel piping attached to two cylinders strapped to his back. No doubt he felt it was not sufficiently burned, for a long flame accompanied by a sinister hiss spurted out of the end of the steel tube. The twisted hand of the corpse, the fingers outstretched towards the sky as if begging for divine protection, disintegrated under the powerful heat. That made the soldier laugh. He turned round and went back into the courtyard.

Cases of wine were being piled into the van. Léa remained paralysed, unable to take her eyes off the smouldering corpse. The awful smell of burning flesh reached her nostrils. In the middle of this nightmare, the Saint-Maixant church bell tolled two o'clock. A train went under the viaduct. The tracks at Saint-Pierre-d'Aurillac must have been repaired.

'Léa, you're crushing me . . . I want to go. I'm frightened.'

Charles . . . She had almost forgotten him, he was so much a part of her. She tore herself away from the sight and turned to Charles. He began to cry when he saw the look on her face. She clapped her hand over his mouth and shook him.

'Shut up, or they'll catch us.'

There was a note of such urgency in her voice that he stopped sobbing, but the tears continued flowing down his cheeks, wetting his shirt . . . Further up, by the house, wine ran down the chins of the uniformed brutes. A militiaman lurched drunkenly into the courtyard, clutching a bottle. He undid his flies and, hiccuping with laughter, urinated on the smouldering heap, then turned round and raised the bottle to his lips as if to drink to the health of the woman he had just murdered . . . Léa vomited . . . Charles tugged at her dress . . .

'Come on, let's run away from here.'

He was right, they had to flee. She stood up. NO! Flames were leaping out of the window of her parents' bedroom and from Ruth's. She stood glued to the spot, in full view of the house, unable to take her eyes off her burning home. It was Charles who dragged her away, her head twisted round to watch the house that had been her haven as it had been her father's . . . Léa burned with it.

'Don't look. Come on . . .'

The little boy dragged her with all his strength. How did they manage to reach the road without being seen? The child pulled the bag and the holdall out of the workmen's hut and held them up to Léa who absently took them from him. Now, the flames could be seen from a long way off. The siren of the Saint-Macaire fire-engine wailed its way over the sunny countryside. Suddenly, Léa looked away. Something inside her was dying as the house burned. What was the point of staying when there was nothing left? With a determined gesture, she adjusted the bag on her shoulder, threw away the straw hat she wore to work in the fields, firmly grasped Charles's hand and set off without once looking back.

The Fayards did not return until the following evening.

Thanks to the firemen's dedication, their cottage, the barns, the wine store and the sheds had been saved from the fire. All that was left of the castle were the charred walls. When they arrived, the rescuers were still searching among the rubble. They stopped their sinister task when they saw the couple standing rooted to the spot, staring open-mouthed at the damage. A middle-aged man, his arms and face black with soot, went over to them. He looked at them long and hard and then calmly spat in their faces.

'You're mad, Baudouin,' cried Fayard, 'what on eath's got into you?'

'You bastard, as if you didn't know,' retorted Baudouin, pointing to the ruins.

Fayard gazed at him in apparent bewilderment. Baudouin went for him and grabbed him by his jacket collar.

'Don't you play the innocent, you son of a bitch! So you had nothing to do with the Jerries coming here? So you're not the one who hangs about with them, who sells wine from your boss's cellar to them cheap . . . Oh no! Bastard . . . so it's not you, eh!'

'But I never wanted them to burn down the castle!'

'Oh no! I bet you didn't! You've been wanting to get your hands on it for a long time! My word! It's going to cost you a fortune to rebuild.'

Another man went up to Madame Fayard.

'So, Mélanie, you don't want to know what's become of the ladies of the castle? Hey! Don't shake like that! We haven't got a flame-thrower, not like some people. We've only got fists that we're going to shove in your faces.'

'Calm down, Florent. We don't want to get our hands dirty.'

Mélanie Fayard's eyes bulged with fear under the black straw hat.

'I don't understand a word of what you're saying! We've been to visit my sister in Bazas.'

'Pull the other one, you old liar. You left because you denounced Mademoiselle Léa and Madame d'Argilat to the Gestapo . . .'

'That's not true!'

'. . . and you didn't want to see what they came and did here. Ah! It might have shaken you up to watch Monsieur Delmas's sister roasting like a chicken and to see Mademoiselle Ruth spurting blood all over the place. As for Mademoiselle Léa and the child, we haven't found them! Perhaps they're underneath that lot. It'd be best for them if they were, rather than being taken away by the Germans and those who work for them.'

'We didn't know that Mademoiselle Léa and Charles were back.'

'Then you're the only ones who didn't. The whole of Saint-Macaire knew that they'd come back without Madame d'Argilat who was killed in Lorette . . . And you live next door too. If there were any justice in this world, you should be burned to death as well.'

'Don't get upset, friend. The war's nearly over and people like them will pay, believe you me. They'll be tried and judged by a people's tribunal.'

'People like that don't deserve a trial.'

'We swear it was nothing to do with us! It's true I've had my eye on the estate for a long time, and that I've sold wine to the Germans, but no more than anybody else. How would I have been able to maintain the vineyards if I hadn't sold any wine? How would I have paid the labourers and bought equipment? You tell me.'

'Don't take us for fools. Do you think we don't know how much you pocketed?'

'That's gossip, folk are envious.'

'And your son Mathias. You're not going to tell us he wasn't after the boss's daughter? That he's not trafficking with the Germans in Bordeaux?'

'This is nothing to do with my son . . .'

'We'll have his hide too, but meanwhile, here! Take this . . .'

'Stop!'

Two gendarmes got off their bicycles. One of them addressed the estate manager.

'Fayard, you'll have to come and give a statement and identify the body.'

'What body?'

'We think that it's Madame Bouchardeau.'

'Oh! My God!' exclaimed Mélanie Fayard, burying her face in her handkerchief.

'Come to the police station first thing tomorrow morning, both of you.'

The gendarme turned to Baudouin.

'Have you found any other victims?'

'No, we've sifted through everything. I'd be surprised if there was anyone in there.'

'Thank goodness! Although we were told there was a young girl and a child in the house. What's happened to them?'

Baudouin shrugged helplessly.

'Right, that's enough!'

'Have you informed the relatives in Bordeaux?'

'The mayor took charge of doing so. Luc Delmas should be arriving tomorrow.'

'Perhaps he'll have news of his niece. And the priest, has he been told?'

'You must be joking. You know that he's wanted by the French police and the Gestapo! If you know where he is, denounce him, there's a fat reward waiting.'

'Who do you think I am? I don't stoop to that sort of thing. Not a day goes by when we don't receive anonymous letters denouncing Jews, Resistance fighters, people who supposedly hide English airmen or listen to the BBC. Soon, the same people will be denouncing girls who are an easy lay and who go dancing on Sundays with German soldiers in the Saint-Macaire caves.'

'And they'll be right to do so,' said a spotty youth with a pronounced squint.

'You say that out of jealousy, Cross-Eyes.'

'Don't call me Cross-Eyes! They're all whores, girls who dance with Germans! If they only danced with them it wouldn't be so bad, but they screw them, while their fiancés are prisoners, or Resistance fighters, or doing compulsory labour. Wait till the war's over, we'll show those bitches. That'll teach them to have it off with the Germans.'

'I wouldn't like to be in their shoes when you and your friends get your hands on them. Now lads, home you go. There's nothing more to be done round here.'

Bernadette Bouchardeau's body was buried in the Delmas family vault on the morning of 22nd July in the presence of Luc Delmas, his son and numerous people, many of whom had come to demonstrate their disapproval and their anger. A police van was parked under the linden trees in the square. Near Toulouse Lautrec's tomb, two plain-clothes policemen scrutinized every single person who had come to offer the lawyer their condolences. The Fayards stayed far apart from the others, not daring to go too close, for they were well aware of the hostility of most of those present towards them. It was Luc Delmas who went over to them and shook their hands with a cordiality that everybody found exaggerated. The ceremony took place without incident.

In Langon hospital, Ruth still hovered between life and death.

Chapter 12

The 28th July 1944 was the day on which Grand-Clément, his wife and one of his friends were executed.

Since Noël and Renaudin's deaths, Grand-Clément had known that his days were numbered. He placed himself under the protection of Dohse who offered him a villa in Pyla. He stayed there for a while with his wife, Lucette, under the name of Lefrançais. He was discovered in this little seaside resort by Meirilhac, sent by Colonel Passy to investigate the circumstances in which Hypotenuse had died. Meirilhac informed Colonel Triangle of his mission and made contact with Jean Charlin who still considered Grand-Clément to be the leader of the south-west Resistance section. Charlin agreed to broadcast a message to 'his' leader. Charlin and Grand-Clément met in the Rue du Hautoir in Bordeaux at the Volant-Doré restaurant. There Charlin told Grand-Clément that London wished to hear what he had to say to exonerate himself from the accusations of treason that had been received against him and that a certain 'Lysander' would take him over to England. Grand-Clément was cornered, and, not knowing what to do, agreed to meet Meirilhac.

To allay Dohse's suspicions, they arranged a fake kidnapping of Grand-Clément's friend and bodyguard, Marc Duluguet. On 24th July, Meirilhac and three Resistance fighters from the group led by Georges, who was the chief of the 3rd division of Aristide's troops, went to Grand-Clément's house, overturned the furniture and fired shots to make the kidnapping look realistic . . . Grand-Clément demanded that his wife and Duluguet accompany him. Madame Duluguet promised not to tell the German police until after they had left.

They were taken to Léognan and the following morning they were handed over to Georges who interrogated them. At first, Grand-Clément refused to answer, asking to be taken to London as promised. Then, no doubt because he feared immediate reprisals against himself and his companions from the men who were convinced of his treason, he agreed to answer Georges's questions and admitted he had delivered supplies of arms to the Germans, and that he had been indirectly responsible for three thousand arrests and three hundred executions. A statement was drawn up and signed.

On 28th July, the three prisoners, heavily escorted, were taken to Belin, to the home of a member of the Resistance, Frank Cazenave. A large number of Resistance fighters surrounded the house. At around one o'clock, Aristide, Dédé le Basque and Lancelot arrived. When Grand-Clément saw the English agent appear he realized that he was done for. Aristide called together the members of the tribunal whose task it was to judge him. Grand-Clément replied to a fresh interrogation, adding that it was to protect the life of his wife and his family that he had accepted Dohse's offer. The prisoners were taken out while the jury deliberated.

They voted unanimously to put Grand-Clément to death. After much discussion, his wife and friend were also sentenced to death.

In the late afternoon, the former Resistance member stepped into a front-wheel drive vehicle with Aristide and two guards. The other two prisoners were put into a second car. They were stopped by militiamen at a road block. Lancelot got out of the car and gave a 'Heil Hitler' salute. Thinking that they were something to do with the Gestapo, the militiamen let the cars through. Grand-Clément had not budged. The cars drew up in a wood near Muret. There, Aristide informed the prisoners of their sentence.

It all happened very quickly: Dédé le Basque dragged Grand-Clément into a sheepfold and shot him. Lancelot executed Marc Duluguet and Aristide took charge of a task that nobody wanted to carry out.

Georges's men buried the bodies in the woods.

Aristide sent a report to Colonel Buckmaster informing him that justice had been done.

Chapter 13

Léa was lying on a beach towel on the hard cobblestones along the banks of the Seine. Her eyes were closed and despite her discomfort, the sound of the water evoked the waves breaking on the sand in Biscarrosse, and she could hear the cries of the seagulls and the children. The sun's warmth gently numbed her, and her body came to life again as she could feel the pleasant burning. She stretched contentedly. There was a feeling almost of unreality, as in a far-off mist, verging on guilt, at basking in such pleasure after the horrors of the last few days. Something inside her told her that she should, above all, try not to think about it, to pretend it had never happened, that it was a nightmare from which she would awaken without any recollection.

She half opened her eyes. A seagull flew across her field of vision, winging rapidly through the cloudless blue sky. A child laughed and clapped its hands. The fishermen, motionless under their caps and straw hats, stared at their bobbing red, yellow and white floats. She could hear the gentle lapping of the water. A Sunday painter was mixing his colours. A boat went past with young girls in pastel-coloured dresses on board. Not far away, an accordionist was playing a popular tune. Everything was peaceful and harmonious. Léa turned over on to her stomach and began to read the book Laure had recommended so enthusiastically.

What an unbearable creature that Scarlett O'Hara was! But as for Rhett Butler! What a man!

'Do you like it?' asked Françoise.

'Mmm, mmm . . .'

'Don't disturb her, can't you see she's dancing with the

handsome Rhett,' said Laure with the utmost seriousness. 'Pass me *Silhouettes*.'

'Wait a minute, I'm just looking at the children's clothes. I'd love to have a little girl so I could dress her in pretty things!'

'You've become very frivolous since you've come to Paris and you have your clothes made by the top couturiers. You're so different from the Françoise of Montillac! You're not anything like the little nurse from Langon who was so proper.'

'It's unkind of you to reproach me for being frivolous. What do you expect me to do? Lock myself up in my apartment and draw the curtains and wait for the war to end? Go to Germany like some of the other women in my position? Where would I go? To Otto's father's house? He'd kick me out! Anyway, is he still alive? And what about Otto, where's he? Perhaps he's dead, or seriously wounded at this very moment.'

'I'm sorry, I didn't mean to hurt you. Look how Charles is playing with little Pierre. Anyone would think they were brothers.'

'Yes, they are sweet. Here, you can have *Silhouettes*.'

Françoise stood up and smoothing her blue woollen swimsuit, she went over to the pushchair where her little boy was sitting.

'Have you read Lucien François's article?' asked Laure. '*Speaking out against briefs: back to real lingerie*, it's hysterically funny, listen to this:

'*The censors will no doubt frown at our concern, at a time like this, over such a trivial subject, which even verges on debauchery: feminine underwear. We are inclined to agree with them. But it is not entirely a laughing matter if we consider that the fashion for bras and briefs which has come to us from abroad has caused the redundancy of thousands of workers in the lace and lingerie industries, both of which are well and truly French . . .*

'Well and truly French! I bet he thinks that if French soldiers have lost the war, it's because their wives are wearing English or American briefs! Listen to the end:

'*There are no strong nations that do not have feminine wives giving support to truly virile men. It is when the sexes begin to resemble each other that, naturally, a race begins to deteriorate. Androgynous women in briefs were the comrades of young men sporting frilly shirts. In a couple with a true woman in cream silk camiknickers, there is no danger that she will ever wear the trousers!*

'Don't you find it incredible that they can be talking about knickers when there's no electricity, no gas, no metro from today, Saturday at one o'clock p.m. until the same time on Monday, when Estelle has to queue up from seven o'clock in the morning outside the grocer's in the hope of being able to buy dried peas, when we've been eating salted mackerel for three days and the air-raids are killing thousands of people? It's unbelievable! What times! What do you think, Léa?'

Léa, who had put down her book to listen to her sister, shrugged.

'It's no more incredible than lazing around in swimsuits on the banks of the Seine or going to the Moulin Rouge this evening to listen to Edith Piaf while people are fighting in Normandy, Brittany, Russia and the Pacific. What's incredible is that all three of us are still alive . . . I'm hungry. Françoise, will you pass me a sandwich?'

'There'll be a riot if anyone sees us eating sandwiches with real bread and real sausage. Don't you agree, Laure?'

'They should learn to get by, like me. Don't think it's easy to get hold of bread and sausage in Paris on 5th August 1944.'

'I can believe that,' said Léa, greedily biting into the sandwich Françoise gave her. 'With your business sense, you're the one who should have looked after Monti . . .'

Her face went pale as she stumbled over the word she had sworn never to utter again. Laure realized her distress and threw her arms round her sister's shoulders.

'You'll see, we'll rebuild Montillac . . .'

'Never! Never! You weren't there, you didn't see it! You didn't see Aunt Bernadette being burned to death . . . She never did anyone any harm . . . And what about Ruth?'

'Be quiet, you're upsetting yourself. There's no point dwelling on all that horror. Forget it.'

'Forget it! It's easy for you to say that! What do you know about the war? Only your little black market deals . . .'

'Stop arguing, everyone's staring at you . . . Let's go,' said Françoise, gathering her belongings.

'You two go home if you like, I'm staying here for a while. Take Charles with you.'

'Léa, I want to stay with you.'

'No darling, be a good boy and go home with the others. I want to be alone for a while.'

The little boy gazed at her with a strange intensity. He took the young girl's hand and squeezed it hard.

'Will you come back soon?'

'Very soon, I promise.'

'Be back by half-past two. The show starts at half-past three. It'll take us at least half an hour to cycle to the Moulin Rouge. It's uphill all the way.'

'Don't worry, I'll be there on time.'

Without taking any further notice of her sisters or the children, Léa stretched out again and closed her eyes. But the images which sprang to her mind were so horrific that she opened them again very quickly.

A bather stood up and dived into the Seine, leaving his newspaper on the bank and slightly splashing Léa. She picked up the paper. It was Marcel Déat's right-wing *L'Oeuvre*. She absently read the article entitled 'Variety of fauna to be found in the Resistance' in which he vented his spleen on the communists, the Gaullists, the socialists and other 'vermin'. She learned that a hundred and ninety American bars had been closed down at the request of the French militia, who were outraged at the immoral nature of these places of entertainment. She learned that an exhibition was opening in the Grand Palais on 'The Soul of the Camps' and that Doctor Goebbels had declared: *'The German people should rise up en masse to force the hand of destiny.'* She discovered that German marines, aboard special machines, had destroyed thirteen Anglo-American ships, that a French Assault

Brigade of the Waffen SS was involved on the Eastern Front and that today the horse races were being held at Vincennes and on Sunday at Auteuil. On the Paris stock exchange, the market had been improving. The Führer and Doctor Goebbels had sent a telegram to the writer Knut Hamsun to congratulate him on his eighty-fifth birthday. The next recruiting board for French volunteers for the Waffen SS would take place on Monday 7th August at 9 a.m. and the recruiting board for the Legion of French volunteers against Bolshevism would take place at the La Reine barracks in Versailles. A children's château was to be named after Philippe Henriot. The following day, at three o'clock p.m., a swimming championship was to be held between the Austerlitz Bridge and the Alexandre III Bridge. Elvire Popesco was playing at the Apollo in *My Cousin from Warsaw*, Jane Sourza and Raymond Souplex were playing in *On the Seat* at the Casino de Paris, and at Luna Park you could go and applaud Georgius, Georgette Plana and many others, and Edith Piaf . . .

Léa flung down the newspaper, slipped a printed floral rayon dress, a present from Françoise, over her red and white two-piece swimsuit and fastened her white linen sandals with wooden platform soles. She ran up the steps that led from the embankment to the street.

On 11th August, there was a wireless announcement about the death of Saint-Exupéry, who had been shot in the south of France during a night flight. The announcer deplored the fact that the writer had gone over to the camp of France's enemies.

That same day, Léa found a letter which had been slipped under the door, from Laurent to Camille, care of the Montpleynet sisters. Overwhelmed, she opened it with trembling hands:

'My darling wife,
    Here I am at last, back on French soil. I can't find the words to tell you of the joy and the emotion my comrades and I felt as we landed. I saw even the toughest men fall

163

to their knees and kiss the earth with tears running down their cheeks. Others slipped into their pockets a little sand from that Normandy beach which the allied forces had the privilege of trampling before us. How long it seems to have taken for this day to come! We thought it would never happen.

'I spent my first night on the seat of a jeep. I only slept for four hours but I woke up feeling fresh as a daisy. I said to myself that I was on the same soil, under the same sky, and that soon I would be hugging you and Charles. I've never been so happy! It was a grey morning when we landed in Sainte-Mère-Eglise with General Leclerc who jabbed at the sand with his walking-stick in disbelief. I heard him murmur: "It's a funny feeling . . . " and then he said aloud: "It's a damned wonderful feeling . . . " We were jostled by photographers from the army cinematographic unit who wanted to photograph General Walker of America shaking hands with our General Leclerc, who agreed with bad grace, refusing to go back to the jetty.

'I accompanied him to the IIIrd American Army HQ to which the 2nd Armoured Division is attached. It was there that we met General Patton. What a contrast between the two men! The one, with his large, cowboy features, a whisky lover who wears Colts on his hips like in the films, and the other, the aristocrat, with two stars on his cap – the third has been waiting to be sewn on for a year – his raincoat tightly belted over his English gaiters. It was a job getting him to remove the haversack he always wears bouncing around on his back. Patton was in excellent spirits. The German Front had finally been crushed in Avranches. We passed through Avranches on our way to Le Mans. It was like the end of the world. Civilians were wandering through the devastated streets searching among the rubble. In the fields were crowds of mournful prisoners, and the bodies of American, Canadian, English and German soldiers were all piled up together. In the villages we went through, young girls held out flowers, bread and bottles of wine or cider to us. We were torn between the joy of the liberated and the despair of those who had lost everything.

'On the 10th, without stopping to rest, we attacked amid chaos. The fighting was fierce. We lost twenty-three men, and nearly thirty were wounded. Fourteen tanks were either destroyed or lost. The following day, in Champfleur, the General was in command of the approach manoeuvre. All day, either from his jeep or his scout car, he urged his men into battle, heedless of the bullets and shells exploding all around them. At the end of this second day of fighting, he was happy. We had liberated about thirty villages and advanced twenty-five miles or so. We were so exhausted, we slept on the ground. Not for long: at about two o'clock in the morning, German shells fell into the field where Leclerc was sleeping, destroying a half-track and killing his two servants. That put an end to our night's sleep for all of us. Between 10th and 12th August, the 2nd Armoured Division killed eight hundred Germans, took more than a thousand prisoners and destroyed fifteen Panzers. In the Forest of Ecouves, the enemy soldiers were surrendering in their thousands.

'On Friday 13th, we attacked the village of Cercueil. It was as I was going down towards Ecouché that I witnessed the worst carnage of all. We were trying to get on to the main road, the N24b. I was behind a tank driven by a friend of mine, Georges Buis, who was in command of the vanguard. Beyond the fields bordered by hedgerows, the road was visible, blocked by enemy vehicles stretching as far as the eye could see. They seemed to be floating above the greenery. For a few seconds, everything hung in suspense. Then, it was the apocalypse. The barrels of all our tanks belched out fire and the air was thick with smoke and screams. A detachment managed to make its way through the mounds of twisted corpses, mutilated bodies and flaming tanks and cross over the main road and seize our objective: the bridge over the Orne.'

Laurent signed off with the usual endearments full of tenderness for his wife and son. Léa carefully folded the letter up again. On the wireless, they announced that Drieu La Rochelle had tried to commit suicide. The telephone rang.

'Hello . . . Ruth . . . Is that really you?'

'Yes, my love, it's me.'

Léa, who had not cried once since Camille's death, felt warm, salty tears streaming down her cheeks at the sound of the feeble but clearly recognizable voice of the woman she had believed dead. All she managed to stammer was:

'Oh, Ruth! Ruth . . .'

Françoise and Laure were both impatient to speak to their former governess too. They also wept for joy. Soon, all the inhabitants of the apartment in the Rue de l'Université were sobbing their hearts out. Laure was the first to dry her eyes, exclaiming:

'That's the first piece of good news we've had for a long time. Let's celebrate.'

She went to fetch a bottle of champagne from what she called her 'cellar'.

'It'll be a bit warm, but never mind. Estelle, bring some glasses and come and have a drink with us.'

Even Charles was allowed to have a 'little drop' as Aunt Lisa would say.

'It didn't even occur to us to ask her what had become of Montillac,' said Laure, draining her glass.

'That's true,' thought Léa, 'I was so delighted to hear she was alive, I forgot all about Montillac. It's better that way. Montillac is dead as far as I'm concerned. What does it matter what's left of it . . . too much blood has already been spilled on that soil . . . Fayard's welcome to it, I'm no longer interested in it.'

'Do you realize, Madame Françoise, forty francs for a kilo of potatoes! Three hours queuing up in Saint-Germain market to bring back two kilos. Butter? There isn't any to be had for love nor money. At a thousand francs a kilo, you have to be a millionaire to be able to afford it,' exclaimed Estelle.

'Don't worry,' reassured Laure, 'I'll get some butter tomorrow. I've got some bars of soap and some tobacco which I can exchange for groceries.'

166

The elderly servant gazed at the girl admiringly.

'I don't know how you do it, Mademoiselle Laure. If it weren't for you, we'd have all starved to death ages ago. Lucky you didn't listen to Mademoiselle Albertine.'

'Hold you tongue, Estelle. I should have been stricter with Laure and refused to accept the goods she gets on the . . . the . . .'

'Say it, aunt: on the black market. Yes, I do, I get things on the black market. I don't want to die of hunger while we're waiting for the allied troops to land. I don't steal anything, I exchange things and make a small profit. I trade. All my friends are doing the same.'

'That doesn't make it any better, child. So many wretched folk are suffering and have lost everything. I'm ashamed of being so well-off.'

Lisa, who had kept quiet until then, suddenly became purple in the face and turned on her sister:

'Well-off! I hope you say that in jest? Well-off indeed! No coffee, no tea, no chocolate, no meat, not even any decent bread! Last winter we didn't even have a fire. And all because mademoiselle refuses to have enough to eat or keep warm because the unemployed, the prisoners and the very poor have nothing at all! But our depriving ourselves won't make them any less cold or hungry!'

'I'm only too well aware of that, but we must show solidarity somehow.'

'There's no such thing as solidarity any more,' snapped Lisa.

'How can you say that?' murmured Albertine while a tear trickled down her wrinkled cheek, leaving a trail on her pale face-powder.

That tear subdued Lisa's anger. She rushed over to her sister and apologized. They withdrew into Albertine's room, arm in arm.

'It's always the same,' said Laure, 'if one of them begins to cry, the other comforts her . . . What are you doing this afternoon?'

'Are you talking to me?' queried Léa.

'Yes.'

167

'I promised I'd take Charles to the Luxemburg Gardens for a ride on the roundabout.'

'What about you, Françoise?'

'I'm going home. A friend of Otto's is supposed to be telephoning me this evening to give me news of him.'

'You've got plenty of time.'

'Not really. Now that the metro has shut down altogether, I've got to walk. It'll take me at least two hours. What are you planning to do?'

'I don't know. Now they've closed down all the American bars, my friends and I are at a bit of a loose end. I'm going to see if the gang are at Trocadéro.'

'Shall we leave together?'

'No, you're on foot and I'd rather cycle.'

'As you like. I'll call you this evening if there's any news of Otto.'

With his little hand in Léa's, Charles walked quietly by her side. From time to time, he squeezed her hand a little harder until she responded by squeezing his, to say: I'm here, don't be afraid. That reassured him. He was so terrified at the idea that she might disappear like his mother.

When they had walked away from the blazing house, hand in hand, he had sensed that there were certain things he should not speak to her about, and that mummy was one of the subjects he must not mention to Léa. Léa, who loved his mummy as much as he did. Poor mummy! Why had she screamed so loudly when he ran towards her the day the Germans were shooting everywhere? He remembered hurting, and feeling his mummy hugging him, and then letting go of him, and then nothing.

When he asked, they told him mummy would come back soon. But he knew that wasn't true, that she had gone a long way away, a long, long way away . . . Maybe she was even in heaven . . . So? Mummy?

The little boy stopped in his tracks, his mouth suddenly dry, his body soaked in perspiration. Why had he stopped just at that spot, in front of the apartment block on the Boulevard Raspail where Camille had lived? Léa pictured the young woman opening the door to her with that gentle smile on her face that made her so appealing. Her hand locked with Charles's until they were one . . . He looked up, she looked down . . . Slowly, without letting go of his hand, she knelt down to his height and hugged him close for a long time.

A German soldier, with his orderly at his heels, stopped to look at them with a tender smile.

'I've got a little boy the same age. He's not as lucky as yours, his mother was killed in an air-raid along with my eldest daughter,' he said in correct but laboured French as he stroked Charles's hair.

The child recoiled as if he had been shot.

'Filthy Jerry! Don't you touch me!'

The German blanched and withdrew his hand. The orderly sprang forward.

'Are you insulting the captain?'

'Forget it, Karl. It's natural for the French to dislike us. Forgive me, madame, I allowed myself to become too sentimental. For a moment, I forgot about the war and the damage it has done to both our countries. That'll all be over soon. Farewell, madame.'

The man clicked his heels and strode off towards the Hotel Lutétia above which the swastika flag still fluttered.

Chapter 14

It was the afternoon of 15th August. A large crowd was hurrying under the trees of the Luxemburg Gardens and around the pond. The hired sailing boats were swaying in the summer breeze. Idle strollers walked past the senate house without a second glance, ignoring the sentries behind their sandbags and barriers of barbed wire. Children with their mothers were queuing up for the puppet show. The roundabout was taken by storm and so were the donkey carts and ponies. Anyone would have thought it was a Saturday or Sunday in June, in the middle of the school term, there were so many children everywhere. Most of them were deprived of their summer holidays, partly due to the rail strike, but mainly because the fighting was drawing closer to the capital. The ten to twelve-year-olds' favourite game was war, but they all wanted to play French soldiers and none of them wanted to be the Germans. The young gang leaders had to draw lots. The 'Germans' fought somewhat reluctantly against the 'French'.

Charles had three rides on the roundabout but did not manage to catch a hoop on his stick. He wanted an ice-cream. At the Boulevard Saint-Michel entrance to the park, a brightly painted ice-cream van in the shape of a carriage was selling so-called strawberry ices. On the bandstand, a green-uniformed band was playing Strauss waltzes. There were yellow and black notices pinned on some of the trees, signed by the new military governor of Paris, General von Choltitz, calling on the population to remain calm, and announcing that the strictest and harshest measures of repression would be taken in the case of disobedience, sabotage or attacks.

But most people reading these notices just smiled. On the midday news, they had announced the allied landing in Provence. Some people even claimed that the Americans were at the gates of Paris because they had heard the cannon. Others were on their way back from Notre-Dame where they had attended the commemorative ceremony of Louis XIII's vow, although this had been banned by General von Choltitz.

At the request of the bishops, the Parisians turned out in full force to defy the ban. The crowds were so dense that the cathedral would not hold them all, and they thronged into the square where, outside the main door, a platform had been erected, and the same ceremony took place as inside. The procession came out of one side door and went in again through another. The crowd responded fervently to the litanies intoned by a missionary from the platform:

'Saint Joan of Arc, liberator of our country . . . pray for us . . . Saint Geneviève, patron saint of Paris . . . pray for us . . . Saint Mary, Mother of God, guardian of France . . . pray for us . . .'

The missionary interrupted his adjurations for a moment to listen to an urgent message from the priest. Those who were standing near the dais saw his face light up. Many fell to their knees when, in a resonant voice, he cried: 'We have been informed that the allied troops have landed in Provence. Pray, my dear brethren, that Marseilles and Toulon be spared destruction. Our Father, who art in heaven, hallowed be thy name, thy kingdom come . . .' Emotion reached fever pitch when Cardinal Suhard made an improvised speech in which he talked of 'the last ordeal we have to face'. A handful of German soldiers standing outside the General Hospital and the police headquarters watched the whole scene without turning a hair. There was one odd detail: there was not a single police officer to be seen in the area. The Paris police force had come out on strike that morning in response to the disarming of their colleagues in the suburban police stations of Asnières and Saint-Denis.

The day after Assumption Day, the right-wing magazine *Je Suis Partout*, which had been suspended, reappeared, announcing that the following issue would be out on Friday 25th August. Truckloads of militiamen began to pour out of the capital, heading eastwards. In the Avenue de l'Opéra, the Champs-Elysées and the Boulevard Saint-Michel, German soldiers paraded with a band at their head, singing at the tops of their voices while passers-by watched scornfully. 'It's the beginning of the end,' they sneered.

On the 17th, the inhabitants had difficulty containing their delight as buses, trucks, ambulances and cars crammed full of mournful, haggard-looking Germans left the city. Behind drove a motley collection of vehicles: carts, horses and traps, delivery tricycles and even wheelbarrows piled high with loot: wireless sets, typewriters, paintings, armchairs, beds, trunks, suitcases and, perched on the top, the inevitable mattresses, reminding the Parisians of their own exodus on the roads of France.

Ah! What a pleasure it was to see the invincible army in tatters! Where were those splendid suntanned conquerors of June 1940? What had become of their impeccable uniforms? Worn out after four years of war in the Russian Steppes? The deserts of Africa? In the armchairs of the Hotel Meurice, the Crillon or the Intercontinental? People sat on the chairs in the Champs-Elysées gardens and never tired of watching them drive past. They counted the cars and trucks for amusement. They continued to smile when very youthful or very ancient soldiers marched past, bundled up in tunics that were either too loose or too tight, unshaven and unkempt, trailing their guns or carrying heavy packages of food or materials that many had no hesitation in selling to the Parisians.

Laure and Léa were cycling along the embankment. There was a sort of euphoria in the air, despite the tension in some districts, the noise of the engines, the shouts, the smoke from the files belonging to the Gestapo and the authorities that were made into huge bonfires on the pavements, the aggravation of the fleeing soldiers and the curfew at nine o'clock in the evening. A limousine overtook the sisters. Inside, young women with hair that was a shade too blonde and clothes that were a shade too elegant were snuggling up to a general wearing a monocle.

The fishermen and bathers were out in full force along the banks of the Seine. In the bright summer sunshine, sailing boats swayed on the water. The whole city was on tenterhooks. The sisters had to dismount from their cycles to cross the Pont Royal bridge which was cordoned off with barbed wire.

Back at their aunts' apartment, Charles was impatiently waiting to give Léa the drawing he had been working on all morning. Estelle was complaining about her poor old legs covered in varicose veins 'because of the queues'. Lisa was very agitated: on the twelve o'clock news, the BBC had said that the Americans had reached Rambouillet in the suburbs of Paris. Albertine seemed preoccupied.

Thanks to Laure's reserves, supper, consisting of sardines in oil and real gingerbread, seemed like a feast. At half-past ten that evening, the electricity was turned on again until midnight, bringing a disappointment for Lisa: the radio announced that the Americans were not in Rambouillet, but in Chartres and Dreux, a lot further away.

Just before curfew, some SS officers had fired a volley of machine-gun shots at the onlookers who were watching the Germans moving their files out of the Trianon Hotel in the Rue de Vaugirard. In the Place de la Sorbonne and the Boulevard Saint-Michel, several people had been killed or wounded.

The Parisians' sleep was disturbed by the occupying forces blowing up the ammunition depots.

'There are no newspapers this morning,' the vendor told Léa when she went to the kiosk outside the Deux Magots café on the Boulevard Saint-Germain. 'Things look bad for the collaborators. Look at the expression on the face of that chap in glasses. That's Robert Brasillach, he's on his way to the café Flore for a coffee. He's never looked exactly healthy, but for the last two days, he's been looking really ill. If I were in his shoes, I'd get out with my Jerry pals while I could.'

So this was the famous Brasillach whom Raphaël had so admired?

He looked like a sickly brat.

Léa took a table on the terrace not far from him and ordered a coffee. The elderly waiter in a long white apron replied that he could not bring her anything hot as the gas had been cut off. She made do with a revolting mint cordial.

At the next table, a young man of about thirty, tall, dark and wearing thick-lensed spectacles, was writing in an exercise book in a neat, round handwriting. Another young man, thin and blond, went over to join him.

'Hello, Claude, already at work?'

'You could say that. What's new?'

'There were quite a few incidents in the area yesterday. The Germans opened fire in the Rue de Buci and in the Boulevard Saint-Germain.'

'Any deaths?'

'Yes, quite a few. How's your father?'

'Fine. He's in Vémars. I'm going to see him tomorrow.'

A series of deafening explosions prevented Léa from hearing the rest of their conversation.

'There go the ammunition depots,' observed one of them when the noise had stopped.

'They've blown up arms stores near the Eiffel Tower and in several cafés. It'll be over soon. The collaborators are fleeing like rats leaving a sinking ship. We shan't be hearing Jean Hérold-Paquis's voice any more, Radio Journal is dead. The Luchaires, Rebatets, Bucards, Cousteaus and the Bonnards, the Gestapo's pals, are all on their way to Germany. He's the only one left, and I'd like to know why,' said the blond young man pointing to Brasillach.

'Maybe it's his way of being honourable. I can't bring myself to hate him. I feel sorry for him.'

'Why did you used to hate him?'

'Oh, it's an old score to do with a disgusting article he published in 1937 about my father.'

'I remember, he called it: "The critical age of Monsieur Mauriac".'*

---

* A reference to the writer François Mauriac

'Yes, Brasillach's base insults hurt me a lot. I wanted to go and beat him up.'

Léa put some money on the table and rose to leave. The two young men gazed after her.

'Pretty girl.'

'Yes, very pretty.'

If it had not been for the ammunition depots being blown up in the distance, that rather muggy morning of 18th August 1944 would have been like any other summer's day. Everything was quiet. The few passers-by ambled slowly along like tourists. Young girls cycled past wearing light summer frocks and smiling. In front of the church of Saint-Germain-des-Prés, a group of young people were involved in a heated discussion. In the window of the Divan bookshop, a few faded copies of Martineau's review were beginning to turn yellow. In the little church square, an old woman was unfolding a newspaper parcel containing cat food. She placed it at the foot of a tree and called:

'Pussy . . . pussy . . . come on, my pets.'

In the Place Furstenburg, some tramps were arguing over the last drop of plonk. In the Rue de Seine, two concierges were standing on their doorsteps mulling over the events of the previous day. On the corner of the Rue de Buci, the fruit and vegetable stalls were hopelessly bare, but that did not deter the queues of determined housewives. The Rue Dauphine was deserted. In the Rue Saint-André-des-Arts, children were chasing each other with sticks, pretending they were guns, and hiding in the recesses of the Cour de Rohan.

'Bang, bang! Surrender or I'll shoot you.'

Léa wandered aimlessly through the streets.

She ended up in the Place Saint-Michel. People were crowding round a plane tree. She elbowed her way through the crowd. A little white notice headed by two crossed tricolours was pinned to the tree. It read:

Provisional government of the French Republic.

   The Allies are at the gates of Paris. Prepare yourselves for the

175

*final battle against the invaders. Fighting has already begun in
Paris.*

*Wait until you receive orders before going into action. Instruc-
tions will either be posted up in public places or broadcast on the
wireless. The combat will take place in one district at a time.*

There was not one Parisian who was unaware that over the
coming days, hours even, their city would either be liberated
or destroyed. Some began making active preparations. Most
people were determined not to budge from their homes and
to wait for the departure of the Germans before celebrating.

As for Léa, her feelings were a mixture of hatred, fear,
revenge and oblivion. She swung from one state to another
with such rapidity that she suffered from nervous exhaustion.
Her nights were troubled and sometimes she could not sleep
at all. This was beginning to show on her face and there were
dark shadows under her eyes. She wore her long curly hair
up and this emphasized the delicacy of her features.

She had to get a grip on herself and contact the Resistance
group mentioned by the young doctor in Langon who had
drive them to Bordeaux and seen them on to one of the last
trains to leave for Paris. It had been a turbulent journey
lasting two days, due to the railway tracks being broken and
the frequent air-raids during which the passengers had to
leave the train and fling themselves flat on their faces in the
fields. Léa had absently followed everyone else, oblivious of
the danger and Charles's grumbling. He had clung to her
hand constantly. The warm welcome of her aunts and sisters
had not reawakened her interest. She felt numb and indifferent to her surroundings. Only the sound of Ruth's voice
had brought her out of her apathy. The tears she had shed
helped her regain her desire to live, but did not restore that
self-confidence which had been her former strength.

She wandered through Paris until early evening. The whole
city was in a state of suspense. It was hunger that finally
made her set off homewards just before curfew. All Estelle
had to offer her was a little cold mashed potato and a piece
of dry Camembert. Albertine de Montpleynet, relieved to see
her, did not scold her for staying out so late. Charles, who

had not wanted to go to bed before she returned, fell asleep holding her hand.

Nightmares kept Léa awake for most of the night. She did not manage to drift off to sleep until dawn.

Chapter 15

'Wake up, wake up . . .'

Laure shook Léa until she sat up in bed. Léa stared blankly at her sister.

'Wake up, The Free French have taken over the police headquarters and there's fighting going on all over Paris. The Americans are coming. Get dressed.'

Laure, breathless, was waving her arms around excitedly.

'What are you talking about?'

'The Gaullists are occupying the police headquarters. The police are fighting alongside them.'

'Who told you that?'

'A friend of mine called Franck. You don't know him. He lives in a huge apartment on the Boulevard Saint-Michel. It overlooks the boulevard, the river and the Rue de la Huchette. He telephoned me. He and some other friends danced and drank all night. They all slept at his place because of the curfew. When he went to close the shutters at about seven o'clock, he noticed men, alone or in pairs, crossing Saint-Michel bridge and making their way towards Notre-Dame. There were so many of them, he was intrigued. He went out into the street. He followed them and ended up in front of the cathedral where a thousand or more people were chatting in low voices. From what they were saying, he gathered they were plain-clothes police officers. A van arrived. A few guns and five or six sub-machine guns were handed out to the men. An order was given and they marched on the main entrance to the police headquarters. Franck followed the crowd. The door opened and they silently invaded the big quadrangle. A large chap in a houndstooth suit wearing a

178

tricolour armband climbed on to the roof of a car shouting: "In the name of the Republic, in the name of General de Gaulle, I take possession of the police headquarters!" The civil servants allowed themselves to be disarmed without offering the slightest resistance. They raised the flag and sang the *Marseillaise*. Franck, who's not the sentimental type, told me he was moved to tears. Apparently, they've appointed a new Prefect, Charles Lizet, I think. Come on, let's go and see, it'll be fun.'

'Fun, not really. Interesting, perhaps,' replied Léa, getting out of bed.

'Gosh, do you sleep completely naked?'

'I forgot to pack a nightdress when I left. Leave me, I want to have a wash.'

'Hurry up, I'll wait for you in the kitchen.'

'All right. Whatever you do, don't say anything to our aunts.'

'Of course I won't. I'm not daft.'

The helmeted German soldiers who drove past in an open van on the Boulevard Saint-Germain, clasping their guns, shouted and wolf-whistled at the two pretty girls on their bicycles.

'They don't seem too worried,' said Léa looking round.

Now, the empty road stretched out in front of them. On the corner of the Rue du Dragon, a German aimed his sub-machine gun at them.

'Abhauen ider ich schiesse!'*

There were half-empty cups and glasses on the tables of the Deux Magots and the Flore waiting for customers who had taken refuge inside to return. In the Rue de Rennes, a handful of people were scattering in all directions. There was a short burst of gunfire and two of them crumpled to the ground. At Mabillon, young people in white coats with Red Cross armbands were rushing in the direction of the shooting. At Odéon, a tank was blocking the road. They turned into the Rue de Buci. Most of the shops had lowered their metal

* Go away or I'll shoot

179

blinds. Café proprietors were hastily pulling in the chairs and men wearing tricolour armbands were rushing past. One of them shouted:

'Go home, things are going to hot up round here.'

Everything was strangely quiet in the Rue Saint-André-des-Arts. A concierge was sweeping her doorstep as she did every morning. The man from the bookshop was having a drink with the printer from the Rue Séguier at the bar in the café-cum-tobacconist's, and the sweetshop owner was busy dusting the jars full of imitation sweets out of habit. In the Boulevard-Saint-Michel, some people were strolling about looking very cheerful as the French flag fluttered over the police headquarters and Notre-Dame.

Laure and Léa were greeted with joyful cries when they entered Franck's apartment.

'I've brought my sister Léa who I've told you so much about.'

'Well done. Hello Léa. Is it true that you're a Resistance heroine?'

'Don't believe everything Laure tells you. She always exaggerates.'

'I didn't exaggerate . . .'

'Shut up. I don't want to talk about all that.'

'As you like. Resistance heroine or not, you're welcome. Come and look.'

The young man led her over to one of the high windows of the vast lounge.

'Look, we've got ringside seats. My mother will be sorry she left for the country. She wouldn't have wanted to miss such a performance for the world. I'm sure she'd have invited all her beautiful friends. For the time being, it's all a bit quiet. What do you think? It's a good view, isn't it?'

'Yes, it's very nice.'

'Franck, have you got any food in the place? We left in such a hurry that we didn't have time for breakfast.'

'You know your way to the kitchen. You won't go short of anything at Franck's place. There's some slightly stale bread, some ham, sausage, pâtés, cold chicken, a few tasty little delicacies, wine, champagne and plenty of whisky.'

'Are you running a grocery?' asked Léa sarcastically.

'I could open one, little lady, but I prefer dealing in silk stockings, perfume and cigarettes. Do you smoke? English or American cigarettes? There's a choice. Which do you prefer?'

'American, but I'd rather eat first.'

'Your wish is my command. Hey! You lot, bring food and wine for the princess. Would your majesty deign to drink to our future liberators?'

For the first time since she had entered his home, Léa looked at the young man. He had a friendly boy-next-door face, looked like the sort you could confide in, share secrets with, but who could never be considered as a man. He was not very tall and was lost in a suit with ridiculously broad shoulders. The trousers were too short, showing his white socks and the inevitable triple-soled shoes of the perfect fashionable young man. His hair was cut in the latest style and a large lock fell over his rather plain face with its childlike expression. This kid, according to Laure, was one of the kings of wheeler-dealing, and had, unbeknown to his parents, amassed a small fortune from his black market trading. He was generous, and willingly treated his friends and his friends' friends. Doubtless satisfied with her appraisal, Léa deigned to bestow a smile on him.

'Good idea, let's drink to the liberation of Paris.'

Sitting on the window-ledge, she was amazed to be drinking champagne in this rebel city as it prepared for battle.

Agents of the passive defence organization were crossing the Place Saint-Michel, shouting that curfew would begin at two o'clock that afternoon.

'It's not true,' said a boy coming into the room. 'I dropped into my local police station and they told me they didn't know what was going on. The Free French don't know either. Oh, a new face. Hello, I'm Jacques.'

'Hello, I'm Léa. Where have you been?'

'All over the place. A lot of the town halls are in the hands of the communists . . .'

'How do you know?'

'It's a rumour going round. They're the only ones who are sufficiently organized and armed. In the Rue de Rivoli, Rue du Louvre and at Châtelet, République and in the Avenue de la Grande Armée, the Red Cross have set up first-aid posts. The hunt for weapons has begun. He who has a knife, relieves a German soldier of his revolver or his gun. With a gun, he seizes a sub-machine gun, he holds up an ammunition truck and distributes the contents among his comrades. "Each to his own Jerry" is the motto for new recruits.'

'Are you going to fight?' asked Léa.

'Why not! We'll be the heroes of tomorrow . . . I'll think about it when I've had some food.'

The whole group, five boys and three girls, gathered in the kitchen where Laure and a pretty blonde girl called Muriel had laid the table.

'What about some music to liven things up?'

'Oh yes! Put on the Andrews Sisters,' said Muriel.

'All right. Which song do you want?'

' "Pennsylvania Polka" or "Sonny Boy".'

'How did you get hold of those records?' asked Léa. 'I thought American music was banned.'

'We've got our sources. We'll tell you when the war's over.'

The shrill tones of the Andrews Sisters rang out through the apartment. The meal was very high-spirited, everybody cracking jokes and adding to the general mirth. They were all so young and carefree that Léa caught herself laughing at one of their jokes under the approving gaze of Franck who poured her another glass of wine.

He rose to wind up the gramophone. In the relative silence, a burst of gunfire could suddenly be heard.

'Quick, come over here, the Germans are attacking!'

They all rushed to the windows.

In the Boulevard du Palais, the occupants of three trucks were shooting at the door of the police headquarters and three tanks were advancing on Notre-Dame. Shots rang out from the law courts and a few of the attackers fell. The trucks disappeared in the direction of Châtelet. Shells exploded. Shortly afterwards, trucks drew up in the Boulevard du Palais. From their vantage point, the young people saw men in shirtsleeves, armed with guns or revolvers, hiding in the entrances to the metro and in the Café du Départ in front of which they mounted a machine gun.

A truck coming over Saint-Michel bridge was their first target. The truck stopped, while another crashed into the Rôtisserie Périgourdine at the corner of the Quai des Grands-Augustins. This was greeted with cries of joy from the spectators. Free French soldiers ran to collect the body which they hid on the steps leading down to the Seine, while the swimmers on the other side of the river, sunbathing against the wall of the Quai des Orfèvres, looked on fascinated. Over towards Châtelet, the black smoke of a burning truck spiralled upwards. A front-wheel drive vehicle, marked with the 'V' of victory and the Cross of Lorraine, turned round on the Quai Saint-Michel with a great screeching of tyres, followed by an ambulance and a fire-engine. From the square in front of Notre-Dame, three tanks were preparing to attack the police headquarters.

'They'll never last out,' said Franck, 'they've hardly got any ammunition and a few sandbags won't be much protection against shells.'

A group of teenagers ran along the embankment carrying an old machine gun that Franck identified as a Hotchkiss. One of them was wearing a cartridge belt over his shoulders. His name was Jeannot. He was fifteen years old and he was unaware that he was going to die soon, on the Quai de Montebello, his neck ripped open by a tracer bullet . . .

A petrol bomb hurled from one of the windows of the police headquarters landed in the open turret of a tank which blew up instantaneously. The shouts of joy from the besieged occupants echoed across the river and combined with those of the inhabitants of the Quai Saint-Michel who, leaning out of their windows oblivious of the danger, did not miss a scrap of the show. A group of German prisoners went past with their hands up, escorted by Free French soldiers. In the square, a passer-by was hit by a stray bullet. A German, covered in blood, was shooting in all directions as he pivoted around. A bullet split his skull open. For a few horribly long seconds, he continued advancing before collapsing on the ground. Léa was the only one to avert her eyes.

An explosion rocked the area. A truck carrying petrol had just crashed into the wall of the Notre-Dame-Hotel. The flames caught the blind and leapt up to attack the façade. Free French fighters abandoned their posts to try and move the truck and protect the ancient building. Luckily, it was not long before the wailing of the fire-engines could be heard.

One of the boys in the apartment decided to make the most of a lull in the fighting and go out for a walk. He returned after an hour, saying a truce had been agreed to enable both sides to gather up the wounded and the dead. This good news was greeted, as was appropriate, by the opening of a bottle of champagne which went to join its fellow bottles in the bath tub in one of the bathrooms.

The evening looked as if it was going to be heavy and stormy. The Parisians had once more taken possession of the streets of the capital and were wandering about, occasionally lingering in front of a pool of blood which had not yet dried, becoming suddenly pensive and silent.

'Drat, we forgot to tell our aunts where we are,' cried Laure, dashing over to the telephone.

The sky over the Pont-Neuf bridge was looking increasingly threatening.

'Aunt Albertine wants us to go home immediately. Apparently, Charles is running a high temperature . . .'

'Hasn't she called the doctor?'

'Old Doctor Leroy isn't answering and the others refuse to come out.'

'Right. I'm going. Are you coming with me?'

'No. I'd rather stay here. Call me if you need me. Franck, will you give Léa the telephone number here?'

'Yes, I'll see her home. I'll be back in less than an hour. I'm borrowing your bicycle.'

Chapter 16

Léa spent the entire night at the delirious child's bedside. In the morning, she wrapped him in a blanket, borrowed the concierge's ancient pram and set off with Charles for the nearest hospital.

Even after the storm that night, there were still angry black clouds in the sky. A smell of dust rose from the wet roads. The streets were deserted that damp Sunday morning, and a heavy, ominous silence reigned . . .

Léa went to the Laënnec Hospital in the Rue de Sèvres where the houseman on duty took the child from her. He was obviously incapable of diagnosing what was wrong, advising Léa to leave him there until his boss arrived and return later. When she refused to leave Charles's side, he gave the little patient some medicine and showed them to a room containing two beds.

It was late afternoon when she was wakened by the sound of voices.

'Well, young lady, you were sleeping like a log. Isn't this your child?'

'No.'

'Where are his parents?'

'What's wrong with him, doctor?'

'A type of acute laryngitis, complicated by the beginnings of congestion of the lungs.'

'Is it serious?'

'It may be. We would keep him here if we could.'

'Is that not possible?'

'A lot of the staff are absent. You haven't answered my question: where are his parents?'

'His mother was killed by the Germans and his father is with General de Gaulle.'

'Poor little thing.'

'Léa . . . Léa . . .'

'I'm here, darling.'

Charles clutched her and groaned. The doctor watched anxiously.

'Take him home and do exactly as I prescribe. Do you know how to give injections?'

'No.'

'You'll learn.'

'But . . .'

'It's not very difficult.'

The door suddenly flew open.

'Doctor, they're bringing in some injured children.'

'How serious?'

'They're wounded in the stomach and legs.'

'I'm coming. Take them round to the operating theatre. You see, mademoiselle, that's what I was afraid of: the arrival of the wounded when there aren't even enough of us to treat the sick.'

The doctor finished writing out the prescription. 'Ask the nurse at reception for the address of the duty chemist and leave her your address. Tomorrow morning, I'll try and drop by or I'll send one of my colleagues.'

'Doctor, he isn't going to . . .'

'No, he's a tough little chap, he'll get over this, don't worry. Give him his medicine very regularly and watch his temperature.'

For the following three days, Léa only snatched the odd few hours' sleep. She was completely cut off from the outside world. All that mattered was the rhythm of the child's breathing. She found herself mumbling naïve prayers. Her hands no longer shook when she gave him his injections. At dawn on 23rd August, his temperature dropped and the little boy, who had lost a lot of weight, said in a feeble voice:

'I'm hungry.'

Léa smothered him with kisses and he smiled a weary, happy smile.

'What's happening?' asked Albertine, opening the door.

'It's wonderful! Charles is better, he's asking for something to eat.'

'That is good news. Luckily, Laure managed to get hold of some milk and biscuits. I'll ask Estelle to rustle up something for him.'

He nibbled a biscuit and drank half his milk. Then he suddenly dropped off to sleep again under the watchful eye of the four women who left the room on tiptoe.

'Is there any water? I feel like a bath,' asked Léa.

'Yes, but it's cold, as usual.'

Cold? The bath water was freezing. But even if it had been colder still, Léa would have dived in with pleasure, to soak away the anxiety which had clung to her skin like dirt since she had sensed death hanging over Charles. Determined to save him, she had felt the critical moments when the body loses a grip on its defences, and, like a faith healer, she had tried to breathe life into him by placing her hands on his body and letting her strength flow into him. The strain had left her exhausted. Now, she sensed that he was going to be all right.

The anxiety and weariness dissolved in the water which was so cold it gave her goose flesh. She covered the loofah with lather from a lily of the valley scented soap, a present from Laure, and scrubbed herself vigorously. She had no shampoo so she washed her hair with the soap and rinsed it in vinegar to make it shine.

She studied herself critically in the large mirror in an ornate gilt frame which gave the simple white tiled bathroom an air of luxury.

'I'm nothing but skin and bone,' she said aloud.

There was no doubt she had lost a lot of weight, but the image reflected in the mirror was far from displeasing. She smugly caressed her breasts, her nipples erect from the cold, arched her back and thought she heard François Tavernier's voice murmur admiringly:

'What an arse!'

She blushed as a thrill of pleasure ran through her at this memory. She slipped on a towelling bathrobe and energetically rubbed her hair dry. In the hall, the telephone rang.

'Léa, it's Laure, she wants to speak to you,' shouted Albertine outside the bathroom door.

'Coming.'

She ran out, her hair dishevelled, and took the receiver.

'Hello, Léa? Aunt Albertine tells me Charles is better . . . is it true?'

'Yes, his temperature's down . . . he ate a little this morning . . . Could you get me some more milk?'

'It's getting harder and harder with the general strike on. The truck drivers refuse to drive out to the provinces. The only thing we can definitely get hold of is meat, thanks to the Free French forces who seized three and a half thousand tonnes stocked by the Germans in the cold stores at Bercy and Vaugirard. That I can get, but I need tickets, the black market is under close scrutiny at the moment . . .'

'I'll drop by and bring you some.'

'Be very careful,' Laure warned. 'The situation's changed since Saturday. There has been a lot of fighting in the Latin Quarter over the last two days. There are barricades all over the place and militiamen and Germans are hiding on the rooftops sniping at passers-by. There are hundreds of deaths every day and they're all piling up at the morgue. With this heat, you can imagine the stench around Notre-Dame-des-Victoires where Mass is celebrated. That's where they're keeping the coffins that are waiting to be taken to Pantin cemetery. They're buried in the rebels' section. The Red Cross people are marvellous. Not only do they help the wounded, but they've also replaced the striking firemen . . . Have you heard from Françoise?'

'No, I don't think so . . .'

'I'm worried about her. Yesterday, in the Place Saint-Michel, the crowd lynched a collaborator. It was a dreadful sight . . . The women were the worst . . . They beat him with whatever they could lay their hands on, screaming hysterically . . . I heard they gouged out his eyes with a bar from a broken chair . . . It was awful. You should have heard his screams! The worst thing was the onlookers who stood there laughing, or who pushed away the Free French soldiers who tried to intervene. When they'd had enough of beating him up, they dispersed with blood on their hands and clothing, leaving a disgusting mess on the pavement . . . Hello! Are you still there?'

'Yes, why are you telling me all this? What's it got to do with Françoise?'

It was Laure's turn to say nothing while Léa shouted:

'Hello! Hello! Can you hear me?'

'Yes, I can hear you.'

'Well?'

'They're also arresting women who've slept with Germans.'

'What do they do to them?'

'Apparently, they shave their heads . . .'

'Shave their heads!'

'Yes. It's happened in certain districts. They hang the hair on the railings and paint swastikas on the women's bald heads. They're usually prostitutes and kept women, denounced by their neighbours.'

'But Françoise isn't one of them!'

'I know, but don't imagine they're going to make those sort of distinctions! I only hope she took my advice and left for Germany with little Pierre.'

'Have you telephoned her place?'

'Of course, but there's no reply. The last time I spoke to her was on Monday morning, she'd just had a visit from a German officer who'd come to fetch her to take her to a requisitioned hotel. They're putting all the women in her situation there. She refused to go with him.'

'What's the name of the hotel?'

'I don't know, I can't remember.'

'We must phone round all the hotels.'

'Do you realize how many there are in Paris?'

'No, but it doesn't matter. First of all we'll call all those in the Michelin guide. Has Franck got one?'

'Yes, I think so . . .'

'While you're waiting for me, start calling those at the end

189

of the list. I'll ask our aunts to begin at the top and to call us if they find anything. See you in a minute.'

'Take care . . .'

Léa had already hung up.

The Montpleynet sisters became very agitated when Léa explained the situation to them, but Albertine soon sat down and picked up the telephone.

'Hello, is that the Crillon?'

'Look, Aunt Albertine, I'd be surprised if they were at the Crillon, the Majestic, the Meurice, the Continental or the Lutétia which are all occupied by the Germans!'

The Rue de l'Université was completely deserted. In front of the Faculty of Medicine in the Rue des Saints-Pères, the charred remains of a truck lay in the road, daubed with the Cross of Lorraine. The Rue Jacob was equally quiet. Léa was about to turn into the Rue de Seine and head for the river via the Rue Guénégaud, when she recalled the arrest of Sarah Mulstein . . . She had not been that way since that sinister night. She carried on towards the Rue de Buci. There, a long queue of housewives had been waiting outside the baker's since dawn. Léa noted that despite the weariness and food shortages, people were in high spirits for the first time in four years. The air itself felt lighter. In the Rue Dauphine, a young man in a vest, his gun slung over his shoulder, was cycling along with a bundle of newspapers under his arm shouting:

'Buy *l'Humanité!** Mademoiselle, do you want a paper?' he asked, drawing level with her.

'Are the papers out again?'

'They have been since Monday. Here you are . . . Two francs please. Thank you. Don't go near the Pont-Neuf, the Germans are shooting at the barricade. Earlier this morning some bastards in a Free French registered car shot at some patriots. Two were killed. The Jerries ran off down the Rue Christine. Goodbye.'

Léa leaned against a doorway and read:

---

* Communist daily newspaper

The whole of Paris is at the barricades . . . ! The commander of the Free French for the Paris area appeals for mass relief of the Parisian people . . . Everyone, men, women and children, must help fortify the streets, apartment blocks and public buildings. The whole population must join in with courage and selflessness to support the glorious Free French. Form PATRIOTIC MILITIA groups everywhere! Attack is the best form of defence. Harass the enemy! NOT ONE JERRY MUST LEAVE REBEL PARIS ALIVE! The battle is developing on all war fronts . . . Battle is raging all day long in the 1st, 4th, 5th and 6th districts, the patriots are gaining the upper hand everywhere . . . The war of the entire nation against the hated Boche . . . Communist women fight for the liberation of Paris . . . How a young girl was tortured by the militia . . . Join the party of the massacred . . . !

In the Place Saint-André-des-Arts, there were a lot of people, waving and shouting. Men who were no longer young, women, a lot of women, young and old, all wearing the same expression of hatred, their mouths contorted with anger, spitting abuse . . . Bare arms were raised, hands were clutched, the fingers like claws. Bastard! Collaborator! Swine! Traitor! Murderer! A tall blond man was struggling in the midst of these furies. Painted nails ripped open his cheek . . . He cried:

'I'm from Alsace!'

'From Alsace my arse!' retorted a voice with a heavy Parisian accent.

That made the crowd laugh.

From the window occupied by the Free French, a man in vaguely military attire was trying to make himself heard. A young girl thumbed her nose at him. A faded blonde with a wide black hairband shouted:

'He's a Jerry! I know him! I'm sure . . . kill him!'

She grabbed the blond man's hair while another spat in his face and another tried to unbutton his trousers, snickering:

'Let's see if he's got any balls, the scum!'

A ripple of laughter went through the mob who began chanting;

'Strip him! Strip the Jerry!'

Dazed, he repeated as he tried to break free from the claws:

'I'm from Alsace!'

Blood was now streaming from his nose and cheeks. One of his eyes was closed. He fell under a hail of blows and kicks . . . One caught him on the nose . . . he stumbled to his feet . . . a young boy wearing a Free French armband tried to intervene. Three men seized his arm, picked him up and deposited him near to where Léa was standing. She was unable to take her eyes off the massacre . . . She did not realize it, but for some time she had been swaying backwards and forwards in the way that blind people often do. In her head, her thoughts were going round and round and bursting into disjointed fragments . . . From the bleeding hole that had once been a mouth, came a gurgling sound:

'I . . . I'm fr . . . from Alshashe . . .'

Overcome with nausea, Léa turned away from the spectacle. The Free French boy was still there. He was very young. Tears were streaming down his pale face, leaving a glistening trail. Their eyes met . . .

'Léa!'

'Pierrot!'

They flung themselves into each other's arms, trembling with horror and disgust. Léa was the first to free herself.

'They're going to kill him.'

'There's nothing we can do about it. There are too many of them.'

'You're in the Free French army, go and get your comrades!'

'They won't come. Yesterday, one of them was nearly lynched in the place of a collaborator he had tried to defend.'

'That's dreadful.'

'Come on, don't watch . . . Come on, let's get away from here . . . We'll go to Colonel Lizé's HQ in the Rue Guénégaud.'

'I don't want to go to the Rue Guénégaud,' shrieked Léa.

Pierrot Delmas was surprised at her violent reaction.

'Well, I have to go there, I act as go-between for Colonel Lisé and Colonel Rol.'

'Who's Rol?'

He stared at her with a mixture of astonishment and disapproval.

'Haven't you heard of Colonel Rol . . . ? He's the leader of the uprising, the Free French chief.'

'And Lizé?'

'Colonel Lizé is another leader. I don't understand very well, it's to do with politics. All I know is that Rol is a communist.'

'Your father would be pleased if he could see you now,' she said with a sad laugh.

'Don't talk to me about my father, he's a collaborator. As far as I'm concerned, he's dead.'

While he was talking, he led his cousin towards the Rue Gît-le-Coeur. He stopped in front of the dirty window of a little grocery, walked up the three steps and knocked at the door.

'We're closed,' grumbled a voice within.

'Open up, it's Pierrot from Bordeaux.'

The door opened a crack.

'It's you. Come in, son . . . who's she?'

'This is my cousin Léa.'

The grocery was also a restaurant. The walls were covered with old photographs, traditional prints, engravings and some fairly good portraits of Napoleon, all covered in a brown sheen. The room was divided in two by a short wooden counter serving as both bar and as a showcase for groceries. Now, it only displayed huge artificial cans of food. The dining-room was at the back, its tables covered with red and white gingham cloths. There was an enormous ancient black stove with gleaming copper hotplates. On it stood an alcohol burner and simmering away in a pot was something that smelled remarkably like rabbit stew. The smell was almost too much for Léa.

'Look out, your cousin's going to faint,' cried the woman who had opened the door to them.

Pierrot helped her to a chair and made her sip a thimbleful

of brandy offered by the owner. A little colour came back into her cheeks and her head stopped spinning.

'Are you feeling better? Here, drink some more.'

'No, thank you.'

She looked about her. It was like stepping back to the beginning of the century. She was sure the food must have been good there before the war, you could tell from the lovingly cared-for stove. She felt reassured. Where the cooking was good, the people could not be altogether bad.

'You must be hungry,' scolded the woman, going over to the stove.

'Oh yes!' exclaimed Pierrot, who had not eaten a proper meal for several days.

'No thank you, madame, I'll just have a glass of water.'

'You'll regret it, Madame Laetitia'a a wonderful cook, in spite of the rationing.'

He sat down to a steaming plate piled high with a blackish-coloured stew.

'I don't understand how you can find the stomach for food,' said Léa indignantly.

Pierrot blushed under the grime on his face. He dropped the forkful of food he was about to put into his mouth and looked so forlorn that she wished she had kept her mouth shut.

'I'm sorry . . . go ahead and eat . . . Tell me how you came to be here.'

With his mouth full, he began his story.

'When I learned that my father wanted to send me to the Jesuits with orders that I should be forbidden to leave the seminary, I decided to join the Resistance. I'll spare you the details of my journey – hiding in goods wagons, nights spent in ditches to avoid the police and pilfering food from the fields. At Limoges station, I was chased by militiamen. I was able to get away thanks to the railway workers. They hid me for several days in an old carriage in a siding. There were so many Germans and militiamen checking every single passenger and every employee that they couldn't let me out. Finally, one day, they hid me in a cattle truck on a goods train that was going to Eymoutiers . . .'

'Eymoutiers . . . is that near Limoges?'

'Yes, why? Do you know it?'

'No, but I had a Jewish friend who was in hiding there for a while. Go on.'

'In Eymoutiers, I was taken care of by some more railway workers who took me to their chief, Colonel Guingouin, also known as Le Grand, or Raoul. What a man! He terrorized the Germans in the area. His HQ was in the forest of Châteauneuf. Unfortunately, with the arrival of winter, we had to abandon the Trois-Chevaux camp. It was about time too, for, a few days later, three thousand German soldiers swooped down on the forest. The Germans nicknamed the area "little Russia", they were so afraid of ambushes. They had lost a lot of men. During those six months, I acted as liaison agent between the different camps. I know every village and every wood like the back of my hand. Thanks to Guingouin's organization, we were properly clothed and fed. Most of the local population was on our side. I wish I could have gone with him on sabotage operations and convoy attacks, but he said I was too young. At the beginning of the month, he sent me here with a message for Colonel Rol. The strike, and then the uprising, prevented me from leaving. There, that's my story.'

Léa stared at her cousin in admiration. How he had grown up!

'What about you? How long have you been in Paris?'

'Since the beginning of the month as well.'

'How's everybody at Montillac? Has Camille heard from Laurent? And what about Aunt Bernadette? Ruth? Mathias? . . . What's the matter?'

Léa sat with her head in her hands, mechanically rubbing her forehead.

'What's the matter?' repeated Pierrot anxiously.

'Camille and Aunt Bernadette are dead. There is no Montillac any more.'

'What on earth are you talking about?'

'The Germans and the militia killed them and burned the house down . . .'

They sat in silence for a long time. A noisy group entered

the grocery-cum-restaurant, jolting them out of their macabre musing.

'Oh! There you are, Pierrot! We've been looking every-where for you. We were afraid you'd suffered the same fate as the collaborator who said he was from Alsace.'

'Perhaps he was!'

The boy, who was not much older than Pierrot, turned towards Léa, surprised by the anger in her voice.

'Perhaps he was, but the population has suffered so much that it's natural for people to want revenge.'

'Natural! . . . Do you find such brutal slaughter natural?'

'What about the Germans, didn't they behave like butchers? Do you know how many of our comrades they murdered at the waterfall in the Boulogne woods last week? No? Thirty-five, all the same age as you . . . Magisson, nine-teen years old . . . Verdeaux, nineteen . . . Smet, twenty . . . Schlosser, twenty-two . . . Dudraisal, nick-named Philo, twenty-one . . . the Bernard brothers, twenty and twenty-four . . . do you want me to go on?'

'I know as well as you do what they're capable of, I've seen them at work. But that's no reason to behave even worse than them!'

They were both pale as they sat glowering at each other. Pierrot intervened.

'Leave her alone, she's right.'

'Perhaps, but this is no time to say so.'

'You'll see, it'll never be the right moment.'

'Léa, be quiet. Are you coming with me to Colonel Lizé's HQ?'

'No, Laure's expecting me. We're staying with my aunts, phone me . . . I want to see you again and talk to you.'

'I'll call you or drop in the minute I'm free. Give my love to Laure.'

They parted company outside the shop.

It took Léa almost an hour to cross the Place Saint-Michel. Snipers hidden on the rooftops were shooting at anyone who ventured out. Two people had been killed.

The huge apartment looked as though it had been hit by a hurricane. It was now occupied by fifteen or so Free French fighters. The only people left from the little group of friends were Laure, the pretty Muriel and Franck. They greeted her eagerly.

'Have you managed to find Françoise?'

'Not yet. We've called about twenty hotels, but haven't had any luck so far.'

'Keep trying. I bumped into Pierrot in the street.'

'Pierrot?'

'Yes, our little cousin.'

'Uncle Luc's son?'

'Yes.'

'How wonderful! What's he doing here?'

'He's got an armband and a big revolver.'

In the kitchen, two young people were preparing petrol bombs according to Fréderic Joliot-Curie's recipe, publicized by Colonel Rol:

All you need is a bottle filled with three-quarters petrol and a quarter sulphuric acid. Cork it and stick on a label coated with potassium chlorate. When the bottle breaks, the potassium chlorate comes into contact with the contents and the mixture bursts into flames.

It was a powerful weapon against tanks.

A shattering explosion sent them all racing to the windows. The defenders of the Rue de la Huchette were climbing over their barricade to see what was happening. The baker's wife cried:

'The Jerries are blowing up Paris!'

The rumour spread through the Latin Quarter like wildfire, creating panic and confusion. In the west of Paris, over the Champs-Elysées, rose a thick column of smoke. They all withdrew, waiting for further explosions. But apart from a few isolated shots from around the Luxemburg gardens, everything remained calm.

Gradually, the fighters and the curious returned to their habits of the last few days. A group of about fifteen German prisoners was escorted through the area by three armed Free French soldiers. They were being taken to join their comrades in the quadrangle of the police headquarters. Their clothes were crumpled and they marched with their hands on their heads. Suddenly, a motorcycle combination came hurtling down the Quai des Grands-Augustins at top speed and rammed the group. There was a burst of gunfire and one of the French soldiers fell. A cry rose up from behind the barricade. A young boy scaled it and threw a petrol bomb at the two German riders. He did not live to see the result of his heroic deed. Another round of shots sent him crumpling on top of the assorted heap of bodies. A huge flame flared up in front of the motorcycle combination. The driver was unable to avoid it. The two men were burned to death in a trice. Witnesses watched the vehicle career crazily into a bookstall along the embankment, the two riders engulfed in multicoloured flames. For a few seconds, everything stood still apart from the inferno from which an accusing hand protruded, pointing up at the sky.

Gripping the window-ledge, Léa relived her aunt's ordeal with the same dreadful feeling of helplessness. Both the German and the elderly woman had made the same appealing gesture as they died. Did death by fire make them reach closer to God?

Then everything happened at once. From behind the barricade in the Place Saint-André-des-Arts and from the neighbouring narrow streets, a yelling crowd assembled and rushed towards the prisoners. They had looked on petrified while their fellow countrymen burned to death. The two surviving Free French soldiers tried to intervene, but they were swept aside by the human tide. One of them ran off to get help from the police headquarters. By the time he returned with a dozen police officers, three Germans had been killed. One of them had had his eyes gouged out, another had no nose left and the third had no face at all. Their wounded comrades were left in a desperate huddle. These big, strong men, who had fought on the Russian front, were crying like babies. The arrival of the police, some of whom were in uniform, calmed the mob's hysteria. And those people, good folk at heart no doubt, turned away, reeling from the exhilaration of the carnage which most of them soon put out of their minds. The spectators who had helplessly witnessed the massacre, unable to do anything about it, would never forget it as long as they lived.

An appalled silence reigned in the big apartment. The young people did not dare look at each other, while the Resistance fighters, sitting on the floor with their guns in their laps, bowed their heads. Franck and his friends stood staring at the wall in front of them. The arrival of a 'lieutenant' helped ease the tension.

'The Boche have set fire to the Grand Palais!'

'So that's what the explosion and the smoke were!'

'But there was a circus in there!'

'Yes, Houcke's Circus. I don't know if the rescuers managed to get the animals out. The horses bolted. One of them was shot at the roundabout in the Champs-Elysées and – you won't believe this – I saw men and women rushing up with knives to carve it up, completely heedless of the bullets whistling past. Some were even holding plates! When I left, there wasn't much left.'

'You should have brought us a piece.'

'You must be joking! They'd have stabbed me, that lot would!'

He said that in a guttural Parisian accent which made everyone laugh.

'Can you picture the fellows sitting there with nice white napkins round their necks, eating raw meat with their little fingers crooked, while the Jerries stand there holding starving lions on leads!'

After the tension of the last hour, it did them good to laugh. They began to laugh and joke like young people again.

In the square below, they were gathering up the French and German corpses and ferrying the injured to the General Hospital.

The rest of the afternoon was spent telephoning Paris hotels.

'No, there's no Madame Delmas with a child, nor are there any women sent to stay here by gentlemen.'

The two sisters were on the point of giving up.

'Just try this one, the Hotel Régina, the number's Opéra 74 02,' said Léa.

Laure did so.

'Hello, is that the Hotel Régina . . . ?'

'Then we'll call Albertine and see if she's found anything.'

'Hello . . . yes . . . that's right . . . What do you mean it's not possible? You have orders . . .'

Léa snatched the receiver.

'Put me through to Madame Delmas. I don't give a damn about your orders . . . put me through at once. Hello . . . hello . . . who's speaking? Lieutenant, put me through to Madame Delmas . . . I'm her sister . . . She'll call me back . . . without fail? We're very worried . . . Thank you.'

'Thank God we've found her!'

'Yes, but we still haven't been able to speak to her. I hope that German didn't lie to me and that he'll give her my message. I'm going home. Are you coming with me?'

'No, I'd rather stay here. Keep me posted.'

A Resistance fighter escorted Léa to the other side of the Place Saint-Michel. The boy left her outside the Clavreuil bookshop.

After the gunfire and screams of the Latin Quarter, the Rue Jacob and the Rue de l'Université were oases of silence. Charles, who had spent most of the day sleeping, greeted her with a show of affection which she reciprocated with a weary tenderness.

She had brought a pint of milk and a few lumps of sugar, some bread and a little meat from Franck's place. Estelle pounced on the packet of food as if it were treasure. Then began the vigil by the telephone.

By the time it finally rang, at about ten o'clock that evening, Léa and her aunts had heard on the BBC that Paris had been liberated! Just then, a burst of machine gunfire shattered the silence of that quiet district. Albertine de Montpleynet drew her slender hand across her forehead and said in her inimitable way:

'Well, those gentlemen in London seem very ill-informed.'

'But it must be true if they say so,' said the naïve Lisa

who believed everything the voices that came out of the wireless set said, whether they were collaborators or Resistance fighters.

The ringing of the telephone prevented Léa from being rude to her dear aunt.

'Hello . . . is that you Françoise? Are you all right? Why didn't you come here? Hello . . . hello . . . don't hang up . . . Can you hear me? You'll call back tomorrow? Lots of love . . . speak to you tomorrow, good night . . .'

Léa replaced the receiver with a feeling of apprehension. Françoise ought not to stay there. The Hotel Régina was in danger of being attacked at any time. She would go and fetch her sister the very next day.

Despite her anxiety, she slept soundly.

Chapter 17

When Léa awoke, the sky over Paris was grey. In the small bed next to hers, Charles was sleeping, a peaceful expression on his gaunt little face. 'He looks so like Camille,' she thought as she stroked his fine blond hair. She slipped on a blue cotton bathrobe and went into the kitchen. For once, the gas was working and she heated up some milk while sipping half a bowlful of 'coffee' made earlier by Estelle, which was still hot. She could hear the crackling of the wireless set coming from Lisa's room. Charles's sleepy little face appeared in the doorway.

'Will you get back to bed! You're still ill, you'll catch cold.'

'No, I'm better, I'm hungry.'

'Sit down and I'll give you some milk and biscuits.'

'Can we go for a walk later?'

'No, darling, it's still too soon and there's a war going on outside.'

'I want to go out and kill the horrid Jerries who hurt my mummy.'

Léa sighed as she watched the determined little boy who talked of killing while he sat calmly drinking his milk.

'Only grown-ups fight wars.'

'So why do they shoot children?'

Léa could not find an answer to the four-year-old's question.

'Is my daddy in the war?'

'Yes, he's with General de Gaulle.'

'When's he coming home?'

'Very soon.'

'It's a long time.'

He was right, it had been a long time. It had lasted for four years! Four years of pretending to carry on living to keep from utter despair. Nothing but deaths! Nothing but suffering during those four years!

'Daddy'll be sad when he finds out mummy's dead.'

So he did know! For the last two months, he had been pretending to believe her garbled explanations!

'Yes, he'll be very sad, but we'll be there to comfort him. You'll have to give him lots and lots of love.'

'But you'll be there too, and you'll love him too. You will love my daddy, won't you?'

She thought she heard Camille's voice: 'Promise me you'll look after Charles if anything happens to me . . . and Laurent too.' Laurent, whom she loved tenderly as a brother, as a very dear friend, but no longer as a lover. Even now, she was astonished how that love, which she had always believed was eternal, had changed! Did love always die before the loved one? It was Raphaël who had said that with reference to Chateaubriand challenging the little message of hope from the lovesick Juliette Récamier: 'Sometimes, in a strong soul, love lives long enough to be transformed into passionate friendship, to become a duty, to take on the qualities of a virtue. Then it loses its innate weakness and lives on its immortal principles.'

Supposing he was right?

'Léa, you will love my daddy, won't you?'

It was raining. Léa tied an old Hermès headscarf over her hair and set off in the direction of the Pont-Royal bridge.

She had tried telephoning the Hotel Régina but there had been no reply. She decided to go there directly without telling her aunts.

The streets were silent and empty and, from time to time, shhe could hear the shooting. On the bridge, the young German sentries let her through. The Tuileries gardens were nothing but a huge, muddy wasteland, with ruts where the tall trees lay. In the distance, the Obelisk and the Arc de Triomphe made the shape of a cross against the dark sky.

She was unable to force her way through the barrier on the Rue de Rivoli. An NCO agreed, however, to go and make inquiries at the Hotel Régina whose façade towered above the statue of Joan of Arc. The man returned: all the women had left the hotel very early that morning. Nobody knew where they were. Léa thanked him and left, distraught.

She saw Red Cross vehicles driving along the embankment and two cars full of Free French soldiers singing partisan songs. Near the Rue Guénégaud, two young men wearing Resistance armbands stopped her violently by grabbing her handlebars.

'Where are you going?'

Their familiarity annoyed Léa.

'It's none of your business!'

A resounding slap sent her reeling.

'Answer politely when you're spoken to. Believe you me, you won't feel so smart after a visit to the local hairdresser's.'

'Let me go.'

'Watch out darling, or we'll get angry. Nobody gets past us without proving they're clean. There are some important people in the area, so we have to be on the lookout for spies. Now, tell us where you're going.'

Léa realized that it was no use being stubborn.

'I'm going to join some friends at the Place Saint-Michel.'

'At the barricade in the Rue de la Huchette?'

'Yes, in the apartment above it.'

'Léa, what are you doing here?'

'Pierrot, will you ask them to let me through?'

'Leave her alone, I know her, she's my cousin.'

'All right. We were only carrying out orders.'

'Come on, I'll introduce you to a pal of mine who's guarding the barricade.'

It was some barricade! All the metal bedsteads in the area must have been requisitioned and the cellars emptied of old furniture: there were radiators, bent bicycles, pushchairs, barrels, crates and birdcages stabilized with sandbags. There was even an antique copper bath tub. The barricade was built around a truck which had lost its wheels and doors. This mountain of old iron was reinforced with market stalls and hand carts which served as supports for the gunmen. They passed along a narrow path fashioned along the top of the parapet. Shots rang out from a building on the Ile de la Cité.

'Careful! Hide!'

Léa and Pierrot found refuge in one of the rounded recesses in the bridge where two men were crouching. Léa recognized the short-sighted young man from the Café Flore and smiled at him. He recognized her too and returned her smile.

'They're shooting from the roof of the City Hotel,' he said, pointing in that direction.

'It's been going on since this morning,' said Pierrot. 'But we think he's a lone gunman, probably a militiaman. Look, there are some comrades on the rooftops.'

The figures of armed Resistance fighters were silhouetted against the sky which was still dark.

'Are you the one who lives in the Place Dauphine?' the barricade leader asked the bespectacled young man's companion.

'Yes.'

'What's your name?'

'Henri Berri.'

'And yours?'

'Claude Mauriac.'

'Perhaps he's the son of our neighbour at Montillac,' thought Léa. She did not have time to ask him; the leader signalled to them that they could advance, shouting to the Resistance gunmen:

'Don't shoot!'

The two men ran off in the direction of the Place Dauphine while the two cousins went back behind the barricade. Pierrot had not let go of the bicycle.

'You shouldn't be running around like that, you might get hit by a stray bullet . . . There, what was I telling you!'

A woman had just fallen to the ground along the embankment. Injured, she dragged herself over to the shelter of a tree. Two young people in white coats rushed out of the Rue des Grands-Augustins carrying a stretcher. A young girl was waving a Red Cross flag. Heedless of the bullets, they picked up the injured woman and ran off towards the makeshift first-aid post set up by Dr Debré.

'Let's take the side street, it's not so dangerous.'

Everything was quiet in the Rue de Savoie. Resistance fighters were on guard outside an ancient eighteenth-century mansion.

'It's the headquarters of one of the Resistance leaders,' Pierrot informed Léa.

'You've got to help me find Françoise.'

'That whore!'

Léa stopped in her tracks, astonished at his abusiveness.

'Do you realize what you're asking me to do?' he continued. 'Helping you to find a collaborator, who has betrayed her country . . .'

'That's enough. Françoise is neither a collaborator nor a whore, she's a sad young girl who had the misfortune to fall in love with a German when our countries were at war. She doesn't deserve to be shot for that.'

'Perhaps not shot, but she does deserve to have her head shorn and to be sent to prison.'

'Shorn! You must be mad! I'd rather die than have my head shaved.'

'Hair grows again,' he sneered.

He skilfully ducked Léa's slap.

They could hear laughter, shouting and clapping coming from the Rue Saint-André-des-Arts. The crowd was pushing along a balding man in his fifties. They had removed his trousers and he cut a pathetic, rather grotesque figure in his stockinged feet. One of his socks, held up by garters, had a hole in it. He was carrying his trousers and shoes. Behind him was a fat girl in a blue flowered dress, her shaven head painted with a white swastika. She was sobbing. Léa felt a surge of shame. Pierrot hung his head. They stood rooted to the spot for a while. The young boy put his arm round her.

'Come on, let's go and look for her. We'll go to Colonel Rol's headquarters.'

They never reached the underground headquarters at Denfert-Rochereau.

Near the barricades at the crossroads of Boulevard Saint-

Michel and Boulevard Saint-Germain, nicknamed 'The Crossroads of Death', a grenade flung from a rooftop exploded in front of them. Léa, who was walking a few paces behind, felt a sort of scratching down her face. As in a slow motion film, she saw Pierrot fly through the air and flutter gracefully down. People dressed in white were hovering over them. The grey sky was spinning and the trees were closing in on her.

'There, it's nothing serious. You can go home.'

Léa sat up, feeling a little giddy. The young doctor helped her down from the first-aid table. His features were drawn and he looked utterly exhausted.

'Next.'

A man with a stomach wound was laid on the table.

'Where's my cousin?'

'I don't know,' replied the doctor, 'ask at reception.'

Until evening, Léa wandered up and down the corridors of the Hôtel-Dieu Hospital in her bloodstained dress with a huge bandage on her head, searching desperately for Pierrot. Nobody was able to tell her what had become of him. The nurses who had taken her there were nowhere to be found.

'Come back tomorrow,' they all said.

With death in her soul, she resigned herself to leaving the hospital. A police officer with a Resistance armband took pity on her and escorted her through the obstacle course in front of Notre-Dame, leaving her in the Rue Saint-Jacques at the corner of the Rue de la Huchette, where a Resistance fighter took charge of her and accompanied her to the apartment in the Boulevard Saint-Michel.

Franck was alone in the apartment. Without a word, he showed her to his room, ran a bath and helped her undress. While the bath was running, he made her a cup of tea which she drank through chattering teeth for the water was cold. He put her to bed in a bathrobe that was several sizes too large for her, and held her hand until she fell asleep. They had not exchanged a single word.

*

'Bleed! Bleed! Blood-letting is just as good in August as it is in May!'

The cry of the Tavannes on Saint Bartholomew's night during the massacre of the Protestants on 22nd August 1572 rang incessantly in Léa's ears.

That morning, while preparing Charles's breakfast, she had looked at the date and seen that it was Saint Bartholomew's day. That had reminded her of Brantôme's *Life of Charles IX*, which she had read after devouring Alexandre Dumas's *The Lady of Montsoreau*, *The Forty-Five* and *Queen Margot*, where she had read that sinister sentence. In her dream, Germans were muddled up with men in the pay of the Guise, shorn women, Admiral de Coligny, Free French soldiers and the future Henry IV, bodies thrown into the Seine, bodies burned with flame-throwers and Charles IX firing an arquebus from his bedroom window in the Louvre palace.

'Wake up! Wake up!'

Léa was almost as white as the bandages on her head. She opened her eyes.

'What do you want?'

Franck was very agitated. He had lost his usual composure. He was twiddling the knobs on the wireless set in his room.

'Listen!'

'Parisians, rejoice! We have come to inform you that you have been delivered . . . Leclerc's division has entered Paris. They will reach the Town Hall in a few minutes! Do not leave your wireless sets . . . you are about to hear the great voice we have all been waiting for. We are wild with joy! Our programme is coming to you direct, we are speaking in bad conditions, we haven't eaten for three days . . . There are comrades who've been fighting and who haven't eaten for three days and who are coming back to the microphone . . . Perhaps we're drunk, but drunk with joy, with happiness, at recovering our beloved city . . .'

Léa got up and went over to Franck. He impetuously flung his arms round her.

*

'We've just received a piece of information: it's very brief: at 9.15, at the postern of Les Peupliers, a column of French, Spanish and Moroccans was sighted . . . Where is the postern of Les Peupliers?

'In Gentilly!

'The postern of Les Peupliers is in Issy . . .

'Here they are, they've arrived . . . at this very moment, at the head of General Leclerc's troops, two armoured cars have reached the square in front of the Town Hall . . . General de Gaulle will be in one of them! What is certain is that the allied troops have arrived at the police headquarters and the Town Hall and it's likely that General de Gaulle is here too . . . Open your windows . . . put out the flags . . .

'I've just received a phone call from the Secretary of Information. He requests me to ask all the priests who are listening to this programme to ring the church bells immediately. I repeat, and I authenticate: this is Schaeffer, head of the French National Radio, the radio that took over the air four days ago, under the German occupation. I have been duly mandated by the General Secretary for Information of the Provisional Government of the Republic to speak to the priests who are listening and who can be informed immediately. To them, I say: ring the bells full peal to announce the arrival of the Allies in Paris . . .'

Franck and Léa stood there hugging each other, laughing and crying. They rushed over to the window. All round the Place Saint-Michel shutters were flying open, and one by one the lights were switched on. Camouflage and passive defence went to the winds. Now it was time for light and rejoicing. People from all over Paris flocked to the square, hugging and kissing each other. wireless sets turned up full volume blared out the *Marseillaise*. In the square, everybody stood still and joined in:

Aux armes citoyens . . . !

To the west, a huge fire made the dark clouds rolling across the sky glow red.

Léa and Franck joined in without even realizing it, carried away by the emotion of the moment. They were hugging each other so hard they could barely breathe.

Suddenly, the first bells pealed out, shy at first, then becoming bolder, ringing out through the sky where a gloomy dusk was gathering over the last day of the Occupation of Paris. The bells of Saint-Séverin replied to the first peal, then those of Saint-Julien-le-Pauvre, joined by the bells of Saint-Germain-des-Prés, the Sacré Coeur, Saint-Etienne-du-Mont, Saint-Germain-l'Auxerrois, Saint-Sulpice, Sainte-Geneviève, Saint-Eustache and finally the deep chimes of Notre Dame could be heard, stirring the city to wild excitement.

It was 9.22 p.m. and Captain Raymond Dronne had just drawn up outside the Town Hall in his jeep, nicknamed 'Death to fools', with fifteen half-tracks and three Sherman tanks, the Montmirail, the Champaubert and the Romilly. A hundred and thirty men were setting foot on the soil of their capital for the first time in four years.

The emotional announcer started spouting lines from Victor Hugo:

> *Reveillez-vous! Assez de honte;*
> *Redevenez la grande France!*
> *Redevenez le grand Paris!**

Down below, in the square, people had made a bonfire and were dancing round it. Suddenly, shots rang out. They all froze, then ran off shouting in all directions.

Léa and Franck let go of each other's hands. On the wireless, the formerly enthusiastic voice was stammering:

'*We were perhaps a little over-hasty . . . It is not yet all over . . . it is best to keep your windows closed. Do not let yourselves be killed unnecessarily . . .*'

Around the square, one by one the lights went off, the shutters were closed again, fear returned . . .

'*We remind you of the precautions for passive defence prescribed*

---

* Awake! Enough shame;
  Become the great France once more!
  Become the great Paris once more!

by Colonel Rol . . . Find other ways to express your happiness . . .'

One by one, the bells stopped chiming, except one shrill peal defying the boom of the cannon firing at Longchamp. Then it too held its tongue. The cannon ceased as well and, finally, so did the shooting around the Town Hall.

It was night over Paris. All around the Luxemburg Palace and the Odeon district, which was said to be mined, furtive shadows carrying heavy loads made their way down to the cellars. The liberation of Paris was not yet over.

A terrible storm broke in the middle of the night. Léa stayed up for a long time contemplating the chaos in the sky where one flash of lightning followed another and the thunder crashed and rolled. It lit up the Pont-Neuf which looked like a toy bridge straddling the still, black ribbon of the Seine. Large drops of rain soon began to fall, riddling the surface of the water.

Chapter 18

At eight o'clock the following morning, Laure came bursting into the room where Léa was sleeping.

'They're coming! They're coming!'

Léa awoke with a start and sat up trembling.

'Who?'

'Leclerc and his men! They're coming! They're at the Porte d'Orléans! Get up, we're going to meet them . . . what's the matter? Are you hurt?'

'It's not serious. Have you any news of Pierrot or Françoise?'

'No, I thought you would have.'

Noiselessly, Léa began to cry.

'Don't cry, we'll find them. Come on, get up, let's watch them march past.'

A 'fifi', as the Free French soldiers were affectionately known, came rushing in shouting:

'They're in the Rue Saint-Jacques!'

He had gone before the words were out of his mouth.

'Did you hear, they're just around the corner! Hurry up.'

'I'm sure he's dead!'

'Who on earth are you talking about?'

'Pierrot.'

'Pierrot!'

There was a knock at the half-open door. It was Franck.

'Don't stand in front of the window, you might get hit by a stray bullet,' he said, pushing Laure into the middle of the room.

'Have you any news of Pierrot?' asked Léa, getting out of bed.

'No, I've tried several hospitals, but none of the injured picked up in the Latin Quarter corresponds to the description of your cousin.'

'But he must be somewhere, either dead of alive.'

'What happened?' Laure wanted to know.

'Léa and your cousin were injured yesterday at the "Crossroads of Death". Léa was taken to the Hôtel-Dieu. We've no idea what happened to Pierrot.'

The three young people remained silent for a long time.

Franck had changed a great deal over those last few days. He seemed more mature. He had lost his remaining happy-go-lucky boyishness from watching too many young people of his age die, both friends and enemies.

'Don't worry, we'll find him.'

None of them believed it for one moment. Laure was the first to speak.

'General Leclerc's troops are in the Rue Saint-Jacques. Let's go.'

Léa had a hasty wash and removed her bandage, leaving just a small dressing. Her dress was unwearable, it was torn and bloodstained. Franck rummaged in his mother's wardrobe and came back with an armful of colourful dresses.

'They'll probably be a bit big for you but with a belt they should be all right.'

Léa chose a blue floral print dress with a Jeanne Lafaurie label. It had short sleeves. She tied a blue scarf over her head to hide the dressing and slipped on her white platform-soled sandals.

It was a gorgeous day. People were rushing from all directions towards the Rue Saint-Jacques. Women in dressing-gowns hastily slung over their nightdresses, men who had not had time to shave, young mothers carrying their children, kids weaving between people's legs, veterans of the Great War wearing their decorations, students, workers and shop assistants running to greet the Leclerc division.

The Rue Saint-Jacques was a great river of joy on which floated Colonel Billotte's majestic Shermans, decked with bouquets and flags, with thousands of hands reaching out to touch them. Young girls climbed up on to the tanks and kissed the soldiers, not noticing how dirty they were. The crowd waved deliriously, blowing kisses to the victors, holding out their children, crying, laughing and shouting:

'Bravo! Long live France! Thank you! Long live de Gaulle! Bravo! Bravo!'

Laure leapt up on to an armoured car and kissed the driver who joyously struggled. Franck clapped as if he would burst and hailed the soldiers.

Léa felt an outsider in this happy throng. She was almost indifferent. The tanks with their striking names inched past: Austerlitz, Verdun, Saint-Cyr, El Alamein, Mort-Homme, Exupérance . . . Exupérance? Standing by the turret of his tank, a radiant officer with a grimy face was waving to the crowds. His glance swept over Léa.

'Laurent!'

Her cry pierced the rumbling of the engines and the shouts of the crowd. She tried to reach him, but an elbow caught her wounded head and she briefly lost consciousness. A Resistance fighter came to her rescue and managed to steer her away from the throng.

She recovered in a little café in the Rue de la Huchette.

'Here, love, have a little tipple, that'll put you right. It's a good one, I've been saving it for the Victory celebrations.'

Léa took the small glass and drained the amber liquid in one gulp. It exploded in her mouth and at once she felt better.

'Nothing like a good drop of armagnac to bring back the colour to a young girl's cheeks. Another drop?'

So Laurent was there! When she had caught sight of him, her heart had begun to race as it used to when she thought she was in love with him . . . Perhaps she still loved him? With the help of the alcohol, she saw the world through rose-tinted spectacles. It was all over. Shots rang out.

'Go home, watch out for gunmen on the rooftops.'

The street emptied as if by magic, bringing Léa down to earth again. Laurent was there all right, but Camille was dead. At the thought of having to break the news to him, she felt faint again. To have to deal with his grief seemed beyond her strength. Let someone else tell him. She was ashamed of her cowardice and blushed. She should be the one to tell him. Camille would not have wanted it otherwise.

Tanks had drawn up in the square in front of Notre-Dame, but she could not see the one called Exupérance. A column of armoured cars was driving along the embankment. The Parisians were commenting on what they saw:

'Did you see those? If we'd had those in '40, we wouldn't have lost the war.'

'Are you sure they're French, with uniforms like that?'

'It's the American uniform . . . it is more practical than puttees . . .'

'All the same, we can't recognize our own soldiers . . .'

'Who cares about their uniform, English, American or Russian? What matters is that they've arrived. Long live de Gaulle! Long live France!'

Léa walked along the embankment, oblivious of the crush, suffering from such profound exhaustion that she was incapable of thinking coherently. Her fuzzy thoughts were going round and round inside her head.

'Laurent's alive! What's happened to Pierrot? I've lost Laure and Franck . . . I must tell my aunts . . . Have they heard from Françoise . . . ? Has Charles had any milk today . . . ?

'Laurent's back! How am I going to tell him about Camille? Why is everybody clapping? Ah! yes, Leclerc's soldiers are here . . . Laurent's with them . . . What about François, where's he . . . ?'

'Excuse me, mademoiselle,' said a news reporter with a cine-camera on his shoulder, who had just bumped into her.

She had reached the Place Saint-Michel. She went up to Franck's apartment but there was no sign of him or of Laure. Fifteen or so 'fifis' were occupying the flat. She tried, unsuccessfully, to speak to them. In their excitement, they were incapable of listening to a word she said. But she had to leave a message, as the telephone, which had worked throughout the last few crazy days, seemed to have gone on strike. In Franck's mother's bedroom, she found a lipstick with which she wrote on all the mirrors in the apartment:

'I've gone back to my aunts'. Perhaps Laurent, Françoise and Pierrot will be there.'

That thought had struck her as she climbed the stairs. She had rushed to the telephone, full of hope, but when the line had remained dead, she decided to return to the Rue de l'Université.

The tanks . . . ! The tanks were all in the Place Saint-Michel, surrounded by a rapturous crowd who greeted them with cheers and applause. Léa elbowed her way through to the nearest tank, climbed up on one of the wheels and jumped up on to the turret.

'Do you know where Lieutenant d'Argilat is?'

'No, I haven't seen the captain since we left Porte d'Orléans.'

In the middle of the tumult, orders rang out.

'Get down, we're going to attack the Senate House.'

'Please, if you see him, tell him that Exupérance . . .'

'That's the name of his tank!'

'I know. Tell him Exupérance is in Paris at her aunts.'

'All right, but in exchange, I want a kiss.'

Léa willingly kissed him.

'You won't forget, will you?'

'Is he your boyfriend? He's lucky to have such a good friend. I give my word, I shan't forget. Unless I'm killed, of course.'

That remark upset her. Of course, if he was killed . . .

She jumped down from the Sherman and watched the tanks manoeuvring. They set off down the narrow Rue Saint-André-des-Arts, cheered on by the crowds lining the pavements in front of the shops with their metal blinds lowered, some of which bore chalk messages: 'Warning: Free French car no . . . is occupied by four militiamen. Shoot them.'

The column turned left and headed in the direction of Odéon. Léa continued down the Rue de Buci. 'It's only midday,' she thought as she looked at the hands of the clock both on the figure twelve. The cafés had opened their doors again. She had a shandy in the bar in the Rue Bourbon-le-Château among the local residents who were commenting on the latest events. One of them claimed he had seen tanks and American trucks on the Pont-Neuf.

A few French flags were hanging out of various apartment windows. People stood on the doorsteps exchanging opinions, darting the occasional anxious glance up at the rooftops.

In the Rue de l'Université, the door of her aunts' apartment was wide open. In the hall was an unusual mess. 'My God! Charles!' she thought, rushing to his room. He was sitting on his bed, quietly leafing through a picture book which had belonged to Léa's mother. His tired little face lit up.

'You're back! I was so scared you wouldn't come back.'

'Darling, how can you say such a thing! I'd never leave you. Have you had breakfast?'

'Yes, but it wasn't very nice. It's a lovely day. Can we go out for a walk?'

'Not today. The war's still going on outside.'

'I know, I heard shots and people shouting earlier. Aunt Albertine even went out crying.'

'I bet she's heard that Pierrot's dead,' thought Léa.

'I'll be back, I'm going to see Aunt Lisa.'

She found Lisa and Estelle crying in the kitchen.

'Here you are at last!' exclaimed her aunt.

'What's the matter? What's going on?'

The two women sobbed all the more. They opened their mouths but no sound came out.

'Will you please tell me what the matter is.'

Estelle managed to gasp:

'Mademoiselle Françoise . . .'

Léa felt shivers run up and down her spine.

'What about Françoise? What's happened to her?'

'She's been . . . arrested . . .'

'When?'

Estelle shrugged.

'The woman from the dairy in the Rue du Bac came and told us,' said Lisa in one breath. 'Albertine left at once without even putting her hat on.'

In other circumstances that remark would have amused

217

Léa. But Albertine not stopping to put her hat on was an indication that it was something very serious.

'Where has she gone?'

'To the square in front of the church.'

'How long ago did she leave?'

'About half an hour.'

'I'm going too. Look after Charles.'

'Don't go! Don't go!' cried Lisa clutching her sleeve.

Wordlessly, Léa shook herself free and left the apartment.

Chapter 19

It was a glorious day, and there was a carnival atmosphere in the air. In the street, pretty girls in short, flimsy dresses, wearing rosettes or little tricolours in their hair, walked past laughing. Elegant women, usually seen at Sunday Mass, had abandoned their habitual haughtiness. Elderly women on the arms of elderly gentlemen walked with a new-found spring in their step. They were all hurrying in the direction of the square.

Although she knew what she was about to see, Léa stopped in her tracks in amazement. The square was a sea of faces.

At the top of the steps leading up to the church, which had witnessed other scenes in the past, a drama was being enacted before a jeering, crowing, mocking audience who were encouraging the participants with shouts and gestures. The stage, which was extremely bare, was impressive because of its very simplicity. There were a few benches, a straw-bottomed chair, and, pinned to the door of the sanctuary with a dagger, was a large sheet of paper on which was written in black ink:

FREE HAIRCUTS HERE. The play had already begun. The actors were playing their parts to perfection. The host, a fat man in his shirt sleeves with an Free French armband, was barking out the crimes of the actresses:

'Look at the Michaud woman, who denounced her husband to the Gestapo. Does she deserve the indulgence of the people's tribunal?'

'No, no,' yelled the audience.

'Sooooo . . .'

'Shaaaaave her head! Ha! ha! ha!'

A wave of laughter rippled through the crowd.

On the improvised stage, the attendants of the popular tribunal forced the Michaud woman to sit down on the chair. The 'hairdresser' appeared armed with a pair of large dressmaking scissors which he twirled and snapped shut above her head, undulating like Maurice Chevalier singing:

> 'Avez-vous vu le nouveau chapeau de Zozo,
> C'est un chapeau un chapeau rigolo
> Sur le devant on a mis une p'tite plume de paon.
> Sur le côté un amour de perroquet'*

Near Léa, a fat girl wearing the white overalls of a dairy worker or butcher stood clutching a fireman's arm, writhing and hiccuping with laughter.

'I'm going to wet myself in a minute . . . Ha! ha! ha! I tell you, I'm going to wet my knickers . . . Ha! ha! ha! I've wet myself!'

The crowd roared with laughter, swaying from side to side. Léa felt seasick. She saw the long locks of hair being held up, like the tail or ears of a bull in the ring, greeted by cries that reminded her of a corrida. Hands were outstretched to rab those sad trophies.

After most of the hair had been cut, her head was shaved.

The woman collapsed on the chair, her face puffy, streaked with spittle and tears. She was suffering the just and deserved punishment for having, perhaps, denounced her husband to the Gestapo. What did it matter that she said he had joined the Resistance in Corrèze to avoid doing compulsory labour. Had not a neighbour overheard her telling a German soldier who asked her for directions . . .

Léa could feel the cold metal of the clippers against her skull . . . Several women standing near her had fallen silent. One of them wiped away a tear, perhaps out of a feeling of

---

* Have you seen Zozo's new hat
  It's a funny funny hat
  With a little peacock feather in front
  And a darling little parrot on the side

solidarity, at last, with this humiliated creature, who looked ridiculous with her tiny head poking out of the neck of a floral dress, wearing round her neck a placard on which a clumsy hand had written: WHORE WHO SOLD OUT HER HUSBAND.

Two men raised the woman from the chair and pushed her over to join those who had already been shorn, who made room for her on their bench. She sat near a mother cradling her child.

Léa scanned the women who still had their hair, desperately seeking Françoise.

A tall, elegant, dark-haired girl took her place on the chair. 'Look, ladies and gentlemen. She looks as though butter wouldn't melt in her mouth. Well, ladies and gentlemen, she's a bitch who preferred to give her arse to the Germans than to a brave Frenchman. What does she deserve?'

'To be shooooorn . . .'

It was a game, a farce, a comedy, a mystery play like the ones that used to take place outside churches for the edification of the faithful. But this was neither the *Mystery of the Mad Virgins and the Good Virgins*, nor was it the *Game of Marriage or of the Leafy Canopies*, but it was certainly the *Mystery of the Passion*. It was not the version that had been enacted in Valenciennes in 1597, for which the audience paid two farthings, but it was that of those wonderful and absurd, cowardly and magnanimous, brave and stupid, heroic and foolish days France experienced during the early days of liberation.

The elegant dark-haired woman was not crying. She sat up very straight, her face pale and proud. A curl fell on to her white hands which were crossed on her knees. Her fingers closed over the warm lock. The crowd fell silent. They were expecting cries and tears. All she did was smile scornfully while fingers released the handful of hair. A disappointed mumble ran through the crowd.

Irritated by her dignity, the 'hairdresser' wielded the scissors with more brutality than usual, hurting his client. Blood ran down her cheek.

'Oh!' gasped the crowd.

221

Léa clenched her fists and looked away. Was nobody going to put a stop to this abomination? Luckily Françoise was not among them. But . . . ?

The woman who was rocking the child looked up. She reminded Léa of Françoise when she emerged from the water after bathing in the Garonne . . . Her heart thudded painfully. No . . . no . . . that wasn't her sister sitting up there! 'I'm glad mummy and daddy are dead, it would have been too much for them,' she thought. A hand was placed on her arm. It was Albertine. The elderly woman's face reflected all the horror in the world. Léa put her arm round her shoulders, astonished at being the one to comfort her aunt, and at how the woman seemed to have shrunk.

The woman's head was shorn. The victim sat up and cast such a scornful look at the crowd that they grumbled and a few insults were hurled at her, while she haughtily joined the other women on the bench, ignoring the bloodstains on her dress.

Another woman, this time screaming and crying, was dragged to the chair, where she fell to her knees stammering:

'Forgive me . . . forgive me . . . I won't do it again . . . forgive me . . .'

The scissors snapped threateningly above her head.

'That's enough. Be quiet.'

A young man in golfing breeches, armed with a gun, leapt up the steps. The 'hairdresser' appeared to know him as he simply said as he grabbed a handful of the unfortunate woman's hair:

'Let us get on with our job.'

He snipped off the thick ringlet.

The boy brought the barrel of the gun down on the fingers of the brute, who dropped the scissors.

'You have no right to do this. If these women are guilty, they will be given a fair trial. You must hand them over to the police.'

Finally, uniformed police officers came out of the police station which was squeezed between the church and an apartment block.

'Move along . . . move along . . . there's nothing to

see . . . Go home . . . There's nothing to see . . . Don't worry, these women will get the punishment they deserve.'

The square gradually emptied and the police officers took the women inside the police station while the dispensers of justice adjusted their armbands, their cartridge belts or their revolvers and went on their way laughing. Soon, everyone had disappeared, and only Léa and her aunt remained rooted to the spot. In unison, they turned to face the police station.

Inside the cramped building, utter chaos reigned. The police officers had no idea what to do with the crying women, some of whom lay prostrate. The young man in golf breeches was on the telephone. He hung up.

'Headquarters are sending a bus to take them . . .'

'Where? To the station in La Roquette?' asked a police officer.

'No, we're taking them to the Vélodrome d'Hiver with a Free French escort.'

'That's funny,' laughed another, 'that's where they took the Jews.'

Léa recalled what Sarah Mulstein had written to her about the round-up of Jews in the famous stadium and stared in amazement at the officer who found it 'funny'.

'Go home, ladies, you have no business here.'

'I've come to fetch my niece, monsieur.'

The men gaped in astonishment at this white-haired old lady who said with quiet dignity: 'I've come to fetch my niece.' She had a cheek.

'That isn't possible, madame. These women are accused of collaborating with the enemy, they must be tried by the competent authority.'

Léa suddenly saw Françoise and little Pierre.

'Françoise!'

She looked up blankly, without appearing to recognize her sister.

'Françoise, it's me, Léa. It's over. We've come to take you home.'

'That is out of the question, mademoiselle. This person was arrested in the company of the mistresses of German officers . . .'

'I never slept with a German,' shouted the Michaud woman, 'we met those women in the street, we've been put in with them by mistake.'

'Be quiet, the court will be the judge of that. Would you ladies kindly leave.'

'Please monsieur. I can answer for her. She's my niece, monsieur, I've known her since she was tiny . . .'

'Don't keep on at me, madame.'

'You're not going to put her in prison with her child?'

The young man looked from Françoise and her son to Mademoiselle de Montpleynet. He seemed perplexed.

'I don't know about the child . . . I'll agree to allow you to take him, if she'll let you.'

Little Pierre, who had recognized Léa, held his arms out to her.

'Do you want us to look after him?'

Without a word, Françoise held him out to her sister.

'Leave us your names and addresses,' said the eldest police officer.

'When will we be able to visit her?'

'I don't know, madame. You'll have to wait. You will be informed.'

Françoise held out her hand to Léa.

'What do you want?'

'Oh, I should have thought of it before,' Léa thought as she removed her blue headscarf. She tenderly knotted it under her sister's chin.

Chapter 20

Léa accompanied her aunt and Françoise's son to the apartment, then she ran out again like a fugitive and got on her bicycle. She wanted to be alone, to try and think about everything that had happened, and above all, to find Laurent.

The Boulevard Saint-Germain was like a promenade as far as the church of Saint-Germain-des-Prés. All the local residents were out walking. After the Rue Bonaparte, the atmosphere was different. The carefree strollers were replaced by groups wearing armbands and carrying guns, young people in white coats marked with a red cross and housewives hugging the walls in their search for a shop that might be open in the Rue de Buci. One of them stopped Léa and clung to her handlebars.

'Don't go past the Rue de Seine. For the last three days, the Germans have been firing shells at the Senate House. They go from one street to the next. Several people have been killed or injured.'

'Thank you, madame. I'm trying to get to the Place Saint-Michel. Which way should I go?'

'If I were you, I wouldn't go. It's very dangerous all around that area. Leclerc's men are going to attack the Luxemburg Palace . . .'

As if to confirm the woman's warning, a shell burst in front of the fishmonger's, shattering the remaining windows and injuring three passers-by in the legs and face.

Pushing her bicycle, Léa returned the way she had come and went to sit down in the little square at the foot of the former archbishop's palace. All the benches were taken up by people sleeping. Boys and girls, ensconced in the sandpit, were passing a bottle round. Léa sat apart from the others, leaning up against a tree. She closed her eyes, trying to order her thoughts; there were so many horrific images chasing each other round in her mind. She shook her head vigorously and then started banging it against the trunk with increasing violence to banish those unbearable images. She was unaware of the tears streaming down her face.

'Stop it, you'll hurt yourself!'

A dirty, sticky little hand had caught her head and was holding it still.

'Here, have a drink, it'll do you good.'

Léa snatched the bottle and drank straight from it so avidly that wine trickled down her neck.

'That's pretty good going for a girl,' said the kid, who could not have been more than fifteen, as he took the almost empty bottle from her. 'Nothing like a good bottle of plonk to cheer you up. It's Burgundy, we nicked it from the wine merchant's. Do you want a cigarette?'

Léa nodded.

She dragged on the cigarette with pleasure, inhaling one puff after another, as she felt herself becoming slightly tipsy.

'Feeling better? Good. Here, we've got some water from the fountain, wash your face.'

While she did as he suggested, he continued to question her:

'Why are you crying? Have you lost your boyfriend? Your father then? You don't want to talk? Never mind! Here, have another drink. You're pretty, you know.'

The admiration in the boy's voice made her smile.

'There, you're much prettier when you smile. Don't you think so, the rest of you?'

The boys agreed noisily, jostling and sniggering stupidly. The only girl in the group conspicuously looked away.

'Your girlfriend's jealous.'

'Rita? Never mind, it doesn't matter. What's your name?'

'Léa. What's yours?'

'Marcel. My friends call me Cécel. These are my mates. That's Alphonse, he's Polo, that's Vonvon, and he's Fanfan, and the fat one's . . .'

'Shut up, I'm not fat!'

Léa and the others burst out laughing.

'He doesn't like us saying he's fat, and yet he's not exactly thin, in spite of rationing. His name's Minou, and she's Rita.'

They all shook her hand except Rita, who contented herself with a nod.

'We're from the thirteenth district. We haven't been home since the 19th.'

'Your parents must be worried about you?'

'Don't worry about them, they don't worry about us. The last we heard of them, they were playing heroes and fighting for the Republic. As for us, we've been acting as messengers for Colonel Rol and Colonel Fabien since the beginning . . .'

'So you know my cousin, Pierrot Delmas, from Bordeaux,' Léa broke in excitedly.

'It's possible, but there are a lot of us.'

'He was wounded yesterday in the Boulevard Saint-Michel. Nobody's seen him since.'

'Oh no! You're not going to start crying again. I promise we'll go and look for your cousin. What does he look like?'

'He's about my height, with dark brown hair and blue eyes . . .'

'What was he wearing?'

'Khaki trousers, a green and blue checked shirt, a grey cotton jacket and he was wearing an armband and carrying a revolver.'

'Vonvon, go to the sewers and find out about this chap. We'll meet at you-know-where this evening. Rita, you check the hospitals on the left bank and Minou, you do the right bank. Meet you same time, same place. Is that clear?'

'Yes, boss!'

'Are you the boss?'

'That's right! Fanfan, you go the Rue Abbé-de-l'Epée with Polo and see whether Fabien needs us. Say hello to my brother while you're about it.'

'I doubt if I'll see him, he'll be fighting at the Senate House.'

'Is your brother in the police?'

'No, he's a metal worker. When they wanted to send him

227

to work in Germany in '43, he joined the Resistance in the Upper Saône region. That's where he met Fabien, alias Albert, alias Captain Henri and after his escape, Commander Patrie. For a while, he distributed leaflets, kept a lookout and acted as liaison officer. After September, he took part in all the sabotage actions in the area. As part of the Liberté group, he blew up the Conflandey lock and attacked a German post near Semondans where three Germans were killed. He sabotaged railway lines and blew up bridges and engines, all under Fabien's orders. Today, Fabien announced that he was going to take the Luxemburg Palace. He'll do it, you'll see, especially now Leclerc and his men are here to give him a hand.'

His enthusiasm took Léa's mind off things for a while.

'I'm famished,' said Alphonse, 'let's go for a bite to eat.'

'Good idea. Are you coming with us?'

'I don't know.'

'Don't think about it too long, it's not good for you. You must eat, that'll clear your brain.'

'You're right. Where are we going?'

'To the Rue du Dragon. A friend of my father's is a waitress in a bar there. The owner's got a soft spot for me and the grub isn't too bad . . . Bring your bicycle otherwise it'll get nicked.'

Cécel's father's friend showed them to a little table under a spiral staircase. She brought them a thick split-pea purée with sausages and a carafe of wine. After two mouthfuls, Léa pushed her plate away, unable to eat.

'Aren't you hungry?'

'No,' she replied, draining her glass.

She drank two or three glasses in a row, under the fascinated gaze of Cécel and Alphonse.

All afternoon, Léa and her new friends sat drinking a horrifying mixture of wines, liqueurs and spirits. At about five o'clock, Fanfan came rushing into the bistro, so breathless that he could hardly speak.

'They've signed . . . it's over . . . Choltitz has signed the capitulation . . .'

'Hurray!'

'So? Is the war over?'

'Go on, tell us, who else signed?'

'Wait for it: we signed too.'

'You're kidding,' said Cécel huskily.

'No I'm not kidding. Colonel Rol, the leader of the Ile de France Free French Forces, signed the act of surrender with General Leclerc and General von Choltitz.'

'Bravo, let's celebrate . . . !'

'Don't you think you've had enough to drink?'

'You can't drink too much when you're celebrating victory.'

'Don't talk of victory too soon. They're still fighting over at the Luxemburg Palace, in the barracks in the Place de la République, in the Bourbon Palace, in certain metro stations and in the suburbs.'

'I'm not worried, Fabien will clear all that up. How are things going?'

'Well. Leclerc's tanks are holding the Rue de Vaugirard, The Free French and the Moroccan Spahis have entered the gardens via the Rue Auguste-Comte entrance, and police cars with loudspeakers are driving around the area warning that they'll be bombing it at about seven o'clock tonight if the Germans don't surrender. The cease-fire starts at 6.35 p.m. But I don't think we'll need to send the planes in. Are you coming with me?'

'We can't leave her here like this.'

'I want to come with you,' stuttered Léa.

'You must be mad! Look at the state you're in!'

'I want to fight with the tanks.'

'Come on, we're not going to hang around for a bird who's had too much to drink.'

'I'm not drunk! I'm a bit tipsy because I've been celebrating the arrival of our valiant heroes . . .'

'Off you go, I'll look after her,' said the waitress. 'Get up, dear. You're going to lie down upstairs.'

'All right, but I want a little drink.'

'You go upstairs and I'll bring you something to drink.'

'You will look after her, promise?'

'You know you can rely on me, Cécel. My word, anyone would think you'd fallen in love . . . I know someone who won't be very pleased about that.'

The boy shrugged as he left the restaurant.

They managed to haul Léa into the upstairs room which served as store room, living-room and bedroom. As soon as her head touched the pillow, she fell asleep with her mouth open and soon she was gently snoring.

Chapter 21

She slept until the evening. The noise from the restaurant could be heard through the half-open door. There was great excitement. Léa sat up. She had a terrible hangover.

'What on earth am I doing here?' she asked aloud.

She could hear footsteps coming up the spiral staircase. The door swung open to reveal Rita and Alphonse. Rita was looking at her with an insane expression.

'Why did you let him go? Why?' she screamed, rushing headlong at Léa with her fist raised. Léa ducked, but not quickly enough. Rita punched her in the face which made her headache even worse and revived the pain of her wound. She slid off the bed, her head in her hands, groaning. The girl flew at her, grabbed her by the hair and slapped her furiously.

'Stop it,' grumbled Alphonse.

'Get out of here, I'm going to beat the hell out of this bitch.'

'Stop it, I tell you. Cécel wouldn't have wanted you to do this,' said Alphonse, trying to restrain her.

Her hand remained suspended in mid air. Her fingers slowly loosened their grip on Léa's hair which flopped limply round her face.

Rita's eyes went from Léa's slumped body to Alphonse's face, as if she were trying to understand what was happening to her.

Alphonse clumsily put his arm round her. He tried to comfort her:

'It's not her fault. When Cécel saw his brother injured, he went beserk.'

'I'd rather he'd slept with her instead . . .' Rita stammered.

Léa had managed to get to her feet. She stared blankly at them for she had no idea what this was all about.

'What happened?'

Before answering, the boy blew his nose noisily.

'Cécel was shot in the Rue de Tournon.'

'Oh no!'

Rita looked her straight in the eyes and blurted out:

'Oh yes! And your cousin's dead too!'

'Shut up, Rita!'

'Why should I? Why should I be the only one to suffer?'

'How do you know?'

'From one of Colonel Rol's lieutenants. Your cousin was taken to Val-de-Grâce. That's where they found him. You'd do better to go home.'

'Poor Cécel, how did it happen?'

'We'd just gone into the combat zone. In the Rue Garancière we met his brother, Clément, who yelled at us to take cover. Cécel didn't want to and we followed them, keeping close to the walls in the Rue Vaugirard. Bullets were flying all over the place. A Jerry came out from behind a burning tank and machine-gunned everything in sight. Clément was hit in the legs. He hung around for a moment and the Fritz just took his time and emptied his gun into him. Then he went off towards the Senate House. Cécel yelled like mad . . . I tried to hold him back. He leapt out, without a gun, picked up his brother's and started chasing the fellow with the sub-machine gun. He stopped, turned round and I think he was smiling. They aimed their guns at the same time . . . Cécel got him in the face . . . He blasted my mate to smithereens . . . There, that's what happened!'

The three young people stood there helplessly, crying like lost children over the fifteen-year-old boy who had just died on a sunny August afternoon in 1944, on the day Paris was liberated.

Rita and Alphonse dried their eyes and went out without a word. Left alone, Léa flung herself sobbing on to the bed.

She kept seeing Cécel and her cousin's faces. Their laughter was ringing in her ears.

'They're dead! They're dead!' she sobbed into the pillow.

Paris joyfully dismantled the barricades. There was wine, laughter and gaiety. The sun was shining. On the Pont-Neuf, people were dancing to the music of an accordion. Girls wore their hair piled up in complicated chignons or loose on their shoulders. They twirled round in the arms of Free French soldiers or Leclerc's men, who had been given late passes. In the Rue Mazarine, the Rue Dauphine and the Rue de l'Ancienne Comédie, the pavements were covered with broken glass. Along the embankment, and in the Place Saint-Michel, the charred remains of burnt-out cars, trucks and tanks were a reminder of the violence of the fighting. In places, humble bunches of flowers left in the road marked the spot where a man, a woman or a child had died. Some people fell to their knees by the brown stains.

Léa walked slowly down the Quai des Grands-Augustins, trailing her hands along the stone walls and wooden bookstalls that were still warm from the afternoon sun. In the Place Saint-Michel, tanks were manoeuvring to the cheers of the crowd. Leaning against the parapet, Léa watched them go past, feeling unhappy and bewildered. The setting sun caught her hair, making it look like a fiery halo. The soldiers yelled to her from their tanks, signalling to her to come and join the other girls who had climbed up and were flocking round them.

'Léa!'

She heard someone shout her name above the din and looked round to see where it could have come from.

'Léa!'

A man was waving to her from his tank.

'Laurent!'

She had to fight her way through the crowd to reach him. He stopped his tank and held out a hand to help her up. Taking no notice of his men's amused grins, he hugged her and babbled her name. To Léa, everything felt unreal: what was she doing standing on a tank that was heading for the

Town Hall in the glorious sunset, in the arms of a soldier who smelled so strongly of gunpowder, oil, grease and sweat that she felt quite dizzy? It was Laurent! Laurent who was telling her how happy he was to find her looking so beautiful on this blessed day, how happy he was to see his wife and son again. What was he talking about? She didn't understand . . . Now wasn't the time to talk of unpleasant things . . . They were there, well and truly alive, laughing and crying in each other's arms. Something was screaming deep down inside her, like a caged animal that wanted to get out. How was she going to tell him? Later . . . I'll tell him tomorrow . . .

At Châtelet, American tanks joined Leclerc's as the Parisians cheered and waved.

'Long live America!'

'Long live France!'

'Long live de Gaulle!'

The passionate enthusiasm of the crowd was contagious. Léa began to feel excited. She snuggled closer to Laurent.

The tank Exupérance stopped by the Saint-Jacques tower where Captain Buis was waiting.

'Well, d'Argilat, you haven't wasted any time!'

'It's not what you think, Buis . . .'

'I don't think anything, I'm merely making an observation.'

Laurent jumped down from the tank and held out his arms. Léa slid down into them.

Couples were forming all around them. Laughter was becoming shriller, words more serious, gestures more precise and there was no doubt as to the meaning of the looks being exchanged. Everybody was preparing to celebrate the liberation of Paris in the simplest and most natural way: by making love.

Léa looked up into Laurent's eyes.

'Camille is dead.'

It was like an explosion. Everything burst, then died, around Laurent. All that remained were the cold, dim lights which crowned the objects and figures moving with dreamlike slowness with a faint glow . . . It was like a night of freezing fog in the middle of August, out of which the dead were rising . . . What did they care about a French soldier in an American uniform leaning on his tank which bore the name of a forgotten saint and crying his heart out? Nothing. They happened to be passing, perhaps awakened by the blaring music, or the lovers' sighs which echoed from east to west, from the banks of the Seine to the back street doorways, making Paris the capital of pleasure that night.

Léa watched the man she had loved suffering. She felt tremendous pity but was incapable of comforting him: she was so deprived herself. She had no strength or hope left.

'Charles is fine.'

That was all she had managed to say.

'What's the matter with you, old chap? Bad news?' asked Captain Buis, placing his hand on his comrade's shoulder.

Laurent stood up, making no effort to conceal the tears streaming down his grimy face.

'I've just heard that my wife is dead.'

'I'm so sorry. How did she die?'

'I don't know,' he replied, turning to Léa with an inquiring look.

'She was killed by the Germans and the militiamen when they attacked a farm where the Resistance were hiding.'

The three of them remained silent, strangers to the merriment that was going on all around them. Buis was the first to pull himself together.

'Come on, the boss wants to see you.'

'Coming . . . Léa, where's my son?'

'He's with me, at my aunts' in the Rue de l'Université.'

'I'll try and get leave tomorrow. Give Charles my love.'

'Goodbye, mademoiselle, I'll look after him.'

Numb with exhaustion and grief, Léa dragged herself along the Rue Jacob, jostled by passers-by drunk with happiness and wine. In the Rue de l'Université, she remained sitting on the stairs for ages, too weak to climb them. The light went on: 'Well, well, the electricity's been switched back on,' she thought. She managed to haul herself up to her aunts' apartment and ring the bell.

'Coming! Coming! Who is it? This is no time to ring the bell! Mademoiselle Léa! Haven't you got your key? What's the matter? Oh my God! Mademoiselle Albertine! Mademoiselle Lisa!'

'What's the matter, Estelle?'

'Léa! Quick, Lisa, Laure . . .'

Helped by her sister and her niece, Albertine carried Léa on to the divan in the parlour. Léa's pallor, her pinched nostrils and freezing hands frightened Lisa.

Albertine bathed her forehead with cold water. Her nostrils relaxed and her face trembled. Her eyes opened and slowly she looked round the room. What a nightmare she'd had! Who was the child Laure was holding? Why did she cry as she kissed the baby's soft blond hair? Where was the baby's mother?

'NO!'

Her cry of despair made the four women jump and woke the baby, and Charles, who came pattering into the room rubbing his eyes. He clambered on to the divan and snuggled up to her.

'Don't be frightened, I'm here.'

'He's been crying all day and calling for her,' whispered Estelle to Lisa, 'and now he's comforting her. What a funny child!'

Léa raised her hands to her forehead and groaned.

'Estelle, will you prepare some herb tea for Mademoiselle Léa and bring some aspirin.'

'Very well, mademoiselle.'

'Calm down, darling. We were so worried.'

'Have you any news of Françoise?'

'No,' replied Laure. 'When Aunt Albertine telephoned me to tell me what had happened, I came as quickly as I could. Frank and one of his friends searched everywhere they thought they might find Françoise, but they couldn't find out a thing. We don't know where she is. What about you, where have you been?'

Léa ignored her question.

'I saw Laurent.'

'Oh! Some good news at last.'

'Pierrot's dead.'

Laure said nothing. She already knew.

'Poor thing,' said Lisa, 'I'll pray for him.'

The elderly spinster did not see the look of hatred Léa shot her.

'Have you got a cigarette?' Léa asked her sister.

'Here,' said Laure, tossing over a packet with a red circle on it.

'Lucky Strike. I've never smoked one of these.'

Estelle brought in the herb tea sweetened with honey which she had managed to obtain from the haberdasher in the Rue de Seine, and some aspirin tablets.

Albertine picked up Charles, who had fallen asleep, while Lisa put Françoise's baby to bed. The two sisters sat sipping herb tea and smoking in silence.

Chapter 22

The sound of people shouting and singing came floating in through the open windows. It was unusual for this quiet district. Laure got up and switched on the wireless.

'Listen, we are about to broadcast General de Gaulle's speech from outside the Town Hall.

'Why should we hide the emotion which holds us all in its grip, all of us, men and women, who are here, at home, in Paris. A Paris which rose up to liberate itself and succeeded in doing so with its own hands. No! We will not hide that deep and sacred emotion. There are moments which are greater than any of our own lives . . .

'Paris! Paris violated! Paris broken! Paris tortured! But now, Paris liberated! Liberated by its own citizens, liberated by its own people with the assistance of the Armies of France, with the help and support of the whole nation, of fighting France, of the only France, the true France, of eternal France.

'Well! Now the enemy who was holding Paris has surrendered into our hands, France can come home, to Paris. She comes home bloody but resolute. She comes home enlightened by this great lesson, but more certain than ever before of her duties and her rights.'

There was a power cut, silencing the voice of the man who, for four years, had been the symbol of hope for France. That evening, he was governing France from the Ministry of War which the Germans had vacated only a few hours earlier.

Laure lit the oil lamp on the little table beside the divan where her sister was lying.

'I'm going to bed and you should do the same. We'll see if we can sort things out tomorrow.'

'Yes, we'll see . . . goodnight.'

'Goodnight.'

The yellow glow from the oil lamp emphasized the silence of the parlour whose old-fashioned charm reminded Léa a little of Montillac. She sighed and lit another cigarette. As she put the packet down on the table, she noticed the headlines in the newspaper lying there: FRENCH TROOPS ARRIVED AT THE TOWN HALL, YESTERDAY, AT 10 P.M. The leader article was signed François Mauriac and she began reading:

'In the saddest hour of our fate, French hope resided in one man; it died through the voice of that man – of that man alone. How many French people came to share his solitude then, those who had understood in their own fashion the meaning of: giving oneself to France?'

The print swam before Léa's eyes.

'The Fourth Republic is the daughter of martyrs. It was born from bloodshed, the blood of martyrs. This blood, of communists, nationals, Christians and Jews has baptized us all with that same baptism of which General de Gaulle remains the living symbol . . . We have no illusions about mankind . . . I am reminded of the lines of old Hugo which have often soothed my grief during these four years:
"O libre France enfin surgie!
O robe blanche après l'orgie!" '*

The paper slipped from Léa's hands: she was asleep.

Once again, she was being pursued by the ghost of the man from Orléans, this time armed with a giant pair of scissors.

---

* Oh free France finally arisen!
Oh white gown after the orgy!

Just as he reached her, she woke up soaked in perspiration. She was unable to fall asleep again until dawn.

It was the smell of coffee – real coffee . . . ? Where on earth did it come from, that rare commodity enticing her from her restless sleep? Strangely, apart from a slight headache, she felt fine. Laure came in bearing a tray on which stood a steaming cup of coffee.

'Coffee?'

'You could call it that. Laurent brought it.'

'Laurent's here?'

'Yes, he's in your room with Charles.'

Léa shot out of bed.

'No, don't go in. Charles is telling him how his mother died. Here, drink this while it's hot.'

'It tastes like real coffee. What is it?'

'It's powder made from coffee. Apparently, it's American.'

'Still no news of Françoise?'

'No, but Franck telephoned. He met someone who's in charge of the arrests, an old friend of his father's . . .'

'I thought his father was more or less a collaborator?'

'Yes, so is the other chap.'

'I don't understand.'

'It's quite simple. When the rebels began to gain the upper hand, a lot of collaborators changed sides and went over to the Free French. Some are even said to have shown great courage. When Franck met his father's friend, wearing an armband with the Lorraine cross on it, he was surprised. When the collaborator recognized him, he was afraid he'd give him away. That's why he agreed to find out where Françoise was being detained. If all goes well, we should have news by this evening.'

'What about Pierrot?'

'His body's at the morgue, Albertine and I went to identify it yesterday.'

'Yesterday? But you didn't say anything to me about it.'

'What would have been the point? We'll have to inform Uncle Luc. Aunt Albertine promised she'd tell him as soon as the telephone lines between Paris and Bordeaux are open.'

There was a knock at the door.

'Come in.'

It was Laurent, holding Charles. Their eyes were red.

'Léa, daddy's back.'

'Hello, Léa. General Leclerc is waiting for me, I can't stay any longer. I'll come back after the procession down the Champs-Elysées. Thank you for everything,' he added, kissing her on the forehead. 'See you this evening, Charles.'

'I want to ride on your tank with you.'

'I'm afraid you can't, darling. Another time.'

The little boy began to grizzle. Léa hugged him.

'Don't cry. We'll go and watch daddy later on.'

'Promise?'

'Yes.'

Laurent kissed his son goodbye and left.

'How unhappy he looks,' thought Léa.

A huge red, white and blue flag was fluttering over the Arc de Triomphe. The weather was glorious and there was not a cloud in the sky. More than a million Parisians lined the route where General de Gaulle, Generals Leclerc, Juin and Koenig, the Resistance leaders and the Free French were to parade. The streets were a sea of faces, stretching from the Place de l'Etoile to the Place de la Concorde and all the way to Notre-Dame. The small American news plane circled above the crowds. Léa and Laure, each holding one of Charles's hands, gradually began to share the general euphoria.

'Here they are! Here they come!'

From their vantage point on the balustrade of the Tuileries gardens, overlooking the Place de la Concorde, they could see a great river, with flags and banners bobbing everywhere, surging towards them. A tall man marched in front, alone, preceded by four French tanks: Lauraguais, Limagne, Limousin and Vercelon. He was General de Gaulle. The procession came to a halt while the military band played the *Marseillaise* and the *Marche Lorraine*. The words rose from thousands of lips.

'Long live de Gaulle! Long live France!'

The General saluted the crowds with both hands and then

climbed into the vast convertible black Renault that had been used by Field-Marshal Pétain on his last visit to Paris. Just then, shots rang out.

'The bastards are shooting from the roofs!'

'Lie down.'

People flung themselves to the ground while the armed marshals pushed the women and children to safety behind the tanks and half-tracks.

'What a shambles,' thought Léa as she contemplated the Place de la Concorde – which was now a tangled mass of panic-stricken bodies, tucked-up skirts, fallen bicycles, barbed wire blocks, jeeps and tanks – before crouching down behind the balustrade where she had been dragged by Laure and Charles, who was thrilled. Resistance fighters retaliated in the direction from which the shots had been fired. More intense shooting seemed to be coming from the Gare d'Orsay station and the Rue de Rivoli. The shooting stopped as suddenly as it had begun. The Parisians stood up again and looked around sheepishly.

The two sisters ran across the Tuileries gardens which had been transformed into a parade ground, holding on to Charles, who found the whole performance highly entertaining.

'Aren't you tired?' fussed Léa.

'No, no,' he laughed. 'I want to see daddy on his tank.'

They were about to cross the Avenue Paul-Déroulède, opposite the Arc du Carrousel, when the shooting started up again. They fell to their stomachs on a lawn. Around them, the crowd panicked and chaos ensued as people tried to run away. There was such confusion that the Free French on the other side of the river began shooting at their own men in the Tuileries and the latter, thinking it was an attack by the militia, shot back.

'It would be too ironic to die here,' thought Léa, getting to her feet, after a hail of bullets hit the ground not far away.

Near the Louvre, they met Franck, wheeling his bicycle. Laure sat Charles on the carrier and they made their way towards Notre-Dame.

*

Charles was the proudest and happiest of little boys. He was looking down on the world from the turret of his daddy's tank.

They had come across Laurent at the Town Hall as he rode back from the Place de la Concorde. He told them he would be leaving again in less than an hour.

'You wouldn't guess it from Paris, but in the northern suburbs, the fighting is still going on.'

'But didn't the Germans sign the act of surrender?'

'It's valid for those under the orders of General von Choltitz, but not for the others, or at least, that's what their leaders say. They've taken over Le Bourget and Montmorency forest. They have troops who have just cycled in from the Calais area at their disposal, and tanks from General Major Wahle's 47th Infantry Division . . .'

'Daddy, show me how it works.'

Léa, who had climbed up on to the tank, rapped Charles's knuckles.

'Don't touch anything, you'll blow us all up.'

Laurent laughed mirthlessly. He kissed his son, picked him up and handed him down to Franck, ignoring his protests.

'Take good care of him, Léa. I'll come back and see you as soon as possible. We'll talk about Camille. I want to know everything about her death.'

Charles and the three young people watched the tank manoeuvring. They followed it as far as the Boulevard Sébastopol.

Franck saw them back to the Rue de l'Université and promised to return that evening with news of Françoise and some food.

Charles was worn out from the walk and he complained of a headache. Estelle took his temperature and found he was slightly feverish. The elderly maid grumbled that she had warned them . . . that he ought not to go out yet, that he had not fully recovered yet. Léa put him to bed and stayed with him, his little hand clutching hers, until he dropped off. No doubt she had overestimated her own strength, for she too fell asleep.

An insistent rumbling woke her up. Léa looked at her watch: 11.30 p.m.! The bedroom was dark, the rumbling grew louder. Planes . . . There were planes flying over Paris, probably allied forces planes on their way to bomb the front. The sirens began to wail. The planes seemed to be flying very low. Léa rushed over to the window.

She had not seen so many planes at one time since Orléans. The hail of tracer bullets, the occasional anti-aircraft shots did not seem to have anything to do with them. Suddenly, huge explosions from the Town Hall and Les Halles shattered the night, lighting up the sky.

'We've got to go down into the shelters,' cried Albertine, opening the door, carrying Françoise's baby.

Lisa and Estelle went running down the corridor, their hair dishevelled.

'Go down without me, take Charles with you.'

The little boy, still sleepy, clutched her.

'I don't want to . . . I want to stay with you . . .'

'All right, you can stay here.'

Charles snuggled up to her in one of the large comfortable armchairs in the parlour and fell asleep again. Léa smoked a cigarette while German bombs dropped on the centre of Paris, killing seven nurses in the Bichat hospital and destroying part of the wine market, causing a fire that lit up the capital like a firework display.

At around midnight, the sirens sounded the end of the air-raid. The wail of fire-engines and ambulances replaced the sound of bombs exploding. Everybody went back to bed, but not for long. There was another air-raid warning at about 3 a.m. and once again the Parisians were dragged out of bed.

The following morning, it was discovered that about a hundred people had been killed and five hundred wounded. For those who had believed the war was over, it was a rude awakening.

At dawn on 27th August 1944, Paris was licking its wounds.

That Sunday morning, Mass was said at a barricade surrounded by flags in the Boulevard Saint-Michel by a Free French chaplain, a priest in the Haute-Savoie Resistance, before a large, solemn gathering.

Léa refused to accompany her aunts to High Mass in the church of Saint-Germain-des-Prés.

After several attempts, Albertine de Montpleynet managed to get through to Luc Delmas. The line was very crackly and she had to shout to make herself heard.

'Hello . . . hello . . . can you hear me? This is Mademoiselle de Montpleynet . . . I'm the young Delmas girls' aunt . . . Yes, they're here with me . . . They're very well . . . I'm calling you about your son . . . Yes, Pierrot . . . No . . . no . . . he has been killed . . . I'm so sorry . . . by the Germans . . . Alas, it is possible . . . I went to identify the body yesterday . . . I don't know . . . he was with Léa, in the Boulevard Saint-Michel . . . I'll go and see . . . she was wounded . . . Hold the line . . . Léa, it's your uncle, he wants a word with you.'

'I have nothing to say to him. It's his fault Pierrot was killed.'

'That's unfair, the man is desperate.'

'Serves him right.'

'Léa, you have no right to talk like that. He's your father's brother, don't forget. If you won't do it out of Christian charity, do it out of humanity in memory of your parents.'

Why was she talking about her parents? They were dead, like Camille! Like Pierrot!

'Hello,' she said, snatching the receiver from her aunt's hand. 'Hello . . . yes, this is Léa . . . I bumped into him by chance, a few days ago, he'd been in the Resistance for a year, with the communists. He was sent to Paris to act as go-between for the leaders of the uprising. He was killed by a grenade . . . no, I don't know if he suffered, I was injured and we were taken to different hospitals. Hello . . . hello . . . don't hang up . . . Hello, who's speaking? Philippe . . . yes, it's dreadful . . . Here we've been liberated, what's happening in Bordeaux? . . . What? . . . You hope the

Germans will repulse the Americans! . . . I'm afraid you don't realize that Germany's lost the war and that sooner or later, people like you and your father are likely to get shot . . . No, it wouldn't make me happy, I wouldn't care. Pierrot's dead . . . Oh yes! I have changed. What should we do about the funeral? . . . Call me back at my aunts' . . . the number's Littré 3525 . . . Have you any news of Uncle Adrien?'

Léa hung up, suddenly subdued.

'Aunt Albertine, it's dreadful hearing him cry,' she said in a tiny voice.

Chapter 23

September 1944 was to be a month of decisions for Léa.

In fact, everything began on the evening of 30th August.

At about eight o'clock, the telephone rang. It was Albertine who answered it:

'Hello . . . yes, my niece is here, who's speaking? . . . Pardon? I can't quite hear you . . . Monsieur Tavernier . . . François Tavernier? Hello, Monsieur Tavernier . . . Where are you? . . . In Paris! When did you get here? . . . With General de Gaulle! I'm so glad to hear your voice, monsieur . . . Yes, Léa's very well . . . Madame d'Argilat? Alas! She is dead, I'm afraid . . . Yes, it's dreadful. Her little boy is here. We saw his father a few days ago, he's fighting in the north of Paris at the moment . . . Hold on and I'll call Léa. Léa! . . . telephone.'

She walked in wearing her bathrobe, her hair wet.

'Who is it?'

'Monsieur Tavernier.'

'Franç . . .'

'Yes. What's the matter, pet? You're not going to faint, are you?'

Her blood was racing so fast that she ached all over.

'No, I'm all right,' she said in a strangled voice as she sat down before picking up the receiver.

Albertine de Montpleynet looked at her with a mixture of tenderness and anxiety. She would have given anything in the world to see Isabelle's daughter happy at last.

'Aunt, I'd like to be alone.'

'Of course, darling, I'm sorry.'

Léa did not dare pick up the receiver although she could hear François impatiently repeating 'hello' on the other end.

'Hello, François? Yes . . . yes . . . No . . . I'm not crying . . . No, I assure you . . . Where? At the War Ministry? Where's that? 14 Rue Saint-Dominique? . . . I'm on my way . . . I'll just dry my hair . . . François . . . All right, all right . . . I shan't waste a second . . .'

Léa hung up, mad with joy. She was laughing and crying both at once. She felt like sinking to her knees and thanking God. He was alive . . .

Since Camille's death, she had tried to forget about him, for she could not bear having to suffer the loss of another loved one. When she had seen Laurent again, the happiness she had felt almost convinced her she had succeeded in putting François out of her mind. But the mere sound of his voice was enough to send a thrill through her body as if she were being caressed. Oh, to be in his arms, to forget all the horrors, forget about the war, not to think about death, only pleasure . . . Drat! Her hair was not dry yet, she was going to look a fright.

She rushed into her room, rubbing her hair vigorously. She rummaged around in the wardrobe trying to find a dress. What had happened to her blue dress that suited her so well? It was nowhere to be found. It was probably in the dirty linen basket.

'Laure, Laure . . .'

'Yes? Stop yelling. What do you want?'

'Can I borrow your green and red dress?'

'But it's brand new!'

'Precisely. Oh please, lend it to me . . . I promise I'll be very careful with it.'

'All right, I'll lend it to you as a special favour. Where are you going?'

'I'm meeting François Tavernier.'

'What? Has he come back?'

'Yes.'

'Lucky you! Hurry up! Don't keep him waiting . . . I'll go and get my dress.'

When Laure came back, Léa was standing there naked dusting her body with talcum powder.

'You're so beautiful!'

'No more than you.'

'Yes you are, all my friends say so. Here, slip the dress on . . . Careful, the material is very delicate.'

Laure helped her on with the flimsy chiffon dress with a plunging neckline and short puffed sleeves. The tight waist made the short gathered skirt seem even fuller.

'I say, you're doing all right! A Jacques Fath dress!'

'I got it in exchange for five kilos of butter and five litres of oil.'

'That's cheap.'

'Do you think so? Butter is rarer than couturier dresses, and after liberation, we'll be able to get all the German officers' ex-mistresses' dresses for nothing.'

'You're so funny! Who would have thought the little country lass from Bordeaux, who was so in love with Field-Marshal Pétain, would end up as a black market dealer?'

'So what? Anybody can make a mistake. So I was wrong about Pétain. You could be wrong about de Gaulle. And as for the black market, if it hadn't been for me, you wouldn't have been able to eat every day.'

'It's true, and I'm the first to admit it. I'm simply admiring your business sense. As for de Gaulle, it's a good thing he was there . . .'

'Time will tell. He's a military man, like the rest of them.'

Léa shrugged and said nothing.

'Still no news of Françoise?'

'No, Franck is still looking. Mention it to François Tavernier, he's bound to know what to do. What shall we do about Pierrot?'

'I don't know. Ask Aunt Albertine.'

'What time are you coming back?'

'I don't know. Tell the aunts I'm going out and look after Charles.'

'What did your last slave die of?' teased Laure, pretending to be annoyed.

'Enjoy yourself and be careful with my dress.'

249

'I'll look after it as if it were the crown jewels, because I don't know where I'd find five kilos of butter and five litres of oil to buy you another one.'

'It's gone up. Now it'd be six kilos of butter and ten litres of oil.'

'If you carry on like that, you'll make a fortune.'

'I'm banking on it. Hurry up, I can hear Lisa. If she sees you going out, she'll keep you talking for an hour: where are you going? With whom? Is he suitable? and so on.'

'I'm on my way. Thanks . . .'

She galloped down the stairs with such speed that she missed her footing and landed in a heap on the hall floor. As she fell, she badly twisted her wrist.

'Shit!'

'What foul language from such lovely lips!'

'How stupid! . . . Franck! . . . Is that you? . . . You can't see a thing with these wretched power cuts.'

'Yes, it's me.'

'Help me up.'

She let out a cry as she got to her feet.

'Have you hurt yourself?'

'It's not serious. What have you got there? It looks very heavy.'

'It's supplies for Laure. I've found out where your sister is.'

'Why didn't you say so?'

'You didn't give me a chance.'

'Well?'

'She's in the Vélodrome d'Hiver stadium. That's where the Free French have put all the collaborators.'

'Can one get in easily?'

'Yes, if you've been shorn.'

'That's not funny.'

'I'm sorry. No, it isn't easy to get in. There's a bunch of rowdies hanging round the gates all the time yelling insults, striking and spitting at the people taken there. Lawyers, even when they're accompanied by a Free French chief, are insulted like the rest of them.'

250

'Go and find out. I'm meeting a friend who's close to de Gaulle. I'll talk to him about it.'

'Ask him to use all his influence to get her out of there. Apparently conditions inside are terrible. It's not a good idea for you to walk around on your own at night. Shall I accompany you?'

'No thank you. I'm going to the Rue Saint-Dominique. It's not far. Thanks for finding out about Françoise. I'll call you tomorrow to keep you posted.'

'Until tomorrow then. Enjoy yourself.'

Léa did not hear him, she was already halfway down the street.

At the War Ministry, as soon as she gave her name, the orderly had her shown to the first floor. She was ushered into a large drawing-room which still bore the traces of its previous occupants. There was a portrait of the Führer which had been removed from the wall and left in a corner, and everywhere were strewn flags and papers bearing the swastika. There were boxes crammed with files and documents. Evidence of a hasty departure.

'The Major has been informed that you are here. He regrets he has to keep you waiting for a few moments, but he is with the General. Here are some newspapers for you to look at.'

There were dozens of newspapers from all over France scattered on one of the tables: *La Nation, Les Allobroges, Le Franc-Tireur, Libération, Combat, Défence de la France, La Marseillaise, L'Aisne Nouvelle, Lyon Libéré, L'Humanité, Le Patriote Niçoise, Le Libre Poitou, La Petite Gironde* . . . Bordeaux had been liberated! The Free French had entered the city at 6.30 that morning. On the front page of *La Petite Gironde*, she read the first day's agenda for the South-West Regional Liberation Council headed by the regional military delegate, Triangle (Colonel Gaillard) and the delegate from the War Office Major, Roger Landes (Aristide), for the Free French. Aristide! So he was alive! Adrien was doubtless with him. 'BORDEAUX CELEBRATES LIBERATION' read the headlines of a paper which she had never seen before. It was strange, it had the same address and the same crowing cock symbol as *La Petite Gironde* of Monday 28th August, but it was called *Sud-Ouest*.

She was so absorbed in her own thoughts that she did not hear him come into the room. She found herself in his arms before she knew what was happening.

'Let . . . François!'

'It's you . . . it's you . . .'

It was as though a wave swept over them, released them, rolled over them, pounded, crushed and shattered them. They reeled across the room in each other's arms, their lips glued together, unaware that they were no longer alone.

'Well Tavernier, is this your urgent appointment?'

'Forgive me, General, but as you can see, it was of the most vital importance.'

'So I see. Mademoiselle is charming. When you've finished your business, let us say in one hour's time, come and join me.'

'Very good, General. Thank you General.'

Dumbfounded, Léa watched the tall figure return to his office.

'Was that really him?' she stammered.

'Yes.'

'I'm embarrassed!'

'There's no need to be. He's a man too, you know.'

'Precisely.'

'Meanwhile, we've got one hour ahead of us, and his blessing.'

'You mean . . . ?'

'Yes.'

She blushed to the roots of her hair. He burst out laughing.

'Stop laughing, it's not funny. What on earth will he think of me?'

'Don't worry, he's already forgotten you. Come here, I want you.'

Forgetting her embarrassment, Léa allowed him to drag her up to the second floor.

'This is the General's office,' he whispered as they passed a door guarded by a young soldier.

At the end of the corridor, after trying several doors, François finally found what he was looking for.

It was a narrow store room lit by a high skylight. It was full of rolled carpets and carefully folded wall hangings. It was stiflingly hot and the air reeked of dust and mothballs. Tavernier pushed Léa over on to a pile of expensive carpets and fell on top of her.

'Wait, kiss me.'

'Later, I've had too many hard-ons thinking about you and your pretty little arse. I can't wait any longer . . .'

He feverishly tried to rip off her underwear.

'Shit, they're made from pre-war material,' he cursed as he yanked them off.

'Stop it, you'll tear my dress.'

'I'll buy you ten dresses! Ah!'

He penetrated her with a violence which made her cry out in pain and anger.

'You're hurting me . . . stop it . . .'

'I'd rather die!'

She struggled, trying to break free of his painful thrusting. 'Bastard!'

'Again, that's the first word you've said to me.'

'Bastard! Bastard! Bas . . .'

François's desire was contagious. They were like two animals groaning and biting, bringing each other to a quick climax.

This hasty pleasure did not satisfy their desire. Without pausing, they made love again, feeling an ecstasy coursing through their veins unlike anything that either of them could remember ever experiencing before. Limp and satiated, they flopped down on to the purple hangings which seemed to want to envelop them.

They lay in silence for a long time, listening to the echoes of pleasure in their bodies. François raised himself on to his elbow and studied her. He had rarely seen such abandon in making love. Once he had taken her, she submitted to his desires without the slightest shame. He brushed her puffy lips. A thin light filtered through Léa's eyelids, arousing an unbearable emotion in him.

'Look at me.'

Her beautiful eyes slowly opened to reveal a misty expression, a heartrending sadness. He misunderstood her melancholy.

'Are you angry with me?'

She shook her tousled head, while large tears rolled on to the amaranth velvet.

'I love you, darling, don't cry.'

'I was so afraid . . .' she managed to stutter.

'It's all over. I'm here.'

She angrily sat up and pushed him away.

'No it isn't over. All over the place, people are killing and humiliating others . . .'

'I know. Calm down. You can tell me all about it later. I know about Camille . . .'

'You know about Camille? Do you know about Pierrot? About Raoul? About Françoise? . . .'

'Françoise?'

'She was arrested and shorn by the Free French.'

'How do you know they were Free French?'

'They were wearing armbands.'

'A lot of rather dubious characters have infiltrated the Free French. The General knows all about it. Everything will be done to restore law and order and punish the guilty.'

'I don't know if it is dubious characters, as you call them, who have infiltrated the liberators of Paris, but I can assure you that most of the audience who watched my sister being shorn had a whale of a time and thought it perfectly natural to punish in that manner.'

'You're still as beautiful when you're angry, my dear.'

'Oh!'

'I'm sorry. Then what happened to her?'

'They took her to the Vélodrome d'Hiver stadium.'

'She's in good company, anybody who's anybody is there: Sacha Guitry, Mary Marquet . . . don't worry, we'll get her out of there. Good God! I have to leave you, the General's waiting for me. I'll call you in the morning. Be good until then.'

He went out, buttoning up his flies.

'François!'

'Yes? he asked, retracing his steps.

'I'm glad to see you again.'

He picked her up and hugged her, kissing her with a tenderness that never ceased to surprise her.

Léa lay there deep in thought, listening to his footsteps die away. With this man, one minute she felt completely safe, and the next, in great danger. She was not in the habit of analysing her feelings yet there she was, lying in a store room in the War Ministry, trying to unravel the causes of her conflicting feelings. 'He frightens me. I'm being stupid, why should I be so afraid, he's never done anything to give me cause for anxiety . . . Maybe I'm afraid he doesn't love me any more? That he'll leave me . . . Yes, of course, I dread that, but I sense that it's not the reason . . . It's almost physical . . . I tremble with fear when he calls me "angel" . . . and yet I'm so attracted to him that I'd follow him anywhere . . . But what about him? He says he loves me, but each time we see each other again, he jumps on top of me without saying anything other than "Come on, I want you . . . " I must admit that it excites me, but I rather like those "caresses of the soul" as Raphaël Mahl and Balzac called words . . . It's strange, why does he always manage to make me angry? . . . Earlier on, when we were talking about Pierrot and Françoise . . . It's as though, subconsciously, I were holding him responsible for what happened to them . . . I don't understand . . . perhaps it's because he's a man whose words, attitudes and connections are ambiguous and I suspect that kind of man of being responsible for the war . . . I know that's ridiculous . . . I'm sure Camille would know . . . I miss her . . . I feel the same sense of being abandoned, of absence as after mummy's death . . . When I think that I betrayed Camille . . . that I wanted to steal her husband! . . . Forgive me, Camille . . . there are so many things I didn't tell you . . . That you didn't tell me either . . . and now it's too late . . . too late . . . Oh! That's enough crying! Tears are no use . . . no use . . .'

Léa angrily tried to smooth her crumpled dress, in vain.

'Ah! these wartime materials!' A fine sight she'd be, walking past the orderly in this outfit. Finally, she had to make up her mind to leave the carpet store room. She opened the door a fraction, hastily glanced right and left then, feeling bolder, sneaked down the corridor and walked down the staircase with the greatest dignity. The entrance hall was full of young men, soldiers and Free French, who watched the pretty girl with dishevelled hair and a creased dress walk past and felt envious of the man who had got her into that state. She held her head up high without appearing to notice the wolf whistles that accompanied her exit, but once she was in the street, she took to her heels, red with shame and mad with anger.

Back at her aunts' apartment, Charles greeted her noisily.
'What? Aren't you in bed yet?'
'Papa's here! Papa's here!'
The child wanted to drag her into the parlour.
'Wait a minute, I'm going to get changed.'
'No, come on.'
'In a minute, darling.'
'Papa! Papa! It's Léa. She won't come in!'
Laurent's tall, lean figure appeared in the doorway.
She kissed him. How tired he looked!
'Wait a minute, I'm just going to get changed.'
Too late: Laure had just arrived.
'Here you are at last! My dress! Look at the state of it!'
'I'm sorry, I fell downstairs.'
'Fell downstairs?'
Embarrassed, Léa fled to the seclusion of her own room. It was going to be hard explaining things to her sister.

When she entered the parlour, Albertine gave her a harsh look.
'You know I don't like you going out in the evening without telling us.'
'I'm sorry. I went to see François Tavernier about Françoise. He's going to deal with it. I saw General de Gaulle,' she added to change the subject.

'What's he like?'

Léa told them of her brief glimpse, omitting the details of the circumstances . . .

The Montpleynet sisters retired, exhausted from so much excitement.

'Monsieur d'Argilat, your room is ready.'

'Thank you, mademoiselle, thank you for everything.'

'You're welcome. Goodnight everybody.'

Laure went over to her sister and whispered:

'I hope it was worth it, otherwise I'd never forgive you for ruining my dress.'

Léa's blushes were enough to satisfy her.

'Goodnight, I'm going to bed. Playing nanny has worn me out. Goodnight, Laurent, sleep well. Come on Charles, it's bedtime.'

'No, I want to stay with daddy.'

Laurent picked up the little boy and held him close.

'Oh! Daddy, keep me with you.'

'I'll always keep you with me, but now it's late and you must go to bed. I'll come and tuck you in.'

'Léa too.'

'Yes of course, Léa too.'

'To bed, you rascal.'

'Thank you, Laure, goodnight.'

'Goodnight.'

Alone together, Léa and Laurent sat in silence for a while, smoking American cigarettes. Laurent rose and walked over to the open window. He stood gazing at the starry sky. Without turning round, he asked:

'Tell me how Camille died . . .'

Chapter 24

'Mademoiselle Albertine, there's a phone call for you.'

'Thank you, Estelle.'

'Hello . . . yes . . . speaking . . . Hello monsieur . . . Of course I agree to take in my niece and act as her guarantor . . . When? Later today! . . . How can I thank you, Monsieur Tavernier? . . . By permitting Léa to have dinner with you? I think that'll be difficult today if her sister is coming back . . . Shall I call her? She's still asleep, she sat up very late talking with Monsieur d'Argilat . . . fine, I'll tell her that you'll call back this evening.'

Albertine de Montpleynet replaced the receiver and went back to her room in a pensive mood. She shut the door quietly behind her and went to sit in the old nineteenth-century armchair she was so fond of. Her heart was pounding. Her hands, which had become moist, gripped the armrests. Gradually, her delight at the thought of seeing Françoise again gave way to an overwhelming sense of anguish. How would the other residents, the local shop-keepers and their friends react when they saw her and knew that she had been shorn because she was the mistress of a German officer? All her life, Albertine had conformed to society, now she felt cut off from it. Already, during the final months of the Occupation, she had not been spared snide remarks about Françoise's German 'fiancé', and about Laure's activities. Lisa, who was more of a socialite, suffered more than she did from it. She had been so upset that she had given up her weekly bridge parties.

Albertine reproached herself for not being firm enough with Isabelle's three daughters. Since their parents' deaths, she had felt responsible for them. She admitted that she had been completely overwhelmed by events and the very different but equally stubborn characters of her nieces. 'I wasn't up to the task, I wasn't able to keep those girls out of trouble. What would their mother say? Whatever will become of poor Françoise after this ordeal? Otto is bound to have been killed . . . Unmarried mother, that's what she'll be called if not worse . . . And what about her darling little boy? Oh! My God! Have pity on us . . . Give Françoise the strength to rise above her grief and her shame . . . Forgive me, You gave me a mission which I have not fulfilled . . . Forgive me, Lord.'

Albertine was crying, her face buried in her hands. She was so engrossed in her troubles that she did not hear the door open.

'Aunt darling, what's the matter?'

Kneeling at the elderly spinster's feet, Léa tried to prise open her blotchy hands.

'Aunt Albertine, please, calm down.'

Finally, her fingers parted. Léa was shattered when she saw the grief-stricken face of this woman who rarely showed her feelings and whose expression was normally rather cold. She felt a mixture of pity and doubt. What? Even Albertine who was so strong, so reserved, so dignified? . . . Once again, her world of childhood certainties was shaken, leaving her feeling helpless. When she had watched Montillac burning, something inside her had been destroyed, isolating her in her despair, leaving her only the strength to survive and protect Camille's son. Last night, she had worn herself out trying to comfort Laurent. But can you console another person when you yourself are inconsolable? And what about now? What could she say to reassure this woman she loved so dearly? Camille would have known. It was Albertine who found the words.

'Get up, darling. I'm a silly old woman . . . I was just tired for a moment . . . I have no right to complain, so many people have suffered so much more than I have.'

She carefully wiped her eyes, adding:

259

'Monsieur Tavernier telephoned. Françoise should be here this afternoon.'

'Is that why you were crying?'

'Yes and no. Don't misunderstand me, I'm delighted she's coming back, but all the same, I'm a little worried.'

'Did he say anything about me?'

'He wanted to invite you to dinner. I told him it wasn't possible today.'

'Why did you say that?'

Albertine stood up, looking severe.

'Your sister needs all our affection. I thought it best for you to be here.'

Lé hung her head. She was weary, so weary.

'Anyway, he'll phone you this evening . . . Don't mention anything to Lisa, she'll be upset. You know her, she's a simple, direct soul. She's even more perturbed than I am by all that's going on and it's affecting her health. Promise me?'

Léa kissed her aunt.

'I promise. Can I ask your advice about something?'

'Of course, child. What about?'

'Well, I . . .'

She stopped. What was the point of talking about that, it was all so confused in her mind.

'Why have you stopped? . . . Is it so hard to talk about?'

'I've decided to join the Red Cross.'

'The Red . . .'

If Léa had said 'I want to join,' rather than 'I've decided to join,' perhaps she would not have plunged head first into this adventure. But, having said she had made a decision, she would not go back on it, prevented by her stubborn pride.

'Did you hear? I said I've decided to join the Red Cross.'

'But you're not a nurse!' exclaimed Mademoiselle de Montpleynet.

'I shan't join as a nurse, but as a driver.'

'But why do that when we all need you here? And what about Montillac? Have you thought about Montillac?'

'Montillac has been burned down!'

'It can be rebuilt again!'

'How? We haven't any money!'

'The notaries . . .'

'The place is mortgaged up to the hilt, for Christ's sake!'

'Léa!'

'Oh! Please! The days of refined language are over, like Montillac.'

'Think of your sisters, and Charles, whom you love as if he were your own.'

'My sisters will manage very well without me. Look at Laure, she's an excellent businesswoman. As for Charles, he has his father now.'

'When did you make this decision? And why?'

'When? I really don't know . . . Last night perhaps, on seeing Laurent's grief, on reliving Camille's death, and that of Aunt Bernadette, Sidonie, Raoul Lefèvre, Pierrot and so many others. I want to follow General Leclerc's troops, I want to enter Germany with him, I wish I were a man and could have a gun and fight . . . I wish I could kill them by the hundred . . .'

'Be quiet, child, you are quite mad.'

Léa was beside herself, her face rad and drawn, her eyes shining with hatred, her mouth contorted.

'Maybe I am, but I want to see them suffer, I want to be present at their defeat, I want to see them dragging themselves along the roads while the bombs are falling all around them, I want to see their stomachs burst open, their eyes ripped out, their children burned . . . I want to see their towns destroyed, their houses razed to the ground . . . Above all, I want to see them humiliated as they humiliated us, I want to see them being servile as we were forced to be, I want to see them on their knees . . . I want them to be wiped out . . .'

Her shouting had alerted Laurent, who had listened unseen to the vile language coming from the mouth of this lovely girl.

She was verging on hysteria.

'Ah . . . !'

A slap halted the delirious torrent. Léa stared at Laurent

in amazement: she would never have believed him capable of slapping a woman.

'Watch out, she's going to faint,' cried Albertine. Laurent rushed to her side, but Léa had already regained her balance.

'It's nothing, I'm perfectly all right.'

'I'm sorry . . .'

'It's all right, I'd have done the same,' she said, staring out of the window.

'Monsieur d'Argilat, do you know what Léa was telling me?'

'No?'

'That she was going to join the Red Cross!'

Laurent went over to Léa and made her turn round and face him.

'Is that true?'

How anxious he sounded!

'Yes.'

He drew her to him and hugged her close.

'After all, perhaps you're right . . .'

Albertine de Montpleynet left the room with a shrug.

Left alone, Laurent and Léa remained silent for a long time.

He went over to her and gently tilted back her head. She offered a stubborn resistance.

'Why?'

Oh, that lost child look! How he wished he could chase all the horrors from her memory and give her back that carefreeness that made her so appealing. But he was too immersed in his own suffering to be of much help to her. He guessed that her decision to join the Red Cross was mainly determined by her confusion in the face of a future that looked bleak and difficult.

'Why?' he repeated.

'Because I want to die.'

In other circumstances, he would have burst out laughing at such youthful vehemence, but now . . .

'Don't be silly, you've got your whole life ahead of you . . .'

'You sound like my aunts!'

'I'm only being sensible.'

'Sensible! Let's see who's sensible! Do you know who's sensible? I don't. Ever since this war began, I haven't seen anything sensible happen, everything has been utterly absurd. And are the crowds who lynch women and shave their heads sensible?'

'I grant that the situation around us is absurd, but don't add to the absurdity by making a decision that is so out of character. Think, in a few months, the war will be completely over. We will have to build everything afresh, we must live as we did before . . .'

'Will you be able to carry on as before? After what they did to Camille?'

Laurent's face was contorted with pain.

'I'll have to. I have to think of Charles.'

'It's all right for you, you have Charles. I've got nothing.'

'You have Montillac.'

'I never want to hear another word about Montillac. I hate that place. I'll never set foot there again.'

'How you've changed overnight. I thought you were happy to see François Tavernier again. He's the right man for you.'

'François Tavernier only thinks about . . .'

'What man wouldn't when he looks at you.'

'You wouldn't!'

The memory of the one night they had spent together in the pink brick cellar in Toulouse was so sharp that they both blushed.

'He loves you. Camille told me so. She thought you loved him too.'

'Camille was wrong.'

'Camille was rarely wrong.'

'Don't talk about her any more. She's dead . . . dead . . . so is Montillac . . . Leave me alone, Laurent. Please, I want to be by myself.'

He left the room, gently closing the door behind him.

Léa clutched her head, her mouth open in a long silent scream which echoed throughout her being, making her tremble. She fell to her knees by the armchair and bit into the antique tapestry seat, stuttering in a broken voice: 'It hurts . . . I can't stand it any more . . . they're attacking me from all sides . . . They want to take me with them . . . No! No! What I said to Laurent wasn't true. I don't want to die! But every night, they call me . . . they try to catch me . . . I can feel their icy hands, with blood dripping from them . . . Oh! Those fingers! . . . I'm frightened . . . And that smell of burning flesh, that charred body that wouldn't stop wriggling, those screams! . . . Oh! Sarah! Your poor disfigured face . . . I feel as though you're talking to me from Hell . . . Sidonie . . . I can hear the honey of your home-made sweets in your voice. I can't get your tortured old body out of my mind. Have pity . . . be quiet . . . Raoul? Oh! You're kind, you are. I can sense you want me to live, that you have taken with you our pathetic gestures of love . . . Aunt Bernadette, oh! Please . . . don't scream like that . . . ah! Those flames devouring you, ah! . . . Raphaël . . . go away . . . have pity! They're burning me too . . . I'm sorry, Aunt Bernadette, I'm sorry . . . Mummy! . . . Protect me . . . tell them to go away . . . they want me to follow them . . . Mummy, tell Pierrot to leave me alone . . . it's not my fault I wasn't killed when he was . . . now it's La Sifflette . . . Monsieur and Madame Debray . . . and Father Terrible . . . and the little children in Orleans and their mother . . . and . . . oh! No . . . that man! That man I killed . . . help! Mummy . . . he's got me . . . Papa . . . Don't let him . . . the blood . . . all that blood . . . There are so many of them . . .'

'Léa, Léa, calm down . . . it's all over. Quick, call a doctor!'

She was inert and drenched with perspiration. François Tavernier picked her up and carried her into her bedroom while Laurent d'Argilat tried to contact a doctor.

'Call Dr Prost at the War Ministry, he's a friend of mine. Tell him to come at once.'

François firmly sent the de Montpleynet sisters and Laure away. Out of his mind with worry, he gazed at the unconscious body of the woman he loved. From time to time she was racked with a violent spasm. He lay down on top of her and spoke softly to her.

'My little love . . . don't be afraid any more, my sweet, beautiful darling. I'm here . . . I'll look after you . . . there, darling . . .'

His soothing voice seemed to calm her. He undressed her. He was moved by the beauty, which somehow seemed both strong and frail, of that body which filled him with wonder each time he made love to her. Even at present, in the helplessness of illness, she was moving and desirable. It was vital to get her away from Paris so she would be able to regain her health. Good God! Where on earth was Prost?

'D'Argilat!'

Laurent pushed open the door.

'Yes?'

'Did you speak to Prost?'

'He's on his way. How is she?'

'A bit quieter. Has anything particular happened since yesterday?'

'Not that I know of. She told me about the circumstances of my wife's death . . .'

'I'm sorry, old chap, I wanted to say how . . . I was very fond of your wife. I had an enormous amount of respect for her . . .'

'Thank you. We'll talk about it later.'

'I think the doctor's here.'

'I didn't hear the bell.'

'You forget there's a power cut. There was a knock on the door.'

They could hear the sound of voices.

'In here, doctor. Please step inside.'

A shortish man with the shoulders of a wrestler and a bull's neck, wearing the uniform and stripes of a captain, came into the room and went over to Tavernier.

'What's going on?'

'Your Parisian colleagues don't answer the telephone, so I thought of you.'

'Are you ill?'

'No I'm not, it's this young lady.'

'Charming.'

'This is no time for joking.'

'All right, where can I wash my hands?'

'There, doctor,' said Albertine, showing him the bathroom.

'Stop pacing up and down, Monsieur Tavernier, you're making me giddy.'

'I'm sorry, mademoiselle, but I'm worried. He's been examining her for at least an hour.'

'Not an hour, dear monsieur, only ten minutes.'

'Ten minutes, an hour, it's the same, it's too long.'

The parlour was like a dentist's waiting-room. Laure was holding Françoise's baby in her lap. Laurent was standing, holding Charles. The child kept asking in a small voice which was becoming increasingly anxious:

'She isn't going to die, is she? Daddy, she isn't going to die?'

Lisa, who was fanning herself with her tearstained handkerchief, murmured:

'Mother Mary have pity on us.'

As for Albertine, she sat bolt upright, her eyes closed. From the way her lips were moving, one could tell she was praying. Finally the door swung open and the captain beckoned her to follow him. but François pushed her aside and went into the room.

'Monsieur Tavernier!'

He took no notice and rushed to Léa's bedside. She seemed to be asleep.

Reassured, he turned to Prost.

'Well?'

The doctor ignored him and addressed Albertine.

'Does she suffer from blackouts?'

'No, not that I'm aware of. She's my niece, doctor, but she's only been staying here for two months.'

'Do you know if she had fainting fits when she was a child?'

'No, monsieur. Oh! Yes, when her fiancé died, she remained unconscious for several days.'

'How long?'

'I don't remember, two or three days.'

'I see she has a couple of head injuries. Were there any after-effects?'

'I don't think so.'

'Does she suffer from frequent headaches?'

'She has occasional migraines which are so bad that she has to go to bed.'

'But that's all in the past,' groaned François Tavernier, 'what's wrong with her now?'

'She's in a vigilant coma.'

'What's that?'

'She's in a coma, but a vigilant coma, which means she reacts to some things and some types of pain. Mademoiselle, don't be surprised if she groans and struggles. Her mind is not entirely comatose.'

'What must we do?'

'Nothing.'

'What do you mean, nothing?'

'I mean nothing. We must be patient.'

'For how long?'

'I have no idea . . . two days . . . four days . . . a week or more, it depends.'

'It depends on what?' asked François.

'On nature, or God if you prefer.'

'God can get stuffed, and so can you . . . you're a lousy doctor, you're not even capable of treating her.'

'Stop yelling. She needs peace and quiet. My prescription is that you get lost.'

'Gentlemen, please . . .'

'Forgive us, mademoiselle. You heard, there's nothing else we can do but wait. Make her drink regularly, try and get her to swallow a little soup and watch her temperature. Do you have a family doctor?'

'Yes, but we don't know what's happened to him.'

'I'll come back tomorrow if you haven't found one of my colleagues by then. I want someone to stay with her round the clock. You need a nurse.'

'That will not be necessary, doctor. There are enough of us to take it in turns.'

'Perfect. Are you coming, Tavernier?'

'No, I'm staying here for a while. I'll come and see you later.'

'Don't forget we've got a press conference in an hour.'

'I don't give a damn.'

'Tell that to the General . . . Goodbye, Mademoiselle, don't worry, she's strong, she'll get over it.'

'Please God, doctor.'

Chapter 25

When Léa opened her eyes in the shuttered room, twelve days had gone by. The first person she saw by her beside was Françoise, who was gazing at her from behind a fringe of hair protruding from an elegant turban of autumnal hues. She was not even surprised: hair grew so fast.

'Léa, can you hear me?'

'Yes. I feel as though I've been asleep for ages.'

Françoise burst out laughing and crying at the same time.

'You've been asleep for a week.'

'What?'

'You've been in a coma for twelve days.'

'Twelve days! Are you sure? Lots of things must have happened . . . tell me.'

'No, you mustn't tire yourself. I'm going to call the others and tell them you've finally come round . . .'

'No! Wait! I'm not tired. I don't remember very clearly . . . the last thing I recall is Aunt Albertine telling me you were coming home and since then . . . twelve days have gone by! When did you come back?'

'The afternoon you fell ill. François Tavernier came to fetch me from the Vélodrome d'Hiver. I couldn't believe my ears when a Free French soldier called me and said: "You're free, you bitch!" If only you could have seen the joy on the faces of the other prisoners. An actress, who hadn't been shorn, cut off a lock of her hair and slipped it under my headscarf . . .'

'Ah! I understand.'

'. . . and kissed me. I was so moved by her gesture that I burst into tears. I was given lots of little errands and letters

269

to take to their families. Luckily, they didn't have time to search my bag. François Tavernier snatched it away from a dirty, spotty, "colonel" who got a kick out of humiliating the prisoners. He felt a right fool when he saw the sheet of headed notepaper from the War Ministry with three or four signatures and as many stamps ordering my immediate release. François pushed me into a car decorated with a red, white and blue pennant bearing the Cross of Lorraine, driven by a uniformed chauffeur, saying:

' "Hurry up, I'm afraid they'll find out that one of these documents isn't quite in order." ' I was so amazed at his cheek, you could have knocked me down with a feather. Luckily, it worked long enough for me to be finally struck off the purge list.'

'What's that?'

'It's true, you don't know what's been going on. They're purging, that means they're arresting people, interrogating, judging and sentencing all those who had relations with the Germans, close or distant. It includes businessmen, members of parliament, writers, actors, newspaper editors, hoteliers, prostitutes, typists . . . everybody, in other words.'

'And what do they do to them?'

'They're released, or some of them are imprisoned pending execution.'

'Who's been arrested?'

'Among those whose names might mean something to you are Pierre Fresnay, Mary Marquet, Arletty, Ginette Leclerc, Sacha Guitry, Jérôme Carcopino, Brasillach . . . others are wanted, like Céline, Rebatet and Drieu La Rochelle. Every day, *Le Figaro* publishes a list of wanted names.'

'It serves most of them right.'

'Doubtless it does, but many of them are arrested on the denunciation of a jealous colleague, a bad-tempered concierge or for the simple pleasure of harming someone.'

Léa closed her eyes. She did not want to embark on that kind of discussion with her sister.

'You're tired! Don't talk any more. I'm going to tell . . .'

'No! How's Charles?'

'Fine. He hasn't stopped asking after you, especially since his father left.'

'Laurent's left?' she cried, sitting up suddenly.

'Calm down, you'll make yourself ill again.'

'Where is he?'

'He left with the 2nd Armoured Division on the morning of the 8th. They've gone eastwards.'

'How was he?'

'Not very happy. He was desperately sad to leave you in such a state and abandon his son.'

'Didn't he leave any message for me?'

'Yes, he left a letter.'

'Go and get it.'

'It's here, in your writing desk.'

Françoise opened a drawer and handed the letter to her sister. But Léa was so nervous that she was unable to tear open the envelope.

'Open it and read it to me.'

'Dearest Léa,

If you are reading these lines, you must be better. I suffered terribly seeing you unconscious and sitting there unable to help you and bring you back among us. I have left Charles with your aunts and sisters, but now you're better, I'm asking you to look after him. Please don't refuse, he loves you as a mother and needs you. I know it's a heavy responsibility, but you are strong enough to shoulder it, you have already proved as much. I hope you have abandoned your crazy plan to join the Red Cross. Your place is with your family, with my son and your sisters. Go back to Montillac. I have written to the notary who deals with my father's affairs and instructed him to sell some land to help you rebuild.

I'm both happy and sad to go off and fight again. Happy, because in military action, it is easier for me to forget the horror of losing Camille, and sad because I'm leaving Charles and you. Love and kisses.

Laurent.

PS I'll let you know where to write to me as soon as I can.'

'He's right, you're mad to want to join the Red Cross.'

'It's none of your business. I'll do as I please.'

'But why?'

'I don't want to stay here. I feel so awful here. I need to sort my ideas out.'

'Léa! You're back to your old self again. Doctor, my niece is better.'

'So it seems, mademoiselle. Well, child, did you want to play at Sleeping Beauty? I'm sorry I'm not Prince Charming. How do you feel?'

'Fine, doctor.'

The old family doctor, who had finally resurfaced, examined his young patient.

'Perfect . . . perfect. Your blood pressure is normal, so is your heart. In a few days' time, you'll be able to gambol about in the woods with your Prince Charming. He's been worrying himself silly about you.'

Léa shot an inquiring glance at her sister.

Françoise's silence implied: 'As if you didn't know.'

'I'd like to get up.'

'Not until you've regained your strength. If you set foot out of bed, your legs would give way under you. What you need is lots of healthy food.'

'Lots? That's easier said than done,' said Françoise bitterly.

'I know, madame, but you'll have to find a way. You can rely on Prince Charming, he's a resourceful man and he'll go to any lengths to help his sweetheart's family. Joking aside, have I made myself quite clear, mademoiselle? This young lady must have meat every day, dairy products, fish, eggs . . .'

'In other words, doctor, everything that can't be found in the shops.'

'Monsieur Tavernier will get hold of it, don't worry.'

'I'll show you out, doctor.'

After Albertine and the doctor had left the room, Léa let out

272

a peal of weak laughter. Aunt Lisa's old suitor was still a tease and ever optimistic.

'Did François drop by at all?'

'François! Every day, several times a day, and he telephoned at least once between each visit to find out how you were.'

'Today, he hasn't given any sign of life for at least an hour,' Léa said obstinately.

'That's unkind. He spent the night at your bedside whenever he could get away, talking to you and cradling you, without getting a wink of sleep. It was heartbreaking watching him leave in the morning, looking so disconsolate, unshaven and red-eyed, after gulping down the cup of coffee I brought him. Sometimes, Charles would wait for him outside your door. François would let him in and they would have long conversations at the foot of your bed. When they came out, they both seemed more cheerful. Charles has adopted François, he calls him my big buddy. You're lucky to be loved like that.'

Léa was moved by the sadness in her voice. She felt guilty for showing such indifference to her sister's plight. She studied her face closely for the first time since her return to Paris. How the young nurse from Langon had changed! Now she was a young woman bravely accepting the consequences of her love for a German officer. What had happened to that aura of beauty that had once lit up the rather plain features of a daughter of the provincial bourgeoisie? The coquetry of a young girl in love discovering the pleasures of the capital? The glowing pride of a young mother walking along the banks of the Seine showing off her baby?

Léa scrutinized this stranger who was her sister, noticing the bitter lines either side of her mouth, which was clamped shut as if to keep in a secret, her hollow cheeks with clumsily applied rouge only emphasizing their pallor, her roving eyes, constantly anxious, and that turban with the ridiculous lock of hair which resembled a hairpiece on an ageing actress from the silent movies. And her hands . . . ? Those poor hands which she convulsively clasped. Perhaps it was those trembling fingers which made Léa realize the full extent of her

273

sister's physical and moral suffering. She felt like embracing her and begging her forgiveness for being so selfish, but a sudden shyness prevented her. Her heart full of pity, she asked:

'Have you heard from Otto?'

Léa stifled a cry at Françoise's sudden transformation. She had turned grey, and her entire body crumpled. She seemed like an old woman. She slowly removed her turban and sat there looking ridiculous with her bald head, which had a moth-eaten appearance, exposed. Her eyes were wide open and yet they were blind as she silently wept.

Léa was overcome with nausea as she flung herself down on to her pillow.

The two sisters remained prostrate for a long time. Léa's nausea had subsided and she sat up and crawled across the bed to her sister whom, as a child, she had bullied. She stroked her wet face in a gesture both of compassion and disgust. She could not utter a single word of consolation. In silence, with the help of a sheet, she wiped the tears and smudged makeup from Françoise's face until she stopped crying.

'Thank you,' said Françoise simply as she replaced her turban. 'I'll go and fetch the aunts . . . No, I haven't heard from Otto.'

Léa suddenly felt exhausted. She lay down again and closed her eyes.

When Albertine and Lisa came into the room, she was already asleep.

Chapter 26

That evening, she woke to find a different face peering into hers.

'François!'

They poured into their kiss everything that they had never and would never be able to say to each other. When they drew apart, they had both regained that will to live which made them capable of rising above the harshest ordeals.

'I say, my lovely, you'll have to fill out a bit: you know I don't like skinny women.'

'That's going to be a job with the food shortages.'

'Don't worry about such domestic trivialities. I'll deal with those.'

'How will you manage it? Will your black market dealer friends be continuing their fruitful little business?'

'I see that being ill hasn't affected your sharp tongue. I like that. My friends, as you call them, have vanished into thin air and at this very moment are probably in palaces in Baden-Baden, or Spanish inns, but others who are equally resourceful have taken their place. Estelle is making you some chicken broth, a soft-boiled egg and some cream cheese which I think you'll like. And to wash it all down, a vintage Lafite-Rothschild.'

'That won't help me fill out much.'

'Kipling said that too much haste killed the yellow serpent.'

'It's good of you to compare me to a serpent.'

'You're the most charming little viper I've ever met,' he replied, stroking her hair. 'I'll send a hairdresser over tomorrow, your hair feels like straw. In the meantime, you're going to have a bath.

François bathed her, which of course aroused him. They returned to her room and locked the door before satisfying their desire. Then he tucked her up in bed.

They devoured the supper Estelle had prepared and drained the bottle of Lafite. The wine brought back the colour to Léa's cheeks and made her eyes sparkle. The expression in François's eyes clearly betrayed his intention of carrying on where they had left off before supper, the intensity of his desire having brought their lovemaking to a rapid climax. But this was not possible as Françoise came banging on the door shouting:

'Open up! Open up!'

Tavernier rushed across the room and caught the wild-eyed young woman in his arms. She yelled:

'The Fayards have been found at the bottom of a well!'

Laure followed, looking distraught.

'They were murdered and thrown into the well in the lower vineyard.'

'Who told you that?'

'Ruth called.'

'Who did it?' asked Léa, who knew the answer.

'The Resistance.'

For a few seconds, the only sound was Françoise's panting.

'Apparently, in Langon, Saint-Macaire and La Réole, the most horrendous things have been going on. They've been shaving women's heads, dragging them through the streets and spitting on them. People are being hung from trees, tortured and killed.'

'How awful,' groaned Lisa who had entered the room unnoticed.

'Why doesn't anybody stop them?' cried Léa.

'General de Gaulle is trying to. Have you forgotten the tortures the Germans inflicted on women and children? I don't know if you are aware that we're on the brink of revolution, and it's going to take all the General's authority to stop it from erupting as the communists wish. That's why he's trying to set up a government of national unanimity.'

276

'With the communists?' asked Françoise aggressively.

'They fought by our side, it's only natural . . .'

'I know, the party suffered heavy losses . . .'

'Don't complain! Of all the French troops, they're the ones who fought the Germans most effectively and who paid the highest price.'

'But even so, to include them in the government . . .' said Lisa in a small voice.

'We had to. Isn't right for all the parties in the Resistance to be represented? Similarly, we would be just as surprised not to find politicians who differ from each other as much as Jeanneney, Frenay, Bidault, Tillon, Capitan, Teitgen, Mendès-France, Pleven . . .'

'Perhaps you're right. We're so ignorant about politics,' said Laure.

'Has anyone heard from Uncle Luc and his son Philippe?'

'Not really,' replied Laure in a faltering voice.

'Tell me, what did Ruth say?'

'There are conflicting rumours going round. Some say Uncle Luc's been arrested and taken to Fort Hâ, others say that he and Philippe have been killed.'

'How?'

'That we don't know. Some say they were hanged, others say they were lynched and others maintain they were shot. Communications between Bordeaux and Langon haven't really been re-established.'

'Is there any news of Uncle Adrien?'

'No, not a word. But they have found Albert.'

'Alive?' cried Léa.

'No, dead. He was tortured by the Gestapo.'

'Poor Mireille . . . Does the death of Fayard and his wife avenge his death? Taking a life has never brought anyone back to life . . . and yet we still want to kill those who assassinated the ones we love . . .'

'Do you remember Maurice Fiaux?' Laure asked Léa.

'How could I ever forget such a swine?'

'He was executed on the order of the Resistance.'

Her little sister, who had once thought she was in love

277

with the young murderer, sounded so unmoved as she spoke. How many more deaths? When would it all end?

'How's Ruth?'

'Not too bad. She's slowly recovering from her injuries, but the circumstances of Albert and the Fayards' deaths have upset her terribly. Over the phone she kept repeating "Men are mad, men are mad." Apparently, the Fayards' death was atrocious. They pushed them along with the tips of their pitchforks, beating them with sticks, dragging them through the vineyard to the well, then they tied them up and threw them in. They let out a long wail in unison . . .'

'I can hear their joint scream,' breathed Léa, 'until the final gasp . . . Ah! Mathias, I didn't want that to happen!'

Léa was drenched in perspiration and her teeth were chattering. She sank back on the pillows.

'We're mad to talk about that in front of her. Get out and let her rest.'

They left the room as if in a state of shock.

François wiped Léa's brow, murmuring soothing words of affection in her ear. Gradually, she calmed down and fell asleep exhausted.

Despite these shocks, Léa recovered very quickly. On Sunday 24th September, François Tavernier took advantage of General de Gaulle's visit to the headquarters of de Lattre de Tassigny at the Front, and took Léa to get some fresh air in the forest of Marly-le-Roi. They had a terrible lunch in a reputable restaurant in Saint-Germain-en-Laye but that did not deter them from enjoying the woods and romping on the soft moss which welcomed their impatient bodies.

That evening, during an excellent dinner in a luxurious restaurant in the Champs-Elysées, he told her he would soon be going away again.

'Where are you going?'

'The General has made me his official envoy.'

'To do what?'

'I can't tell you. But it shouldn't be for longer than a month or two.'

'A month or two! You're not serious.'

'The war isn't over.'

'Don't leave me, François!'

'I have to.'

'I want to come with you.'

He let out a loud laugh which caused heads to turn and a waiter to come over.

'Does monsieur require anything else?'

'Yes, a bottle of your best champagne.'

'What are we drinking to?' snapped Léa.

'To you, my love. To your lovely eyes, to your recovery, to life . . .'

But when he saw that Léa was inconsolable, he became serious.

'Don't worry, everything will be all right.'

'I don't know why, but I'm more afraid now than during the four years of occupation.'

'That's only natural. A new world is emerging that will have different qualities, and different faults too, from the other one. You're frightened of this unknown new world. But I know you're capable of coming to grips with it. Go back to Montillac and rebuild it. That's the task you should set yourself while you wait for me.'

'I shan't go back to Montillac, or if I do, it'll be in many, many years' time. And who says I'm going to spend my time waiting for you? Maybe you want me to take up knitting for the prisoners, make up parcels for the orphans, visit the sick . . .'

'Oh! Yes! I can just see you leaning over the poor wounded, comforting the weeping widow, depriving yourself so as to add a few biscuits or a toy to a parcel . . . Ouch!'

A violent kick from Léa had hit home.

'That'll teach you!'

'What a beast you are! You haven't got the vocation. You'll never be a real woman . . .'

'How dare you say that I'm not a real woman,' she flashed, sitting up straight and arching her back, her nostrils quivering with rage.

He could not help it, he had to tease her. She was never more desirable than when she was angry. There was no doubt about it, she was a real woman, just as he liked them, both free and submissive, coquettish and natural, brave and weak, happy and wistful, sensual and modest. Modest? . . . not really, if anything, she was provocative. She did not behave like a well brought-up young Frenchwoman, but more like the heroines of American films, enticing and prim but capable of sitting on a chair with their skirts hitched up to reveal the tops of their stockings, or leaning over to let you glimpse their cleavage. Léa was one of those. He knew how she liked to arouse men's desire. She blossomed under their gaze. It did not make him jealous, but rather amused and slightly irritated him.

'I was only joking and you know it.'

The arrival of the wine waiter with the champagne created a distraction. They drank in silence, engrossed in their own thoughts.

Léa was the first to speak.

'When are you leaving?'

'The day after tomorrow.'

She blanched and shuddered, then drained her glass in one gulp.

'So soon!'

She said it with such simplicity that he almost rose to his feet and took her in his arms.

'Come on!'

He paid the bill and got up.

They ran across the Champs-Elysées. In the Rue Balzac, she asked;

'Where are we going?'

'To a hotel.'

Desire surged through her body. She would like to have protested, to have been shocked by his offhandedness and tell him that she did not want to be treated like a whore, but none of that would have been true. He behaved exactly as she would have wished.

The hotel where he took her was a *maison de rendezvous*, where lovers met. There was too much pink drapery, too many crystal chandeliers, too many plush carpets and the sounds were too muffled. There were too many mirrors, doors with the names of flowers on them and lewd staff wearing expressions of indifference. The perfume of the previous occupant lingered in the room with its enormous four-poster bed. A suitably comely maid entered with a pile of thick pink towels. On the wall was quite a pretty engraving, representing Fragonard's *Le Verrou*, which Léa found amusing. The same print had hung in her father's study at Montillac.

'Come here, quick.'

She shared his impatience. She flung off her clothes and was the first to be undressed. Without even bothering to remove the pink satin bedspread, she lay down and offered herself to him.

The soft light from the pink silk lampshades shed a gentle glow over the bodies of the two lovers who lay smoking in silence. Léa's body seemed to be made of a soft, delicate substance, while François's appeared to be made of a raw material the colour of terracotta. The young woman raised herself up on her elbow and her finger traced a long scar reaching from his heart to his groin.

'You haven't been injured anywhere else since the Spanish Civil war?'

'Nothing serious. A bullet in the shoulder. Would you love me if I was all scarred?'

'It would suit your sort.'

'And what is my sort?'

'Bad, as my uncle Luc would say. You should have heard him say: that child's a bad sort.'

'I couldn't agree more, you're a very bad sort.'

'Oh . . . !'

She hammered her fists on his chest, but soon found her hands pinned behind her and her legs immobilized under François.

'And now? What are you going to do? You're at my mercy. Do you love me?'

'Let me go! I shan't answer you while . . .'

'While what?'

'No François! I've got to go home.'

'We've got plenty of time.'

'No, no, I'm frightened of getting pregnant!'

François Tavernier froze.

'Now you're telling me!'

'I only just thought of it.'

He burst out laughing, making her jump.

'You should have thought of it sooner. I'd love to have a baby with you.'

'You're mad!'

'Mad about you, my beauty.'

'Let me go . . . I don't want a baby!'

'Too late!'

At first Léa struggled, then pretended, and then was completely overwhelmed by the pleasure she always experienced with this man, although she was reluctant to admit it.

After they had made love, François was worried about this baby business. He had meant it when he said he wanted to have a child with her, but in the present circumstances, it would be crazy. He had tried to warn her several times, asking if he should take precautions, and she had always been evasive. Selfishly, he had considered the matter closed, and now she was telling him she was frightened of getting pregnant. What a thoughtless creature she was! What would he do if she were pregnant? He knew a back-street abortionist near the metro Cambronne, but he would not let her filthy hands near Léa's stomach for anything in the world. There was only one solution: marry her.

For many years, he had rebelled at the thought of marriage: he was too fond of women and his freedom. But, when it came to Léa, the idea had already occurred to him. But what about her? Would she agree? He could not be certain. In that area, she was different from all the other girls; she was not waiting for a husband to come along, apart from a schoolgirl crush on Laurent d'Argilat, a desire that had been fanned by the latter's engagement to Camille. What a wonderful woman she had become, but she was so strange, so unpredictable! She would switch from laughter to tears or from the greatest audacity to the deepest fear. He put that down to the experiences she had lived through during the last few years, but was not entirely convinced.

'Help me join the Red Cross.'

And she was still going on about that! What the devil did she think she was going to do wading around in the mud, the blood and the horror?

'The Red Cross doesn't need you. I'm perfectly aware that lots of young ladies from good families join, but it's not a tea-party.'

'I know. I'm absolutely serious. Help me.'

It was true, she seemed utterly in earnest. His heart missed a beat. Supposing it was a means of getting away from him? Of drawing closer to Laurent?

'Why, sweetheart?'

'Run me a bath.'

He obeyed and stayed in the bathroom for a long time looking at his reflection in the mirror, saying: 'watch it, old chap, you're as much in danger of losing her as you are of ending up getting hitched.'

'Why?' he asked, walking back into the bedroom.

'I'm not really sure. Something is pushing me into it.'

'Make an effort, it's not a decision to be taken lightly.'

'I'm not taking it lightly even if I'm not sure why I want to do it . . . I could reel off lots of reasons, all of them excellent . . . but . . . I don't want to see my sisters any more, or my aunts . . .'

'Charles has been entrusted to your care by his father.'

'That's the only thing that might have stopped me . . . Françoise will take better care of him than I will.'

'But he loves you!'

'I know . . . don't say it! I want to go. I feel stifled here . . . I don't feel anything in common with anybody . . .'

'Not even with me?'

'With you it's . . . how can I say? . . . It's wonderful, while I'm in your arms. Then . . . it's as though all the things I'm frightened of were going to come down on me and swallow me up . . .'

'But Léa, you know very well they're fantasies . . .'

'Maybe, but that doesn't make any difference . . . Please, if you love me, help me.'

There was such distress and determination in her request. He held her close and stroked her head which was buzzing with so many painful contradictions.

'I'll do as you wish . . . if you had a little patience, if you trusted me a little, I'd chase away all those ghosts . . . It breaks my heart to see you like this and not be able to do anything about it. But if you think that's the best way of recovering your sanity, I'll help you.'

'Oh! Thank you! Drat! The bath!'

Chapter 27

The following morning, François telephoned Léa to say that he had arranged an appointment for her with the officer of the French Red Cross who was in charge of recruitment and that upon his request, Monsieur de Bourbon-Busset would act as her guarantor.

'Who is this gentleman?'

'He's the man who, on 24th August, set up the General Commission for the repatriation of prisoners of war, deportees and refugees. In addition to that, he is the managing director of the French Red Cross. You couldn't have a higher recommendation.'

'Tell him he won't regret it, and thank him.'

'You have an appointment tomorrow morning at 9 a.m. at 21, Rue Octave-Feuillet. It's in the sixteenth district. Don't forget to bring all your papers. You will be interviewed by Madame de Peyerimhoff. Be on time. Apparently she's a stickler for punctuality.'

'Thank you, you're wonderful.'

'Don't thank me. I don't enjoy doing this. But I realize your heart's set on the idea. You're as stubborn as a mule. I'm leaving first thing in the morning. I beseech you to spend this evening with me.'

'It's going to be hard to persuade my aunts to allow me out.'

'Don't worry, I'll deal with them. I'll come and pick you up at seven. Dress up.'

Léa's heart was racing when she hung up. She did not like the idea of his departure. A nagging anxiety skulked in the back of her mind. It was stronger than her fears for Laurent in the midst of all the fighting. She fell weak at the thought that something might happen to François. Although she had not heard from Laurent since he had left, she reassured herself with the thought that if he were injured – for she refused to think about the worst – they would be the first to hear about it.

The flowers and the chocolates sent the de Montpleynet sisters into raptures. Albertine simply said that Léa had not fully recovered from her illness yet and she should not be home too late. François Tavernier promised and drove her away in a luxury car confiscated from a prominent black market dealer. He took her to a small recently opened restaurant in Montparnasse. The place reminded her a little of the clandestine restaurant in the Rue Saint-Jacques.

'What became of your friends Marthe and Marcel Andrieu? And their son René?'

'After René's arrest . . .'

'Was René arrested?'

'Yes. Tortured and deported. Marthe and Jeannette went back to the country with the little one at the beginning of last summer. Marcel stayed in Paris. He was denounced as a collaborator by his concierge. The local chief of police came, and as he had been one of their best clients he cleared Marcel, saying he was a member of the Resistance.'

'Wasn't he?'

'Yes and no. He helped and entertained a number of Resistance fighters, but he never wanted to join a network. René was a member though.'

'Poor Marthe.'

'Let's drink to her health, she'd like that.'

The meal was delicious and restored Léa's high spirits. Once again Tavernier admired her vitality.

He told her he had opened a bank account in her name at the Société Générale on the Boulevard Saint-Michel. She merely thanked him and said no more. She thought: 'I'll be able to buy myself some new shoes.'

That evening, they made love with a slowness and tenderness that was unusual for them. It was as though they were savouring every inch of each other's bodies. Their pleasure rose, nonchalant and irrepressible, to submerge them in a tenderness that was almost painful, bringing tears to their eyes. To grip him better, she wrapped her legs around his and only opened them, satisfied, when she felt her lover became aroused again. Once more, their pleasure transported them out of the present.

They fell asleep for a few minutes in each other's arms. Léa was the first to awaken and she lay there studying this man who was about to leave her. Something told her she would not be seeing him again for a long time. She drank her fill of that face which, relaxed in sleep, looked like that of a youth. How old was he? She had never asked him. How could she know so little about him when they had known each other for several years? What was it that made her refrain from finding out who he really was? Now, she wanted to know everything about him: about his childhood, his youth. Did he have any brothers or sisters? What were his parents like? Were they still alive? Why had he fought in Spain? What role did he play? Did he know her uncle Adrien well? Who were the women he had loved? What had been his profession before the war? And what would he do once it was over? So many questions that would remain unanswered since he was leaving the next day.

How handsome he was! Handsome . . . ? Yes, those rugged features, that brutal jaw, softened by a wonderful mouth with full, well-defined lips, those thick eyebrows which emphasized an expression that was sometimes hard, and the next minute tender or ironic. That irony had often hurt her, even if behind it she could sense a passionate interest in anything that affected her. The memory of those expressions distressed her.

She caressed his broad shoulders, her fingers disappeared among the hairs on his chest and slid down his stomach where his strong grip immobilized her hand.

'Caught you, sweetheart, taking advantage of a poor man while he's asleep.'

Through his half-open eyelids he scrutinized her with an

acuteness that belied his lighthearted words. Embarrassed by his intensity, she tried to withdraw her hand.

'Carry on, I like seeing you lean over me like that.'

Without flinching, she continued her progress towards his genitals. She took his penis in her hands and caressed it until it grew hard between her fingers. Léa straddled her lover's body and slowly lowered herself down on top of him.

She made love to him, controlling his pleasure, slowing down when she felt him on the brink of climaxing and watching the effect on François's face.

'I'm your mistress,' she said defiantly.

Their bodies were locked together. They did not take their eyes off each other, allowing the other to see them in that least controllable, least discreet state, at the moment when pleasure contorts and disfigures the loved one's features. Léa arched her back as she came, supported by François's outstretched arms. He revelled in the sight before exploding inside her, as they looked into the depths of each other's eyes.

How long did they remain like that, as if suspended in time? With a cry, she fell down on top of him and held him tight. Thus entwined, he rocked her for the duration of the spasm that had seized her.

She finally quietened down and remained as if unconscious for a moment. He bathed her forehead and temples with a damp towel and began wiping her stomach and thighs.

'It's cold,' she murmured, pushing him away.

He dressed her as though she were a little child. He gave up trying to brush her tangled hair. When she stood up, she was as limp as a rag doll.

Deeply moved, he carried her to the car, and then up to her room. When he put her to bed, naked, she was already asleep, with that smile that sometimes hovers around the corners of a baby's mouth when it is dreaming.

He tore himself away from his contemplation, which was becoming too painful, and tiptoed out of the apartment in the Rue de l'Université like a thief.

Chapter 28

Bordeaux,
Tuesday 22nd August 1944
Dear Léa,

I am writing this letter without knowing whether you'll receive it, either because I'll tear it up before I finish it or because the postal service isn't working any more.

We collaborators, militiamen, Gestapo supporters or volunteers to go and fight in Germany are preparing our departure amid total chaos. You should see all those people who not so long ago paraded through Bordeaux. Now, they're making themselves scarce and skulk along the streets. A lot of them try to join the Resistance, but the Resistance chaps are suspicious of last-minute recruits. Since the allied landing, they've been queuing to join up in their thousands. Just wait till the war's over, the biggest heroes of the Free French will be the collaborators who've changed sides now the boot's on the other foot. They make me sick! If the situation changed again, they'd come running back to Field-Marshal Pétain's fold.

As for me, I've decided otherwise. I'm going to fight for this lost cause. I'll be like the heroes in the thrillers we used to read when we were children. Do you remember how we loved them, those knights in shining armour who had made a pact with the devil. Of course, they always lost, but what a price they exacted for their defeat!

I'm telling you all this so that you understand that it's not political ideals that made me sign up with the Waffen SS. There's nothing left for me here, there's no future for me. Once the war is over, the victors will have only one thought in their heads: revenge. I'm no sheep waiting to go to the slaughterhouse. The only thing I'm afraid of is that they'll take it out on my parents. My father's received several threats, and he's been mistakenly accused of setting fire to Montillac and killing your aunt.

Maurice Fiaux's body has been found. He was executed by the Resistance. Aristide also had Grand-Clément and his wife executed. They're in control of the area. I saw your cousin Philippe last week and I advised him to hide in a safe place. He said his father wouldn't hear of it, for he had nothing to be ashamed of. That's not what some people in Bordeaux think. Here, we're following what's happening in Paris very closely. I suppose you're out there fighting on the barricades. It would not have taken much for me to be by your side.

As this is perhaps the last letter I'll ever write you, I want to apologize for the way I behaved towards you, but I was crazy about you. I know that's no excuse, but it's important for me to say it. I also want you to remember me only for the happy times we spent together as children. What I'll remember of you are our races through the vineyards, playing hide-and-seek in the chapels of Verdelais, our swims in the Garonne and our tussles in the hay. Think of me occasionally and remember you are the only woman I've ever loved. I will always love you and keep you in my heart until the very end.

> Your faithful friend,
> Mathias

PS Later this afternoon, at ten past five, a train of German railway workers is leaving Bordeaux for Germany. A carriage is reserved for us.

Mathias! Where was he now? Dead or alive? His letter had taken nearly three months to reach her. The postal service was not really back to normal yet. There had been no news from either Laurent or François. Léa was not unduly worried, for she was fully preoccupied with her training as a driver for the Red Cross.

The day Tavernier had left, she had kept the appointment in the Rue Octave-Feuillet. She overslept and just had time to slip on a dress. The crowded metro seemed to take forever. When she finally reached the Pompe station, she elbowed her way out and rushed to the exit. It was ten past nine.

Madame de Peyerimhoff was immaculate in her well-tailored uniform. She gave Léa a cold reception.

'You are late.'

'Yes, I apologize, madame.'

'You have been recommended by our director. Do you know him?'

'No.'

'I see,' she said disdainfully.

Léa hung her head.

'Do you always wear that hairstyle?'

She blushed like a child who had been caught out.

'Is it the latest fashion? Well, if you like that sort of thing . . . However, I would advise you, if we accept you, to wear your hair in a style that is more in keeping with our uniform. Can you drive?'

'Yes, madame.'

'Change a wheel? Do mechanical repairs?'

'No.'

'I see. We'd have to teach you everything. Presumably, you don't know how to give first aid to the wounded either?'

Léa could feel herself flaring up. This woman with her airs and graces was getting on her nerves!

'No, madame.'

'Why do you want to join the Red Cross?'

'To serve my country.'

Whew! She had done well to listen to Françoise. Her answer seemed to please Madame de Peyerimhoff, who said, in a gentler tone:

'Good. If we decide to accept you, you will have to go on a six-week training course during which you'll learn basic mechanics and how to give first aid to the wounded that you'll be transporting. After that, we will send you wherever you are needed most.'

'When will I hear whether I've been accepted?'

'Later on this week. We have a lot of applicants and we only want to take those who seem capable of fulfilling their duties. If you are accepted, you will be notified.'

The interview concluded with a vigorous handshake.

Five days later, Léa ate her first meal with the other new recruits at the training centre in the Rue François-Ier. Right from the start, she showed a particular aptitude for changing wheels, cleaning spark plugs and carrying out minor mechanical repairs. Alix Auboineau, who was in charge of the ambulance garage in the Rue de Passy, complimented her in front of her companions. One of them said knowingly:

'You're in the redskin chief's good books.'

'Why do you call him that?'

'It was Claire Mauriac who nicknamed him.'

'The daughter of . . . ?'

'Yes, she's in Béziers, where she's doing a wonderful job. I hope she'll come back soon.'

It was doubtless thanks to the friendly atmosphere and comradeship, and the training course which she was enjoying, that Léa was able to cope with the dread and the horror of Ruth's letter which arrived on 7th October.

'Verdelais,
2nd October 1944
My darlings,

I've been putting off writing to you every day for the last two weeks. What I have to tell you is so dreadful that I am having difficulty holding the pen, which is why this letter is so messy.

My lovely little ones. You're going to have to be very brave after you've read the following. Albert is dead. His body was found buried in the garden of the villa occupied by the Germans in Le Bouscat. The autopsy revealed that he had probably committed suicide by hanging himself, after being tortured. Mireille is extraordinarily brave. She hasn't shed a single tear, and yet she still hasn't heard a word from her son. The funeral was in Saint-Macaire and was attended by the Mayor of Bordeaux and a large number of Resistance fighters. On this occasion, unfortunately, we witnessed a shameful spectacle: blows and insults aimed at supposed collaborators. Since the horrendous deaths of Madame Bouchardeau and the Fayards, the slightest hostile cry sets me off shivering and it lasts for several hours. The doctor says it'll get better in time.

Your uncle Luc and his son were lynched by the crowd in Bordeaux . . .'

'Oh! My God!'

Lisa de Montpleynet was overcome with nausea and had to rush to the bathroom, while the others sat there stupefied. When Lisa returned, pale and dishevelled, her hair damp, they were all frozen in the same positions. The elderly spinster placed her hand on her sister's arm. That affectionate gesture made Albertine pull herself together.

'Continue, Léa,' she said in a quivering voice.

The young women had to make several attempts before she could utter the gruesome words:

'. . . and their bodies were paraded through the streets and then ditched in the Quai de la Monnaie. The apartment and Luc's practice were looted. It's appalling! Their elderly housekeeper, Madame Dupuis, came to visit me in hospital. She said that since he'd heard about Pierrot's death, your uncle hadn't been the same. He aged ten years in the space of a few days. Philippe and Monsieur Giraud, the longest-serving employee at the practice, tried in vain to persuade him to go somewhere safe where he was not known. He refused, but advised his son to leave. Your cousin would not go as long as his father stayed. Madame Dupuis is convinced your uncle stayed to get himself killed . . . My darlings, I know how upset you must be. Forgive me. The hardest part is yet to come . . .

'No, not him,' groaned Léa who had broken off in mid-sentence several times.

'Who else is dead?' asked Françoise.

'Here, you read it, I don't want to see his name . . .'

'The police came to ask me to identify a body. With them was a shortish man in uniform, accompanied by two Free French soldiers. The three men examined the corpse. Each one in turn identified him. When it was my turn, I felt faint. "You have to," said the superintendent, "you're the only member of the Delmas family in the area." So I looked. Part of his face had been gnawed away by animals, but the other half was immediately recognizable. It was your uncle Adrien . . .'

A cry escaped Léa and she sank to the floor, stammering:
'I knew it . . . I knew it . . .'
Albertine and Laure helped her up and carried her to the settee.
'Lisa, call the doctor!'
'How did he die?' she managed to utter, pushing away the hands supporting her.
'Françoise will finish the letter later. Now you know the worst. Why torture yourselves even more?' said Albertine.
'No! Finish the letter.'

'. . . the forensic doctor concluded it was suicide . . .'

'Suicide?' they cried.
'A priest . . . ? That's impossible,' declared Albertine, crossing herself.
Léa sat huddled up, her teeth chattering, shattered with grief. 'I knew it,' she thought. 'I should have understood when he hinted to me that he'd lost his faith . . . But why did he do that? . . . He was brave . . . He played an important part in the Resistance . . . It's so unlike him . . .' She tried to reject the notion of suicide with all her being but something told her it was true.
Albertine and Lisa had fallen to their knees and joined their hands together in prayer. For these fervent believers, there was no greater crime in the Catholic religion than suicide. The idea that this man was damned not only caused them deep sorrow, it also challenged the very foundations of his preaching. They had heard his words ring out through

294

the vaults of Notre Dame and he had had more influence on their consciences than their own priest. Through this monstrous deed, Father Delmas refuted the notion of a Christian God. They could see that quite plainly.

It was Laure who picked up the letter which had fallen from Françoise's hands and continued reading:

'None of us wanted to believe it, but we soon had to accept the evidence of the chief of police and particularly the doctor. Your poor uncle was buried in the family vault in Verdelais cemetery, near the remains of your aunt and your parents. There was no Mass and no benediction. It would have been the funeral of an outcast if it had not been for all the flowers. I'm staying with my friend Simone in Verdelais. I'll remain here until I recover my health. Then, if you like, I'll come and join you. The grape harvest began two days ago. It'll be a good harvest but the wine will only be average. I had to hire German prisoners to help. They are so afraid of the Resistance that they work very hard. Some decisions need to be taken as to the future of the estate and the rebuilding of the house. I've started going through Fayard's papers, but I can't make head or tail of them. The notary is dead, we'll have to find another one. Think about it.

Darlings, forgive me once again for bringing you all this terrible news and know that I remain your devoted friend.

All my love,
Ruth.'

'It's true, it's the grape harvest, I'd completely forgotten,' thought Léa.

All that day, they remained locked in their own rooms. Charles and little Pierre sought refuge in Estelle's kitchen.

Léa missed her topography class. Albertine telephoned Madame de Peyerimhoff to explain briefly the reasons for her niece's absence.

During the following days, Léa experienced a female solidarity that she would never have dreamed existed.

After practising on the roads full of potholes in the forest of Marly-le-Roi, Léa turned out to be an excellent driver and an excellent mechanic. The head of the garage in the Rue de Passy said that after the war, she would have no trouble finding a job in a garage. On the other hand, she was reluctant and clumsy when it came to giving first aid.

'Be careful,' shouted the doctor in charge of the class, 'if you lift someone with a stomach injury like that, their intestines will fall out . . . Gently, you're handling this one, who's definitely got a spine injury, as if he were a sack of potatoes . . . I wouldn't like to fall into your clutches . . .'

In the evenings, she met Laure and her chums who were dealing in cigarettes, whisky, petrol and stockings with the American soldiers. On some days, they danced until one o'clock in the morning, spurred on by a desire to live, and to live now, that was shared by most boys and girls of their age. Although she was very popular with the young men, Léa did not respond to the advances of the soldiers who had come from afar to take part in the liberation of Paris. She flirted, laughed and drank with them but remained strangely distant, appearing to be present while her mind was somewhere else, far away and inaccessible. In the arms of these forward young men, she behaved provocatively for as long as the dance lasted. In fact, one day she was slapped by a tall black sergeant who did not appreciate her coquetry.

It was in this atmosphere that Laurent's first letter arrived on 7th November. It was dated 28th October.

Dearest Léa,

I heard that you are better from François Tavernier who has arrived on an assignment under General Leclerc. I was so overjoyed that I was at a loss for words . . . He also told me that you were persisting in your decision to join the Red Cross. You know that I don't entirely approve of the idea, but everyone is master of their own destiny. Thank your aunts on my behalf for everything they have done for Charles. Tell them to talk to him about me, and as for you, as long as you're with him, talk to him about his mother.

Since 22nd September, we've been up to our knees in

296

mud. The Paris buses which were used to transport the battalions of Parisian Free French soldiers incorporated into the 2nd Armoured Division, are in it up to their axles. We had to abandon two vehicles and give up the idea of getting them across the Meurthe. The others were towed by Shermans. The Parisian kids say it gives them a taste of Pan Am. You should see the poor blighters, wading about in the sludge, with only sandals or plimsolls on their feet, dressed in an assortment of odd bits of clothing, with no helmets and sharing one gun between two. They are patrolling the woods. Although they complain loudly about everything, they never recoil in the face of a mission. We are almost constantly under mortar fire. The enemy is no longer short of ammunition as in August. We're marking time until the real offensive. We in the armoured tanks don't like that. We've stupidly lost two outstanding officers whom we met in Africa and who had become close friends: Captain Dubut and Captain Geoffroy. The angriest person is my friend Georges Buis who feels as though he's beginning to put down roots in this place. He moans about it, saying that it's no place for a knight to be turned into a clay statue.

In the mess, morale is sinking. They can already see themselves spending the winter in this "wretched country". Buis and I went for a spin over the lines in one of the artillery's Piper-cubs to break the monotony. A demoralizing sight through a sheet of rain. We are prouder of the few miles' progress we make in one day than of the enemy prisoners we've captured. Even Captain Déré, a veteran of Tunisia, a cheerful fifty-year-old, is talking about joining the expeditionary corps leaving for Indochina "to see a bit of countryside at least". It's no longer the enthusiasm of the liberation, but rather a feeling of total disarray. It's time they let us see a bit of action, otherwise the 2nd Armoured Division will fall apart.

I've just re-read this letter and I've given you a pretty dismal picture of the 2nd Armoured Division. It's not quite like that. Since we left Paris, we have indeed seen some fighting. No doubt the awful weather and this period of intertia are responsible for my disenchantment.

From the corner of the mess table where I'm writing to you by the light of a hurricane lamp, I can see the rain bucketing down through the tent "window". This rain is enough to depress even the most hardened characters.

I won't bore you with my chatter any longer. I hoped to feel the ray of sunshine of your beauty in writing to you, but the darkness of melancholy is weighing down on me and on these lines. Forgive me. Give my love to my darling son.

> With all my affection,
> Laurent.

He was well, in spite of the dark depression she could feel throughout the letter. What about François? Why didn't he give any sign of life? She had been to the War Ministry, where they had not been able to give her any news of Major Tavernier.

On 20th November, Léa passed her examination, despite the disastrous stretcher-bearing test which had finished with the nurse who was playing the wounded soldier falling off the stretcher. She carefully stowed away her Red Cross ambulance driver's certificate after the speeches by Madame de Peyerimhoff, Alix Auboineau and the doctor who had taught them first aid.

Three days later, she was sent to Amiens to Mademoiselle de Guillencourt's castle, which served as the Red Cross headquarters. There, she threw herself into saving civilians: children mutilated by mines, the dying back from the Front, and fleeing Belgian and French families, sick with cold, hunger and dysentery. At first, she thought she would not be able to stand it, but a girl called Jeanine Ivoy who was so tiny that she'd had to have a uniform specially made, took her under her wing and inspired her with courage.

Towards the end of December, Léa finally received some mail from Paris. There was a letter from Françoise, one from

Albertine, one from Laurent and one from François. She rushed to her room which she shared with Jeanine Ivoy and tore open François's letter which was dated 17th December.

Sweetheart,
I don't know whether this letter will reach you. I spoke to Laure on the telephone a few hours ago and she told me you were in Amiens but didn't know if you were still there. After my first assignment, the General has given me another one. Now, he's sending me . . . I can't tell you where, but just wait till I see you again! I'll find a way of turning up, in Amiens or elsewhere. I miss you terribly, I'm dying to hold you in my arms and go far away from Europe with you. When all this is over, I'll take you to visit some friends of mine in Brazil. We'll spend our days on the beach, making love and forgetting the last four years. Take good care of yourself and don't be cross with me for this short note. A plane is waiting to take me to my destination. Did I tell you I love you? Well I do. Love and kisses all over.

François.

As she read, her body recalled her lover's caresses. A thrill of pleasure shot through her.
I love him too.
With a happy sigh, she slipped the letter inside her blouse, next to her skin, so that she could feel the sheet of paper his hand had touched next to her breast.
She opened Françoise's letter.

Dearest little sister,
Here in Paris we're surviving thanks to Laure's dealings which bring us some coal and food. She sends her love and says she's fine. Ruth has come to live with us. You wouldn't recognize her. She's an old woman now and the slightest sound makes her jump out of her skin. We've appointed a new notary to take care of our affairs. He's found a trustworthy man to look after the Montillac vineyards. But when spring comes, we have to decide whether

or not to sell. Laure and I are inclined to sell, there are too many unhappy memories associated with the house and the estate. We don't have the money to rebuild the house and knowing that it is in ruins is very distressing. What choice have we?

Pierre is well. He's galloping all over the place now. He's only got six teeth and I'm beginning to worry that something might be wrong with him. Charles is too good and too quiet for a boy his age. He often asks for you, especially at night. Apart from that, he's fine. Our aunts are growing older but they're always so kind to us. My hair's growing back and soon I'll be able to go out without the turban. I haven't heard a word from Otto, but I know he's alive. It's dreadful not knowing anything about the one you love and not being able to talk about it to anyone, except Laure from time to time.

Ruth greeted the news that Strasbourg had been liberated with emotion, as you can imagine. They're still purging like mad. It's not always the guiltiest who are sentenced. Everybody listens to the French broadcasts from Baden-Baden where we can hear the familiar voices of Brinon, Déat, Luchaire, and so on. The other day, there was a Resistance gala at the Comédie-Française and a poem by Paul Claudel praising General de Gaulle was read. It was my first outing. I noticed several prettily turbaned heads among the audience . . . Near me, a journalist said to his neighbour that the poem had been written in 1942 in praise of Feild-Marshal Pétain and that it had been slightly adapted to suit the circumstances:

'*Monsieur le Maréchal, voici cette France entre vos bras et qui n'a que vous et qui ressuscite à voix basse.*

France, écoute ce vieil homme sur toi qui se penche et qui te parle comme un père'*

It's funny, don't you think? Laure dragged me to the

---

* Monsieur le Maréchal, here, lying in your arms, is that France who has nobody but you and who is coming back to life with a whisper.

France, listen to this old man leaning over you and speaking to you as a father.

Crillon bar which is full of ladies in uniform and English and American officers from different regiments, all vying to be the most elegant. I recognized the ex-mistress of a German general on the arm of an English colonel. She recognized me too and winked as if to say: Life goes on!

Petiot has finally been arrested, he was a lieutenant or captain in the Free French Forces!

We're preparing the children's Christmas presents. We're going to miss you. Lots of love and kisses,

Your loving sister,
Françoise.

Françoise seemed to be coping with the situation. In a way, it would be better for her safety and peace of mind if Otto were dead. She was strong enough to bring up her son on her own. What did it matter what happened to Montillac? The mere idea of having to think about it was unpleasant. She had to forget, blot out everything that had been her reason for existence.

Albertine's letter only contained advice and the news that she would be sending her woollen stockings and warm under-wear for Christmas. They would be most welcome, for the light gaberdine Red Cross uniform was not sufficient protection against the wind that howled across the plain.

Léa toyed with Laurent's letter for ages before finally deciding to open it.

Dearest Léa,

I hope you're not suffering as much from the cold as we are. When General Leclerc saw that his men were freezing, he ordered rabbit-skin waistcoats to be made for them, and we're all very grateful to him. After the rain and the mud came the snow and ice. The vehicles are suffering from it as much as the men. No doubt you've been following our progress in the press. After the capture of Baccarat, we drank champagne in goblets engraved with a gloved fist that were made for Goering. I met Colonel Fabien, a communist and former member of the Inter-national Brigades and assistant to Colonel Rol-Tanguy, the

301

head of the Free French of the Ile de France region during the liberation of Paris. He's a strange man, always dressed in jodhpurs and a tunic buttoned up to the neck. He followed the 2nd Armoured Division with three thousand men, nearly all from the Paris suburbs, together with the Free French from all over the country, but in particular from Janson de Sailly's group. The Paris Brigade, which is attached to the 3rd Corps of the American Army (Patton), has been given the name of the Lorraine Tactical Company. On their request, it was attached to the 1st Army, under General Lattre. On 10th December, in Vesoul, the General inspected the new recruits, some of whom have only just turned seventeen. They do not always find integration easy. They have difficulty taking orders from certain officers and NCOs, especially those with brand new uniforms. They call them the "mothballites", a nickname which needs no explanation.

Fabien is an endearing character. He joined the International Brigades when he was seventeen and was wounded. It was he who killed that German officer on 30th November 1942 in the République metro station. He was arrested and tortured but he escaped and carried on fighting in the Resistance. His father was shot by the Germans and his wife deported.

The days leading up to the capture of Strasbourg were very trying for all of us. Buis said it was because of the bad weather that the men were quarrelsome, picking fights at the drop of a hat. During the entire time, General Leclerc was in a filthy mood, pacing up and down the damp rooms of the Birkenwald château, the same castle where Foucauld's future father spent his holidays. At dawn on 23rd November, it was raining cats and dogs and the General was mechanically banging his stick on the floor and frowning, with that twitching in his right cheek that showed he was in a state of great agitation. It wasn't until half-past ten that a motorcyclist went into the room where all the officers were gathered. His numb hand held out a piece of yellow paper sent by Rouvillois. The message was written in code: "Cloth is in iodine". That meant he had entered Strasbourg. General Leclerc let out a great guffaw: "Come on, we're on our way," he cried.

Luckily, we suffered very few losses, but one in particular devastated several of us. The death of the chaplain, Father Houchet, who had been with Leclerc ever since Tchad. When he heard the news, the General rushed to the hospital in the middle of the night. I saw him brush away a tear when he saw the remains of the man whose faith, whose cheerfulness, kindness and untiring devotion had made him the most liked and respected man in the division. The following day, the soldiers who were supposed to carry the coffin weren't able to get to the chapel, and so it was we officers who carried it. On Sunday 26th, the standard of the 12th Cavalry fluttered over the Place Kléber before a silent, sparse crowd. We could sense great tension in the air. Then, gradually, windows opened, flags were waved, a muffled *Marseillaise* rose from the streets and then died away. It was only when General Leclerc arrived that the population gave free rein to their jubilation.

After five days, we left to meet up with the 1st French Army which had conquered Belfort and Mulhouse. The Germans were now isolated and had been driven back to the Rhine. When I say we were on our way again . . . ! Like a donkey going backwards as my father would have said. Leclerc's men had no desire to be incorporated into the 1st Army. The weather was appalling. Rain, snow, storms: luckily the morale of the 2nd Armoured Division can resist anything. We even kept our sense of humour. To give you an example: the other day, we were sheltering in a little station, the sort where you see departure written on one side and arrival on the other. Over the rails came a volley of 88s, which is rather unusual as the Germans haven't got much ammunition left. When we got up again, Georges Buis said to La Horie and me, as he dusted himself down with one hand and pointed to the hole made by the shells with the other: "They're such conformists, the Germans." We burst out laughing because the shells had come in from the arrival side. These schoolboy jokes, sometimes in the middle of the worst fighting, this comradeship that I would have called barracks humour before, help prevent me from going mad when I think of the suffering and death of Camille. Some nights, when the cold is so intense it keeps me awake, I see her gentle face leaning over me. Then I have the feeling she's calling me, that she's saying: "Come. Come and join me . . . don't leave me alone . . . " I feel as though I'm being pulled by a supernatural power.

But I'm so stupid! Forgive me, dear little Léa, I'm making you sad, you loved her too. How is Charles? But perhaps you're not with him? Perhaps you are also in one of those places where people are dying . . . if you aren't, talk to him about his mother and me, make up happy childhood memories for him. Soon it'll be Christmas. Do you realize! I haven't spend one Christmas with my son since he was born! Spoil him and don't be stingy with the sweets, the toys or the candles on the tree. Tell him his daddy will be thinking of him even more than usual that evening.

> Your affectionate friend,
> Laurent.'

At the thought of being a long way away from her loved ones for that first Christmas in a partially liberated France, Léa began sobbing like a child. All her memories of an indulged child came flooding back: religious fervour at midnight Mass in the freezing church in Verdelais or under the mediaeval vaults of Saint-Macaire, her emotion before the crib, and the angel collection-box which nodded its head and played the first bars of 'Away in a manger' when you put a coin in the jar it was holding. She remembered the mixture of fear and joy when she saw the illuminated Christmas tree which had appeared miraculously in the courtyard outside the house, her beating heart and cries and laughter as she opened the drawing-room door . . . and there, near the hearth where a fire of dead vines blazed, would be the presents from Father Christmas, a mountain of brightly-coloured parcels. After a moment's hesitation, a second's feigned surprise, the three sisters would rush over to the stockings, pushing and shoving each other out of the way, screeching like wild animals. They would set to, ripping off the wrapping paper, pulling off ribbons, jumping up and down in their excitement and rushing over to kiss their parents and Ruth, whom they suspected were hand in glove with Father Christmas! Later, when they were older, they enjoyed the same happy times at home and would not have spent Christmas anywhere else for the world. The war had put an end to all that . . . Thanks to Léa's efforts, Christmas was maintained under the Occupation and, although it was a sad affair, without many presents or the usual sparkle, they still celebrated. It was the first Christmas Léa was spending away from home. At that moment, nothing seemed more terrible. She forgot the suffering around her, the war that was still going on and all the dead who had been part of her life.

'What's the matter? Bad news?' inquired Jeanine Ivoy, coming into the room.

Choked with tears and hiccups, all Léa could manage was to shake her head.

'So what are you upsetting yourself for?'

'Because . . . it's Christmas . . .' she managed to stutter.

Jeanine stood gaping in astonishment at her ravishing friend and suddenly she too began to cry. How long it takes to outgrow childhood! They cried for a few minutes without daring to look at each other, then their eyes met and they both suddenly burst out laughing and threw themselves into each other's arms.

On 24th December, they returned late, exhausted from ferrying the injured to the local hospitals. They climbed up the steps dragging their feet. The hall was in darkness, but there were bright lights and the sound of cheerful, animated chatter rising above the jazz music coming from the drawing-room. That was not how they usually spent their evenings there. Intrigued, they pushed open the door and were amazed to see an enormous Christmas tree with fairy lights and cotton-wool snow decorating its branches. A huge fire was

305

crackling merrily in the hearth. A man was leaning against the mantelpiece holding a glass. He stepped forward, smiling.

'You're the last, come in quickly and close the door.'

Léa slowly shut the door and then turned round, her hands behind her back, still gripping the sculptured copper doorknob whose ridges were digging into her palms. She leaned against the door for support as, walking towards her as if through a mist, came the man who always managed to disconcert her.

François Tavernier had the greatest difficulty prising Léa's hands away from the doorhandle. The owner of the castle walked over to them.

'Mademoiselle Delmas, get a grip on yourself, you've turned quite pale. Doubtless it's the excitement of seeing your fiancé again.'

Her fiancé? What was she talking about? The owner continued:

'Thanks to Major Tavernier, we'll be able to have a real Christmas. He brought everything we need for our Christmas party with him in his car. Go and get changed, you're all muddy.'

Tavernier bowed to the elderly lady and said with his most charming smile:

'May I accompany Mademoiselle Delmas?'

'Of course, Major, meanwhile we'll finish setting the table.'

Léa allowed him to lead her away like a sleepwalker.

'Where's your room?'

'Upstairs.'

When they reached her room, he fell on top of her, showering her with kisses.

She submitted, incapable of responding. He became aware of her passivity and drew back. He held her at arm's length and studied her.

'I hoped for a more enthusiastic welcome.'

Suddenly, she flared up.

'You turn up without warning when I thought you'd gone to the devil . . . you . . . you introduce yourself as my fiancé . . . you leap on top of me and . . . what's so funny?'

'That's more like it. It's not like you to be so passive.'

She blushed and struggled as his arms enfolded her again.

'Calm down, we haven't got long. I'm in danger of being court-martialled for coming to see you. I'm supposed to be in Colmar.'

'Why did you say I was your fiancé?'

'So that my unexpected visit wouldn't shock them and so I'd be allowed to see you alone. Kiss me.'

She was crazy to quibble like that. She had been so over-joyed to see him, she thought she would die. She returned his kisses and dragged him over to one of the beds.

'Come on,' she said.

They made love clumsily, as if they were being timed. But their bodies adjusted to the haste and very soon, their pleasure made them forget the time.

There was a discreet knock at the door and they came down to earth with a bump. Giggling, they smoothed their clothing.

'Come in,' said Léa.

Her room-mate's tiny head appeared round the door.

'I'm sorry, I've got to get changed,' she said without daring to look at them.

'Please go ahead. It is I who apologize for having delayed Léa. I'll leave you.'

The two girls got undressed without exchanging a word.

The champagne, oysters and foie gras that François Tavernier had brought made the meal extremely lively. By the time it was over, most of the guests were slightly drunk. Shortly after midnight, François stood up to take his leave.

'So soon?' they chorused, with the exception of Léa who hung her head.

'Alas, I must be back by the morning. Carry on celebrating without me. Darling, will you walk to the car with me?'

'Goodbye Major, thank you for everything.'

Outside, a blizzard was raging. The front-wheel drive vehicle was covered with a thick blanket of snow. François opened the door and pushed Léa inside. His icy hands felt their way underneath her skirt until they found her warm stomach.

'Unbutton my trousers.'

'No,' she said as she complied.

Hampered by their clothes, they made love with a violence, a brutality belied by the tender words they murmured in each other's ears.

Breathless, they gazed at each other in the flickering glow of the car light. As they sat in silence, they both tried to engrave the image of the other in their memories. No doubt it was the cold, but it seemed to Léa that a tear rolled down and mingled with her lover's hair.

A nearby clock struck two. François shivered and got out of the car.

'I've got to leave.'

He started up the engine. Standing near the door, Léa trembled, wrapped in a blanket smelling of petrol. Leaving the engine running, he hugged her.

'Where are you going?' she asked.

'To Alsace.'

'Alone?'

'No, my orderly's waiting for me in a bar. Sweetheart, we'll see each other again soon. After Alsace, I'm going to Russia as an observer on behalf of General de Gaulle.'

'But why you?'

'Probably for a perfectly simple reason: I speak Russian.'

He spoke Russian! He'd never told her. But there were so many things she didn't know about him. One lifetime wasn't long enough to get to know him.

'François . . . !'

'Be quiet. If you speak, I won't have the courage to leave. Just tell yourself that I'll always know where to find you. Now, tell me something that'll help me be patient when I think of you.'

'I love you.'

'That's what I wanted to hear. You're so stingy with your "I love you's". Now go back inside quickly, you're frozen.'

'No! Kiss me!'

He kissed her . . .

'Go on, scram!'

He pushed her away with such violence that she fell over.

He repressed the urge to go to her aid. As the car pulled away it sent a shower of snow over Léa, who still lay where she had fallen in the snow.

It was only a few seconds later that one of her friends, concerned that she had not reappeared, found her huddled up, almost buried under the snow. Helped by the castle handyman, she carried her up to her room where she made her drink a steaming grog and put her to bed with a hot-water bottle under a pile of blankets.

She slept until midday the next morning.

Chapter 29

On 6th February, the day after the Treaty of Yalta, Léa received two crumpled letters which had been forwarded by the Red Cross. One was from Laurent, dated 3rd January.

Dearest Léa,

I've come, as usual, to wish you a happy new year. I hope 1945 brings you happiness. You, of all people, are made for it. You have a will to live that is capable of rising above the worst torments. As for me, I feel the desire to live ebbing away. I am fighting this morbid state of mind as hard as I can, by thinking of Charles, but very soon my morose thoughts take me back to the happy times in the past which have been lost forever.

Here, in this universe of mud and rain, the transition from life to death has become an everyday occurrence. The modesty of men who have agreed to die for a just cause is one of the things I have found most moving since we began fighting. On the eve of an attack when we know many of us will fall, that we might be among the dead, the atmosphere in the camp is that of restrained fervour. Men exchange letters, shave closely and speak in low voices. They know, even before their superiors, that an attack will be taking place. There's no need for a warning bell. If you could only see how beautiful the expression on a man's face is when he is thinking that tomorrow . . . it's as though he has been cleansed of any stains. It's as if he were looking beyond the visible, beyond himself. That too is war, that silent solidarity, that dignity which makes men valiant knights, legendary beings, heroes. They are people who, taken as individuals, would perhaps not be of great interest, but here, through their great sacrifice, they join the ranks of the heroes of the battles of Austerlitz and the Marne in the annals of history.

These words coming from me will no doubt astonish you, as they astonish me. No doubt, if I had not joined Leclerc, if I weren't in the 2nd Armoured Division, I would have spoken differently as a confirmed pacifist. But one cannot live with impunity alongside people who are dying by the thousand for the freedom not only of France but also the world, without having second thoughts about certain judgements favoured by an easy life and a horror of violence.

In my last letter, I wrote to you about Colonel Fabien. Well, he's dead. He was killed stupidly by a mine, with three of his comrades on 27th December. I keep thinking about his little daughter.

If the same thing should happen to me, do not forget that Camille and I have entrusted you with our child. Before leaving, I made you his legal guardian in my will. Talk to him about war, but so that he grows up to hate it. Tell him, though, not to bear a grudge against the German people: they made a mistake. I knew the Germans well before the war, I spoke their language, I listened to their music, I read their poets, I admired their courage. Often, my friends from Berlin and I would drink to the United States of Europe. After so much horror, it needs men and women to pick up that idea and make it happen.

Dearest Léa, I pray to God to keep you at the beginning of this new year, and to heap His blessings on you.

> With all that is left of my love,
> Your friend,
> Laurent.

'He's going to die,' murmured Léa with dazed weariness.

She turned the second letter over and over in her hands. Like the first, it was covered with postmarks. She did not recognize the handwriting. Finally, she made up her mind and tore open the envelope. On reading the name at the bottom, Léa understood and, without shedding a tear, began to read.

Mademoiselle,

Nobody likes to be the bearer of bad news. Yet, out of friendship and because I gave my word, I have to tell you this sad news. Captain Laurent d'Argilat died on 28th January. At the same time, sixteen officers of the Tactical Company were killed as well as Commander Puig and Lieutenant-Colonel Putz. It occurred during the capture of Grussenheim which cost the 2nd Armoured Division more lives than the capture of Salerno and Strasbourg.

We had orders to cross the Ill and reach the Rhine, and divide the pocket of Germans down the middle starting from Sélestat. The snow was two feet deep. The temperature was below freezing. The vast white plain, broken by the occasional copse, criss-crossed with canals and rivers, made a perfect target for the Horniss, Jagpanthers, and 88s. The 3rd Company engaged the enemy first and took the famous 177 crossroads. The 2nd went beyond it and was given orders to take Grussenheim at all costs. At the rear, the rest of the regiment followed the fighting eagerly, quaking for their comrades but at the same time envying them. The units which weren't engaged voluntarily took off their ammunition belts to help those in front reload their guns with greater speed. It was during this attack that our friend was killed. His tank blew up a few yards away from mine. The force of the blast ejected his body.

Later, we went back to fetch him. He looked as though he were asleep, his expression was peaceful and there were no wounds visible on his body. He is lying in the village cemetery until he can be transported to the family vault. All his comrades miss him. He went out to meet death. Perhaps he wanted it? If I told you what he did in Herbsheim, you would believe me because I'm telling you, but you would be flabbergasted. The way one courts death is very personal. It is secret. People of calibre, who commit suicide and who thus advance to the threshold of the sacred, usually leave a note saying nothing other than: "Do not try to understand, I myself do not know why . . ." I do not think we really know why we risk our lives in war. We do it because it is the done thing. Laurent did not leave any letters and it is best that way. "A fine officer", a colonel said. From his sceptical lips, that is a great compliment. But for me, he was more than that, he was a man who was brave enough not to reveal his weaknesses.

Mademoiselle, I share your sorrow and commiserate with your grief.

Yours in friendship,
Georges Buis.

And so he had gone to join Camille. Despite her chagrin, Léa could not help feeling that it was a good thing. True, there was Charles, and it was almost a sort of cowardice to have abandoned him with no other family than the Delmas, but Laurent had wanted to die . . .

'Mademoiselle Delmas, we wish to inform you of your next assignment. You have been selected to drive a seriously wounded British officer from Brussels to Cannes where he will be spending a few weeks convalescing on the shores of the Mediterranean.'

Léa could hardly contain her joy. Every day, her work was becoming increasingly painful. Driving along the roads full of ruts and potholes was not pleasant, but collecting the wounded, not forgetting the limbs lying around, giving them first aid, hearing their groans, seeing their tears on amputation, listening to them calling their mothers before they died, snatching newborn babies out of the rubble, living in the mud, blood, pus and excrement was a horror that repeated itself day in and day out.

Since she had learned of Laurent's death, her nightmares had returned with a vengeance. Not a night went by without images of Camille crawling towards her child, the man from Orleans with his knife or Bernadette Bouchardeau's screams of agony. Blood during the day and blood at night. She lived in terror of going to sleep and in anguish on awakening. Perhaps she would have coped with it better if her new companions, apart from Jeanine Ivoy, had not vented their jealousy on her and ragged her constantly. She was given all the worst duties: cleaning shoes, washing the ambulances, sweeping the offices. At first, she had agreed to do all these things, thinking it was part of her job, but she very soon realized that this was not so. When she objected, it was made clear to her that they could manage perfectly well without her services. And so her astonishment was all the greater at being assigned such an important and pleasant mission.

'I see you are surprised,' continued the woman, 'it is only due to your knowledge of English. You do speak English, don't you? It is stated in your file.'

Léa nodded, dreading that she would be asked to say a few sentences in the language of Churchill. She had a little schoolgirl English and it was several years since she had studied.

'You will leave tomorrow with a convoy on its way to Belgium. When you reach Brussels, contact the Red Cross headquarters. You will find all the necessary information in this briefcase as well as the appropriate documents enabling you to travel across Belgium and France. You are on leave until your departure. I wish you a safe journey.'

'Thank you, madame. Goodbye.'

Léa took advantage of her afternoon of freedom to go and have her hair done in a hairdressing salon which had been set up in a barracks not far from the castle. When she emerged, with her hair shorter and clean, she felt a new woman and was slightly more optimistic about the future. That night, she did not have any nightmares.

The following morning, she bade the girls goodbye, feeling no regrets at leaving the north.

Chapter 30

Léa would have believed she was on holiday if it had not been for the wounded being pushed in little carriages and the crowds dressed predominantly in the uniforms of the allied forces. For a month, she had been leading a life of idleness and parties in the company of her wounded soldier.

Sir George McClintock, a colonel in His Majesty's army, was of Irish origin. He preferred Bourbon to tea, playing cards to playing soldiers, and smoked fat cigars. His sense of humour was second to none, his bravery was tantamount to folly and he was a womanizer, according to his comrades. On top of all that, he was very rich. This was the man Léa was supposed to be taking care of. He had been wounded in the Ardennes offensive near Dinan, and had seen death from such close quarters that he intended to make the most of every single day that was left of his life. As soon as he was able to walk again, with the help of crutches, Léa's life became a whirlwind: cocktail parties, garden parties, dances, picnics, trips out to sea and excursions in the country. He wanted her by his side all time, saying that the minute he set eyes on her, he had known that his life was going to be turned upside down by this little French girl with dishevelled hair, a provocative mouth, proud and anxious eyes and a figure he guessed was ravishing under her badly tailored uniform. He had insisted, in return for a few fistfuls of pound notes, that she have a room close to his at the Hotel Majestic.

For the first few days, he had been tired and slept most of the time. On the evening of the fifth day, he asked to be taken down to the hotel dining-room. He made a face when he saw Léa take her place opposite him wearing her uniform,

315

her blouse immaculate, her tie carefully knotted and her plastic shoes shining.

'Haven't you got anything else to wear?' he asked her in disgust, in that accent which had so charmed Léa at first.

She blushed, feeling ugly.

'I don't have anything else. If you're embarrassed to be seen with me, I can eat in my room.'

'Forgive my, my dear, I didn't mean to hurt you. You look charming in your uniform, but it is a bit monotonous.'

The following day, the couturiers and shoemakers of Cannes descended on the hotel. She started by refusing, but gave in when she saw their evening dresses, one in particular of black chiffon, another in green taffeta, and splendid Italian slippers in "real" leather, an unheard-of luxury! As the evenings were still a little chilly, the colonel insisted she take a short silver fox fur cape too.

The following day, she accompanied him to the garden party thrown by the American Club. He was proud of her conquests. They all vied to bring her a glass of champagne, orange juice or lemonade, a plate of cakes, dessert or fruit. Léa laughed, and became as coquettish as the spoilt young carefree girl she had been before the war.

At the beginning of March, George McClintock received a letter summoning him back to England. Léa begged him to take her with him, she would not return to Amiens for anything in the world.

'You still need me,' she told him.

'I'll always need you, now,' he said with uncharacteristic gravity.

'You see!' she replied flippantly.

He smiled and said there would be a lot of red tape. It was no easy task to obtain the permission of the Cannes Red Cross, then that of Paris. Léa's assignment bore an impressive number of stamps.

Despite the air-raids and frequent air-raid warnings, and the atmosphere of fear, the week in London turned out to be as frenzied as the time spent in Cannes. It was as if all the young people, the eldest of whom were under thirty, flung themselves into dancing, courting and drinking sessions with a kind of frantic compulsion, as if trying to make up for lost time, and to forget the war, which was not yet over, in alcohol and cigarette smoke.

A letter from Mathias, forwarded from Paris by Laure, which had reached France after a roundabout journey through Switzerland, was handed to her on her breakfast tray between the tea and bacon and eggs.

It was impossible to make out the date on the envelope and Mathias had forgotten to date his letter.

My beloved,

'Honour is fidelity'. That's what is carved on the archway at the entrance to Wildflecken camp where I have joined the French Waffen SS. I have adopted this motto when I think of you. It's the motto of the Waffen SS. The camp is situated on a wooded mountainside in the middle of a beautifully kept park. There are a few small buildings dotted among the greenery along the impeccably kept paths that lead to the Adolf Hitler Platz. Iron discipline rules and training is tough. At first, many men fainted during the exercises, but now, we all have the bodies of athletes. Those who can't keep up are sent to other units. This discipline is necessary to control four or five thousand young men who are eager to fight. I like it like that, it helps me not to think of you too much. In November, we were joined by two thousand militiamen. They swore allegiance to Hitler, some of them reluctantly, on 12th November in the presence of Darnand and Degrelle. It was bitterly cold. The troops paraded in perfect order in a howling blizzard. Brigadeführer Krukenberg and Oberführer Puaud inspected the troops. But what impressed the Frank-guard most, was our chaplain, Monsignor Mayol de Lupé's speech, which he delivered on horseback. He wore the full dress uniform of a Waffen SS officer and his cross gleamed on his chest. He took no notice of the snow blowing in his old, weatherbeaten face and he spoke of the Führer as he spoke of God, and his benediction resembled the Nazi salute. In these extraordinary surroundings, above which fluttered the tricolour, the Reich's war flag and the black standard of the SS, the militiamen, their arms outstretched, repeated after three of their comrades who had stepped forward opposite an officer holding an unsheathed sword: "I swear to obey Adolf Hitler, head of the Waffen SS, as a loyal and faithful soldier in the fight against Bolshevism." I noticed that not all arms were raised.

I'll never forget the day I took the oath. The phrasing was not exactly the same. It took place with great solemnity, between two oak trees, according to German custom. There were two crossed daggers on which our motto was engraved. An officer took the oath on behalf of all of us, in German. We repeated after him in French: "I swear, Adolf Hitler, Führer and reformer of Europe, to be faithful and brave. I swear to obey you and the leaders you have appointed until death. So help me God!" I'll never forget as long as I live the first time I did the Hitler salute, shouting *"Heil Hitler!"* That day, I felt I was severing myself from my past for ever.

Here, officers and simple soldiers receive the same treatment. There are no privileges. There is no officers' mess. We all eat the same food in the same place. If there's a round of schnaps, the soldiers are served first and the rest is shared among the officers. The higher your rank, the more tasks you have to perform. During the weekly dinners, called *Kamaradschaft*, the humblest soldier has the right to laugh at his superiors, and anyone who tries to punish him will be heavily sanctioned. That's what we French find the most astonishing, we're so used to standing to attention while listening to our superiors and being billeted in barracks while they lounge around in gilded drawing-rooms. Here, they are making new men out of us. Life in Wildflecken is very tough: we have to get up at six and lights out is at eight p.m.

Our training is hellish: icy showers, parade, Hitler salute, coffee and then a relentless series of exercises, manoeuvres, hikes . . . The only rest we get is during the theory classes on arms and strategy. In the evening, I collapse on to my bed and, invariably, I'm dragged out again when the whistle blows for nocturnal exercises. We have to rig ourselves out, groping around in the dark, and go out into the freezing night that chills you to the marrow. For the last two weeks, I haven't slept for more than four hours in a row. I feel as though I've had nothing to eat – I miss those sumptuous high teas at Montillac. At lunch-time it's cabbage soup and potatoes, sausages at five o'clock and a little margarine on sticky black bread . . . I'm amazed that it's enough to build us up and keep us clear-headed. And even the most French of Frenchmen among us seem to adapt to this regime.

However, it's not all a bed of roses and for a while, the atmosphere has been deteriorating, mainly because of the militiamen, many of whom are unable to get used to it. Nearly every day, since the formation of the Charlemagne Brigade, French SS men have deserted to go and join units leaving for the Front. That's how some of them end up with the Wiking and Totenkopf divisions.

Our commander is Oberführer Edgar Puaud, who was formerly on the Russian Front. For the last few days, I have been a real SS: my blood group has been tattooed under my left armpit. That means, if we're injured, we stand a greater chance of being saved, but if we're taken prisoner, we are more likely to be killed. We are all impatient to leave for the Front. We think it's only a matter of days now.

Yesterday, some comrades managed to get hold of some German wine and smuggle it into the camp. It's strictly forbidden of course. Just as we were about to open the bottles, we were almost caught by Brigadeführer Kruken-berg. I don't think he was taken in because as he went out, I heard him say: "Ah! Those Frenchmen!" After he had gone, we drank to his health. The wine, a white wine, a little dry but very fruity, wasn't bad at all. Of course, it's nowhere near as good as Montillac wine. I wonder if the grape harvest was good and if it took place in the best conditions.

Where are you? I can't imagine you anywhere other than Montillac. You're at home on that soil. If you receive this long letter, and if you have the patience to read it to the end, it'll be as though we've sat down and had a long chat. Don't forget me and remember, I'll think of you right to the very last.

Mathias.

The tea was cold and the marmalade had a strange taste. Léa tried to imagine Mathias in his SS uniform but could not picture it. It seemed to her that at the root of all this, there had been an incredible misunderstanding that had turned a kind, cheerful boy into a little brute who would do anything. But was that any more absurd than her being in London in a luxurious old hotel with its windows replaced by greaseproof paper? There was a knock at the door.

'So, you've had news from home, have you?' asked George McClintock, coming into her room.

The Englishman's cheerful face brought a sad smile to her lips.

'What's the matter? Is something wrong?'

'No, no, it's nothing.'

'Up you get! We're leaving.'

'Where are we going?'

'To Germany.'

'To Germany!'

'Yes, I have to join the 2nd Army.'

'But you've barely recovered!'

'A doctor friend of mine has pronounced me fit for service. I can't see myself staying here while my comrades are getting themselves killed.'

'What about me? What am I supposed to do? Do I wait patiently here until the end of the war, do I go back to Amiens or the Paris office?'

'Not at all, you're coming with me.'

'I'm coming with . . .'

'Yes, one of my friends is, what's the word? . . . director of the British Red Cross . . .'

'You certainly do have a lot of friends.'

'Yes, it comes in useful sometimes. I told him about your great knowledge of mechanics and your remarkable competence in nursing the wounded.'

'As long as he takes your word for it and doesn't put me to the test.'

'The person who's in charge of the ambulance drivers here is a friend of Madame de Peyerimhoff's. In a few days, you should be receiving notification of your temporary transfer to our Red Cross.'

Léa flung off her covers and kissed the Englishman on both cheeks.

'You're wonderful, George. How did you guess I wanted to go to Germany?'

'You've been talking about nothing else ever since we got here.'

A week later, Léa received her orders to serve under the G. P., Hughes Glyn Hughes, head of the medical team of the 2nd British Army. On the night of 5th April, she landed near Duisburg, about forty miles from the front.

That was the beginning of her descent into hell.

Chapter 31

A few hundred miles away, Mathias was also going through hell.

On 12th January 1945, three million formidably armed Russian soldiers, backed by tanks and planes, set off on a march from the Baltic to Czechoslovakia to wipe out the remains of the proud army of the Reich once and for all.

On 17th February, the Charlemagne Waffen SS, which had become a division, left for the Front. They reached Hammerstein, a large market town in Pomerania, on 22nd February. It was bitterly cold and an icy wind swept this landscape of lakes and woods. They pitched camp in an old Wehrmacht camp, which had been transformed into a stalag, pending the arrival of the heavy artillery. In the distance the booming of cannonfire could be heard.

Mathias's regiment, the 57th, was installed to the southeast of the town. The minute he arrived, Obersturmführer Feunay went off to inspect the positions with Oberjunker Labourdette and Mathias. After the cold, the thaw arrived overnight, transforming the dirt tracks into a quagmire where the horses sank up to their knees and the carts weighed down with heavy material and crates of ammunition got stuck. It took dozens of men to heave the vehicles out of the clay. At dusk, which soon fell, the temperature dropped to freezing again. All along their route stretched endless convoys of refugees fleeing the Russians. Old people, women and children tramped along in the mud, distraught and silent. Among them were a few Latvian SS, dirty and dishevelled, their hands in their pockets and their expressions vacant.

The first battle took place near Heinrichswalde. It quickly

turned into a massacre. They were outnumbered ten to one in the face of the Soviet tanks. Shells and torpedoes crushed the French SS positions. Close to Mathias, one of his comrades, his leg ripped off, was bleeding to death. Feunay gave orders to carry on.

All night, fresh convoys arrived at Hammerstein station and headed straight for the Front. Very soon, the companies of the 58th regiment found themselves being bombarded. At dawn, thousands of Russians advanced on them, shouting as they came. Twice they managed to repulse them, but they were soon overwhelmed by sheer numbers. The order was given to retreat. The survivors assembled and waited. In battle, communication was difficult. The Charlemagne division had gone to the front line without a single radio set. The vans went backwards and forwards from one company to another, conveying orders from the staff. At around midday, the noise of the tanks was deafening. The French dug themselves into holes, camouflaged at the edge of the forest. Feunay's men tried to join the 58th regiment through the woods, but all they came across were a few remnants wandering among the trees, dragging the wounded. During the evening, they reached the camp near Hammerstein from which they had set out that morning. Exhausted, they gulped down a bowl of split-pea soup and immediately fell asleep on the lice-ridden pallets in their huts.

Out of the four thousand five hundred men who had left Wildflecken, one thousand five hundred had died or disappeared. For a battle that had only lasted two days, it was a heavy toll. The survivors from the Charlemagne division managed to gather in Neustettin, a little town of sixteen thousand inhabitants, swamped by refugees and soldiers. The news of Jacques Doriot's death demoralized those who had joined up in his footsteps. On 5th March, in Körlin, they fought with the fury of despair, alongside a company from the Wehrmacht. Not far from Mathias, a German tank blew up. A soldier emerged and ran in a straight line, his uniform blazing. The division's doctor-lieutenant threw himself on him to put out the flames. Mathias joined him and helped him drag the man to safety. He was moaning softly. He had lost his helmet and his back was entirely burned. 'Poor fellow,' thought Mathias, returning to the battle. Suddenly, he froze in his tracks and retraced his footsteps. He leaned over the dying man, cleaned his face with a handful of snow and wiped it with a grimy cloth. It was him all right.

'Captain Kramer, can you hear me?'

The wounded man's face quivered when he heard his name on the lips of a Frenchman. He painfully opened his eyes and gazed at the German soldier who was unrecognizable under the muck and grime.

'Captain Kramer, I'm Mathias, from Montillac.'

'Montillac . . .'

'Yes, you remember, Léa . . .'

'Françoise . . .'

'Yes.'

'Françoise . . . my son . . .'

Otto tried to raise himself up, but was unable to. He said in a voice which grew feebler with every word:

'Look . . . in my pocket . . . my papers . . . and a letter . . . it's for Françoise. If . . . you survive . . . give it to her . . . the papers too . . . Swear you will . . .'

'I swear I'll give them to her.'

Mathias searched Otto's tunic. He removed a wallet, carefully wrapped in a piece of oilcloth which reminded him of the one in the kitchen in Montillac, and slipped it under his shirt next to his skin. The dying man did not take his eyes off him. He nodded. The Russians were drawing closer. Mathias had to leave. Otto attempted to speak and Mathias guessed rather than heard what he was trying to say:

'What . . . is a Frenchman . . . doing here?'

He shrugged. What could he answer?

The Brigadeführer gave the order to evacuate. Mathias's battalion tried to escape in the direction of the Oder and then Belgard. Bassompierre's stayed behind to blockade the enemy.

The 57th regiment advanced under cover of the still, freezing night, by the light of the candles which illuminated Körlin. They hid by day and inched their way forward in the dark, only a stone's throw from the 'Ruskies' as they called them. Battles were short and violent. Ammunition was growing scarce and their horses had either died or bolted. For a while, their only food had been what they could steal from German houses where women and girls who had been raped wept. When there was no food left in the villages, they ate raw beetroot which gave them dysentery. They slept huddled close together for warmth. They awoke covered in lice. The grime accumulated in the folds of their skin. Some liked to joke that it helped keep them warm and frightened the lice away. They advanced like robots, their faces a mask of weariness, their eyes bloodshot with heavy shadows. The enemy was everywhere, harrying them relentlessly.

The temperature suddenly rose and the fields were covered in delicate green. In a forest, where they had stopped, exhausted, they walked on a carpet of violets. Mathias lay down and inhaled their fragrance. With Léa, it had always been a great event when the first violets of spring appeared in the sheltered part of the grotto. As a child, he would make them into bunches whose perfume filled the little girl's bedroom. With his calloused hands, he began to gather the flowers under the mocking gaze of his comrades. Then, as if driven by an instinctive force, they all started picking violets which they carefully slipped into their wallets with their papers. This cheered them up. They began to hope that spring would flower for them too.

'We're filthy,' one of them remarked.

They looked at each other. It was true they were filthy. At the edge of the wood ran a river. They tore off their grubby uniforms, shook their clothes from which fell huge lice, and leapt into the water. It was freezing! As they had no soap, they scrubbed themselves with handfuls of earth. They rubbed themselves vigorously, shrieking with laughter like children. They dried themselves by chasing each other naked among the trees. Feunay watched them pensively. Their socks had worn out ages ago. They had all adopted the 'Russian sock', a square of material under the sole, folded first over the toes, then the left-hand flap was folded over and lastly the right. You pulled hard on the back. If the flaps were crossed properly, it was easy to pull on your boots. It protected and held the foot in place admirably.

They reached Belgard, which was in flames, at two o'clock in the morning. They crossed the cemetery and vanished into the night. At about four o'clock, Oberführer Puaud arrived in Belgard with the main body of the division, about three thousand men. Scattered Russian outposts welcomed them with machine guns and mortars. The Waffen SS slipped into the town, retaliating. Those who crossed the central square in Belgard by the light of the flames, had to step over the bodies of hundreds of old people, women and children.

Puaud, who had an ankle wound, advanced like a sleepwalker, his face ruddier than usual. In the countryside, the firing had ceased, replaced by the rumbling of engines and the creaking of tanks which resounded eerily across the plain. The enemy was everywhere. The Charlemagne division moved through the fog. When the mist lifted in the morning, they found themselves surrounded by Soviet armoured tanks, in the middle of a vast bare stretch of land. They were dumbfounded. Time stood still for a second, there was total silence . . . then, suddenly, the massacre began. In less than two hours, most of the Charlemagne division had been neutralized . . . The wounded were finished off and the survivors were rounded up and shepherded off in the direction of the prisoner of war camps. A few men managed to flee into the woods.

The five hundred men in Mathias's battalion reached Meseritz castle in a pitiful state. They were wounded and suffering from dysentery, but happy and proud of their leaders who had temporarily got them away from the fiery furnace. They left the following day, setting off into the sunshine, de-loused and cleanshaven with their guns slung over their shoulders. They had been joined by two hundred and fifty survivors of the 58th regiment, the Holstein SS, a Hungarian regiment and the SS Nordland division as they made their way to the Oder estuary under the orders of Krukenberg. They crossed the Rega just south of Treptow and reached Horst, on the coast, late that afternoon. Along the way, refugees mingled with the exhausted soldiers as they waited for boats to take them to Sweden.

At nightfall, Mathias and a few of his companions reached Rewahl, a small seaside resort. Just as in Horst, the town was overflowing with refugees and routed soldiers. This crowd was in a state of frenzy: side by side with dazed and mournful creatures, young women made love with whoever came along, allowing themselves to be caressed by grimy, lice-infested men, while swigging schnaps. Children watched them impassively, while their parents continued their desperate course without seeing them. On the iodine air of the Baltic wafted the musty smell of engines, the stench of pus and blood, the sweetish odour of sperm, the stink of shit, that of thousands of unwashed bodies and, strongest of all, the persistent smell of cabbage soup that was being dished out to the terrified crowds.

'The Russians are coming . . . ! Hurry up!'

Men, women, trucks, horses and tanks all collided, fighting, jostling, knocking over, crushing and killing anything that got in the way of their flight. The sea front was one long procession of damned souls, trying to escape the fires of hell. Mothers who had lost their minds, clutching a dead child to their skinny breasts, girls flinging themselves from cliff tops to avoid being raped, men pushing their wives under tanks, soldiers firing at the truck drivers so they could take their places . . . children screaming . . . horses whinnying . . . dogs whining . . . the sound of the sea . . . the rumble of a cannon . . . the whistle of shells . . . mines blowing up . . . death . . . death . . . death . . .

The Charlemagne division marched on, fighting and getting drunk when they came across wine. Following the hordes of refugees, they advanced westwards along the beaches, hit by shells from time to time that sent the mutilated bodies flying skywards amid a shower of sand. The crowd trudged on, indifferent to the screams of the wounded and the groans of the dying.

They joined the German lines at Dievenow late at night on 9th March. The following day, at dawn, the Russians bombarded them, attacked and were repelled. In the afternoon, the men were taken into the German Supply Corps arms depot. They were thrilled to finger the automatic 32-shot guns and pranced about in the new uniforms, chain-smoking the cigarettes they did not want to leave behind for the enemy.

Finally, their boots struck the wood and iron of the pontoon bridge slung over the Oder. With Brigadeführer Krukenberg in his new gloves and Obersturmführer Feunay at their head, they filed over in orderly fashion, leaving behind the 'furnace' where ninety per cent of their number had been lost.

The following day, the Führer's headquarters sent out a communiqué praising the role played by the survivors of the Charlemagne division in the liberation of the Pomeranian refugees. That made them feel very proud. They left Swine-münde singing:

> La où nous passons, que tout tremble
> Et le diable y rit avec nous.
> Ha, Ha, Ha, Ha, Ha, Ha, Ha!
> La flamme reste pure
> Et notre parole s'appelle fidélité!*

At last, about eight hundred volunteers out of the seven thousand who had left Wildflecken were assembled two hundred and fifty miles from Berlin in the little town of Neustrelitz and the neighbouring villages of Zinow, Karpin, Goldenbaum and Rödlin.

Krukenberg summoned the officers and asked them to keep only those who volunteered for future battles. The others would form a battalion of workers who were to leave Karpin at once. Three hundred men left under a single officer. Those who had chosen to stay signed an oath swearing absolute fidelity to the Führer until death.

---

* Wherever we go, let everything quake
And the devil's laughing with us
Ha, Ha, Ha, Ha, Ha, Ha, Ha!
The flame remains pure
And our motto is fidelity!

The Charlemagne division was not spared the boredom and ill humour that befalls an army during the wait to go into battle. Those men, who had shown such solidarity during the ordeals they had just survived, courageous to the point of recklessness in the face of the enemy, picked quarrels with each other at the slightest provocation. The main source of their present discontent was the food: half a pound of bread, an ounce of margarine, soup that was either too salty or too sweet, imitation coffee and two cigarettes a day each. The strict German discipline was not severe enough to constrain the French, who joked about the secret weapons that were going to save the Reich. Nobody believed in the victory of the Reich.

The division's morale reached its lowest when, in mid-April, four volunteers were shot for stealing supplies from a warehouse. They died without a single cry of protest after receiving absolution from the priest of the LVF, a replacement for Monsignor Mayol de Lupé who had retired to a German monastery.

On 20th April, in honour of Hitler's birthday, the men were given biscuits, a blackish substance supposed to be chocolate and three cigarettes. They celebrated the Führer's fifty-sixth year singing and drinking wine that Krukenberg had managed to wheedle from the Supply Corps.

They were shown a film with Zarah Leander, whose husky voice tugged at their heartstrings. After the showing, they watched a newsreel. The German announcer commented on images showing crowds scattering in all directions outside Notre Dame to escape the snipers' bullets on the occasion of de Gaulle's arrival in Paris. He said it was the communists shooting. The French SS left the projection room even more firmly convinced that they were the last bulwark against the communist invasion. Some even pictured themselves being given a hero's welcome by their fellow countrymen, parading down the Champs-Elysées acclaimed by those who saw them as the defenders of the West . . . The more clear-headed among them had no illusions: either way, it was the firing squad, or, at best, long years of prison.

*

On the night of 23rd April, Brigadeführer Krukenberg received orders to go back to Berlin with the French SS of the Charlemagne division.

The officers went to the barracks and made the men line up.

'Volunteers to go to Berlin, step forward!'

They all stepped forward.

In the morning, they were given weapons: grenades, Sturmgewehr and Panzerfaust. They were heavily laden, their chests criss-crossed with cartridge belts, lemon-shaped grenades hanging from their buttons and those with handles looped over their belts. They had never been so well-armed. The four hundred volunteers clambered aboard eight trucks, lent by the Luftwaffe, happy at the thought of defending the Führer. The Germans fleeing their capital watched in amazement as they entered Berlin singing.

Chapter 32

As a result of the Franco-Soviet pact, when the Russian troops entered Germany, the Russian government agreed to the presence of a number of observers whose task was to assess what had been taken from the French arsenals and draw up a list. Both sides pretended to take these assignments seriously. François Tavernier, who was already known to the Russian Secret Service, was one of the officers chosen by the French government. Before he left Paris, Professor Joliot-Curie had clearly outlined the objective of his mission. It was rather more important than chasing around after rusty equipment . . .

Until 15th March, Major Tavernier played a lot of chess, improved his vocabulary of Russian swear-words and got drunk on vodka with an application that earned him the respect of Gheorghi Malenkov, the head of the special department whose job it was to recover German industrial and scientific installations and in particular secret weapons.

The weeks François Tavernier spent running around between the headquarters of the various Soviet armies in Moscow almost got the better of his patience.

The 1st Belorussian army command sent him to the Front at the end of March and ever since he had been champing at the bit, his only distractions being chess and conversations with the General Vassiliev whom he had met in Algiers where he was military attaché.

Finally, the time was ripe for the major offensive against Berlin.

At four o'clock in the morning of 16th April, on the orders

331

of Joukov, three red rockets lit up the banks of the Oder, bathing the land and the sky in purple light for what seemed like an eternity. Suddenly, powerful floodlights were switched on, together with the headlights of the tanks and trucks, while beams from the anti-aircraft projectors swept the enemy lines. A great silence reigned in that light which heralded the end of the world.

Three green rockets were fired and the earth began to quake. Twenty thousand cannons exploded. A hot wind destroyed everything in its path, setting forests ablaze, burning villages and the processions of refugees. In this terrifying din, the high-pitched screams of katiouchka rockets rent the air.

The attack was launched by the 1st Belorussian Front, commanded by Joukov, the 2nd Belorussian Front by Rokossavski and the 1st Ukraine Front by Koniev. One million six hundred thousand men, most of whom were desperate to avenge a father, a brother or a friend who had fallen at the hands of the Nazis, advanced over the plains. The German towns were emptied of their occupants, who left behind them nothing but ashes. Tavernier understood the hatred that inspired the Russian fighters from Stalingrad, Smolensk, Leningrad and Moscow, who had crossed the whole of Russia to reach the Oder. The toll the war had taken on them was the highest in the whole of Europe. To avenge what their mothers, their wives and their daughters had suffered, the Red Army wanted an eye for an eye. Their revenge was total.

The French officer had become fond of these simple men who fought with a complete disregard for danger and who shared their meagre rations with their prisoners. As for the Russians, they were intrigued by this man who spoke their language, drank like a trooper and, although he did not fight, always found himself in the thick of battle. That was how he ended up with a bullet through his thigh.

'Keep still,' said General Vassiliev, visiting him in the country infirmary where they were dressing his leg.

'I'd like to see you in my shoes,' groaned Tavernier. 'Not only have I not found any equipment belonging to us, but you're keeping me out of things. I wonder what I'm doing here since I'm not allowed to fight alongside you.'

'You know very well that orders are orders. The same applies to all the foreign officers who are with our army as observers.'

François turned away, annoyed. If he was going to get himself killed, he'd rather die in combat. He was not cut out to be a civil servant.

Chapter 33

If Léa had been in any doubt as to the necessity of crushing
Nazi Germany, what she experienced on 15th April 1945
reinforced her hatred and disgust.

George McClintock had tried in vain to dissuade her from
accompanying the team of doctors and nurses under Dr
Hughes, head of the 2nd British Army's medical service, to
the camp of Bergen-Belsen which had just been liberated.

'They're short of people, I must go.'

Woods and meadows stretched as far as the eye could see.
The road wound its way towards the pointed steeple towering
over houses surrounded by flowerbeds. This was the village
of Bergen. If it had not been for the tanks, the trucks and
the soldiers posted along the roadside, the war would have
seemed remote.

Suddenly, at a bend in the road, in the middle of a desolate
plain, a nightmare universe rose up with barbed wire fences,
watchtowers and rows of greenish huts. Skeletal figures,
dressed in striped sackcloth, wandered about in the grey
sand. Some of those wraiths came to meet them at the fence,
their bony arms outstretched, trying to smile, while tears ran
down their ravaged faces. These smiles horrified the soldiers
who froze in their tracks as if they feared what they were
about to discover. Dr Hughes gave everyone a cup of hot
coffee, then they entered the camp.

Hanging from the barbed wire fences were half-naked
corpses. On the ground were more corpses, of men, women
and children, naked or covered in rags, wretched remnants
of humanity. The English walked slowly through this

undreamed-of world peopled with creatures who recoiled as they approached, protecting their faces with their hands, or who walked towards them, stiffly, dragging the weight of their own bodies around with difficulty. They advanced slowly with a rustle that resembled the brushing of the feet of thousands of insects.

Léa walked straight ahead, unable to take her eyes off those strange-coloured faces which ranged from dark brown to green to grey or purple.

The crowd of living-dead parted as they approached. They followed a covered way to the left, and then to the right. The reality of the camp was revealed in its full horror. Between the huts, away from the barbed wire fences, ageless creatures crouched in the squalor. Others lay on the ground, inert. Dr Hughes entered one of the huts and signalled to his companions to wait on the threshold. When he emerged, some time later, his face was ashen, his eyes were bulging with terror and his hands were trembling.

'Get them out of there,' he stuttered.

McClintock held Léa back.

'Go and fetch your ambulance and tell the others to follow you with the truck containing the blankets.'

When Léa returned, dozens of women were lying on the ground. A dreadful stench rose from their bodies. They tore off the filthy rags they were wearing. Lice flew out in all directions. They wrapped the wretched skeletons, covered in wounds and their own dirt, in blankets.

The day was spent transporting the poor creatures, cleaning and feeding them. They were nearly all suffering from dysentery and did not have the strength to get up, so they lay in their excrement. A hundred or so of them died very quickly. All night, doctors, nurses and soldiers helped to get the deportees out of their cess-pits. Illuminated by floodlights, the forty-five huts looked like the set from a horror film: tottering skeletons, crazy creatures dancing around fires, contorted, dribbling and leaving blackish trails in their wake. Faces that were no more than prominent cheekbones and huge dilated eyes slowly followed every move their liberators made.

Dr Hughes harassed headquarters to provide him with a hospital with fourteen thousand beds, more doctors, nurses and thousands of tons of medicine and medical equipment immediately, to try and save the fifty-six thousand people interned in the camp of Bergen-Belsen who were suffering from hunger, gastro-enteritis, typhus, typhoid fever or tuberculosis.

The following day, at dawn, they counted a thousand dead among those who had received some treatment. Everything was grey, the sky and the people, the ground was muddy, the huts were the colour of ashes, gestures were weary, rags were hanging everywhere and heaps of refuse lay in the mud. Men and women died without convulsions. It was raining.

Léa and George were making their way towards the camp gate to get a little sleep. They passed a large uncovered ditch, overflowing with matchstick-like corpses whose thinness was horrific. Léa stood rooted to the spot on the edge of the ditch and studied the scene without turning a hair. Those arms, those legs and those faces had belonged to men and women who had laughed, loved and suffered. It seemed inconceivable to her. There was nothing human about that heap of bones, they could not have belonged to living creatures like herself. There was something she could not grasp . . . Why? Why that . . . ? Why them . . . ?

'Come on, Léa, let's go through the woods.'

She gladly followed him.

'There!' she cried, pointing.

Hundreds of bodies were laid out between the pine trees.

A group of German civilians, pushed by English soldiers, were carrying the corpses and laying them next to the others. White-faced, the Germans laid the body of a woman close to where they were standing. Her torn clothing revealed legs covered with bruises, her body nothing but skin and bone. The rain made her face look like that of a drowned person.

'Léa . . .'

The young woman turned to George. But he had wandered off and was talking with one of the soldiers.

'Léa . . .'

Who was calling her in that feeble voice which seemed to be coming out of the earth? She looked down at her feet. The eyes of the woman who looked as though she had drowned were open and she was staring at her. Léa was paralysed by a terrible dread.

'Léa . . .'

She was not dreaming, the woman was calling her. Dominating her fear, she leaned over her. Huge, sunken eyes were glued to hers. Who was this half-dead creature murmuring her name? None of the features of this wretched face was familiar. Her lips were drooping, her hollow cheeks scarred . . . no!

'Sarah!'

Her cry made George and the soldiers spin round. The English officer rushed to her side.

'What's the matter?'

'Sarah! It's Sarah!'

'But this woman is alive!' cried the soldier, hurrying over to them.

McClintock lifted Sarah and ran with her to a tent which had been hastily pitched and turned into a makeshift hospital. The dying woman was laid on a camp bed and her rags were removed and replaced with a blanket. Léa knelt by her side and took her hand.

'You're alive, Sarah, you're alive. We're going to take you far away from here and look after you.'

'None of the people detained here is allowed to leave the camp, mademoiselle,' said the docter.

'Why not?'

'To prevent the spreading of epidemics. We have come across many cases of typhus. Besides, she can't be moved.'

'But . . .'

'Forget it, Léa, you must listen to the doctor. Come and rest, we'll come back later.'

'I don't want to leave her.'

'Be reasonable.'

Léa leaned over and kissed each of the cheeks that had been branded long ago by Masuy.

'You sleep, it's all over now, I'll be back soon.'

They walked towards the canteen in silence. They were given a cup of tea and a slice of cake. They were unable to swallow a mouthful. George held out a packet of Players.

'Help me get her out of here.'

'You heard, we mustn't . . .'

'I don't give a damn about what we mustn't do. We've got to get Sarah out of here.'

'Where do you want to take her?'

'To England.'

'To En . . .'

'Yes, there must be a way.'

'But . . .'

'Find one, please.'

'Oh Léa, we're living in a nightmare. I feel as if I'm going mad.'

'This is no time to start feeling sorry for yourself. Find a plane for England.'

'How on earth . . . ? Of course there are . . .'

'What, tell me quickly!'

'Of course, there are the planes flying the wounded home.'

'There you are! That's a brilliant idea. You arrange it so that I'm appointed to accompany the convoy.'

'It might not be possible . . . the hardest part will be getting her out of the camp. The health service is bound to increase surveillance of the camp gates.'

'We'll find a way. Find out when the next plane's leaving.'

'I will. But promise me you'll get some sleep.'

'All right.'

'Meet you later at your friend's bedside.'

Léa did not have a chance to get any sleep. As soon as she left the canteen, her boss, Miss Johnson, sent her to help transport the sick. It was not until late that evening that she was able to visit Sarah. George was already there. The poor woman was asleep.

'There you are at last! The day after tomorrow,' he whispered, 'there's a flight leaving. The commander is a friend whose life I saved. He's agreed to help us. I've got hold of the uniform of one of our dead comrades. Tomorrow evening, when it's dark, we'll dress Sarah in it and we'll carry her aboard the ambulance that you will bring here during the daytime. You have been designated to transport the wounded. You will accompany them to England where they will be sent to different hospitals up and down the country.'

'But they'll soon see she's a woman.'

'One of my friends, who is the King's physician, will meet the plane. He has been ordered by His Majesty to take care of some of the wounded.'

'You're wonderful!'

'Don't cry victory yet, the hardest part will be getting her out of here alive.'

'What do you mean, alive?'

'Dr Murray doesn't think she'll last the night.'

'I don't believe him,' said Léa, drawing close to the bed.

Sarah was having difficulty breathing, and her bony hands were burning with fever. Leaning over her, Léa studied her intently. The patient slowly opened her eyes. On seeing a face peering into hers, she flinched and tried to recoil.

'Don't be afraid, it's me.'

The ghost of a smile hovered on her lips.

'We're going to get you out of here, but you've got to help us and recover a little strength. You must, do you hear? You must.'

'Mademoiselle, don't tire her. Let her sleep.'

'Goodbye, Sarah, I'll be back tomorrow. Let me go now.'

Léa had difficulty in prising off the fingers that gripped her hand. She went over to the doctor who was examining a ten-year-old child who had escaped from the Revier hospital presided over by the sinister Karl.

'Dr Murray, what is my friend suffering from?'

He gently replaced the covers over the child before turning round. Léa flinched at his angry expression.

'What is your friend suffering from? There's an interesting question! She's suffering from everything! She hasn't got typhus, like this child who was injected with it, but perhaps she was given a syphilis injection, or smallpox, or plague, or perhaps she was sterilized, unless they implanted her womb with a chimpanzee embryo . . .'

339

'Be quiet, doctor!'

'Then don't ask me what she's suffering from. She's suffering and that's enough.'

He turned his back on her and leaned over another bed.

George was waiting for her, chewing on a short pipe that had gone out.

'Your Dr Murray is completely mad.'

'No, but he's likely to go mad. The horrors he's seen here are so appalling, he would never have imagined them possible, or that doctors could assist at certain experiments. His whole world is falling apart.'

'He'll never allow us to take Sarah away.'

'You heard: she hasn't got typhus. I'm going to ask Dr Hughes to transfer her to a hospital for non-contagious patients.'

'And if he won't agree?'

'We'll have to find some other way.'

They found another way. At about five o'clock in the afternoon, George McClintock arrived at Dr Murray's hospital accompanied by a dozen others.

'Here's the team to take your place while you get some rest. Dr Murray, allow me to introduce Dr Collins.'

'But no, Colonel . . .'

'It is an order from the head doctor.'

'Very well, come with me Collins and I'll fill you in on the most urgent cases.'

Luckily, Sarah was not one of these.

After Murray had left, McClintock distracted the attention of the new team. Léa, helped by the colonel's aide-de-camp, dressed Sarah in the stolen uniform. Her fellow sufferers watched every movement without batting an eyelid.

No matter how hard she tried, Sarah was unable to keep upright. Léa and the aide-de-camp supported her between them.

'Another of our men who can't cope with this horror,' said George, putting himself between Doctor Collins and Sarah.

Léa only regained her spirits when they reached the

landing strip. With the help of a nurse, she laid Sarah on a stretcher and carried her on board the plane.

Despite the cries and groans, inside the plane there was almost a holiday atmosphere. For most of these young men, the war was over.

Throughout the journey, Léa clasped Sarah's hand tightly in her own.

Chapter 34

The Berliners looked on in silence as the trucks borrowed from the Nordland division drove past, transporting uniformed SS wearing tricolour badges and singing at the tops of their voices, sometimes in German and sometimes in French:

> *Là où nous passons, les chars brûlent*
> *Et le diable y rit avec nous*
> *Ha, Ha, Ha, Ha, Ha, Ha, Ha!*
> *La flamme reste pure*
> *Et notre parole s'appelle fidélité!**

Women dressed in black rushed up, holding out a child, or a crust of grey bread, young girls blew them kisses. The young soldiers waved, then disappeared from view among the ruins while in the distance the cannon rumbled.

In the evening of 25th April, Mathias ate a tin of asparagus before falling asleep on one of the imitation leather seats in a brasserie in Hermann Platz.

On the same day, on the Elbe, to the south of Berlin, the soldiers of the Vth Army of the 1st Ukrainian Front led by Marshal Koniev, joined up with the Americans from the 1st Army near Torgau.

---

* Wherever we go, tanks burn
And the devil laughs with us
Ha, Ha, Ha, Ha, Ha, Ha, Ha!
The flame remains pure
And our motto is fidelity!

During the night, the Russian aircraft bombarded the town in powerful bursts. The noise of the explosions awakened the defenders of Berlin, who grabbed their guns ready to repulse a Soviet attack. But the planes flew off, leaving a heavy silence behind them.

The following morning, before daybreak, the soldiers made their way to Neukölln Town Hall. The day that was dawning promised to be magnificent. Finally, the order to attack was given.

The Russians fired from all sides. The French SS leapt from doorway to doorway, hugging the walls for protection. With the help of a Panzerfaust, Mathias blew up his first tank.

Throughout the morning, the battle raged, killing about twenty volunteers. Around them, everything was crumbling. Fires blazed, tinging the sky red. Soon the dust was so thick that it was impossible to see more than a few inches. The noise of the engines and tanks made the earth shudder, drowning the cries of the dying and the calls of the wounded.

Hauptsturmführer Feunay, wounded in the foot, continued to command his troops. In the Neukölln Town Hall, which had been transformed into a fortress, the Charlemagne division, reinforced by the boys from the Hitler-Jugend and white-haired veterans, fired from every opening. Soon, they had to face facts, they were surrounded. They could no longer count on the Nordland division's tanks which were out of petrol and ammunition. With a knot in their stomachs, they watched them drive off in the dust.

Feunay gave orders to evacuate the Town Hall and head for Hermann Platz.

The night ended in the cellars of the Opera House.

Total chaos reigned and no efficient plan for the defence of Berlin had been formulated. There were a few remnants of the foreign divisions of the Waffen SS, and a few youths and old men to take on hundreds of thousands of Soviet soldiers.

In the afternoon of 27th April, Mathias blew up three T34 tanks.

Wounded in the head, he was treated in the infirmary in

Hitler's bunker. He managed to reach the underground station Stadtmitte where Krukenberg had transferred his headquarters. Most of the survivors from the Charlemagne division were assembled there. The carriages with broken windows served as an infirmary, offices or supply store. Mathias smoked his first cigarette for two days.

On the station platform, the Brigadeführer awarded Iron Crosses to those who had distinguished themselves in the Neukölln battle. Mathias gazed at his with emotion.

At daybreak on Saturday 28th April, Russian pressure was becoming increasingly strong. The French SS lay in wait concealed behind doorways and windows. The tanks advanced in the grey dawn.

A Panzerfaust was fired and scored a bull's-eye, hitting the first tank. Flames shot up and a series of explosions could be heard followed by an enormous blast which sent lumps of steel flying through the air. All that was left of the T34 was a heap of twisted metal and charred bodies. The tanks advanced relentlessly. Shells rained down. Mathias, his Sturmgewehr on his shoulder, fired at a group of infantrymen. Five of them crumpled to the ground.

'Good work, Fayard,' said Captain Feunay, clapping him on the back.

Wounded in the shoulder, Mathias was taken to the Hotel Adlon which had been converted to a hospital. He was discharged that night, or what should have been night time. The sun had gone down long before. They had lost all sense of time.

The building in which the French were hidden was miraculously still standing. Russian mortars joined the anti-tank cannons. The building collapsed, killing a dozen volunteers. Half-choked, his lungs filled with dust, Mathias scrambled free of the rubble. His wounded shoulder was painful. Fires blazed all around him. The survivors managed to escape to new positions, avoiding the flaming girders, the sections of wall and the bullets. At dawn, they had retreated as far as Puttkammerstrasse.

In the evening, they found themselves near the Kochstrasse

underground station, the outpost for the defence of the chancellery. After a few moments' rest in the battalion headquarters in a huge bombed-out bookshop, they renewed their attack in a mist the colour of blood.

The day of the 30th was similar to the preceding days in that hellish universe where their dreams or disappointments had led them. They fought on, in the belief they were protecting their leader to whom they had sworn fidelity until death. They were protecting nothing but a bunker full of corpses. Hitler and his new bride, Eva Braun, had committed suicide at three-thirty that afternoon. In the evening, the Russians invaded the Reichstag after a furious battle. Lieutenant Berest and two sergeants hoisted the Soviet flag on top of a monument. During the night, General Krebs, chief-of-staff of the Wehrmacht, offered to negotiate the surrender of Berlin with General Tchoukov.

On the evening of 1st May, the French SS had to vacate the bookshop and take refuge in the cellars of the Ministry of Security. By the light of candles, placed in *julturms*, a kind of terracotta candlestick used on the night of the winter solstice, Feunay distributed Iron Crosses which he pinned on the torn, often bloodstained uniforms.

Once again, Mathias had been wounded, this time seriously, in the chest and legs. He had managed to drag himself, in the company of a few other survivors, to Kaiserhof underground station. Helped by his comrades, he hid in Potsdamerplatz station, where he witnessed, from behind a heap of rubble, the capture of Feunay and half a dozen of his comrades. Burning with fever, he was found by a German youth who hid him, with his father's help, in their cellar.

Chapter 35

François Tavernier's friendship with Major Klimenko made it possible for him to follow the Russians' progress in Berlin at close quarters. He was full of admiration for their courage throughout the fighting. He shouted with joy at their side when he saw the red flag fluttering over the Reichstag. The beast had been well and truly slain.

During the evening of 4th May, Tavernier wandered through the devastated Berlin streets. The air was mild, but stank with the smell of corpses buried under the rubble. The charred skeletons of buildings were silhouetted eerily against the clear sky. A very young girl crawled out of the ruins, blinking, her face black with soot, and bumped into him.

'Careful, kid,' he said in French.

The girl looked at him, round-eyed.

'*Sind Sie Franzose?*'

'*Ja,*'

'*Kommen Sie mit!*'*

She took his hand and led him into the ruins. They stepped over fallen masonry and wormed their way down a narrow passage. They made their way down some steps blocked by refuse. She guided him into a candlelit cellar. It was full of people lying prostrate. A young mother rocked her crying child while another adjusted a bandage around a little girl's head.

They cowered fearfully at the sight of François's Russian

---

* 'Are you French?'
'Yes.'
'Come with me.'

uniform, which he had worn since he began following the Red Army. But the girl said a few words which calmed them. She led him to a corner where a wounded man was lying.

'*Franzose*,' she said, pointing to the man whose face was devoured by his beard, his eyes burning with fever, a filthy, bloodstained dressing round his chest. From one of his legs, bound with rags, rose a fetid odour. The man was delirious.

'*Er muss ins Krankenhaus*', said the girl.

'*Dazu ist es zu spät, er liegt im Sterben.*'

'*Nein, Sie müssen ihm helfen!*'*

'Can you hear me, old chap?' he asked in French.

The wounded man stopped groaning and slowly turned towards him.

'I'm thirsty.'

François Tavernier turned to the young girl who shrugged helplessly:

'*Wir haben kein Wasser mehr, mein Vater ist unterwegs um was zu holen.*'†

'In his state, a sip of vodka can't do him any harm, poor creature,' he thought, taking a silver flask from his pocket which he had won from a Russian officer at poker. He gently poured a few drops on the wretched soldier's lips.

'Thank you . . . fidelity . . . it hurts . . .'

'Don't move, I'm going to get help. The war's over, you're no longer in any danger.'

'No,' said the wounded man, clutching his sleeve. 'The Russians will kill me.'

François Tavernier looked at him closely. But of course, he was one of those bastards who fought for the Germans.

'Waffen SS?'

'Yes. Charlemagne . . . the Charlemagne division. I've lost my comrades . . . They're all dead . . . it's stupid dying here . . . water . . .'

The vodka went down the wrong way and he began to

---

* 'He must be taken to hospital.'
'It's too late, he's going to die.'
'No! Help him!'
† 'We have no water left. My father has gone to fetch some.'

choke. Pain rent his chest and he howled, while blood spurted from his mouth.

The young German girl wiped his face tenderly.

'Léa,' he babbled.

*'Ich bin nicht Léa, ich heisse Erika.'**

'Léa . . . forgive me . . .'

'What's your name?' asked Tavernier.

'Léa . . .'

'Er heisst Mathias, seinen Nachnamen kenne ich nicht.'†

François rummaged in the inside pocket of his torn tunic. He fished out a package carefully wrapped in waterproof material and bound with an elastic band. The package contained two military records. Kramer, Otto, he read. That name rang a bell.

'Otto Kramer,' he said aloud.

'He's dead . . . I saw him die . . . He gave me a letter . . . for Françoise . . . must give it to her . . . '

A photograph fell out of the second record.

'Wie hubsch die ist!'‡

François snatched the photograph. Léa was smiling at him, her head resting on the shoulder of a young man whose attitude and expression clearly showed how proud he was to be holding her. On the back, Léa had written: 'Mathias and me at Montillac, August 1939.'

Tavernier had never really known what happened between them, he only knew Mathias was her dearest childhood companion.

The sound of voices could be heard at the cellar entrance. Five or six Russian soldiers came bursting in. The women got to their feet screaming and hugging their children close. An NCO went over to Tavernier. When he recognized the Russian uniform, he saluted.

'Greetings, comrade, who is this?'

'I don't know. He must be taken to hospital, he's seriously wounded.'

---

* 'I'm not Léa. My name's Erika.'
† 'His name's Mathias. He didn't tell me his surname.'
‡ 'How beautiful she is!'

The other sniggered.

'He's had it, there's no point.'

They made the Berliners leave the cellar. As they filed out, Erika darted François a pleading look. Left alone, he gazed at Mathias pensively.

'Léa . . .'

He realized he was still holding the photograph. He slipped it into his pocket with the military records and sat beside the dying man. He lit a cigarette and slid it between his lips.

'Thank you,' whispered Mathias.

They smoked in silence, their thoughts centring on the same woman. From time to time, Mathias let out a groan. A fit of coughing made him spit out the butt. François leaned over and wiped his brow.

'Will you write to Léa . . . her address is in my *soldbuch** . . . tell her I died thinking of her . . .'

He sat up and clutched his companion with extraordinary strength.

'Tell her I loved her . . . that she's the only woman I've ever loved . . . Léa, forgive me . . .'

Mathias's hands slipped. Never again would he see the sun-drenched slopes where he used to chase the girl who had been his sorrow and his joy. In death, he had the expression of an astonished child. Gently, François Tavernier closed his eyes, covered him with a tattered blanket and left.

* military record

Chapter 36

During the night of 7th May, François Tavernier received a telegram informing him of the arrival of General de Lattre de Tassigny in Berlin. He had been appointed by General de Gaulle to represent him at the signing of Germany's capitulation treaty. He asked Tavernier to meet him at Tempelhof airport.

He drove there in a jeep at ten a.m. and waited with a group of Russian officers and General Sokolovski, Field-Marshal Zhukov assistant. Sokolovski was in charge of greeting the delegates from the allied forces who were coming to sign the capitulation.

The guard of honour stood in ranks of twelve, their guns resting on the shoulder of the comrade in front. They paraded faultlessly.

On the dot of twelve o'clock, the DC3 carrying the British delegation arrived escorted by Soviet fighter planes. Admiral Burrough and Air Chief Marshal Tedder stepped out of the plane, followed by three uniformed figures, one of whom was a woman. General Sokolovski walked forward to welcome them. He gallantly kissed the woman's hand.

After the introductions, the battalion paid honour to the guests.

At ten past twelve, the American DC3s touched down on the runway. Sokolovski abandoned the British to go and welcome General Spaatz of the US Air Force. As before, the battalion paid honour while the members of the British delegation made their way to the cars waiting to take them to Karlshorst on the outskirts of Berlin. Tavernier automatically gazed after the attractive figure of the Englishwoman, thinking that she was one of those rare examples of the female sex who looked like a woman in spite of her uniform. There was something familiar in her gait . . .

'Major Tavernier, the French plane is about to land . . . Major, are you listening?'

François pushed the Soviet soldier out of his way and ran after the English group. He got caught up in the crowd and reached the exit only to see the car door close on two lovely legs. The car pulled away before he could get any closer.

'Major . . .'

Tavernier wiped his brow. I keep seeing her everywhere, he thought. What on earth would she be doing in Berlin with the English?

'Major . . .'

'Yes, I'm coming.'

He was just in time. General de Lattre, escorted by Colonel Demetz and Captain Bondoux, was walking towards General Sokolovski.

The cars sped through the still-smouldering ruins of the capital of the Reich. At crossroads, young Russian girls, in impeccable uniforms, bare-kneed above their high boots, were directing the traffic with the help of red and yellow flags. Everywhere, wretched groups of civilians queued up at the fountains and fire hydrants for a little water.

François was listening to Bondoux with only half an ear. When they reached Karlshorst, the French were driven to an NCO training school that was still more or less intact where Marshal Zhukov had his headquarters. From there, they were taken to one of the officers' wings. The furnishings were sparse, but the mattresses on the ground were covered with dazzling white sheets.

General Vassiliev came to greet General de Lattre whom he had met in Algiers. The two men were delighted to meet again. Tavernier took advantage of their reunion to slip off in search of the British delegation. He found Air Chief Marshal Tedder and Admiral Burrough without any difficulty, but there was no sign of the pretty girl who had been with them.

351

Asking these prominent military figures what had happened to her was out of the question.

The rest of the day was devoted to the making of a tricolour flag to be raised alongside the allied flags in the room where the ceremony was to take place. The Russians, full of good-will, made one up from a piece of red cloth borrowed from a Nazi flag, some white canvas and blue serge from a mechanic's overalls. Unfortunately, the result was a Dutch flag! They had to begin all over again. Finally, at eight p.m., the French flag took its place between the British and American flags, topped with the Soviet emblem.

On the dot of midnight, Field-Marshal Zhukov, his chest covered with medals, opened the session. He addressed words of welcome to the allied representatives and then gave the order for the German delegation to be shown in. Field-Marshal Keitel entered in full dress uniform, carrying his staff with which he saluted the assembly in an atmosphere of frosty silence. Nobody stood up. His eyes roved round the room and came to rest on the flags and then on General de Lattre.

'*Ach!*' he grumbled. '*Franzosen sind auch hier! Das hat mir gerade noch gefehlt!*'*

He irritably flung his staff and helmet on the table and sat down. General Stumpf took his seat to his right, and Admiral von Frendenburg to his left. Behind them, six German officers wearing the iron cross studded with two-edged swords and diamonds stood to attention. The authorized photographers' cameras started clicking.

Three-quarters of an hour later, General Keitel left the room. He had just signed the unconditional surrender of Nazi Germany. The six German officers looked devastated and had difficulty holding back their tears.

The night ended with a banquet laid on for the Allies by Field-Marshal Zhukov. When the guests parted company, it was after seven in the morning. François had still not seen the young woman from the airport again.

At nine o'clock, the Russians accompanied their guests

---

* 'Ach! The French are here too! That's all we need!'

back to the airstrip which was decked with the Russian colours and the same ceremony took place as on their arrival. It was then that Tavernier learned that the English and American delegations had departed immediately after the banquet. He took his leave of the French and went back to his post.

When he returned to Berlin, he arranged Mathias's funeral. A month later, he was summoned back to Paris.

The minute he arrived, he rushed over to the Rue de l'Université but nobody was able to give him news of Léa. Her last letter had come from London and was dated 30th April. At the Red Cross headquarters, Madame de Peyerimhoff told him that she was in Germany, in Luneburg where she was regarded as the fiancée of an English officer. Tavernier gave Françoise Otto Kramer's military record that he had found in Mathias's tunic, as well as the letter addressed to her that was inside it. Françoise did not cry. She thanked François and withdrew to her room.

My darling,

This evening, I want to talk to you and forget for a moment the horror of what is going on around me. My comrades are dead and my country has been destroyed. I want to think only of the happy times we spent together. Moments we snatched from the war, moments that were too short. You gave me everything a man could wish for: your love and a son, to whom I was unable to give my name. Raise him with honour and dignity. Teach him to love his unfortunate country and help with the rebuilding of our two nations. At the moment, we are fighting alongside foreigners who have joined the Waffen SS. I find it hard to understand what the poor blighters hope to get out of a fight which is not theirs. I dream of seeing you again, when all this is over, in the Bordeaux region that I have come to love. I like to picture you both, you and our child, in the old house or on the terrace overlooking the vineyards. Go back there, you will find peace. In the long winter evenings, you will sit at the piano and play our favourite tunes. Music is a great source of comfort to the soul.

My beloved wife, I have to leave you now. The Russians are approaching the ruined house where we are sheltering. I'm going back to my tank. These few minutes spent with you have brought me great peace, and dispelled the anguish of the last few days. I'm going into battle strengthened by our love. Farewell,

Otto.

Chapter 37

Léa was back with the French Red Cross after her brief trip to Berlin. François had indeed caught a glimpse of her. There had been a spare seat in the plane bringing the British delegation: they had thought there might be contacts in England with the Red Cross organizations of the allied countries but this turned out to be impossible.

After the 'kidnapping' of Sarah, Léa had become quite a heroine among Field-Marshal Montgomery's circle. They had intervened and asked the Field-Marshal and Léa's superiors to allow her to stay in England for a while.

Sarah had been put in quarantine for fear of typhus, and was gradually regaining her strength in England. There was nothing left of the attractive young woman who had charmed Léa. Now she was a broken woman, old before her time, who began to quake when anybody raised their voice. She refused to talk of the tortures she had suffered. She constantly went over and over her miraculous discovery by Léa with poignant gratitude. When she came out of quarantine, George McClintock took her home to stay with his family. The British officer confided his intention of marrying Léa to her. Sarah replied in a gentle, weary voice:

'She's the wrong person for you.'

George left the room sad and hurt, before returning to Germany.

From then on, he kept a close watch on Léa. She had changed. At the same time, she was more coquettish and more affectionate, staying up all night to drink and dance with the young officers. She was surrounded by a court of admirers who were devoted to her. She treated them with irritating indifference. He pointed out to her that it wasn't very decent of her to behave like that, and she kissed him, saying he was old-fashioned, thinking all the while that he would make an ideal husband. Sometimes, a desire for peace and quiet made her think she might marry the Englishman.

She was sent first to Brussels and then to Luneburg, where she met up with Jeanine Ivoy and made the acquaintance of Claire Mauriac and Mistou Nou de la Houplière. Together, they transported deportees, their youth and beauty giving them fresh hope in life. They had exchanged their caps for round hats, after realizing that their simple headgear reminded their patients of their executioners. Despite, or perhaps because of the horror of the camps, the atmosphere in the French section was very gay.

They reached Berlin at the beginning of August and settled into 96 Kurfürstendamm, in the British sector, in one of the few buildings that had not been too badly damaged in the air-raids. They and their Belgian colleagues were the only people authorized to move freely in the Russian-occupied territories to search for French and Belgian nationals in the camps. More than once, they brought back an English person in their ambulances and in exchange, the British gave them fuel or supplies. One of their most painful tasks was taking children of French or Belgian fathers away from the Germans. Whenever possible, they spent their evenings in the English club, dancing with the officers, or they would sunbathe by the swimming pool of the 'Blue and White'.

Mistou, Claire and Léa shared the same room in Kurfürstendamm. Their comrades called it 'the boudoir' because of their efforts to brighten it up, and particularly because of their beauty, which made some of the girls jealous. The minute they entered one of the allied forces military clubs, all the men would abandon their partners and rush up to them begging for a dance. Mistou's mischievous eyes and brilliant smile broke many hearts. Claire, who had a melancholy beauty, had eyes only for Captain Wiazemsky, who had been liberated by the Russians alongside whom he had fought the rest of the war. He refused requests to return home and took his place in the French army. As for Léa, they had all lost count of how many hearts she had broken.

One evening, returning from a particularly painful mission with Claire and Captain Wiazemsky, Léa bumped into a French officer.

'I'm sorry.'

Too exhausted to reply, she carried on walking.

'Léa!'

She stopped, paralysed as she had been that Christmas Eve . . . The main thing was not to turn round, not to destroy that precarious happiness by turning round.

'Léa!'

He was there, standing in front of her, even taller than she remembered him. She had forgotten how bright his eyes were and his mouth . . .

There were no more ruins, no more thin, grovelling Germans, no more errant wraiths, no more abandoned children, no more blood, no more corpses, no more fears. He was there, alive, so much alive, in her arms. Why was he crying? He was mad to cry on a day like this. Was she crying? She was laughing and crying at the same time, and everybody around them was doing likewise.

Mistou, who had come to join them, blew her nose loudly, murmuring:

'Love's a wonderful thing.'

'Poor McClintock,' said Jeanine.

Claire squeezed her handsome captain's hand.

'I've been looking for you all over the place since May,' François murmured into her hair.

'I had no news of you, I thought you were dead.'

'Didn't your sisters tell you I went to see you in Paris?'

Sniffing, Léa shook her head.

Mistou held out a handkerchief.

'Don't stay there, if the chief sees you, you'll be in trouble. You know he's very particular about the girls' behaviour. Come and join us at the English club later. We're going to have a bath. We stink to high heaven of rotting corpses.'

'Mistou,' cried Claire.

'Well, it's true, isn't it? You even said that you had one of your famous migraines coming on.'

'I'd like to see you with one,' she snapped.

'Thanks, but I'd rather you kept them to yourself. Just thinking about it gives me a headache.'

'Stop bickering,' said Léa. 'Here, this is Jeanine. Do you remember François Tavernier?'

'Not half! Thanks to him, I had the best Christmas of my life. Hello, Major, I'm glad to meet you again.'

'Hello, mademoiselle.'

'Come on girls, we've got to do our report. Don't think you're going to get out of it. See you later, Major.'

Left alone, the two men stared at each other and finally agreed to meet at eight o'clock at the English club.

All those who saw Léa laugh and dance that evening understood that they did not stand a chance. McClintock watched her with a heavy heart. Mistou noticed and went over to him.

'Don't look so miserable, Colonel. Ask me to dance instead.'

When they met on the dance floor, Léa flashed her a grateful smile.

François held her so tight that she could hardly breathe. But she would not have complained for the world. They danced without speaking. They were beyond words. They slid across the floor, without thinking about their movements, following the music instinctively, changing rhythm automatically, their bodies perfectly attuned to each other. As in Paris, at the German embassy, they continued whirling round after the last tune had died away. The laughter and clapping brought them back down to earth. After a few drinks, they left the club.

It was a mild evening. They climbed into a jeep parked near the entrance and drove through the bombed-out city for ages, in silence. They crossed a devastated park where, in the wan moonlight, the twisted, charred tree-trunks looked like an army on the march. François pulled up in Charlottenburgerstrasse. The area around the Victory column looked as if it had been ravaged by leprosy. Only the gilt symbol with outspread wings rose up intact, a pathetic sight in that destroyed city and conquered country.

Gently, François drew Léa to him. They remained entwined without moving, letting the other's warmth steal over them, closing their eyes to savour this unexpected happiness, allowing themselves to be overcome by love and feeling their hearts thumping in bodies that no longer belonged to them. In this sinister setting it was perhaps the first time that their tenderness unfolded and carried them into that slow whirlpool of heightened feelings. For the time being, they felt no desire to make love, they were too overwhelmed by the joy in their bursting hearts.

An owl screeched close by, making them both laugh.

'It's a good sign, the night birds are returning,' said Léa. 'Let's go back.'

They drove past the church which had been built to the glory of Emperor William at the entrance of Kurfürstendamm. The four bell towers rose up, half-destroyed, still dominated by the central bell which looked as if it had been decapitated.

'Are you taking me home already!'

'No my love, only if you want me to. When I left you earlier, I rented a room in an old lady's house not far from here.'

'How did you manage that? There are no rooms to let.'

'I managed.'

He drew up in a small side street near Hohenzollerndamm. The low houses had been spared. François opened a glass-panelled door with a huge key. An oil lamp burned in the hall. A large cat came and rubbed up against their legs. They each took one of the candles lying on top of a chest of drawers and went upstairs giggling. There was a smell of faded roses in their room.

François relieved her of her uniform by candlelight. He slowly slid down the straps of her pink slip. The rustle of silk made their nerves tingle. Léa's skin quivered at the touch of the material. She stepped out of the warm underwear in which his face was buried, avidly breathing in her smell. He restrained himself from tearing off her lace-edged camiknickers. When she was naked, he remained kneeling at her feet for a long time, looking at her. She allowed his gaze to rove over her, devouring her, making her body tremble and her knees go weak. She shivered when his lips touched the inside of her thighs, and made their way up to the hollow of her stomach. Between her legs, she could feel herself open out to receive her lover's kisses. She climaxed standing up with her hands on his head. He carried her over to the bed and undressed without taking his eyes off her. He took her gently. Confident, she let herself be led. When she felt her pleasure rising, she cried:

'Harder, harder!'

He drove her back before dawn. She slipped into the 'boudoir' without wakening her companions.

The following day, they told each other what they had been through since that Christmas near Amiens. François learned of Sarah's rescue and slow recovery in England with a delight that almost made Léa jealous. He dreaded breaking the news of Mathias's death. He began by telling her about Otto and described his visit to Françoise.

'Were you with him when he died?'

'No, I found his military record in the pocket of a French SS who knew him.'

Léa closed her eyes.

'What happened to this Frenchman?'

'He died.'

A tear rolled down her cheek.

'What was his name?'

François took her in his arms and told her in a low voice.

'He died calling you and begging your forgiveness. Cry, darling, cry.'

Léa sobbed like a little girl. How hard it was to grow up.

That evening, she wanted to visit Mathias's grave. She laid a few flowers bought from the little stall on the corner of Konstanzerstrasse on it.

'We'll have his body sent back to France if you like.'

'No, he died here and here he must stay.'

'What are you doing?'

'I'm collecting a little earth to mix it with the earth of Montillac.'

A painful happiness shot through her.

'What's the matter?'

Nothing was the matter. Simply, for the first time in ages, she had just imagined the possibility of returning to her beloved land. It was Mathias who suggested it to her. She frantically filled her hat with earth. When Léa stood up, her eyes had a fresh sparkle.

For a week, they saw each other every day. Claire and Mistou covered up for their comrade's absences and blunders as much as they could. Despite that, the work of the young French Red Cross women in Berlin was greatly admired by all. Jeanine Ivoy, head of the section, wrote to Madame de Peyerimhoff:

> You will see from the report that we've done a good job. We have managed to persuade the British to let us stay longer in their sector, thanks to the work we've been doing for them. In fact, they were refused permission to enter the Russian zone to look for their missing (about thirty thousand people) so, when we go on a mission, we do for them what we would do for our own people. We sometimes come back with hundreds of death certificates or lists of graves found in little villages. We have to divide them up into nationalities. There's so much paperwork!
>
> In each team, there are five drivers and one nurse. The English insisted on reducing the number of personnel as food is very limited.
>
> People continue pouring in from Alsace and Lorraine, and we all share their joy. The poor things suffered so much. For ten days, our girls dressed, fed and treated seven thousand people from Alsace-Lorraine. Their tireless devotion has been praised by both the French and British authorities.
>
> More trainloads of people from Alsace-Lorraine (about

three thousand) are expected any time and the British authorities are also asking for our help over the telephone. The refugees are in very poor physical condition and the French Red Cross is glad to be able to give them moral as well as the material support they need so desperately.

We often see General Keller coming from Moscow. He tells us when to expect the trains. There are so many people in camps in deepest Russia.

We are very lucky to be able to move freely in the Russian zone. They trust us and treat us with the greatest of respect. Last time the hospital train came through, we requested permission from an important general to bring the most serious cases back. He telephoned Moscow while we were in his office. The answer was no, but at least he tried. Our request was not in vain, because this week, the most serious cases will be handed over to us and will leave on the hospital train which has just arrived.

There's a marvellous atmosphere here. I have only praise for the team, particularly Mademoiselles Mauriac, Nou de la Houplière, Delmas, Farret d'Astier and d'Alvery, who are always together, always backing each other up . . .

François Tavernier received orders to return to Paris before flying to the United States. Léa drove him to Tempelhof airport after spending the night in the old German lady's little house. As she watched him board the Dakota, she was overcome with a fit of shivering. The fear she would never see him again nearly made her collapse.

Her companions did all they could to take her mind off it. Mistou and Claire were so good that she regained a little of her old cheerfulness. They visited the chancellery and Hitler's bunker with Captain Wiazemsky. They all came out feeling depressed by that place, strewn with telegrams, charred newspapers, torn portraits of the Führer, boxes with their contents spilling all over the floor and ruined decorations.

Chapter 38

In mid-September, Léa received orders to escort a group of young children to Paris. She left Berlin and her comrades, feeling a mixture of sadness and relief. There was too much devastation, too much suffering, and too much death.

In Paris, Madame de Peyerimhoff granted her leave. She rushed straight to her aunts' flat and found the place locked up. They had left the keys with the concierge who told her they had all gone down to the Gironde region. Léa did not understand.

She had been so looking forward to spending a few days in the capital, and now she found herself taking the first train out. That evening, she dashed to the Gare d'Austerlitz.

The train was packed and uncomfortable. She spent the night wedged between a soldier with wandering hands and a crotchety fat woman. Each time she dozed off, she heard her aunt's screams of pain, or Raoul's groans. How long were these ghosts going to keep haunting her? She was crazy to go back to Montillac. What did she hope to find there? After seeing so many ruins, why add another to the chapter of disasters that had grown longer each year? What was the good of going back, nothing would bring back the dead or the old house.

She reached Bordeaux exhausted and decided to take the first train back to Paris. On the opposite platform, the old Langon train was about to leave. Without stopping to think, she ran for it. A hand reached out from an open door. She jumped on.

Langon station had not changed. Suitcase in hand, she

headed for the little town centre. It was market day. Two policemen were chatting outside the Hotel Oliver.

'But it's little Mademoiselle Delmas!'

Léa looked round.

'Don't you recognize us? We're the ones who took you, your uncle and the poor young woman to La Sifflette's.'

Yes, of course she remembered.

'So, you're home again? Ah! A lot has happened here . . . and not necessarily pleasant things either. Haven't you got your famous bicycle any more? We'll give you a lift . . . We can't leave you to walk, can we Laffont!'

'What a question, Renault! Nobody can say that the French police are lacking in chivalry!'

Léa could not refuse their offer. She clambered into the car.

The two men talked and talked, but she did not hear a word they were saying. She drank in her beloved countryside that she had thought she would never see again, overcome with emotion. They did not insist on taking her further when she asked them to drop her at the foot of La Prioulette hill. She waited until the car had disappeared from view before continuing her way.

It was a beautiful afternoon, the late summer sun turning the grapes golden, and bathing the vineyards in that typical autumn light.

The hill seemed steep, and she slowed her footsteps. Behind the trees was Montillac. With racing heart, she reached the white gates.

There was an unfamiliar smell in the air, the smell of new wood. Familiar sounds reached her ears: the clucking of hens, the barking of a dog, the cooing of turtledoves and the whinnying of a horse. Behind the farm buildings she would see the house. A light breeze ruffled her hair. She continued walking towards it, each stride an effort. The monotonous sound of a saw . . . the sound of hammering . . . A young man's voice singing:

C'est une fleur de Paris
Du vieux Paris qui sourit

364

Car c'est la fleur du retour
*Du retour des beaux jours**

Workmen were tiling the newly timbered roof. Part of it was already finished . . . the kitchen door was open. Inside, the kitchen had not changed one bit. She tottered backwards as she stood in what she and her sisters used to call 'the street' . . . Children's shouts and laughter could be heard from the terrace . . . Léa wanted to flee, to run away from the mirage, but a giant hand was pushing her towards the laughter and shouts. The swing was moving backwards and forwards in its wistaria-covered frame. Time stood still, then took a leap into the past: now, there was a little girl with tousled hair sitting on the swing saying:

'Higher, Mathias, higher.'

Then everything went misty and settled again: the arbours, the rose bushes along the drive, the vines among the cypress trees . . . a train went past in the distance, a bell tolled . . . She recognized her sisters' voices.

Nothing seemed to have changed. Léa walked towards the house . . . A man, holding Charles by the hand, was coming to meet her.

---

* It's a flower from Paris
Of the smiling Paris of yore
It's the flower of return
The return of the good old days

STAR BOOKS BESTSELLERS

	TESSA BARCLAY	
0352315520	**Garland of War**	£1.95
0352317612	**The Wine Widow**	£2.50
0352304251	**A Sower Went Forth**	£2.25
0352308060	**The Stony Places**	£2.25
0352313331	**Harvest of Thorns**	£2.25
0352315857	**The Good Ground**	£1.95
035231687X	**Champagne Girls**	£2.95
	JOANNA BARNES	
0352316969	**Silverwood**	£3.25
	LOIS BATTLE	
035231270X	**War Brides**	£2.75*
0352316640	**Southern Women**	£2.95*

STAR Books are obtainable from many booksellers and newsagents. If you have any difficulty tick the titles you want and fill in the form below.

Name _____

Address _____

_____

Send to: Star Books Cash Sales, P.O. Box 11, Falmouth, Cornwall, TR10 9EN.

Please send a cheque or postal order to the value of the cover price plus:
UK: 55p for the first book, 22p for the second book and 14p for each additional book ordered to the maximum charge of £1.75.

BFPO and EIRE: 55p for the first book, 22p for the second book, 14p per copy for the next 7 books, thereafter 8p per book.

OVERSEAS: £1.00 for the first book and 25p per copy for each additional book.

While every effort is made to keep prices low, it is sometimes necessary to increase prices at short notice. Star Books reserve the right to show new retail prices on covers which may differ from those advertised in the text or elsewhere.

NOT FOR SALE IN CANADA

STAR BOOKS BESTSELLERS

	MICHAEL CARSON	
0352316179	**The Genesis Experiement**	£2.50
	ASHLEY CARTER	
0352317264	**A Darkling Moon**	£2.50*
035231639X	**Embrace The Wind**	£2.25*
0352315717	**Farewell to Blackoaks**	£1.95*
0352316365	**Miz Lucretia of Falconhurst**	£2.50*
	ASHLEY CARTER & KYLE ONSTOTT	
0352317019	**Strange Harvest**	£2.95*
	BERNARD F. CONNERS	
0352315814	**Don't Embarrass The Bureau**	£1.95*
0352314362	**Dancehall**	£2.25*

STAR Books are obtainable from many booksellers and newsagents. If you have any difficulty tick the titles you want and fill in the form below.

Name _____

Address _____

_____

Send to: Star Books Cash Sales, P.O. Box 11, Falmouth, Cornwall, TR10 9EN.

Please send a cheque or postal order to the value of the cover price plus:
UK: 55p for the first book, 22p for the second book and 14p for each additional book ordered to the maximum charge of £1.75.

BFPO and EIRE: 55p for the first book, 22p for the second book, 14p per copy for the next 7 books, thereafter 8p per book.

OVERSEAS: £1.00 for the first book and 25p per copy for each additional book.

While every effort is made to keep prices low, it is sometimes necessary to increase prices at short notice. Star Books reserve the right to show new retail prices on covers which may differ from those advertised in the text or elsewhere.

NOT FOR SALE IN CANADA

STAR BOOKS BESTSELLERS

STAR Books are obtainable from many booksellers and newsagents. If you have any difficulty tick the titles you want and fill in the form below.

Name _____

Address _____

_____

Send to: Star Books Cash Sales, P.O. Box 11, Falmouth, Cornwall, TR10 9EN.

Please send a cheque or postal order to the value of the cover price plus: UK: 55p for the first book, 22p for the second book and 14p for each additional book ordered to the maximum charge of £1.75.

BFPO and EIRE: 55p for the first book, 22p for the second book, 14p per copy for the next 7 books, thereafter 8p per book.

OVERSEAS: £1.00 for the first book and 25p per copy for each additional book.

While every effort is made to keep prices low, it is sometimes necessary to increase prices at short notice. Star Books reserve the right to show new retail prices on covers which may differ from those advertised in the text or elsewhere.

NOT FOR SALE IN CANADA